I
SCREAM
MAN

I SCREAM MAN

A Nut Cracker Investigation

Katherine Ramsland

LEVEL
BEST BOOKS

Author Photo Credit: Kristin Laudenslager

First edition

ISBN: 978-1-68512-172-3

Cover art by Level Best Designs

This book was professionally typeset on Reedsy.
Find out more at reedsy.com

For my first readers: Sue, Sally, and Ruth

Praise for Katherine Ramsland's Books

A thoroughly entertaining and captivating read. *I Scream Man* has all the elements of a great mystery and crime drama, with some paranormal phenomena and a threatening natural disaster adding to the intrigue.As a retired Internal Affairs Investigator and now Private Investigator, I found the storyline and the characters compelling, and relatable. As often happens, what on the surface seems like a simple case is found to be entangled in realms others don't want you looking into. Knowing who you can trust, and who can provide legitimate information, is key, and Annie Hunter possesses that asset. She has assembled a team I would love to work with or share a glass of wine. I look forward to reading more of The Nut Crackers' adventures.—Susan Lysek, private investigator

Missing children get under Annie Hunter's skin. A brilliant forensic psychologist, she is familiar with the secrets and shadows that hide inside the mind, but her search for the disappeared sets her on a propulsive, suspenseful ride through a world more dangerous and mysterious than she expected, especially when it gets personal. Gritty crimes, paranormal explorations, spine-tingling adventures—this twisty thriller grabs hold of the reader and never lets go. *I Scream Man* is the start of an outstanding series featuring Annie and her colorful team of investigators, and I'm anxiously awaiting the next installment.—Ruth Knafo Setton, award-winning author of *The Road to Fez*

Forensic psychologist Annie Hunter leads her team of crackerjack but quirky investigators through an exceptionally convoluted and precarious case involving missing children, the paranormal, and unfinished business

i

that begs for resolution. Author Katherine Ramsland, a renowned expert on forensic psychology, skillfully uses her extraordinary insight into the human mind, and a razor-sharp knowledge of crime-solving forensics to bring to life *I Scream Man*, a cleverly plotted thriller.—Lee Lofland, Author of *Police Procedure and Investigation, a Guide for Writers* and founder of the annual Writers' Police Academy

As Katherine Ramsland leads us down a murderous path that keeps getting darker and more complex, there are many twists and surprises. She uses her unique real-world expertise and experiences to craft intriguing characters and a story that will keep you turning pages well past bedtime. And the thrill ride to the end is one you'll not soon forget.—Shamus Award-nominated J.D. Allen, author of the Sin City investigation series

Praise for Darkest Waters collection
New or classic cases, no one writes with the insight of Katherine Ramsland. Period."—Gregg Olson, *New York Times* bestselling author

Praise for *The Mind of a Murderer*
"Dr. Ramsland writes with a clarity of prose and elegance of style that makes her the envy of forensic commentators and establishes her as a genuine authority in her field."—Host of *Most Evil*, Dr. Michael Stone

Praise for *Ghost: Investigating the Other Side*
"The best book of its kind I've ever read."—Dean Koontz, *New York Times* bestselling author
"Ramsland is a master of foreboding."—*Publishers Weekly*

Chapter One

Missing kids get under my skin. I follow these cases with charts and maps, and hope for a call to consult. I owe someone. I haven't forgotten the day a biker snatched my childhood friend in front of me. She'd looked back, her face begging me for help. They never found her. Neither have I ... yet. So, no matter how tough a case might get, with kids I don't give up. I'll do whatever it takes to get them back to their families.

Like the missing twelve-year-old, Jimmy Broderick. His mother, Lillian, had placed a frantic call to me after he appeared to her in a dream. He'd begged for help. She'd heard that my private investigation agency accepts cases with paranormal features. Hers qualified.

I'm Annie Hunter, a forensic psychologist. I call my agency The Nut Crackers, because we accept hard nuts to crack. I perform psychological assessments and offer profiling with a specialty in questionable suicides. Being a petite, blond female, I work hard to gain respect as a death investigator. I publish books and run a weekly podcast called *Psi Apps*, where I dispense tips and discuss cases. I admit to dabbling in the uncanny, usually to dissect and debunk paranormal reports. Yet I can't ignore those rare events when something weird has certainly occurred.

And that's personal.

I'm looking for my father, Lang Hunter. The medical examiner who read his suicide note thinks he killed himself. So does my mother. But I'm not convinced. He left a note but not a body. So, it could have been a pseudocide—he faked it. He'd researched "vanishments," or people who've gone missing in odd ways. Maybe he learned their secret. Considering the person he'd married—my intolerant mother—this made sense to me. To locate him, I've retraced his travels from journals I found in the Outer Banks house he left to me. I'll use almost anything to reconnect, and a case like Jimmy's, with its paranormal potential, might open new doors. Lillian wanted me to check out a psychic. That's one of my services. Should the guy prove legit—a rare occurrence—I might tap his talent myself.

But I'm not a sole consultant. I have a team, and my work outside the lines attracted just the right people. First came Natra Gawoni, a half-Cherokee trainer of dogs for search-and-rescue, or SAR. I met her on a case in which a man had murdered and skinned the face off his pregnant niece before dumping her dismembered remains in a river. Natra had brought Mika, her black Doberdor sniffer dog. Mika detected traces of blood in the uncle's freshly scrubbed home, which nailed the guy. The cops had tried to undercut us both, which drew us together. After I helped her get through her son's death from opioid addiction, Natra became my info-miner. She's also my confidante and a substitute mom to my daughter, Kamryn.

She's nine. She's fascinated with digital forensics, so my part-time digital examiner, Joe Lochren, provides instruction. He says her nimble mind gives her real talent for rapidly comparing various solutions. But I insist he show her none of the gritty stuff.

Then we have Ayden Scott, my PI. He's a skeptic but always eager to explore cases with ghost stories attached. We'd met over one such tale when he urged me to hire him. I'd considered him an overly tanned blond beach bum who probably thought sleuthing is easy, so I'd turned him down. But then he'd baited me into a staged suicide case that proved his worth. Now, he's indispensable.

Besides my core team, I call on colleagues with specialized skills. This includes paranormalists I respect. My tolerance for the mystical does risk my reputation but it also brings unique opportunities. I can't tell you how many cops and coroners have said, "I don't believe in this stuff, but..." and then admit to me what they'd never tell a partner. This builds trust on both sides, a currency I need.

In truth, some cases *do* resist explanation. That's why I keep exploring. Among my fan base for *Psi Apps* are cold-case sleuths—our "team-sourcers." That's how I learned about Jimmy Broderick. A team-sourcer had referred Lillian to me.

On a video chat, I watched her talk. Lillian styled her thick blonde hair and spoke in a way that suggested upper middle-class. She kept touching her right pearl earring. Her controlled expressions showed training for the proper Southern lady, marred only by the occasional catch in her voice and the puffed skin under her eyes.

The photo she'd sent of Jimmy featured his broad smile and sweet mop of brown hair that curled over his forehead—the kind of kid you want to protect. But Lillian's tangled narrative seemed to hide as much as reveal.

"He's been in some trouble," she admitted. "Mah husband...he resides separately... he thinks Jimmy needs discipline. Two weeks ago, he sent Jimmy to a school or a camp. He won't tell me whe'ah because he thinks Ah'd intahfe'ah."

I can't figure why any woman would let her husband make unilateral decisions about their children, but I kept a straight face. It's not as if being assertive had improved *my* marriage. My former marriage.

Lillian continued. "In mah dreams, Jimmy's cryin' an' pleadin', an' Ah just feel so helpless. It breaks mah heart. Ah must find him. Ah hi'ahed an investigatah he'ah in Savannah. But he gave up. Ah think he's been threatened."

I leaned in. "By your husband?"

"Mah husband would emphatically object, but Ah won't give up. Ah don't see why Jimmy can't send me a note. Ah know somethin's wrong. Ah've heard about a psychic an' Ah want you to tell me if he's worth visitin'. Ah'd go mahself, but Ah don't want mah husband knowin'. He'd be livid. To him, this spirit stuff is the Devil's work."

I could already tell her that most psychics won't give her much more than expensive false hope. They play the probabilities to hook people into revealing information with which they shape a credible narrative. Some even ventriloquize the dead. When told they're wrong, most pivot to blaming paranormal barriers. I accept requests like Lillian's so I can help clients avoid a scam.

Lillian dabbed her eyes. "Do you think mah son is...could he be...?"

I knew where she was going. "Sometimes dreams like this are just ways to deal with anxiety."

"But what if it *is* Jimmy? Don't you think it could be? Ah thought you believed in that stuff."

"Dream images can come from people with so much emotional energy they manage to project it into someone's mind. He could be alive. Don't give up hope."

I knew about dreams of missing people. In the infamous Red Barn murder in England in 1827, a dream had revealed a murder victim's grave, which led to the killer. But for Lillian, I needed a better example. Someone had posted a news article on my *Psi Apps* site about a medium in South Carolina who'd located a kidnapped child. I told this to Lillian, adding, "That child was alive."

"Mah lord! Can you talk to this man?"

"I'll contact him."

"Please do whatevah you can. Talk to both, or anyone else you think could help. Please do it soon. Ah'll pay the fee. Ah need help. Ah think Jimmy's in danjah. He's terrified. He mentioned othahs."

I went alert. "Others?"

"He said help us. *Please.* Help *us.*"

This intrigued me. "I'll make some calls. I'll be in touch."

And I would be. A manifestation of a mother's anxiety wouldn't include such a detail. Lillian's revelation had moved Jimmy's case into a new category.

Chapter Two

Lillian's psychic of choice was Angus McMaster, near Savannah. He gave regular tours of a reputedly haunted property called the Scavenger House. I could join the group and study his moves. North of there, in South Carolina's Lowcountry, I'd find the medium who'd supposedly located the kidnapped child. I hoped to observe both in one trip. First, I prepared.

Natra had collected a folder of clippings on the Lowcountry medium. He called himself Airic. No last name. I guessed it was a stage name, to give the sense of being airy, or ephemeral. A suggestible prompt. So, a possible con. Then we learned he was a *physical* medium, which is quite rare and difficult to fake. Airic's followers claimed some quirk in his chemistry made objects materialize around him. One of our regular team-sourcers, Indigo Rose, had posted that his sitters claimed they could touch floating objects. One had described the rough skin on the back of a dismembered hand.

I skimmed the articles while Natra waited. Typically in jeans, like me, today she wore navy sweats. Mika watched, alert, while Natra braided her brunette hair—a signal for an imminent training session that came with treats. A blurred photo of Airic showed a thin, fortyish white guy with dark hair to his waist. I looked at Natra. "Any evidence he actually helped?"

She shrugged. "Just quotes in the news from the parents. Nothing from him."

"No grandiose bragging?"

"Not that I found."

"That's unique. Any legal record on the case?"

"The kidnapper pled out."

So, a dead-end there. "Did the parents pay him? Maybe their claim about his success is just cognitive consonance to justify the fee."

"He does charge." Natra pointed to a passage she'd highlighted in green. "And reviews are uneven. He doesn't always deliver."

I looked through the comments she'd pulled from the *Psi Apps* site. One person said Airic was autistic and obtuse. Another called him an angel who adapted poorly to our realm. A third dismissed him as demonic. Whatever. I'd never met a medium without a quirk. Didn't matter. If he could make tangible ghosts appear before my eyes and also locate missing kids, I'd accommodate his oddities.

"I called Gail," Natra added. Gail Holzer was our most regular and reliable paranormalist. "She knows about him. Said he has trouble understanding people and his communication skills are minimal. Some kind of language processing issue, and he's disorganized. His handlers manage his sittings. But here's the real problem. Look at the second page."

I scanned it. Airic restricted his séances to an intimate circle of regulars—his "Air-aides." Another red flag. "Air-aides? Sounds like a cult."

"He has a following."

"I can deal with that, but he's not very accessible. Does Gail know anyone who can help me get in?" For me hurdles are merely motivational tests. My motto is, *better to be told no than to lose an opportunity I might get if I pursue it.*

"I'll ask."

While Natra worked on that, I emailed my own query to an address listed for contacting Airic. In it, I explained my awareness of his success with the missing child case and said I had a similar need. I included a link to my *Psi Apps* episode about remote viewers solving a murder. I'd gained entrée more than once with the lure of PR. If he researched me, he'd see I have an audience that would take him seriously.

The next day, chief Air-aide Virginia Kisner responded. My timing was perfect, she said. Airic worked only with multiples of three and one sitter had bailed on their upcoming "storm dancing" session, which was scheduled to tap into an approaching weather front. "Such disturbances make spirit holes," she wrote. She added conditions: no shoes or jewelry, no cameras or recorders, dark cotton clothing only, and complete confidentiality. No problem. I sent back my response: Count me in.

I texted Natra to get this on my calendar. She called back. "You have a conflict. Your follow-up with Harnett's that day."

"Ah, I forgot. And that's important." I thought about it. "Harnett's in South Carolina, too. Maybe I can do both."

Danny Harnett, a fifteen-year-old delinquent, was accused of killing another kid, Mick Keller, in a juvenile facility. I'd performed a clinical evaluation. He'd been difficult, but I still hoped to help him skirt the full force of adult proceedings. I checked a map. Even with the best traffic conditions, I couldn't complete my final eval and also get to Airic's in time. And I *had* to get to Airic's. There might not be another opportunity.

I pulled up my notes on Harnett. He was as lost as any missing kid, just in a different way. He'd denied killing Mick, but the evidence went against him. He was the last one seen with Mick, and he'd allegedly made a threat. His fingerprints were on the hammer that matched the wounds on the victim's bashed-in face. I'd seen the gruesome autopsy photos. They showed a lot of anger. But aside from some enigmatic comments, Danny had given me little to work with.

During my initial clinical interview six weeks earlier, the lanky kid with ash-blond hair had remained aloof, especially when I declined to buy him cigarettes. He seemed to think my eval was pointless. When we did some testing at my second visit, he'd opened up a little but said some odd things.

I'd given him a blank sheet of paper and asked him to draw a person. This is a common projective test meant to identify themes in unresolved emotional issues. Danny had drawn two stick figures. Over them, he'd placed a single eye. He'd pointed at the drawing and whispered that he and Mick had "done things at the witch house for Plat-eye." I'd frowned. Witches and plat-eyes were folklore. Danny had then sketched something in the corner. "It's a set up," he'd mouthed. He'd pointed at his chest. "Know things." As he'd turned his drawing to show me, a corrections officer rapped on the door. Harnett had ripped off that part of the paper and stuffed it into his mouth. His greenish-gray eyes had begged me to say nothing.

So, I'd requested one more meeting. I didn't really need it. I could finish my report without it. Harnett was angry. He'd made threats. His impulsivity score was high, and he had a history of fights with other boys. His case looked grim. But if I could get him to tell me what he'd tried to convey during our second interview, I might be able to keep him in the juvenile system. I still didn't know his side of the story. He had one.

I reached for my phone to reschedule the appointment just as my daughter ran into my office. Kamryn stopped near my desk and put a hand on her slender hip. "Did you find it yet?"

I shook my head. "This is a hard one. I need a hint."

She giggled. She loves to stump me, so we've turned our challenges into an ongoing game. I'd introduced her to the world of codes and riddles, and she'd embraced them with gusto. Joe was right. She had a knack for metacognition, like my father. Kamryn touched her mouth.

I leaned back in my chair. "A word puzzle, right? It'll show me where to find the key?"

She shook her head, making her ponytail swing. "Too easy. First, there's a knot. A special kind of knot."

"What kind?"

"That's part of the puzzle!"

I looked around, letting her take delight in my confusion. She gets ten points for each day I can't figure it out. When she reaches 100, she can set up a physical challenge for me. These are not fun. But I adore her ingenuity.

Kamryn laughed. "You can't just see it! You have to *look* for it." She brushed her fingers over her chestnut hair, toward my bookshelf. She'd picked up the art of gestural subtleties from an Escape Room guide.

"It's in a book?"

"Mom! You have to figure it out!"

Ordinarily, I enjoyed playing with her, but my mind was on my appointment conflict. "One more tip. A little one."

Exasperated, Kamryn said, "Okaaaay…blue."

The rumbling din of a truck outside drew her to the window. She dashed out, leaving me with too few clues to untangle her knot. Like with Danny Harnett. And Jimmy Broderick.

Chapter Three

At my bookshelf, I checked the titles of books with blue covers. Four had been moved close together. Good. I was getting somewhere. *Mental States in Homicide* was the first one, followed by *Intake Strategies, Assessment for Suicide,* and *Kids and Crime.* I cringed at the image of Kamryn handling these books. But I was overthinking. The clue was a word puzzle. Some arrangement of words or letters held the key. She'd merely looked for titles that would work.

Kamryn raced back in, her brown eyes glistening. "Guess who's here!"

"Must be Ayden."

My PI followed her in. His dark tan told me he'd spent the past week outside. He manages several Air-B&Bs, renovates his Rodanthe house, trains for search-and-rescue along the ocean... and surfs. "I'm that predictable?"

"Your truck engine's a giveaway." I gestured toward the window. "And the weather. A tropical storm's forming, so I figured you'd come check my hurricane shutters."

"Should I?"

I shrugged. "We don't know where it's heading."

"I think it'll be a hurricane."

Kamryn clapped her hands. "When?"

Ayden smiled. A weather fanatic, he embraces new recruits. "Maybe a week, maybe less. Depends how fast it moves. They've pulled out the names. This one's Delano."

I crossed my arms. "Well, Delano hasn't yet selected who he'll shower with his blessing, so let's not get worried."

"I'll check the shutters."

"Be my guest. And take her." I pointed to Kamryn. "She needs some weather lessons." I knew his passion would infect her. He'd already pulled her into a sea turtle rescue and shown her how to grow roses in our sandy soil. Kam learns fast. We call her the Rose Whisperer.

"Blue," she told me over her shoulder. "Keep trying."

I watched her ponytail bounce behind her as she ran out to catch Ayden's weather tip. I was grateful for his tutoring. I'd worked hard with her on focus exercises. Not quite ADHD but full of disconnected chatter, she needed constant guidance to stay attuned. Natra viewed her neurodivergence as a talent for mental agility, but I worried it could diminish her chance at future success. I feared, too, she'd become like my father. A brilliant man, he'd followed whims down multiple rabbit holes that had sapped him. His dark moods could be scary. Perhaps one had been deadly. I loved Kam's resilience, but I wanted her to learn to stay on task. To that end, we played these mental games daily.

I redistributed the blue books to look for the clue, but Natra interrupted me. I raised an eyebrow. "Where's Mika?"

She tossed her head toward the window. "With the kids." That's her view of Ayden and his gig-work approach. She handed me a note. "Harnett's attorney called. They're moving him to another facility. The hearing's postponed."

I breathed out. "Good. That gives me more time. I can attend Airic's sitting and see Danny later." I went to my desk and tapped my pile of case folders. I often have a dozen at once, but right now I had just seven clinical cases and only two that involved investigation. Plus Jimmy Broderick, so three in that category.

Natra handed me a schedule. "This could work. I checked the dates for the Scavenger House tours and found an opening after Airic's session. You can storm dance with him, then head to Savannah. The storm won't hit before then."

I nodded. "And I can drop Kam off with Wayne for her week with him."

That's my ex, Wayne Worth, an agent for South Carolina's Law Enforcement Division, known as SLED. He lives near Columbia, six hours away. In the divorce, I got our lake house down that way. Along with shared office space in Charleston, it gives me a base of operation for my cases to the south. Kamryn lives with Wayne during the school year, so I often stay at the lake house to see her. For Kamryn's sake, Wayne and I have settled into a parental alliance, although he gets cranky when my work raises risk. He thought a suicide pact I'd recently questioned in Georgia had this potential.

The parents of Alicia Morton and Marti Girard had hired me to investigate the girls' recent deaths. They'd been at the Angel Oak juvenile facility. I'd done a basic analysis, turning up nothing to suggest foul play, but had received no toxicology report. The coroner, Trey Sullivan, had said there wouldn't be one. He was right, but when I'd probed he'd stonewalled me. I'd told both families they'd need a detailed investigation. A trip to Savannah provided an opportunity to visit Sullivan.

"I'll work from the lake house," I told Natra. "I'll pack for that in case I make headway on the Morton-Girard case. I can't believe I now have four juvenile cases. Let's hope we find Jimmy quickly. Maybe one of these psychics will deliver, but I might run a forensic investigation, too. Lillian has secrets. There's something she's not telling me."

Kamryn ran in, with Mika bounding next to her. Ayden followed.

"I wanna stay for the hurricane!" Kam said. "Can't I?" She leaned over the dog, who licked her face all the way up under her bangs. "See? Mika wants me to. And what about the turtles? We have to check them!"

I held up my hands. "Kam, you're going to your father's soon. You know that. If a hurricane comes, you'll be where it's safe."

She looked crushed. "Why?"

Ayden shook his head, amused. "Like mother, like daughter."

I raised an eyebrow to warn him not to support her beg-a-thon.

"Am I heading back to Georgia?" Ayden asked. "If so, I can take her to Wayne's."

"Maybe. I'm checking something out. We might go for a few days." I gestured around the room to include Natra. "All of us."

Ayden saluted. "Always ready, Boss."

"Pack for a week. I'll know soon. And pack rain gear, just in case."

Over the next couple of days, I prepared for the session. I'd heard about how turbulent weather can escalate paranormal activity but had never seen evidence of it. I did know to ramp up my potassium intake and cut down the calcium. Some groups claim this assists spirit conductance. I got Kamryn ready, too, despite her claim I was being unfair.

Then Wayne threw a wrench into my plans. On the day of my trip to see Airic, he said he'd be working late and asked me to keep Kam till evening. I invited Natra to come along, to watch her. No way was I missing this meeting with a physical medium.

When we arrived at our Lowcountry lodging near Blufton, Kam reminded me of the points she'd accrued over several days from my failure to solve her puzzle. She begrudgingly offered another clue. "It's a two-syllable name."

"Okay. So, there's a knot I can't just see, the color blue, and a two-syllable name."

"If you don't know by midnight, I win. It's the last day."

"I'm working on it."

I handed Natra a list of riddles to keep Kamryn challenged. Then I dressed in a navy T-shirt, jeans, and slip-off sandals to go storm dancing.

Chapter Four

The séance location proved challenging to find. You wouldn't guess from the high-end car dealers and gated communities on the main road in that area that back roads hid rusting mobile homes and ageing shacks. In woodsy places, they weren't easy to find. Nor was the medium's log cabin. I'd missed the landmark—a lightning-split sycamore—and bypassed the dirt driveway to Airic's two-story abode. Backtracking, I saw it, but I arrived late. As I pulled in next to four other cars, I noticed scattered gravestones under the octopus arms of live oaks draped in shrouds of Spanish moss. A light breeze brought a musty bouquet and tickled the branches.

So, Airic operates like this, I thought. *More power of suggestion.* Deep in the woods, near reminders of death, we'd automatically think of ghosts. This man was canny.

A plump, silver-haired woman in a gray blouse and long dark skirt came out to the covered porch and waved me over. She introduced herself as Virginia Kisner and pointed toward a wooden box. "You can place your shoes in here."

Another prop. We'd all be barefoot. Vulnerable. I started a mental list. Even if Airic turned out to be just another psychic fraud, he showed intriguing variances. Good podcast material. But I had to focus on Jimmy Broderick. If Airic seemed legit, I was here to enlist his help.

"The sitting room is dark," Virginia said, "and we dress in dark clothes. We find that spirits need darkness to form. All life starts in seeds or eggs, hidden away. The higher vibrations of light can sometimes disperse fragile forms."

I nodded. "That makes sense." It didn't, but I wasn't here to argue.

"Also, Airic wants me to tell you that since you're a stranger, his entities might decline to attend." She shrugged as if to apologize in advance. "He has spirit guides, you know, but they need certain conditions. They're used to certain people."

"I understand." I'd heard this excuse before. Spirit people always have reasons why their conjuring fails—a headache, an intruder, a reluctant spook, or an atmospheric fluke. But surely experienced people who channeled ghosts regularly could override *my* shortcomings.

"Airic is getting ready," Virginia added, "but he said you can inspect the room. The others are already here. They know how it works. Once he enters the room, he's already engaged with the other side. He'll know you're there, but he won't speak to you."

She opened a solid wooden door that led to a descending set of steps. I stopped. The damp odor hit me, and I nearly turned around. I hadn't expected a cellar, especially not in a Lowcountry building. I hate closed spaces. The only thing worse would be a closed *dark* space filling with water. Swamps were not far from here.

I took a breath. If Airic could show me a ghost, I could subvert my phobias. I grabbed the metal railing and descended toward the quiet murmurs below. The low strains of a musical instrument, like a violin, provided background. I figured the other sitters were envisioning contact with their deceased loved ones. I'd come for a stranger who might still be alive. I didn't really fit.

Tiny overhead lights allowed me to see the layout of the roughly 15-by-20-foot windowless room. *Enclosed.* I directed my focus away from the concrete walls and toward a large wooden chair with leather straps around its arms. Virginia seemed to read my thoughts. "Strapping Airic down keeps him from floating away should he levitate. It also proves he's not using his hands to flick switches or pull cords." She led me over to it and invited me to test the restraints.

I pushed on the firm leather and metal buckles. The oppressive air seemed to thicken. I sensed scrutiny from the devotees. The straps seemed solid, the buckles real. I peered at the dark curtain on a tall wooden box behind the chair. It suggested intriguing things inside—and possibly a trick door for an accomplice to perform Airic's "supernatural" feats.

"That's a spirit cabinet." Virginia gestured for me to examine it. I went over and pushed aside the curtain. Against the wall in one corner of the cramped space, I spotted a small table that held a drum, a bell, a candle, two trumpets, and some paper rolled into tapered tubes. I knew what they were for. So did anyone who'd ever heard of the Spiritualist movement of the 19th century. Mediums like the notorious Fox sisters had offered contact with the dead, attracting thousands of followers before revelations of their fraud dissolved the movement's momentum. Reportedly, the items in this room facilitate spirit communication that's otherwise inaudible. I pressed on the wall to test for a trick door. It didn't yield.

So far, I'd seen the usual contrivances. Even if a spirit showed up, I'd probably doubt its validity. After all, Airic knew from my email what I hoped for. I began to think I'd wasted my time.

With a sense of claustrophobic dread, I sat in an empty chair and nodded toward a gray-haired woman to my right who oozed the sweet scent of lilacs. I leaned slightly away.

Instead of a table in the middle, we sat around a four-foot-wide shallow pool filled with dark water. So, I was now in a dark cellar *with* water, as if they knew what would spook me. Only a little research would have yielded this information since I've revealed my phobias on my podcast. I assumed the pool, which stank of a Lowcountry swamp, would serve as a scrying mirror. Supposedly, a smooth surface yields images of spirits, but in truth, if we stare long enough at still water, our brain automatically forms patterns. It's like seeing a cow in a cloud. Add expectations, such as the hope to see a particular person, and you'll spot familiar features. People who know nothing about perception are wowed.

Virginia darkened the room. A small blue LED illuminated the area over Airic's wooden seat, settling in a spooky way on the faces and hands of those with light skin. A young couple across from me huddled close and held hands. The woman gripped a shaggy-haired doll. Next to them, two males whispered together. I heard the lanky one say, "Maybe he'll stay longer this time." I wondered if he meant Airic...or someone else.

I looked at the closed door from which Airic would emerge and noticed a tiny red light. Virginia had prohibited me from recording the session, but Airic seemed to have his own rules.

"It takes him a while," whispered Lilacs. "He's a little OCD."

I adjusted my seat. Some seancers think an element of fun attracts spirits, so I mentally sorted through the twisters Kamryn had presented on our ride down. "How do you make seven an even number without adding or subtracting? Just remove the s." I smiled as I recalled how she'd giggled over this. That worked. The image of her glee lifted my heart. I was ready.

Lilacs leaned toward me again, her perfume assaulting me. "You'll see something," she whispered. "We always do. Just follow his directions."

Ah! A confederate. She was planting seeds. I looked around for other props. I'd agreed to confidentiality, but I could still spin this stuff for my podcast.

Across the pool, I noticed a young man in a plain black T-shirt. He stared down at the pool. I looked at it, too, and saw motion in the middle that pushed shiny ripples out from the center. *Probably a motor*, I thought. I glanced at Black Shirt. A prickly sensation caressed my neck just as a sliding noise inside the spirit box drew my attention. The curtain moved and Airic emerged.

Chapter Five

He looked younger than his photo, but the blue light caught a silvery streak along the right side of his waist-length black hair. A dark robe cloaked him, and his gaunt face looked serious. I caught the fragrance of camphor, like the Vicks™ I use under my nose during pungent autopsies. Airic sat down and let Virginia buckle the straps over his wrists and legs. Lifting his right arm, he demonstrated the metallic noise it made when the strap moved. I nodded. Airic seemed fragile, as if a spirit truly *could* pass through him. His name, real or contrived, fit.

Airic nodded toward some of us without looking directly at anyone before he raised his face toward the ceiling and took three long breaths. His shoulders slumped and his head fell forward. I'd expected greater theatricality. Aside from the music, the room went silent. All eyes were on Airic. I tried to keep my breathing shallow. Lilacs put her hand on top of mine and squeezed, which made me jump.

In the pool, the ripples swelled. Then the air over the water seemed to form into something dark. I blinked. It looked like a floating fist, but I wasn't sure. The room remained silent, as if no one else had spotted it. I glanced at Black Shirt. He stared at me. I thought he mouthed something. I squinted and shook my head.

The sharp clang of Airic's restraints caught my attention. He sat forward against the straps with a blank expression that suggested a trance... or an act. The room felt tense, expectant. A gust of wind strained at the cellar door. I *hoped* it was wind.

I glanced across the pool. No Black Shirt. I looked around but didn't see him. I felt a slight impression in the air behind me, as if someone's finger hovered just short of touching me. Movement in my hair sent a chill down my back.

Airic remained still, his open eyes vacant. I heard someone whisper, then a sound like a metal rake dragging over the floor. One of the two men across from me began to sing in a low voice, and the doll woman joined in. Singing supposedly helps conduct the energy. Plastic hooks scraped over a rod as the spirit cabinet's curtain slid open. My heart raced. I saw movement across from me in the dark and heard a distant voice in a different language, sharp and quick. To Airic's right, a young woman in a black tank top suddenly giggled.

Airic stirred. He coughed and asked, "Who's here?"

A bell rang inside the cabinet.

"It's Kevin," said the giggler. "He's playing. I'm sure it's him."

The curtain flapped. Airic moved again, clanging his restraints. "He can't get here. He's blocked. He wants to come through."

The sensation of a fingertip at the center of my back made me jerk upright. I caught my breath. Then it was gone. Lilacs sat up next, as if the phantom finger were making the rounds. I peered to my right as far as possible without seeming obvious. No sign of Black Shirt.

"It's dark," Airic said. "They're cold. They're waiting."

"Someone's here who doesn't belong!" Lilacs half-rose from her chair. "Leave now!"

Dampness at my feet made me look down. I couldn't see much, but I felt liquid lick at my bare toes. I pulled my feet up just as a man shouted, "Water!" My heart stopped. I heard a gushing sound as the water rose to my ankles. My twin phobias wound their fingers around my throat. I stood just as Virginia shouted, "Everyone out! It's the sump pump again. Upstairs please! The session is over."

I slipped past the others and sprinted up the steps, relieved to be out. Then I turned around. Seven people emerged, including Virginia. She apologized to everyone. I looked for Black Shirt. He didn't come out. The participants put on their shoes as Virginia closed the door. I mentally calculated. Airic worked with multiples of three. With Black Shirt, I'd seen eight. I was number nine. But Airic would be number ten.

So, who was Black Shirt?

Chapter Six

Retrieving my sandals, I stood on the porch and peered through the rain. The others ran out to their cars while Virginia went into the cabin. No one else came out.

Who *was* that guy? He hadn't looked like the photo of Jimmy. He had to be an Air-aide, a regular, but the others hadn't engaged with him, and he couldn't have blended in unnoticed. There hadn't been enough of us. I needed to speak with Virginia. Or Airic.

I went inside but Virginia waved me off. She said Airic was exhausted. "That session was intense. Something dark came into the room. He couldn't get his helpers through. We would have ended, anyway, because it wasn't leaving. And when you go home, be sure to do a cleansing ritual, so it doesn't attach to you." She offered me a packet of salt.

I asked her about the young man across from me. She twisted her ring. "I don't screen the sitters, Airic does." She touched her right temple. She was hiding something.

"Will you try again?" I asked.

"We'll let you know."

In other words, no, not with me. So, for the moment I couldn't even ask Airic about Jimmy.

I went to my Jeep Liberty. I didn't like this. If Black Shirt were a confederate, Virginia would cover for him. But that would mean Airic was a fraud, and all this stuff about multiples of three and storm dancing was nonsense. This session had been a bust. Strike one.

Back on the road, I drove north. The thickening rain drenched my windshield and soured my mood. I hit several water-filled ruts, further annoying me. I hate to waste my time. I mentally checked Airic off my list. I doubted now that he'd found a missing child. That left the question of why he'd invited me if he were going to just shut me down.

A dark form the size of a kid darted in front of me. I slammed on the brakes and slid into mud. Panicked, I put the Jeep in park to let my heart settle. In the rearview mirror I saw only rain streaming down the back window. I had to get out and go look. Not a great place for that, but I had to see if I'd hurt someone. I grabbed my Glock 42 from my purse, pulled up my parka hood, and opened the door.

Behind my SUV, I saw nothing. I listened but heard only rain smack the dirt road and the leaves overhead. I got back in and drove slowly in reverse. With brightened headlights, I peered into dark spots. I thought I saw a figure. It seemed to watch me, as Black Shirt had done. I gripped the gun, but the shadow dissolved.

Just a perceptual blip, I thought. I'd done a dozen *Psi Apps* on such cognitive quirks. But academic research didn't comfort me out here on a dark, rainy night. Chilled, I stepped on the gas. I couldn't get back to the hotel fast enough.

When I opened the door to our suite, Mika jumped up and barked, fur raised, until she realized it was me. She licked my hand to show she didn't mean it. I touched her collar. Blue. Aha! Kamryn's clues clicked into place. I smiled. M-I-K-A. The first letter of each book title, rearranged, formed the two-syllable name. Just a simple code. I should have seen it.

Kam rushed in from the other room. Her purple pajamas said she was ready for bed. "Mom! Dad didn't come."

I frowned. "Why not?"

Natra followed her in. "He asked if you could keep her another day or two. He's in the field, on a time-sensitive case. He's not going home tonight. He'll call you tomorrow."

I felt Kam's eyes on me, so I forced a smile. "Great. Then we'll find something fun to do tomorrow." I pointed at Mika. "I solved your puzzle. Mika. Two syllables. And it's only 10 o'clock." I leaned down to shift her collar around and found a clump of white string. "Here's the knot, right?"

Kamryn slumped onto the arm of the couch. "You're not all the way there. You have to guess what the knot means, too."

I leaned down and Mika licked my face. I'd taken a knot-tying course with Kam, so I studied the way the strings looped overhand, came around, and tucked in. I recognized it but pretended I didn't. I shook my head.

Kamryn smiled. "So, I win!"

"It's not midnight. I still have time. But one thing I do know. It's time for bed."

"Can't I stay up?"

"If you're in bed in under five minutes, I'll give you a riddle."

Kamryn called for Mika and scampered into the other room.

I let Natra see the exasperation I'd hidden from Kam. She held up her hands. She hates being in the middle of my issues with Wayne. For our daughter, we try to keep things smooth, but he thinks his work trumps mine. It's one of the things that had finally dissolved our seven-year marriage—not to mention his infidelity and tendency to switch plans last-minute.

"I wish he'd said something before we left. He had to know by then." I went over to Mika's water bowl. Kamryn had tied a water knot on Mika's collar. I lifted the bowl to look underneath. A sign taped there said, *You got it!*

I breathed out. "She keeps getting smarter. This one took me a while. I might have to change the rules of this game."

"She'll think her way around those, too."

"That's what I'm afraid of."

I went to check on Kamryn. Mika was curled up on the floor next to her bed. I told Kam I'd found the solution, then gave her the promised puzzle: "I have cities but no houses. I have water but no fish." Then I kissed her, glad to have her with me for another day, and returned to Natra. The television was tuned to a weather channel with the sound off. Bright flashes played across the darkened room.

"How's the storm?" I asked.

"About four days away. It's into the North Atlantic, moving around the

Bahamas. Still not settled on a track." With a tattooed hand, Natra poured a glass of red wine and raised it toward me. "Not to put you in a worse mood, but Harnett's attorney called again. Says he's off the case. They hired someone else."

I stared at her. "Damn it! No wonder that kid's spooked. That's too many changes. How can he trust anyone? Now I'll have to start over." I stopped. "Wait. That attorney hired me. Did he say I was off it, too?"

"He said to send him your report and invoice."

"So, yes, I'm fired." I slumped down on the couch. "That's frustrating. I doubt anyone else will try to help that kid." I took a sip of wine. "So, today's a bust all around. I lost Danny, made no headway on Jimmy, and with Kam still here I can't work on our Georgia cases."

Natra sat forward. "What happened with Airic? You're back sooner than I expected."

I made a face. "It wasn't great. I think my *Psi Apps* caption will be 'medium of the air full of hot air.' I saw hints of fraud, but the session didn't last long enough to confirm it. Water in the cellar forced a shutdown, supposedly by accident or by some dark presence that wouldn't leave. Maybe they realized I wasn't playing and turned on a hidden faucet." I shrugged. "Just can't figure out why they even let me in."

"Crap."

"This one kid acted kinda weird, though. He might've been a plant. I asked Kisner about him, but she claimed she didn't know him. There weren't many people there, so maybe she was lying. It was dark, but she keeps such tight control how could she *not* notice? And he spoiled the numbers. With Airic, we had ten."

Natra sipped her wine. "Maybe he doesn't count himself. What was weird about the kid?"

"He seemed detached. He didn't talk to anyone."

"Doesn't sound like a stooge. They usually manipulate things."

"He might have. When all eyes were on Airic, this kid disappeared. I thought he was behind me, but when the session ended, I couldn't find him. He said something to me. Two or three words. But whatever it was, I couldn't make it out. Anyway, I got nothing on Jimmy. I didn't even talk with Airic about him. I can't charge Lillian when the session was basically canceled."

"Maybe you'll have better luck with McMaster."

"It just feels like I've gone down too many dead ends. Did we get a response from the Georgia attorney?"

"Not yet. Farelly's secretary said he'd call soon."

"She always says that. And he never does."

I watched the storm prediction charts on the TV screen. The weather guy demonstrated with colorful loops the various tracks it could take and the stages it would go through as a hurricane. It was moving around eight miles per hour. One track had it glancing off the coast and heading out to sea, harmless. I liked that one. Another showed landfall right where we were. Well, we probably weren't staying.

I pulled out my phone and saw an email from Virginia Kisner. She'd sent it soon after I'd left. I opened it. The message was short. "Airic wants you to have this." She'd attached a recording.

My heart thumped. I gestured to Natra. "Open the computer. Maybe tonight wasn't a bust after all."

She fired up her laptop. I sent the file. Together we watched the brief clip. When it ended, Natra said, "I don't see anything. Just people sitting in a circle."

I could hardly breathe. I pointed at the dark area where Black Shirt was sitting. I'd half-expected the chair to be empty. But there he was, a fuzzy image in the gloom. "That's the guy, the kid who vanished. Black Shirt."

Natra leaned in. "Looks morose."

"Play it again. Watch only him."

As the clip neared the end, Black Shirt looked up at the camera, his pale face lit in shimmery blue. He mouthed a phrase—the same message I thought he'd aimed at me.

Natra put her hand to her mouth and looked at me, her brown eyes wide. She gave it a voice. *"Find us."*

A chill swept through me. I nodded.

Chapter Seven

The next morning, I tried getting Joe Lochren to clarify the image, but he said he couldn't do it till later. That's the problem with our arrangement. He works fulltime for a cyber security firm and moonlights for me when he can. He thought Kam could help, but I didn't want her to see it. I said I'd wait. I also sent an email to Virginia Kisner to ask about it. I still thought Black Shirt's presence at the sitting had been a set-up. But his message was too similar to Jimmy Broderick's to ignore.

To make up for Kamryn's disappointment over my decision about the storm, I decided to take her to Savannah. She likes ghost stories and she'd make good cover for me as I observed our next ghostbuster. We'd have fun in town, with a meal at a haunted restaurant before we went to the Scavenger House. I rented a car so Natra could take mine to my lake house, where she could coordinate any calls that came in.

I generally avoid grandstanding psychics who speak to groups. They're often just upping their odds of finding someone to dupe. The skilled ones are observant. Their eyes dart to viable targets, looking for defenseless postures and desperate faces. Some hire canvassers to dig up info gleaned from credit cards. They know the more they impress with their "supernatural" precision, the more effective their bait for further paid services.

I'd once watched a "pet psychic" describe to a middle-aged woman how her deceased beagle had loved riding in the car with his head out the window. Even I could have told her that. But she'd nodded at the psychic's "uncanny" vision, then paid $200 for a spirit session with her pet.

This kind of fraud tempts me to dismiss all psychics and mediums. But then I'll have an intriguing encounter. On Jackson Square in New Orleans, an elderly male psychic had beckoned me over to his grimy blanket in front of St. Louis Cathedral. He'd shown the typical signs of a con—persistent chatter, a roving gaze, and a flurry of waves. But then he'd sat up, his bloodshot eyes full of surprise. "There's a cold wind. It's from the west. I see two mountains... someone has died."

I'd felt a chill. A friend of mine "out west," who lived at the foot of the twin San Francisco Peaks, was in dire health. I'd made a call and learned he'd passed that morning. So, even if that psychic had no powers, in that moment he'd seemed to route *something* toward me. These rare encounters make me hope that one day my father might try this way to reconnect. I'm skeptical, but I don't automatically dismiss paranormal possibility.

I reminded myself to be flexible tonight. I had to make a fair evaluation for Lillian Broderick. That's why Kam was a good companion. Her fluid brain popped out surprising comments from things she noticed that I didn't see.

A damp film on my arms foreshadowed a humid evening ahead, but heat never bothered Kam. She just pulled her hair into a ponytail and kept going. She admitted I'd solved her "blue" challenge, but she hadn't worked out mine till I'd offered a clue that set her back five points: "I can be physical or digital." Her eye had lit up. "A map!"

Kam gave me a superior look. "I have one you'll never guess, I know you won't." She giggled. "How can 5-8-1 equal 6?"

I hate math puzzles, but I mentally calculated additions and subtractions. "It can't," I said. "Five plus eight plus one is fourteen, and four plus one is 5." I tried other combinations but never got the numbers to equal six.

Kamryn clapped her hands. "You have to think *differently* about each word. *Each* word."

I tried again but still failed.

"Give up?"

"I yield my points. What's the answer?"

She giggled. "Eight is *ate*, a-t-e, like eating. Five ate one, so he became six."

I shook my head. "Not fair. He just became a fatter five." But it was clever, and I'm the one who'd shown her how to think past the obvious. I conceded.

Satisfied, Kam opened a guidebook. Soon she provided a steady recitation of ghost stories from Savannah.

"You'll hear more tonight," I told her. "And by the way, we're undercover." I thought this would appeal to her. "We're just tourists, ok?"

She nodded absently and leaned into the book. "What's haint blue?"

"What does it say?"

Kam used her finger to trace the passage. "Haint blue was produced on Indigo plantations. Folklore holds that it protects against boo hags." She squinted at me. "Is that a ghost?"

"Sort of. A nasty one. They look like us by day but run around in creepy forms at night to spook and harm people."

Kam nodded. "It says the blue color makes them think they're near water. They can't cross it, so they leave."

"Well, there you have it."

Kam looked up. "Maybe we should paint something haint blue at our house."

"Maybe we should."

We passed the sign for the Georgia border. It reminded me of Alicia and Marti, and what remained to be done on that case. I'd tried to contact Brooke DeBolt, a girl who'd supposedly known about the suicide pact. She'd landed in Angel Oak for hacking into school records. I'd confided my plan to visit her to the families' attorney, Mark Farelly, so I couldn't figure out how the Angel Oak officials had found out. I'd asked for an interview room, but a corrections officer had ushered me into a cluttered office that smelled like cheap coffee and cheaper aftershave.

I could still hear Warden Jared Nash's thick accent as he "invited" me not to come again. A stocky man in a sweat-stained gray uniform shirt that strained the buttons, he'd stepped close to look down his nose. "We he'ah in Savannah ah family. This he'ah case is done. You challenge one'f us, you challenge us awl. We don't take kine'ly to tha'at. So let this be a gentle warnin', dahlin'. Y'all come back he'ah, we'll be watchin'. So, stay in yo own backyahd."

I had every right to be there. However, it was better for my clients that I'd withdrawn. I hadn't even told them. I aimed to try again, but I needed something from Coroner Trey Sullivan, and he wasn't cooperating. Like with Kam's recent puzzle, I had to develop a new angle on this case. They were covering for something.

Chapter Eight

I parked in a lot to board a Scavenger House van with a dozen other people. I checked for messages. Nothing from Natra or Kisner. I turned off my phone.

Kamryn grabbed my arm, wriggling in her seat. "I wanna see a ghost!"

I smiled. We'd had a fun afternoon walking around historic Savannah. Kam had looked up all the ghost stories in her book, telling me with great drama about each haunting. She preferred computers and things she could figure out, but she loved going to new places.

We soon arrived at our destination, a one-story gray frame house that sat several miles down a rough logging road. Darkly ominous woods stood behind it, nearly hiding the ghostly hint of a three-quarters moon. This was the Scavenger House. We gathered in the yard.

"Good evening, everyone!" A short, lean man up in front waved at the group. His sun-darkened skin had surrendered its resilience into sagging folds on his face. I judged from his scrubby gray hair and chin stubble he was in his sixties. He held out his arms as if to embrace us and gestured with two fingers for us to come close. When we did, I smelled pipe tobacco on his black shirt. His raspy voice confirmed his smoking habit.

"I'm Angus McMaster. I'll be your spirit guide tonight." He bounced twice on his bowed legs as he admitted he looked like a steer. His hooded eyes suggested he had secret knowledge we'd have to earn. Angus lifted a bag and pulled out a bunch of bananas. "Everyone needs to ramp up the potassium! We get more spirit energy that way." He passed them around. I split mine with Kam and winked at her. She frowned. I knew her well enough to guess her thoughts: Nothing in her ghost book had mentioned bananas. I didn't bother to explain the potassium enhancement. I just hoped for a better show than I'd gotten with Airic.

There were fourteen in the group. To the side, I noticed a lone dark-haired woman dressed in a white T-shirt and long white skirt. She glowed in the approaching dusk. When Angus invited her forward, she introduced herself as Sarah, his assistant. Her nurturing brown eyes instantly drew me. She smiled at Kamryn, the youngest person present.

Kam leaned so tight against me I smelled the strawberry fragrance of her shampoo. I whispered, "Are you scared?"

She shook her head but grabbed my hand. Hers was cold. I squeezed to reassure her. I remembered being that nervous about ghosts at her age. I'd wanted to see one, but as night approached I'd pull up my covers and hide.

The sound of boots on the weathered front porch drew our attention to a plump brunette in a yellow T-shirt. Angus introduced her as Noreen. She owned the place. I figured she got a percentage of the take for letting us invade her space. She told us which rooms were accessible and which were locked.

"The Scavenger House got its name from vultures." Noreen looked around at each of us and gestured overhead. "On any given day, you'll find groups of turkey vultures on the east part of the roof. I've seen them, sometimes a dozen at once. They stay there for hours. They're liminal birds, which means they're purifiers. They represent the mother spirit, who attends to our troubles before they become destructive. The myths tell us that vultures transform flesh by cleansing it through their bodies. When they roost on a house, like this one, they sense a portal for redistributing energy from physical to spiritual."

Kamryn strained to see, but the roof was empty. Noreen told several stories of spirit sightings, including people's faces at the window when the house was empty. She said she'd had some experiences here, too. One evening, she heard a bumping noise outside the house and saw a buck with a full rack standing on her lawn. It gazed at her until she went back inside. The next morning, she found the buck dead on her porch, from no obvious cause. "I think it saw the vultures," she said. "Maybe it came for the portal."

Noreen stepped aside and invited us to enter. As the others shuffled in, I held Kamryn back. I wanted to stay out of the front lines. Sarah looked over at us before she went in. I wondered if she was concerned about Kam's age. The booker had assured me kids had come on previous outings.

We entered a small room off the kitchen that smelled like meat stew and gathered around Angus. He was a natural-born spellbinder with a gravelly drawl that rolled each word. He lifted his chest and declared, "I have special senses." He made a dramatic flourish. "I know when a ghost is close. But I might not tell you. I'll let you sense it yourself. If you feel something, let me know. I'll tell you if something's there." He predicted we'd feel cold spots and catch sight of people wandering through that weren't in our group. He'd personally seen three. "Look around. See who's here. Then keep your eyes open."

Kam looked at me. I squeezed her shoulders. I wanted her to just have fun. She'd read enough stories to be ready. Angus probably knew how to temper his tales for kids. He'd already used the typical trappings of a spooky campfire talk. If it got too intense, I'd just take her outside.

Angus stepped into the next room and invited us to observe his "special senses" in action. Kam let go of my hand. She darted between several people to find a position in front. I breathed out. She'd entered learning mode. This would be fine. I was about to follow when Sarah came into the kitchen and looked directly at me. Her dark eyes narrowed as if she knew I was no tourist.

Chapter Nine

I noticed the polished indigo stone on Sarah's necklace and smelled a whiff of cinnamon on her skin as she came closer. "I have a message for you." Her soft accent sounded more like a Charleston native than a Lowcountry local. "Do you want to hear it?"

I felt called out. I hoped Lillian hadn't exposed me. "From whom?"

Sarah waved her right hand through the air.

So, not Lillian. I relaxed. "You're a medium?"

"I'm a...mmm... a paratherapist."

That was a new one. "What's that?"

"Sort of like a social worker. I try to help spirits, the ones who get stuck. It's not a business. Just a callin'. I find so many who need help."

This reminded me of a woman who'd once claimed she freed stuck ghosts by sending them through her washing machine. I hoped Sarah wasn't just another poser with a contrived narrative. For Lillian's sake, I had to listen. "Okay, what's the message?"

Her face relaxed. "I don't know what it means, but you might." She cocked her right ear before she looked at me again. "He's aware of you."

This felt raw and...close. "Who?"

"He says you know."

"Maybe." My guard went up. This sounded like fishing for names. "Can you describe him?"

"Teenager. Fifteen, sixteen?"

Okay, that could be Jimmy Broderick. Maybe. Jimmy was twelve, and he looked it. I waited.

"He's determined to get you to do somethin' for him." Sarah shook her head. "No, sorry, he wants you to *know* somethin'." She looked at the floor. "He needs people to know he's innocent, that he wasn't … is it *conscious*?… He wasn't conscious. He didn't understand. People said he was bad, but he's sayin' he wasn't. He's been misrepresented. He wants his mother to know."

I shrugged. "How can I help? I need to hear him."

Sarah waved her right hand in a tight circle. "You can. He says, do mindless stuff. Walking, cleaning, typing… just let him talk while you're not thinkin'. You should grab the first words you hear. Trust 'em."

Right. Not my particular strength.

Then Sarah caught my attention. "There was a murder."

I leaned toward her. "Who? Where?"

"A boy. Maybe another. He keeps sayin' he didn't understand… he didn't know what he'd…what *they'd* do."

"Can he give some details?"

"Not here. It's…" Sarah took a deep breath. "It's north."

Danny Harnett came to mind. But that wasn't my case anymore. Could Jimmy be somewhere north? This spirit boy said to trust what I hear, so I asked, "Does he know Jimmy?"

I could have kicked myself. I'd just fed Sarah a piece of information from which she could build a narrative. I'd given her an opening.

She waited, her eyes moving to the left. "I don't hear that name."

I was already in. I figured I'd keep going. "What about Danny? Does he know Danny?"

Sarah held still, then nodded. "He's saying he does. He says it's not what you think. Look at the pictures."

I cocked my head. "Pictures?"

"Dead. The dead … the death pictures? Something about raining. It's raining. Or… sorry, I don't understand what he's saying. It's a word I don't know."

I *had* looked at the death pictures. The autopsy photos. Danny's alleged victim had been bludgeoned in the head multiple times, causing his brain to swell through cracks in his skull. His face had been badly smashed. I didn't know how another viewing of photos that had turned my stomach could help. But I made a mental note to look again.

Sarah's eyes moved from side to side. "He says you understand how it worked…how *they* work. I hear something about ice cream…or, no … maybe candy?"

I caught my breath. "The *Candy* Man?" Damn! I'd done it again.

Sarah listened and nodded. "I get the number three. Maybe three people."

I wondered if the Candy Man and the "number three" referred to Dean Corll, a sadistic Texas-based killer from the 1970s. I'd written about him, but Sarah couldn't have researched that because I hadn't made this reservation under my name. Corll had made candy, actual candy, but he'd also used booze and drugs to manipulate two teenage boys to procure kids for his S&M torture parties. In the end, he'd always kill the kid, sometimes two at once. One of the teen accomplices, Elmer Wayne Henley, had finally shot Corll and led police to three mass graves containing the bodies of twenty-eight victims.

I shook my head as if I didn't understand. But I recalled that Danny Harnett had hinted at such an arrangement. He'd said he and Mick had "done things" for "Plat-eye." He'd mentioned a witch house and suggested a set-up. I thought he'd sounded paranoid, but this message gave his patchy claims a new twist. I decided to do my own fishing. "Does he mean like Elmer?"

Sarah listened, shook her head, and gestured in a "not so much" way. Then she added, "He seems to be saying, yes, but not as much."

I smelled an odor of wet cotton. "Not as *many*?"

Sarah placed her hands to her throat. "Something here. Choked? Were they choked? Yes. Like…for fun. There were boys, and some girls. Different boys had different dirty jobs. Different people came. Important people. I see files…no, a book, uh…. handwritten. With names and dates." With her hands Sarah approximated a size, about five-by-eight. "He wants you to get it right. Sorry, *set* it right."

"But I can't hear him."

"He says you do hear. You *did* hear. But you didn't understand. He wants you to try. There's abuse. Like he...or someone...was forced..."

This was getting uncomfortable. I despise child abuse. "Can we solve it? The murder?"

Sarah shook her head. "I hear stones... or tones... maybe bones?"

"Bones? So, there are remains?"

She took a deep breath. "I hear... a lot of work. It would be a lot of work. They're hidden. There's water. It's in water. Maybe it's in the river... No, he says no."

I felt annoyed. If some spirit was actually here, I wanted to hear him say these things myself. I wanted to ask questions directly. I *needed* to.

"If you relax," Sarah said, "you can write it. He says to listen."

Ah. That was an idea. "Like automatic writing?" This is where mediums allow spirits to use their hands, holding a pencil or pen, to write or draw the message. Psychography. It usually offers only odd items, but I'd seen it produce leads in two murder cases.

"Yes, like that." Sarah looked tired. "He says he was forced. You understand? He thinks you do." She paused. "I'm getting six. The number six. Like he's been around you, like six weeks? Six months? I'm not sure."

Six weeks. I thought back. That's when I'd been hired to evaluate Danny. But I'd been cut off. "And what should I do?"

Sarah listened. Haltingly, she said, "N-ine...or, no, f-f-find...something. It's faint. Just one word. It? Me?" She shook her head. "He says you know."

I couldn't breathe. *Us* was one word. *Find us.* Black Shirt's message.

Sarah continued. "He was told he was bad by everyone, but he wasn't. All he knew was violence... He was a pretty boy. He got tapped...*trapped.* ...I'm gettin' somethin' about a knee, or...a *key.*"

I felt myself clenching up. I breathed. "Should I seek out someone like you to help?"

"He's sayin' you could use someone. No, he says you *know* someone. But I'm not sure...if it's like me or...Sorry, he's fading. Someone else is pushing him away."

Sarah dropped her head. She seemed to be having trouble. She took two long breaths, as if she were meditating, then stepped back and shook her head. "He's gone, sorry. Just…gone."

I took a moment to ground myself. This is when I grew most impatient with mediums. They lead you right to the point of discovery, then leave you hanging. *What can I say? The spirit left. I can't channel what's not available.* But I wondered why this spirit kid couldn't have told me right away what he wanted, where I should go, and how I could find this book or key. Simple. For all the energy he'd expended to contact me—if that had even happened—he could have spelled out the critical details. Now I had nothing but intrigue.

I reached in my pocket to offer Sarah my card. "If you get anything more, please pass it along to me. This could be important."

I saw Kamryn standing at the door. How much she'd heard I wasn't sure. Sarah gave me an odd look. "There's another one, a girl. Thick red hair. She wants to—"

I glanced at Kam and backed away. "Sorry. It's not for me."

Sarah seemed to understand. She didn't press it. She waved my card as if to say she'd be in touch.

For the next hour, nothing much happened. Angus pointed out cold spots and got scratchy noises on a recorder that he offered as electronic voice phenomena—a ghost voice. Only *he* could decipher it. He told one woman a little boy was standing next to her. Stuff I'd seen before. He was amusing, but he showed no evidence of special senses. I'd have to advise Lillian that McMaster wasn't a viable option for locating Jimmy. Even Sarah, for all the intriguing tidbits, hadn't delivered. Finally, we boarded the van.

I put an arm around Kamryn. "Did you have fun?"

She nodded. "He told good stories. But I didn't see any vultures. Or ghosts. And I ate the banana."

"Well, we can't make them come on command, not even with bananas."

"I just wanna see one. That's all."

Me, too.

The session with Sarah lingered. I didn't know what to think. Had this spirit boy said, *"Find us"*? Like Black Shirt? If so, find *whom*? And where? We already knew where Mick, the murder victim, was. Were there more?

37

Kamryn pressed against me. "What did that lady mean about that red-haired girl?"

"Nothing. Sometimes psychics say vague things to get you talking, and then they pick through it to make you think they know something."

She squinted as if she'd sensed my lie but didn't know how to push. "Who was that kid?"

"Kid?"

"A kid went out the door."

My blood froze, but I tried to stay calm. "What did he look like?"

She raised her left shoulder. "Just a kid, older than me." Kam cocked her head. "You didn't see him?" Then her eyes widened. "Was he a ghost? Like Angus said?"

I caught myself. It was close to her bedtime. I opted for the technical truth. "I didn't see anyone leave."

Kam frowned. Then she shrugged. "He didn't look like a ghost."

Black Shirt. Had he followed me?

Chapter Ten

In the van, I checked again for updates. I couldn't believe Natra's voice message. As of today, my Georgia cases had a new lawyer. Farelly was out. The Mortons and Girards had hired someone named Jackson Raines, a Savannah-based attorney. He wanted to speak to me at once, so Natra had checked him out and told his office where to find me. "This could be good for us," she said. "Follow his lead." I rarely had cases that switched legal representation mid-stream and now I had two in as many days. Since we were on a van, I didn't call back, but I intended to learn more about Raines. If Warden Nash had maneuvered this replacement to further block me, they'd have a fight on their hands.

When the van arrived at the parking lot, I noticed a goldish-orange-lettered cobalt blue Georgia State Patrol car parked near our black Ford Escort. If Raines had sent a cop, he must be in Nash's pocket. As we walked over, the patrol car's door opened, and a pudgy officer stepped out. His stiff manner felt menacing. I grabbed Kamryn's hand and stopped. The officer came up to me and asked, "Dr. Hunter?"

Kam looked at me. I tightened my grip. "Yes."

A second officer emerged and waited.

"What can I do for you?" I asked.

"We'ah gonna have this offisah he'ah take your—"

A honking car horn cut him short as a silver BMW Coupe pulled into the parking lot, flashed its lights, and came toward us. When it stopped, a tall, dark-haired man in a gray suit emerged. He stepped toward the cop with a show of authority. "I'm Jackson Raines, an attorney. Here for Dr.

Hunter." He gestured toward me but remained facing the officers. "Is there something you need?"

The cop narrowed his eyes. "We just want ta speak ta her is awl."

"You can do that through me." He handed over his card. "Unless you mean to arrest her."

Arrest me! I stared at him.

The cop glanced at me and gestured for his partner to get back in the car. When he walked away, Raines turned to me. His dark eyes swept over Kamryn with concern. "Sorry for the drama." He held out a hand. "Jackson Raines. I believe you were told to expect me."

He was a full foot taller than me. I shook his hand. "You're the new attorney on my cases here."

"Yes. And we should speak right away." He watched the patrol car pull away before he said, "We should do this elsewhere. Would you mind following me? It's not far."

I sensed Kamryn watching me. I just wanted to put her in the car and go home. "Can we talk tomorrow?"

Raines gestured in the direction of the road. "They'll follow you. If you're with me, they'll keep their distance."

I urged Kam to get into the car. I didn't like where this was going. When she was out of earshot, I asked, "What's this about? Why would they arrest me?"

"Dr. Hunter, you're being watched. You're in the middle of something more complex than you realize. I'd like to give you some context. It's fifteen minutes from here, and it's on your way."

I was torn. Natra had urged me to trust him. "Okay, I'll follow you. Just don't drive fast and lose me."

"I won't be breaking any laws. We don't need that kind of attention."

In the car, I told Kam we were taking a quick detour.

She nodded. "Is everything okay?"

"I just need to get something for a case. He's the new attorney. This won't take long."

"He seems nice." She raised her arm and lowered it.

"What?"

She raised her arm again. "He said it, Mom. Did you hear it? *With* him." Her arm went down. "Without him."

"Oh. Got it." She loves escape movies. One of her favorites features the hero conveying with this gesture to the doomed damsel that her chances of survival were high with him but low without him. "We're not in that kind of trouble."

I wanted to talk to Natra but not in front of Kam. Raines dressed like an attorney at least, and his olive-tan skin and dark eyes suggested tribal connections. And he actually *had* rescued me. But I didn't know what I was getting into with him, either.

Chapter Eleven

I parked next to him in a brick driveway for a two-story, French-style carriage house with tall arched windows. Not what I'd envisioned for an office. A blue Mini Cooper was already here. On the porch, I saw a slender blond woman with a clipped boyish haircut wearing a beige suit and heels. Her professional garb reassured me.

"Can I come with you?" Kam asked.

"I think so." I got out and Kamryn followed. I kept her close.

Raines introduced the blond. "This is Trish, our digital expert."

Kam perked up. "I know about that! Joe teaches me."

I put an arm around her. "This is Kamryn. She's nine."

She wriggled free. "Ten in two months! I'm good with codes, and I can break a zip tie and untie tricky knots."

Trish looked impressed. "You can do all that?"

"I've practiced." She looked at me. "Right, Mom?"

I nodded. "She actually can. She's our knot expert. And she can get you through an Escape Room faster than anyone I know."

Raines smiled. "Those are handy skills, Kamryn. How would you like to tell Trish more about that? Maybe you can teach her something."

"Sure!"

Trish gestured. "Let's go inside. I'll show you around."

Kam looked at me. "Mom?"

"It's fine. I'll be right behind you."

Raines picked up a banker's box near the door. "Dr. Hunter, I'd like to show you these files. Our Angel Oak cases are linked to others, and we should proceed quickly."

"Mr. Raines, I—"

"Jackson, please. Better yet, Jax. Let's go inside."

I walked ahead to open the door. "I'm Annie. And I need some time to consider all this." Raines was nothing like Farelly, who'd been so hands-off I'd wondered if he'd vanished. Now I had an attorney who was setting the pace—a quick one.

"Of course," he said, "but for now, hear me out. Trish will keep your daughter busy."

Inside, I saw a spacious sitting area with blue-and-white flowered couches to the right of a designer kitchen that featured stainless steel appliances and a gray marble island. Expensive copper pots hung from a wrought iron ceiling rack. I wondered if they'd ever been used. Beige drapes set off pale blue walls with white trim, and another set of couches around a gold-and-glass coffee table near a white fireplace looked pristine. The place oozed elegance and smelled like pine cleaner.

Jax carried his box into a room that served as an office. The antique desk and chairs looked just as tasteful as the other furnishings. Jax gestured around. "We use this place for guests. If what I show you intrigues you enough to stay another day, please consider staying here."

"We accept!" Kam stood at the door. "It's so beautiful, Mom!"

Jax placed several folders on a round table. Kamryn came over. "Look!" She pointed at a folder. "Caryn. Spelled weird, like mine." She gave a sidelong glance toward me to let him know whose fault *that* was.

He looked amused. "Well, Kamryn, for the record, I like your name. It's unique."

She grinned.

Trish came to the door. "I've got some snacks, Kamryn. Hungry?"

"Yes!" She ran out.

"Is that okay?" Trish asked me. "They're healthy."

"That's fine, but not too much."

When they were gone, I asked, "So, what do my cases have to do with those cops tonight?"

"*Our* cases."

"Okay. Our cases. Why are they watching me?"

Jax invited me to take a seat. His near-black irises were impenetrable. "We called your agency today to let you know we've taken over. Your partner, Natra Gawoni, called us back. I work for the Child Support Project, CSP, a law firm for juveniles. I sue on behalf of kids who've been abused in juvenile detention."

That was positive. Much better than Farelly. And Raines had manners. I couldn't imagine him working for Nasty Nash. I pushed through his file folders and spotted Marti Girard and Alicia Morton. I didn't see Jimmy Broderick. Or Danny Harnett.

"We know about your expertise in suicide assessment," Jax continued. "That's what we need, and you're already familiar with the details of these cases. We know your fees and we're prepared to cover them."

I liked the sound of that, but I remained cautious. "What about Farelly? What happened to him? Not that he was any use, but why did the families replace him?"

"We went to them. When we told them about our services and our record of success, they made the switch. We think these cases are related to others we're working, so it made sense for us to acquire them. You can call the families in the morning if you want to be sure."

I figured Natra already had. Tapping the folders for Alicia and Marti, I veiled my next question, in case Kam might be close. "Are the others in the same condition as these two?"

Jax raised an eyebrow. "Eight are...that we know of so far."

"Eight!"

He selected a file to show me. The top page was a summary. A fourteen-year-old boy had died in an accident. The official story didn't match the boy's injuries on multiple points. I closed the folder. "So, eight suspicious incidents like Marti and Alicia. This feels rather dark."

Jax tapped his folders. "The details are here. And this is why certain officials don't want you—or me—looking into it. This involves cover-up, and worse."

"Worse?"

Jax pulled his box over. "I have more cases to go through that I might add. And the girl you've been trying to talk to could end up with these as well." He took another bound stack from the box and removed a file. It bore Brooke DeBolt's name.

My face grew warm. I stared at Jax. Somehow, he'd learned the details of my private investigation. I recalled Nash kicking me out of Angel Oak. He'd discovered the same thing. "How do you know about her?"

Jax sat down. "It's all related to a criminal enterprise network in the juvenile system. It's too involved to explain quickly, so if you'll stay the night, I'll show you the big picture in the morning. And I'll share these files. Everything. I've been researching these cases for years. Your suspicions are on the right track, but no matter what you do, you'll be blocked. We can help each other. You and your daughter will be comfortable here, and it's quite secure."

I seemed to have found the very resource I needed. And he was telling me the corruption I suspected among these corrections officials was real; it was also more widespread—and dangerous—than I'd realized. No wonder cops were watching me. I'd gone fishing for trout and had landed a shark. I *had* to look at these files, if only to decide whether I should stay in. And I had to do that soon. I took a breath and nodded. "We accept."

Chapter Twelve

From our rental car, Jax brought in the overnight bag I'd packed in case I decided to get a room after the Scavenger House tour. Trish had already left. Jax invited me to use the office, but said he'd keep the files until he'd filled me in. Assuring me of surveillance cameras around the property, he gave me his cell number, took mine, and asked, "How early will you be ready tomorrow?"

"How's 7:30?"

Kamryn shook her head. I raised an eyebrow to suggest he ignore her.

"I'll be back in the morning." He wished us a good night. "Please call if you need anything. I live fairly close."

As soon as he left, Kamryn bounced on the sofa and said, "He's cute, Mom!"

I smiled. "He's a little old for you."

"I mean for *you*! Dad's had at least six girlfriends since you split up."

That stung. "I'm not like your dad. And it's time for bed. Go pick your room."

"I already know. The rose room."

"Then, go get ready."

I did find Jackson Raines attractive. He looked about mid-thirties, perhaps a year or so younger than me. He seemed intense but caring, engaged in work on behalf of kids. As long as he was really what he seemed.

Kamryn sprinted up the white circular staircase. She had her father's lean grace and dark hair but my "all-in" personality. I hoped it wouldn't undermine her.

I called Natra to tell her about Raines. "I took your advice. We're staying here tonight so I can look at his files." I gave her the address. "But it seems weird that we're suddenly shedding attorneys."

"Listen! This law firm knows a *lot* about these juvenile treatment facilities. They've sued the one that's been thwarting you in Georgia. Successfully! He's got resources."

"So, we might make progress. Did you call Ayden?"

"He's ready. He'll head down in the morning."

"Tell him to wait."

Natra snorted. "You know him. He's made up his mind."

"What about Joe?"

"He got the tape a little clearer, but I still can't swear by what the kid said."

"I'll look when I'm back. And I'll call Lillian to find out what she wants next. We might have more work than we thought. Did Wayne call? I told him Kam would be ready in the morning, but we'll be down here."

"He didn't call, but JD Riley did, just to say Wayne will call you in the morning."

"He had his *partner* call? That's rich." I heard Kam singing in a bathroom upstairs. "So, what about Raines? What do you know?"

"We got a voice mail from the Child Support Project asking for a call back right away, no matter what time. I looked them up, they're legit, so I called and got Valerie Raines, the director."

Despite my resolve to block romantic thoughts, my heart sank. Was Raines married?

"She said the Girards and Mortons have retained them. She sent over proof, which I've confirmed with them. When I told her you were near Savannah, she seemed concerned. She said cops might hassle you, so she wanted to send someone to give you a hand."

"Just in time, too. Did you look up Jackson Raines?"

"I found a profile in a professional journal. Impressive creds. The George Washington University Law School in D.C. He has a SAR dog, so he's not just an attorney. I have some connections in that world. I'll keep digging."

"He seems genuine. There's a quality about him. Respectful but like he knows he'll get his way. I guess he did, so far, because we're staying. Kam's head over heels. Thinks he's cute."

"What happened with the psychic?"

I'd nearly forgotten about Angus McMaster. I glanced up the stairs. Kamryn stood at the top in an oversized navy T-shirt with "Paris" printed on the front, her long legs bare. She wiped her eye and said, "Goin' to bed."

"I'll be up soon," I told her. "I'm just wrapping things up with Natra."

"Tell her to kiss Mika for me."

"She already did, twice." I waited to hear the door close before I told Natra about Sarah and the boy Kam had seen.

"Maybe he's a neighbor."

"Maybe. It was just strange. I didn't see him, myself, and Sarah didn't seem to notice him. I don't think she's a fraud. She had a way about her, like she was pulling up information she didn't understand rather than trying to manipulate me." I summarized the gist. "But it's two strikes for me. There's nothing on Jimmy Broderick, and McMaster's a dud. We need a new strategy."

We ended the call and I looked in on Kamryn. She breathed evenly, already asleep. A nightlight revealed a room with rose-print curtains and a matching duvet. The room even had a slight rosewater fragrance. No surprise for the Rose Whisperer. I leaned down to kiss her. She didn't move. I left her alone. I was wiped out, too… and worried. I left a riddle on the table next to her in case she woke up. She'd know I'd come in.

I glanced out the window. The light wind pushed clouds away from the expanding moon. Something below caught my eye. Just before the moon dimmed, I saw a large dark shape, like a car, at the end of the long driveway. A glint of light off its right side confirmed it. Had Jax stayed behind? But he'd have told me. And his BMW was silver. I wondered if the cops had put a tracker on my rental. So much for being secure.

I went down, grabbed my Glock, and went out a back door. I stayed in shadows to work my way to the front. But I couldn't see down the drive. I waited for the cloud to slide off the moon before I stepped out for a better look.

The driveway was empty. But *someone* had been there.

Chapter Thirteen

Alert now, with a child to protect, I powered up my tablet to do my own research. If I found any association that even hinted at an acquaintance between Raines and Nash, I'd be out. I found the profile Natra had mentioned, and the photo was the man who'd brought us to this carriage house. However, the information was spare. He'd gotten a scholarship to the George Washington University Law School and had spent three years at a prestigious law firm before he left to join the CSP. The article quoted him about his hope to help reform the state's juvenile corrections system and mentioned an award for his reentry program.

The Child Support Project had been in business for five years, affiliated with a firm that specialized in juvenile law. They sponsored scholarships and awards through Ethan's Project, named for a boy who'd been killed in a Georgia juvenile facility. The photo of CSP's current director, Valerie Raines, showed an attractive woman who knew her way around fashion. With thick auburn hair and fair skin, she didn't resemble Jackson, which dashed any hope she was his sister or cousin.

It wasn't easy to dig up more on Raines. He seemed to hide in plain sight—like how he'd sidestepped some of my questions.

I checked outside again. The driveway was empty. The wind had picked up, so I turned on weather reports. The storm remained elusive about its track. I watched the various predictions until I fell asleep on the couch.

A tone from Natra's early-morning text startled me. I glanced out the window before calling her. She'd learned more about Raines.

"He's got a Creek affiliation, so I called my second cousin in Georgia.

50

He knows things. Jackson's mother was Creek. And get this! His brother, Carter, was a DA's chief investigator and co-founder of the CSP. Three months ago, he was killed. The official story says it was a tragic wrong-place-wrong-time incident, but rumors suggest he was set up."

"That adds a disturbing dimension." *Set up.* Danny had said those words.

"There's more. When Jackson was a teenager, he got in trouble and was sent to juvenile detention, where his case was mishandled."

"I figured he had secrets. Not just secrets. An agenda."

"An attorney helped him, and he ended up in law school. A few years ago, he sued the Juvenile Treatment Associates over a kid who died in custody and won a big settlement, so they're prickly about him. That explains his interest in the Angel Oak cases. That's a JTA facility."

So, he's not friends with Nash, I thought.

"More relevant for us," Natra continued, "his grandfather is a tribal *owala*, a shaman."

I breathed in. *"That's* interesting."

"Shall I drive down with your luggage?"

"No. I'll be back. I want to hear him out and then process it with you and Ayden. It sounds like Raines has made some enemies." I told her about the car in the driveway. "Maybe it wasn't about me. Maybe it was about *him*."

Chapter Fourteen

At 7: 30 a.m., I heard a light knock at the door. I opened it to Valerie Raines in the flesh. She wore a sleeveless blue linen dress that hugged her slim figure and she'd pulled her auburn hair into a perfect twist. She held up a white pastry box. "Good mo'anin'! Ah'm Val. Ah've brought breakfast, although you look as if you won't let a single carb through the door. I hope you have coffee on. We stock that up he'ah, with all the fru-fru to go with."

I did, indeed. Her friendly poise warmed the room, along with the fragrance of fresh baked goods, but she kept her voice low. "Jax said your little daughter is so sweet. Is she still asleep?"

"I'm pretty sure she is."

Valerie lifted a powder blue laptop case that nearly matched her dress. "Let's take this to the sun po'ach, then. We can draw the shades and turn awn the a'ah. It'll cool off fastah 'n' a firebug's blink. Can you fetch us some plates? Ah have napkins. Ah just despise papah, so Ah brought linen. Jax's bringin' his dawg, if you don't mind. He thought it would keep yo'ah daughtah occupied while we talk." She had that breathy 'h' in her 'what' that showed lessons in elocution, but they hadn't erased her accent.

I grabbed three mugs, a tray, and some small plates. "He read her right. She loves dogs."

"Diggah will stay outside. Ah ado'ah him, but Ah must be in court today and Ah won't have his fur makin' me look like an ol' saddle blanket. Listen, I'm so relieved you could stay to see what we'ah doin'. Jax wants you involved, and I trust his judgment."

52

"He doesn't really know me yet."

"Oh, he does. He listens to that radio show you do."

This revelation startled me. She had to mean *Psi Apps*. So, he knew about my atypical investigations. *And* knew of me before he took these cases.

"Ah'll give you the run-down till he gets he'ah. Don't you just love him? He's what you call adoptable. Evah he'ah that term? Of course, you have. Yo'ah a psychologist. People who meet him just want to take him home. Don't you?"

I blushed, but she'd already moved on, chattering in a honeyed drawl that probably won her plenty of male attention. Her expert make-up fell just short of hiding the stress lines around her blue eyes.

"'Course, they ca'yan't have him, so they send us donations," she went on. "Jax did most of the work on this investigation, but we'ah all involved now. With this sto'am comin', we must work quickly." Valerie turned to me, her eyes wide. "Some of these so-called accidents, well, they'ah hahtbreakin'. And a hurricane… Oh, Ah'm so sorry. I'm getting' ahead of mahself, Dr. Hunter. Please fo'give me. Mah prattle just drives mah staff crazy. Ah always think they know what Ah'm talkin' about before I evah explain mahself. But talkin' helps me deal with these things. Ah'm sure you undahstand."

When she paused long enough to open the pastry box, I broke in. "Please, call me Annie."

"Thank you, Ah will. Ah find that fo'malities just get in the way, although sometimes that's a plus, don't you think?" She brought out her computer while I fetched the coffee carafe. Returning, I saw she'd pulled up a complex timeline with names and dates in a variety of colors. I sensed I was getting sucked into something for which I wasn't prepared.

Val cocked her head to give me a stern look. "Do you know of Youth Services International?"

"I do. They privatized many state juvenile facilities and then got hit with lawsuits over abuse. They hadn't done background checks for staff."

"That's right, and we'ah dealin' with a corporation just like that. JTA."

I nodded. "Juvenile Treatment Associates."

"Oh, of course you know that. You just visited one of the facilities."

"Briefly."

She stirred sugar into her coffee. "So, you know what a JRV is? That's the troublemakers. Juveniles at risk fo' violence." She shuddered. "It's just awful. The staff—the *ogres*—use these vicious tactics to keep these kids undah control. We sued them for breakin' a boy's hand. They got fined and his family got money. We won anothah suit when a girl with anorexia was allowed to stahve almost to death. But recently, they've thrown a lot of money around to get themselves immunity."

I set down my coffee. "So, they do buy politicians. I heard that."

"Yes, they do, but the real problem is the'ah multi-state operation. They can easily move kids around. So, a child from he'ah might end up in Seattle, even Alaska! Imagine a poor Jawja boy in that frigid place! And once they get in the system, it's as hard getting' 'em out as suckin' the shugah from sweet tea. They just about nearly dissolve in the'ah. And JTA gets more federal money for JRVs because they supposedly need intensive treatment. You undahstand whe'ah Ah'm goin' with this."

I nodded. "False charges, exaggerated offenses."

"To say the least! Do you know about that kids-for-cash scandal in Pennsylvania?"

I selected a berry scone from the box. "Two judges raked in millions in kickbacks for placing kids with minor infractions into long-term private facilities. But they were convicted."

Her face had flushed. "Which only made things he'ah worse! They were a small paht of this network, hon, just a few grains in a whole box of soiled cat litter. But just those two alone, with their cronies, harmed hundreds of kids. Why, that's just disgraceful! And now our corrupt officials have gone deepah underground. That's what we'ah dealin' with. Grubs in fetid soil."

I sensed I'd stepped into a spider's web that was visible only from the inside. "Jax gave me the impression JTA officials actually kill kids. Is that true?" Stating it so bluntly gave me a bad taste. I thought about the mystery car in the driveway.

Valerie blew on her coffee. "Well, that's his paht. Ah want him ta tell you. Ah didn't believe it at first, Ah can promise you, but he convinced me. He just needs that smokin' gun." She got up to grab sugar. From her briefcase, she removed papers. "These ah copies of the signed forms from yo' clients that allow you to talk to us. They fired the othah attorney."

"Jax told me but didn't say why."

"Oh, hon, that man's one of the grubs. JTA paid him to *block* you."

Chapter Fifteen

Kamryn wandered out to the porch, her fine hair tangled. I was glad she'd pulled on a pair of shorts. She seemed startled to see Valerie and her frown told me I should have warned her. I gave her a hug, introduced them, and told her to get ready for a treat.

"What is it?"

"A *surprise*. You'll like it. Put on a tank top because you'll be outside."

She grabbed a croissant and left.

"Oh, she's so pretty," said Valerie. "You must be proud."

"Thank you, I am." I was still processing Val's bombshell. That's how the Angel Oak warden had known my plans. And why Farelly hadn't answered my calls. I'd left him a detailed message about where I'd be in Georgia yesterday. He must have alerted the cops.

Valerie gestured as if to dismiss my concern. "We assured these families you were deceived, and that we plan to retain you."

"I'll call them and apologize. I can't believe I didn't pick up on it."

"Well, hon, don't blame yo'ahself." Valerie sat down and gestured for me to join her. "Ah'd like to know more about this psychological autopsy method you use in cases like this. The families mentioned it. Ah haven't heard of that."

I sat. "Most people haven't. It's used for cases with questionable elements. Basically, I research the decedent's life and final days to look for mental states and behaviors that might support suicide. I interview people and look at autopsy reports, death scene photos, methods used, things like that. If I don't find the indicators I expect, I'll suggest a deeper investigation."

"Oh, you must get pushback on that."

I nodded. "All the time. Especially if a manner of death has been established, like in our cases. Cops like to think they've done their work, but their ideas about suicide are based on the same myths most people believe. They're not trained on psychological conditions, so they make poor assumptions. And they sure don't like psychologists second-guessing them."

"And how did you conclude that Alicia and Marty had not formed a suicide pact?"

I set down my coffee mug. "I haven't yet. But what you just said about Farelly confirms my suspicions. My initial evaluation supported the coroner's. Then some things didn't seem right. Officials at the detention center showed me the girls' alleged plans, all written down. It seemed consistent with the autopsy reports. But when I interviewed some kids there, I didn't find the kind of close connection I'd expect for a pact. I heard about another girl, Brooke, who was supposedly part of it or knew about it. I wanted to interview her, but the facility blocked me."

Valerie nodded. "What did you do?"

"I contacted the coroner, Trey Sullivan. At first, he said there was nothing to question. He even showed me Alicia's suicide note. But I didn't think it was a suicide note. And the handwriting was different from another item I'd seen of hers."

Valerie leaned forward. "Why did you question the note?"

"It was a poem. It had dark overtones, but that's no surprise, considering where she was. I thought it expressed a need to act, but to *do* something not to kill herself." I sat up. "I thought Sullivan had misinterpreted it. Some investigators think that any scrap of writing found near a body's a suicide note. Even coroners who collect them don't know how to distinguish between fake notes in staged suicides and authentic ones."

Valerie nodded, her eyes narrowed, as if she understood. "But you need mo'ah evidence, don't you?"

"Yes. If they think Brooke was part of it, I need to talk to her. Since they've blocked me, I'd guess she knows something she shouldn't."

"Your work seems so dark. Your husband supports you?"

This abrupt query seemed assuming, even offensive, except that Valerie ran her own agency. I thought she was fishing. And it gave me an opening. "He has nothing to say about it since he's not in the picture. Our work lives clashed, and I had no intention of taking a back seat. Men are competitive. You run a business. Don't you find that?"

Her face softened. "Oh, Cahtah never imagined Ah'd have to manage alone. Neithah did Ah. But he's passed now and Ah'm committed to our mission, so it falls to me. Jax has no patience for office administration."

I'd misjudged her. She'd been married to *Carter* Raines. She was a recent widow. *Very* recent. "I'm so sorry."

She held up a hand, although her eyes had watered. "His work was dangerous. Most of our marriage Ah spent worryin' about what Cahtah was up to. Like sweepin' a dirt road. It wo'ah me out. And the risks he took affected the project. We've lost two attorneys and half a dozen interns."

I realized Valerie hadn't been fishing for info; she'd been seeking assurance of my involvement. I leaned in to show I was listening.

"We think Cahtah was on to somethin' when he was killed," Valerie continued. "The police put out a cov'ah story about a random shootin', but somethin' else happened. He was workin' on—" She stopped and turned her head. "That must be Jax."

I heard Kamryn rush down the steps and out the front door. A dog barked outside, and she squealed in delight.

Valerie gestured toward a door on the porch. "Jax should tell you the rest. Let's go see him."

As we walked out, damp humidity hugged my skin. Jax, in jeans and a green shirt, stood next to a scuffed red Jeep Wrangler. He showed Kamryn how to give commands to his border collie. You can tell a lot about a man from his choice of dog. Border collies are observant problem-solvers, among the best breeds for SAR operations.

Kam gestured. "Digger, sit!" The dog sat at once and looked up for her next command. She crouched low to pet him. "He's so good."

Jax handed her a twisted rag. "Use this to reward him. It's his toy. He doesn't like just anyone. I think he knows you're special." He showed her where the hose was on the side of the house. "Make sure he gets water. You can get him wet. If you want to go inside, just tell him to stay by the door."

Kamryn looked up with a grin. "Okay. And if you need help with digital, come and get me."

"I'll keep that in mind."

I shook hands with Jax and nodded toward the dog. "Brilliant idea. You've won her devotion for life." To Kamryn, I said, "Try to stay in the shade."

Jax strode to his Jeep. He moved like a man who knew he attracted women. He retrieved the box of files. Inside, he accepted a mug of coffee. "Were you comfortable here?"

"Yes, thank you. Kam fell asleep at once."

He raised an eyebrow. "But not you?"

I shrugged. "Naturally vigilant."

His eyes narrowed, but before he could probe, Valerie handed him a plate with a plump blueberry scone. "Ah've given Annie some context." She nodded toward her laptop. "You can take it from he'ah." To me, she said, "Ah'll keep an eye on Kamryn."

When she left, Jax said, "This is hard on her. She was married to my brother, and this project got him killed. For me, it's a way to make his death matter."

"Val said he was on to something."

Jax pulled the stack of files from the box and laid them on the table in front of me. "He was. The connection among these cases. He wanted to find something to help me prove what I suspect. I think he did."

I looked for his own reaction to his brother's death, but I couldn't read it. He had the kind of face, with hooded dark eyes, that even in repose seemed perpetually caught in thought. Then I remembered the car.

"Before you start, I need to ask something. Did you stay for a while last night, in the driveway?"

He looked concerned. "No. Did you see someone?"

"I think so, but it was dark. When the moon came out, I saw a dark car sitting with no lights."

Jax looked concerned. "Why didn't you call me? I would have returned immediately."

"I thought it might be you, but then they left."

"It wasn't a police car?"

"Not an obvious patrol. It was too dark to see well. I wondered if those cops put a tracker on my car. It's a rental, but they got the information, maybe from Farelly, because they were in the right lot."

"They have a large network, Annie, with many informants. I'll have Val look at the security images."

Jax went in to tell her, then returned. "Now I'll show you this." He tapped the laptop to bring up the timeline. "Last night, I mentioned eight cases." He pointed at the names in dark red. "Each is a child who's died under suspicious circumstances in a JTA detention center over the past five years. We're sure there are more and we're going over potential cases of abuse, but the eight we've tracked through their system show a pattern." He glanced at me. "Some involve the same point people."

"A conspiracy?"

"Certainly a cover-up. Except for Marti Girard, all were from families that couldn't afford an attorney or the resources to track their child. The kids had complained of neglect or abuse in official records, and soon they were moved into a status that made them inaccessible. Dangerous or troubled, so they were blocked from visitors. Eventually, they were moved to a distant location."

I thought of Jimmy Broderick. But it was too soon to mention him.

"We've learned that Marti and Alicia were about to cause real trouble. They were going to expose a situation that would have led to arrests and political embarrassment."

I stared at him. "What do you mean?"

He held up a hand. "Let me tell you this in the right order."

I sat back.

Jax picked up a pen to point toward the screen. Again, I noticed the roughness of his knuckles. "What we found is a shell game. Specific children were moved around, which buried their records under several layers. JTA has detention centers in a dozen states now, mostly along the East and West Coasts. It's easy to fabricate offenses to get a child sent from here, for example, to Pennsylvania or New York. Each death on my list has been recorded as a suicide, accident, or illness. Sorry. One was a homicide, called justifiable self-defense." He popped up a color-coded map to show me the states with JTA facilities.

"And you think they're planning to kill others?" I asked. "Soon?"

"Possibly." Jax looked at me with a grave expression. "If you want to stage an accident, dangerous weather's a good cover. We've seen at least one of those."

"This storm?"

"Maybe, if it ramps up." He highlighted Georgia and South Carolina and pointed to a dot near the coast. "This week, two allegedly high-risk juveniles were moved to this facility, which would be vulnerable should the storm sweep along the coast."

He'd used their initials. I didn't see Jimmy's.

"Another will be moved soon. Maybe tomorrow."

I leaned in and saw *D.H.* I wondered if it was Danny. "But why are they killing kids in the first place?"

His eyes narrowed, as if ready to gauge my reaction. "To prevent them from exposing a human trafficking network. Kids for sex."

I couldn't hide my surprise. "What?"

"Carter knew of facility administrators who secretly supplied kids to powerful people whose inclinations would send them to prison. In return, JTA gets protection."

I crossed my arms. I didn't want to believe this, but Sarah had conveyed this message, Danny had hinted at it, and Jax had just confirmed it.

And Danny's initials were on his chart.

Chapter Sixteen

J ax urged me to read the brief file summaries. I scanned three, which filled me with dread. Even when I thought Marti and Alicia's suicides were questionable, I hadn't probed the potential for something this wicked. I felt visible, as if I were the single dark figure on a snowy landscape. "Is this why your brother was killed?"

"I think Carter discovered something that would expose them. He was our investigator, and he made a mistake. He told the wrong person. When he was a homicide detective, he had a partner, Sloane Gilcrest. He'd invited her to help. I think she set him up."

"How?"

Jax went to the door to look outside. Then he turned to me. "Carter had something important. He told me he was going to call Sloane to tell her. Not long afterward, he was shot. At some point that day, he'd sent me a text in our language, Muscogee. *Don't believe.* That's all. Like he knew what was coming and I'd be told lies. He was right. They said he stumbled into a drug deal. Sloane denied hearing from him, but his phone records show she did. And the investigator I hired to examine the crime scene said Carter wasn't killed there. Sloane hadn't even checked this. So, she knew. She was part of it."

"Was she paid?"

"I checked her accounts, but they were a front, like everything else about her. We've been looking for her, but she knows how to cover her trail." Jax sat down.

"And what did Carter find?"

He held up his hands. "I don't know. He thought his phone was tapped, so he wouldn't say, but he assured me it was what I needed. The only thing I was working on was proving the sex ring. Whatever he had, I think he might have hidden it until he could go get it. That was our last conversation."

"Any idea where?"

Jax shrugged. "I don't know what I'm looking for."

"So this woman, Sloane, might have it?"

"Yes."

I leaned toward him. "If they killed your brother and these kids, wouldn't they just kill you, too?"

"If they did, it could reopen Carter's case. They don't want that. Or more attention to *my* suits against them. That gives me some protection. Carter was..." He looked away and his jaw tightened. "He was too close. And it's been three months, so if I had something from him on them, they'd know. I'd have used it."

I tapped the folders. "I still think you pose a greater danger."

He crossed his arms. "They don't know what I've discovered. They did know something about Carter. And he *had* something. I intend to find it. Look, Annie. I know this is daunting. I'd like your help, but you should know the bigger picture. It's not what you signed up for."

Those were my thoughts, too. Ayden, I knew, would jump right in. He loved intrigue like this. Natra would see its importance and seek ways to limit my exposure. But I didn't like being stopped by cops, especially with my daughter in tow. I'd soon send her to Wayne, and I did care about what was happening to these kids, but I had to think hard about this unexpected development. I pointed at the chart. "Those kids being moved. You think they're in imminent danger?"

"At least two are. I tried to acquire their cases, but I've been blocked." He pointed to D.H. "This one's locked down tight. He has an official JTA attorney."

I struggled with confidentiality. But if this kid was Danny, and he was in imminent danger, I couldn't ignore it. "Is his first name Danny?"

Jax cocked his head. "You know him?"

"Never mind. No. It can't be who I'm thinking. I have…had…a client, but he wasn't at a JTA facility."

"You're sure? JTA uses several corporate names. This kid's near Sumter."

I stared at Jax and felt my face flush. He raised an eyebrow. "You do know him. Daniel Wyatt Harnett. His girlfriend's my client." He picked up Caryn Greenwood's folder.

I blinked. "Girlfriend?"

"She's at Sycamore Girls' Academy in South Carolina, moved from Angel Oak. They were arrested together for stealing cars. She's been in and out several times, but he's never been out, not since he was twelve. Two months ago, she asked me to represent him. She said he's being framed for murder."

I swallowed. "They do have physical evidence against him."

Jax leaned toward me. "What does *he* say?"

I hesitated.

Jax nodded. "Right. Confidential. I'll tell you what I think he said. You don't have to confirm it, but if I'm right, you'll want to talk to Caryn."

"I'm not on the case anymore. I really don't think—"

"She's valuable. And she knows Brooke, the girl you've been trying to question."

That got my attention.

Jax held up a finger. "Caryn said Danny and his alleged victim, Mick, were part of this human trafficking network. They were luring other kids into it. Mick was killed because he was making trouble. Danny's about to take the fall."

Another chill. This *was* like the Candy Man. "But… that doesn't make sense. You just said he's in danger of being killed."

"And yet they haven't done it. So, I don't know why they're moving him." Jax stared at me as if he were thinking. "Did he say anything about the ice cream man?"

I couldn't hide my surprise. At the Scavenger House, Sarah had mentioned ice cream. "Where did you hear that?"

"Did he?"

"He didn't, but… someone else did."

64

Jax grabbed a tablet and wrote something. "It's not what you think. It's this." He turned the tablet around to show me. On it I saw four words that made me gasp.

The I Scream Man.

Chapter Seventeen

Jax crossed his arms. "You see? We can help each other. You and I have different pieces of this puzzle, and together we can assemble it."

I pointed to the tablet. "What does it mean?"

"It's a name the kids use when one of them gets moved or disappears."

Energy filled the room as if someone had flicked on a heater. It came from Jax. This work was clearly his passion. He opened a folder and removed several 8x10 photos. I recognized them. Alicia and Marti lay on a steel autopsy table. What marred their youthful beauty were the ugly red ligature marks across their necks.

"*You* already think this was no suicide pact," Jax said, "and *we* know these two were about to expose the I Scream Man."

Another surprise. "So, it's an actual person?"

"We believe it's a group. You've heard of exclusive enclaves for the wealthy, I'm sure. Some are secret. The one we're tracking, the sex ring, is networked to JTA."

I pulled my arms together. Jax noticed.

"Go see Caryn," he urged. "I'll get you in as my psychologist. You can tell her you've seen Danny and ask her about Brooke."

"Jax, I don't know. It's all so …tangled. Don't you see how weird it is that I'm on connected cases?"

"I think you were hired by the same people who decide on attorneys. Maybe they thought you'd get information he won't tell anyone else. They expected you to deliver *pro forma* evaluations, but you didn't. So, they took you off Danny. You went to the Girards and Mortons yourself, not through the attorney. So, they can't bump you off."

"They'll connect me to you."

"They already have. Cops saw us last night."

Valerie interrupted. "Jax, you'll want to see this." To me, she said, "Yo'ah daughtah's so smaht. She came in to get a bowl for the dawg and saw me tryin' to focus these security images. She showed me how. Ah could hahdly see a thing 'til she came in."

Alarmed, I stood up. "She saw the car?"

"Well, she saw it, but Ah don't think she made anythin' of it. I'm so sorry. She wanted to help."

I breathed out. "It's all right. I'm overreacting."

"Ah sent the clip in he'ah." Valerie pointed to the laptop.

Jax brought up the clip. We watched together. I had to admit, Kamryn had done a nice job. When the moon was out, it was easy to see the dark-colored sedan, but I couldn't make out a driver.

Jax looked concerned.

I cocked my head. "Do you recognize it?"

"No, but I think it's a Lexus LS 500. Expensive." He looked at me. "Do you know someone who drives a car like this?"

"No."

"I'll send this clip to Trish. She'll get more information."

Kamryn came in, her phone in her hand. With a look of exasperation, she handed it to me. "Dad wants to talk to you."

I excused myself and went outside, for privacy. I was about to yell at Wayne over his shifting plans, but he slammed me first.

"Why are you getting Kam involved in a case? We discussed this. We made a pact!"

I let Wayne rant for a minute before I interrupted. "She's not involved. She merely showed someone how to enhance a video."

"An attorney. Why are you in Georgia, anyway? Are you working on that case? You shouldn't have taken her!"

His anger seemed oddly out of proportion to what I'd done. I took a breath. "I had plans. You left me scrambling. So, I took her with me to have some fun. I didn't expect to work. Are you ready for her now?"

"Bring her back. I'll arrange childcare."

"If you're working, I'll keep her."

"Fine! But take her back *now*. I'll get her as soon as I can. Clearly, I can't trust you to do the right thing."

Wayne liked to make me feel like the lesser parent. Still, he was right. I'd inadvertently brought Kam into a potentially dangerous situation. I had to undo this.

I looked for her and noticed that Valerie's briefcase was gone. I found Kam in front with Jax and Digger. Jax looked completely comfortable dealing with a kid as he showed her how to make Digger roll over.

"Kam, get your things from upstairs. We're going back."

She looked astonished. "What?"

"Would you please do what I'm asking?"

She knew I meant business. When she was gone, I said to Jax, "I'm sorry. I need to get her back. Her father's upset that she's been exposed to my work."

"Annie, I understand. You didn't expect any of this. I've given you the context. I can send the files digitally."

"Yes, please do. I'll get my team together. I know you're concerned about timing, but it's difficult with a child—"

"Please." Jax pressed his palms together, fingers pointed toward me. "You need time to consider what I've shown you. If you can find a way to be involved, we'll make it work. I'll have Trish send the files. I've made some connections, but maybe you'll see some I missed. I'll take whatever help you can offer. And I'll arrange an escort to make sure no one harasses you."

"An escort?"

"I might have enemies among these cops, but I also have friends."

Chapter Eighteen

The cloudy sky revealed little about our future weather, but I sensed a storm brewing in the car. After I crossed into South Carolina, leaving our Georgia escort behind, Kamryn cocked her head toward me. "Did I do something wrong?"

"No."

"Should I keep my mouth shut about helping?"

I reached over to pat her arm. "Kam, I never want you to feel you have to lie to your father."

"Then why are we leaving? Aren't we gonna work with them?"

I glanced at her. "There's no *we* in this, and your father insists I get you back."

"Why can't *I* decide?"

"Because…you're *nine*. And he's right."

Kamryn put in her earbuds and sat back, cutting me off. She stared out the window, which freed me to think. I needed to know more. Jax had a way of talking as if I were already part of his team. His passion was infectious, and I did care. But the more miles I put behind me, the more doubts arose. *Kids for sex.* Yes, there were such things. And, yes, powerful people had been arrested and sent to prison for it. Some had gotten away with it. But if his suspicions were true, he was challenging a dangerous organization. They might have murdered his brother. I needed Natra's perspective. She'd line up the pros and cons.

At one point, Kamryn removed her earbuds. "Can't Natra watch me so you can go back and work with Jax?"

"Mr. Raines. He's an adult."

"He said I could call him Jax. He doesn't like being called Mr. Raines. And Ayden's an adult and you let me call him Ayden."

"Ok." Kid logic. I couldn't argue.

"Jax is nice. Don't you like him?"

I looked at her, startled. "Of course, I do."

"A little or a lot?"

I blinked. I had to be careful. "He seems like a caring person, but I can't form a complete opinion yet."

"I mean—"

"I know what you mean, Kam, but I barely know him. Adults take longer to decide things like that."

"Dad doesn't."

Ouch! I turned my eyes back to the road. "And how many of his girlfriends have lasted more than three months?"

She raised her shoulders and shook her head. "I hope Linda doesn't. I don't like her."

I wondered if Linda had moved in. A couple of prior girlfriends had, which bothered me. I wanted some voice in the kind of person to whom Wayne exposed our daughter. "Well, you'll need to get along with her for now. You're going to his house."

Kamryn jerked up. "No, no, no, Mom! I thought you said we were going back!" She waved her hand forward as if she could push us all the way through South Carolina to the Outer Banks. "I have to check my roses! And the turtles!"

"Ayden can check your roses. And this has all been arranged. It's not a surprise." I hated this. I wished I didn't have to uproot her. She fell into a pout, earbuds back in. It lasted twenty minutes before she said, "Jax gave me a secret name."

"He did?"

"He said I have a quality and he wanted to give me a name that would remind me when I needed it."

I looked over at her. That seemed like an odd thing for him to do. "Are you going to tell me?"

Kamryn shook her head. "It's *secret*. He said I should tell only those who earn my trust."

"I see! And how would I do that?"

"By trusting *me*. You know, between you and Dad and TV, I'm around this crime stuff all the time. I know what murder is. You don't have to protect me."

Wayne and I had worried about exposing our daughter to the horrors we see. I knew kids her age were reading and watching young adult stories about suicide, rape, abducted children, and sexual abuse. Yet I had to shelter her. I didn't want her to have to stretch into this scary murky world. Just a couple more innocent years, please. Even just one.

I switched lanes to pass a car. "Okay, I'll wait until I'm worthy."

"That might never happen."

"It's possible."

Kamryn frowned. She wanted me to negotiate. I wasn't biting.

"I hate going back and forth, Mom. Why couldn't you and Dad just stay married?"

Because he also had girlfriends every three months when we were married, I thought. "We have different ideas about being happy and we can't achieve that together. And *you* wouldn't be happy if you had to be with two miserable people."

"You always say that."

"And that's all you need to know."

Kamryn vanished into her private world. I let her stew. I knew she'd soon focus on something else. That was the upside of her wide-ranging mind. And *I* had to focus on what I was going to do with Jax.

Chapter Nineteen

My lake house office is a tight fit for my team, but I was glad Ayden had come. He always does his own thing, and I usually benefit. He'd brought his extended cab Ram 2500 truck so he could camp out overnight in the yard. Natra stays in a guesthouse on the trail to the lake. Trish had sent the files, and we spent the afternoon reading them. I wanted Natra and Ayden to make their own notes for an evening discussion. By that time, Joe Lochren would be free if we needed digital analysis.

During a coffee break, I called our paranormalists. Natra had sent Gail the tape of Black Shirt. I described my disappointing experience with Airic.

"That's very strange," she said. "I've heard good things about him."

"Maybe it was an off night. Did you see anything on the tape we missed?"

"We couldn't enhance it any better."

So, a dead end. "I tend to think that kid was a confederate, considering the other contrivances I saw. But I appreciate your help getting me in to Airic's sitting."

There was a brief pause before Gail said, "I didn't. Virginia Kisner told me he won't let someone in he doesn't know."

I sat up. "Then how'd I get in?"

"You must have a secret benefactor."

When I hung up, I went to the computer to look at the tape again. That kid, Black Shirt, had clearly sought my attention. But why did he speak to the camera? It still felt like a set-up, especially with Gail's revelation. *Someone* had wanted me there. Kisner had said no to Gail, and then yes to me? Why? I needed Airic to clear this up.

After dinner, Kam, still miffed, went to Natra's place with Mika so we could work on the files.

Natra offered her assessment first. She thought we were flirting with danger, but the access to Caryn Greenwood intrigued her. "Without another way to Brooke, our investigation stalls, anyway. We either work with Raines and you see Caryn, or we pull out."

Ayden squinted at me. "You're considering that?"

"I don't know. I want us to brainstorm first. If we decide to move forward, we'll head to Georgia as soon as Wayne picks up Kam. I need to go talk with Lillian Broderick, anyway, because we have that case, too."

Ayden tapped the stack of papers Natra had printed out. "I'm impressed with the case organization. These files date back over five years, in several states. Each is in one of three groups. First, we have deaths with questionable features in a JTA facility, like Marti and Alicia; then, we have missing kids who were moved around; and third, we have kids who look vulnerable to becoming one of the other two. Danny's in that group. Of the remaining seven from Raines' files, three have some connection. Two are—or were—in the same facility as our suicide kids, and both are at risk. One, who's missing, was in Golden Larch, the same place they're sending Danny. And one is currently there."

Natra went to the white board on the wall where she'd written the case names and drawn lines with red, blue, green, and black markers. "We need to keep it sorted and focus just on ours." She pointed to *Danny* in purple. "Our first JTA case, although we didn't realize it." Gesturing toward me, she added, "Yours, actually, because it was a forensic evaluation, not an investigation. But what we initially thought were just weird statements from him are now potential links to our Georgia cases. He's accused of murdering Mick Keller, hinting that they'd worked for...." She underlined *The I Scream Man* in red and shook her head. "That's one grim tag." She looked at me. "Brooke DeBolt's file has an asterisk. Know what that means?"

I peered at the board. "I'll have to ask Jax."

Natra pointed to Marti Girard and Alicia Morton. "Raines shows them as 'questionable deaths.' Maybe Caryn Greenwood knows more. I have her in blue, too, though she's Danny's girlfriend." She circled Caryn's name in black and drew an arrow to Danny. "Then, there's Jimmy, in green. He's not on Raines' list, but he's on ours, and he's missing. He went to a juvenile facility or camp of some kind, so we can't rule out a potential connection."

"Even a JTA facility wouldn't necessarily connect him." I pointed at the board. "On the edge of your chart, away from the others, write Black Shirt, maybe in black. I don't know who he is, but we should keep him in mind."

"I think we need Trey Sullivan on our chart, too," Ayden added. "He performed autopsies on Marti and Alicia and gave us the heads-up. And here's a link. Raines' file shows Sullivan on the autopsy of Mick Keller. That's suspicious. Sullivan's in Georgia, but wasn't Mick killed here in South Carolina? Why would Sullivan have done the autopsy?"

I looked through my file on Danny for the autopsy report. "My records show someone else's name. Nate Sempson."

Ayden shrugged. "Maybe our new attorney mixed up some cases."

Natra went to the desktop. "Let's look up Sempson." In a few minutes, she had a report. "He was an ME in North Carolina, but he's been sanctioned for ethics violations. He retired. If he did this autopsy, it had to be freelance."

I leaned back on the sofa. "We need more on the Keller incident *outside* the info they gave me." I got up and went to the whiteboard, pointing at the phrase in red: *I Scream Man*. "This is about a network. We have no idea how many or how powerful they are. I misread Danny when I saw him. He wasn't being obstinate. I think something really scares him. Maybe Caryn knows."

My phone chirped. I grabbed it to look at the text. It was Joe Lochren. *Need to show U something ASAP!*

Chapter Twenty

Natra turned on a large monitor so we could all see. Joe shared his screen to show us the clip we'd sent him of Black Shirt at Airic's sitting.

"I worked on it a little more," he said, "but it's still fuzzy. Best I can do. I saw a photo in the files you sent that looked like him, so I tried a super-imposition." He opened the image of a boy's face. The eyes were closed—an autopsy photo unfamiliar to me. Joe dragged it over a still of the clip, with Black Shirt looking up. "Not an exact match, but the bone structure's close."

It looked *very* close. I peered at it. "Who is it? Is the photo labeled?"

"Yeah, there's a name. Mick Keller."

I shook my head. "No. You have the wrong file."

"That's what it says."

"Then Jax must have put a photo of someone else into Mick's file."

Joe's face came on the screen. "There are several photos of Mick, all labeled with his name, and they all look like this one."

"I saw that, too," Ayden added. "That's from Trey Sullivan."

I grabbed Danny's file. My team hadn't seen these photos because it was a forensic eval. "It can't be Mick. He was bludgeoned in the face. Badly! I had a hard time getting that image out of my head. You couldn't even tell it was—" I caught my breath. "Damn!"

"What?" Ayden asked.

"Danny said it. A set-up. They set *me* up. The photos they gave me for Mick aren't Mick. They must be of someone else. I was supposed to just do the assessment and sign off, but I didn't. So they cut me off." I picked up the file. "This whole thing is probably fake." I turned to the screen. "Thanks, Joe. Can you send me a copy of the superimposition?"

"Sure thing."

Joe signed off, but Ayden stared at the screen. "So, Raines has the real photos of Mick?"

"He must. And the real autopsy report. Sempson probably wasn't even involved."

"Then Sullivan's part of this, like I thought. Raines got them from him. And…"

"And?"

He raised an eyebrow. "And we just saw a potential ID for the kid at Airic's sitting. The one who said, 'Find us.'"

I felt a chill. Ayden and I vie for being the first to make a definitive, provable spirit sighting. But this wasn't it. "I can't say for sure. The image is blurry, and a digital comparison isn't definitive."

He gave me a challenging look. I didn't back down, but he was right. Black Shirt's resemblance to Mick, a dead kid, was eerie. I pulled together Danny's file. "I'll call Jax, see what he says. These connections are getting a little weird."

I went into my bedroom. Now I wondered if the description of Danny's crime was even accurate. A set-up. My heart sped up as I phoned Jax, partly because I'd just experienced some doubt about him. He knew Sullivan, who clearly had some unusual association with these cases. If Jax spun an implausible story about the photos, I'd back out. He'd just replaced an attorney he *said* was working with JTA. Now he aimed for Danny. And he'd known that Danny was at a JTA facility when I hadn't and had suggested that Danny had important information.

Jax answered. "Annie?" He sounded hopeful.

"Hi, Jax. We're discussing the cases and I need to ask you about one of your files. How well do you know the coroner, Trey Sullivan?"

"Pretty well."

"And he gave you these images of Mick Keller's autopsy?"

"Yes, when I looked into representing Danny. He said he did the autopsy."

"That's just it. Why *would* he? According to my file, Mick was killed in South Carolina."

Jax went quiet.

"Does Sullivan know you were going to send these to me?"

"Annie, did something happen?"

"How much do you know about Danny Harnett's case?"

"Just basic facts. What you see in the file. I sent you what I have. Why?"

"Because Mick's autopsy photos in *your* file are not the photos I received for Danny's court evaluation. Not even close."

"Don't say anything else. Not on the phone. I'll drive up. I can come tomorrow afternoon. We'll look at it together."

"I have a better idea. Can you set up an evaluation of Caryn Greenwood for tomorrow? You said she's in South Carolina. That's where I am right now."

"Yes. Sycamore Girls. I'll arrange it and meet you there."

"I don't want to interrupt your work."

"I have other clients there. I can check on them. I'll send you directions to where to meet me."

I felt overheated. I didn't know if it was the adrenaline that always jump-starts a case or the idea of seeing Jax again. I returned to my team to convey what he'd said. "Something's up with this. I need some time to compare my files to those Jax sent us. And I'll go see Caryn Greenwood tomorrow."

Ayden knocked once on the table. "So, we're on."

"For now. I'll try to find a way back into Danny's case. That kid's in trouble. Big trouble. And he has a message. But I can't approach directly. I want JTA to think I'm backing off." I directed Natra to prepare a fake report to send to Danny's former attorney.

"Who's the kid in *your* file?" Ayden asked. "If he's not Mick, then who is he?"

I pointed to Natra's chart. "Add a figure with a question mark."

She did so. Then she looked at me. "What about Lillian Broderick?"

"Call her and tell her I'm still sorting through information. This Airic character might be more interesting than I realized."

I grabbed some assessments for personality and mood evaluations, then picked up Jax's file on Caryn Greenwood. She was 15, I learned, from a small town in Georgia. She'd been caught stealing a car—not for the first time—and landed in Angel Oak. She fought with another girl there, which got her sent to Sycamore, a restrictive facility. I looked at a map, calculated my timing, and sketched out a plan.

Natra came in to have me sign the fake report for Danny. "It's convincing," she said. "Looks like you're accepting the case termination."

I sat back in my chair. "I wonder why this kid's still alive. If they've killed others, why not him, too?"

"Maybe he has something they want."

"He drew something on a piece of paper. I wish I knew what it was. I need to find a way to see him." I signed the report. Natra was nearly out the door when I said, "And one more thing."

She waited.

"Don't let me give Jax the benefit of the doubt just 'cuz he's attractive."

"You suspect him?"

"Not ... outright. But this all feels very rushed. I don't want to make the wrong choices. I think I easily could, especially when I'm with him. He's got a quality. Valerie calls it adoptable, but it's more than that. He's forcefully polite if that makes sense. Just ... help me keep perspective."

"Gotcha."

I got back to work. The trick in any investigation is to know when you have a real clue, not a red herring, and to know the difference between a lead and a rabbit hole. Danny had been a seemingly simple forensic gig; now, he was a key player in a complex investigation that could absorb my other cases.

Chapter Twenty-One

The next morning, we learned that Tropical Storm Delano had drenched the Bahamas and remained on track to threaten our area. It had crept closer to Florida. Wayne *had* to pick up Kamryn. No more excuses. She couldn't come with us to Georgia, and I wanted to get work done before bad weather hit. Wayne had pushed back on the time I'd given him, so we'd compromised at mid-morning.

In my office, I asked my team for further thoughts. "I'm ready to see Caryn, but now's the time to express any other concerns. Let's do a quick run-down. We've got two potential murders to investigate, another kid in danger, and another missing."

Ayden held up a finger. "Maybe more than one."

"Did you find something?"

"Well, we know Danny's alleged victim is someone other than Mick."

I shook my head. "Not really. We know only that the *photos* in Danny's supposed arrest report aren't of Mick. Danny still might have killed Mick, or the other boy, or maybe no one. Two dead boys are associated with him, that much is clear, and these people seem to be using the remains of one to frame him for killing the other. We hope to learn why. And I want to know why Danny didn't tell me the kid in the crime scene photos is *not* Mick? He has to know that."

Natra looked surprised. "You showed him?"

"I did."

"How did he react?"

"He almost never looked straight at me."

"Maybe he thought you were just another colluder."

Ayden cracked a knuckle, a habit I hated. "Or maybe he didn't see Mick killed. So, he didn't know. If the face was smashed, maybe he couldn't tell."

I tapped my pen. "When I rethink my sessions with him, it's clear he knows something more. For one, that it's all a set-up. So, the autopsy photos wouldn't surprise him. Hopefully, Caryn can shed some light. What about Sullivan? Anything there?"

Ayden sat forward. "OK, going on the premise that he's been trying to tip us, I looked for psychological traces."

"Meaning what?"

"Like intentional inconsistencies. Breadcrumbs. What you taught me."

"And…?"

"Annie, I went through every paper in the file. I stayed up late. I read and reread them. All of the autopsy reports in these files are from him. They're not all signed, but I think the handwriting's the same, the way certain letters are formed."

"So, he had jurisdiction. Mick must have been killed in Georgia."

"But Mick was not listed as a resident in a facility in Sullivan's jurisdiction. He *was* in one in South Carolina."

Natra sat down with a mug of tea. "I noticed it, too. I think Sullivan's part of it in some way, unethical if not illegal. Either JTA wants to hide where Mick was killed or Sullivan's getting cases he shouldn't, and he knows it."

"I vote for the second one." Ayden moved his right hand to signal hesitation. "Here's what I think. They wanted *him* on this case. And on other cases. So, I say he's implicated in the staging. I think I should head there and try to dig up more."

Natra cocked her head. "But then why would he give the actual report to Raines? Did he think Raines would give it to us, to help us, or did he not realize Raines would do that?" She looked at me.

I shrugged. "Jackson Raines knows something. For now, we'll treat Sullivan as part of a cover-up, so we'll be careful. But he did tip me to something amiss with the suicide pact." I breathed in. "So, potentially, we have a missing kid, Jimmy, and maybe the elusive Brooke. We also have

Mick's missing remains, and another dead kid, ID unknown. But these last two are not our cases, at least, not for now."

"I did some research," Natra added. "Mick's family held a memorial service, but there was no notice from a funeral home."

Ayden shrugged. "That doesn't mean anything. Didn't Jax say most of these families couldn't afford much?"

"It's possible they only got ashes. Perhaps JTA officials paid for the cremation. That would be emotional leverage while keeping secrets hidden."

I nodded. "Seems possible. But I don't think we should contact the family just yet. You two can go ahead to Georgia. Get set up. Maybe find a hotel near the CSP office. But don't get too close to Sullivan yet. I want to learn what Jax has to say first."

Chapter Twenty-Two

I went to Kamryn's room to make sure she was ready for her father's arrival. I brought a necklace made from a white shell with lavender stripes, her favorite color. Meant for her approaching birthday, I thought it might lift her mood right now.

She wasn't there, so I placed the necklace on her pillow. I went outside and walked around the property. No sign of her. It wasn't like her to not tell me where she was going. I texted her. She didn't answer. I called. Still no answer. I walked around the house again and looked in all the spots I could think of—her favorite chair, the tree swing, the fishing dock. Then I found her pink phone. She'd left it on the porch. I plugged it into a charger. Her bike was here, so she hadn't gone far.

I texted Natra. She joined me with Mika to scan areas around the shore. There were hiking paths, but Kamryn usually took Mika when she hiked. Natra sent Mika to search, but the Doberdor quickly returned and sat in front of her.

"She was upset," I said, "but she wouldn't just..." I couldn't finish the thought.

"She wouldn't."

"Someone seems aware of what I'm doing. Maybe—"

"Don't even think that. Besides, Mika would have barked if a stranger was near the house."

I could hardly breathe. Was the car at the guesthouse a warning? Should I pull out of the JTA cases? We strode back as Ayden came out on the porch. "Find her?"

"No. I'll check her room again."

Mika barked and ran in.

Just then a red Mercedes S550 drove up to the house and stopped. A well-dressed blond woman emerged. It took me a minute to realize it was Linda, Wayne's girlfriend. I'd seen her once when I'd dropped off Kamryn. I tried to control myself when she waved and approached as if we were friends.

"I'm so sorry to just show up," she said. "Wayne got called in early this morning and he's too far away to come when you wanted. So, I offered to pick her up. I hope he called to tell you." She checked her fitness watch. "Oh, he's still in the field. Is Kamryn ready?"

I roiled inside. Typical Wayne. He couldn't be bothered to pick up his daughter himself, or at least let me know. Like having his partner call me instead of doing it himself. And he had to show off his girlfriend, with her perfect skin, lean figure, and the spiked heels I'd never wear for him. I wasn't about to give this woman the satisfaction of knowing he hadn't called.

"I'll look for her," I said.

To my relief, Kamryn was in her room, with Mika. I sent the dog out and gave Kam her phone. I noticed she'd picked up the shell necklace. "Kam, I've been looking everywhere for you! Where'd you go?"

She shrugged and kept her eyes down. It stabbed me in the heart. It didn't usually take her this long to forget why she was mad. I guessed the weather reports about the approaching storm had fed the fire. I took a deep breath. "Linda's here to pick you up. Are you ready?"

Anger deepened her pout. Now she did look at me...with fury. *"Linda!* Where's Dad?"

"I don't know. He sent Linda."

"I'm not going with her!"

"Okay, I'll get Ayden to drive you over. But you have to—"

"No! I don't want to go!" She started to cry but tried not to show me.

I felt helpless. "I'm sorry."

Kam stormed around her room, slamming things into her bag. "Never mind. I'll leave. I don't want to be with you. I *hate* you! I know you don't want me around!"

She lifted her suitcase. When I tried to take it, she swung it away, hitting the doorjamb, and then shoved past me. She was out the door and down the porch stairs before I could catch up. She didn't stop to hug me good-bye. She just got in Linda's car and slammed the door. Linda got in the driver's side. I rushed to the passenger side window to persuade Kam to reconsider or at least let me hug her, but Linda started moving. Kamryn glared at me. She wanted to hurt me as much as she thought I was hurting her.

But I saw something else that made me step back and gasp. It was the expression I'd seen when I was fourteen, when my friend Hailey had flashed me the same look—*do something!*—before Tommy Ray Bruder had whisked her away on his motorcycle. And just like then, I froze.

Linda waved and drove off.

I wiped my face to stop the tears. Natra hugged me. "She'll forgive you."

I just shook my head. I hated this. More to the point, I hated Wayne for this bait-and-switch. He'd never been so callous. Kamryn didn't like this woman. Now she had to spend time alone with her for who knows how long till Wayne got home? With his schedule, that could be a long day.

Ayden stood apart, staring up the now-empty driveway. "I've seen her before."

"She's Wayne's latest girlfriend."

"It was recent."

"Maybe in town?"

He shook his head and turned to me. "Call him. Tell him this isn't right."

"Believe me, I intend to." I looked up the driveway. I should have just opened the door and made Linda stop. I should have assured Kam I loved her.

But I hadn't, and it was too late. Several drops of rain bounced off my face. I had to get on the road. Kids in real trouble needed me now. Kam would be okay.

Chapter Twenty-Three

As I drove, I tried calling Wayne. He didn't pick up, so I left him a blistering message. Then I tried Kam. She didn't answer, but that didn't surprise me. It was too soon. On her voice mail, I mentioned seeing Jax, which I thought would please her. Or, it might just further annoy her. I couldn't shake her strange look. It was like that superimposition Joe had shown us, only with Hailey's face overshadowing Kam's.

Jax had directed me to yet another classy, unoccupied house, already aired out and smelling fresh. He'd done a legal service for the owners, he told me, and they'd given him a key to their summerhouse. Since it was close to the Sycamore Girls' Academy, he stayed here whenever he came up. He clearly had a knack for getting favors.

"You can set up over here." He tapped a round table in a cozy nook. "I've made coffee. I'd like to discuss a strategy before we go over." He set down some mugs.

I told him about Kam. He commiserated. "But she seems pretty resilient."

"She is. And she loves her father. I just wish he'd handled it better. His work's important—he's a SLED agent—but this treatment's inexcusable."

"Did you tell him?"

"Can't reach him. He's been on some investigation for several weeks. So, enough about him. Let's get to work." I spread out my test instruments. "Initially, it's just an interview, to see what works best." I placed a *House-Tree-Person* packet in front of him as he sat down. I'd used this one with Danny, when he'd drawn the eye. The *H-T-P* exercise asks subjects to draw a house, a tree, and a person, with the idea that the same psychological issues will show across all three domains. They might draw everything on one page or each image on a separate page, their choice. Even that seemingly trivial act becomes part of the behavioral map.

Jax looked through my pile as if he knew what each item was. Although lawyers *should* be familiar with psychological tests, they're often not. He tapped the *H-T-P* test. "This is good. She can code things."

"Code?"

"Don't assume the guards respect attorney-client privilege. I have friends at Sycamore, but we're dealing with corrupt officials. They know I'm coming. They're probably watching her."

I put up my hands. "What do you call this network? We need a better name than the I Scream Man."

"Got any ideas?"

"Well, what is it? A network of corrections officials? An enclave of rich deviants? A gang of crooked politicians?"

"All of the above, probably. We just call it ISM. That's the first layer. The handlers. The kids have nicknames for the key figures."

"Fine. ISM. It goes with our other shortcuts. JTA. JRV. At least it doesn't prickle my skin as much. But how can they violate privilege?"

"They have attorneys and cops in their pockets."

I raised an eyebrow. "And you think you can stand up to them?"

"I have a system."

"What, the David-and-Goliath system?"

He smiled. "It feels like that sometimes. But it's more like the thorn-in-the-elephant's-foot. They don't see it coming. We've pierced them already, several times. A large thorn could take them down. I'm close to having that."

I nodded. "Like that law center that hit the Klan with a series of crippling lawsuits."

"Like that, Annie. That's my model."

"But those groups nearly assassinated the director."

Jax tilted his head. "And yet, he's still alive."

I placed my hands on the table. "Okay. You have a plan and you're committed. I agree that we should try to help Danny. I just don't want my daughter in harm's way."

Jax leaned toward me and tapped the top of my hand. "Neither do I."

I grabbed a personality assessment. "If we don't have privacy, I'll work around it. Is Caryn pretty bright?"

"She is. She's a car thief, a good one."

"But she hasn't told you what she knows?"

"She said Danny's in trouble. He smuggled a note to her that she managed to read before a CO confiscated it. When I called her yesterday, she used our code, so she has information she can't say until she sees me."

"How does she communicate with Danny?"

Jax sat back. I cocked my head, waiting.

He breathed out. "She has ways. These places have networks."

I felt blocked. "Ok, full disclosure. I know you have experience with juvenile detention, and not just as an attorney. Obviously, you've changed your life for the better. So, please be open with me."

Jax nodded. "Good. I figured your investigators would turn it up. Yes, I was in detention, several times. That's why I relate to these kids. And care about what happens to them. *And* know how they communicate. What's your plan?"

He'd let me in, a new level of intimacy. That was a good step. So, I laid out my approach. "As you say, hopefully, she'll use these items for covert communication. Danny did."

"I have no doubt. By the way, Brooke's here, too."

I sat back. "I thought she was at Angel Oak."

"They moved her. Changed her status."

This alarmed me. "Because of my inquiry?"

"Possibly."

"Can I see her?"

"No. We don't want undue attention, to us or to her."

"So, she's at risk, too. Why the asterisk by her name on your file?"

"Her role's unclear."

I raised an eyebrow. "They got to her?"

"Maybe. We think she knows the truth about the suicide pact."

"That they were killed?"

"My intel says the girls wanted to expose ISM, but the youngest one let it slip, which got back to the wrong person. Brooke is part of that. She might be a snitch, or she might be a target, but I can't get around her attorney to find out. So, he's paid, afraid or getting laid."

I snorted. "The terrible trio. P-A-L. Nice way to put it."

"Sex is always currency for men in power, and ISM offers it in every deviant form."

"What about Trey Sullivan? Which one is he?"

Jax surprised me when he said, "You need to leave that alone."

I thought I'd misheard. *"Alone?* I think he's helping to frame Danny for murder. I can't leave it alone!"

Jax got up with his coffee and went to a window. His body language telegraphed discomfort. "Trey's in a tough position. He wants to help, but they have leverage. He's in the A category. Afraid. They could ruin him for a stupid mistake he made. So, he does what they require. But he slips me information." He looked at me. "Like the true autopsy photos. You can't let anyone outside your team know about that."

"But how would it work? Unless you saw my file on Danny, you wouldn't have spotted the inconsistency."

"We're working together. I told him. He gave me what he had. He said it was staged."

"Did *you* know I didn't have Mick's actual autopsy photos?"

"No. But I'm not surprised. I think you were hired to be a cog in this machine. When you questioned the suicide case in Georgia—which Trey told me—you made it clear you're not. So, they blocked you."

"Whose autopsy photos were passed off as Mick's? That kid was obviously murdered, too."

"I don't know. I haven't seen your files. But let's try to get Danny out of trouble first, while he's still alive."

I felt as if I were treading water without knowing where I'd jumped in. I just had to trust I'd find solid footing—not a feeling I liked. "So how does this all work in your system?"

"I collect evidence for lawsuits. Each win makes the elephant stumble. Then I put another one in its path. If you stick the beast enough times, you halt its momentum."

"Unless he tramples you first."

Jax gave me a serious look. "We can't let that happen."

Chapter Twenty-Four

Despite the typically arduous protocols for entering a correctional facility, Jax got us through quickly. He clearly had friends there. With smiles and winks, they eased the process. Three female COs seemed especially pleased to see him, and he spent some time chatting them up.

Jax had told me to leave my phone at the house. I didn't like this, but I figured if Kamryn were going to call, she'd check in with Natra or Ayden if she couldn't get me. Or maybe she'd call them first. If Wayne called, he could wait.

Finally, we went into a cramped, windowless room with a table and scratched metal folding chairs. Yellow stains on the beige walls magnified the repulsive stench of residue from cigarette smoke. Outside in the hall, I heard other kids talking. Caryn Greenwood hugged Jax with a grin, but when he left to see other clients, she sat down and pressed her thin arms tight against her sides. I took this as a warning to me to be careful. The girl looked mousy. I thought she hadn't washed her dirty blond hair in days. I doubted she had much to offer.

I explained my procedure and showed her the testing instruments. She looked as if she expected me to pull out a needle and stick her with it. I asked her some preliminary questions about herself, which she answered in as few words as possible, and gave her a pencil and a stack of numbered blank pieces of paper. I asked her to draw a house.

Caryn stared at the paper. Then she picked up the pencil. Glancing at me from under bangs that nearly hid her lifeless hazel eyes, she drew a square box with three windows as her "house." When she included bars on the windows, I knew what she meant. She decorated the tops of each window before she grabbed a separate sheet and drew a hanging tree, with a corpse. I tried to show no reaction. The head was strangely shaped, with a flat right side. To my surprise, she added a second figure on another branch that had long curly hair. Her choices were unusual. This had to be code.

I pushed the stack of paper toward her. "Now draw a person."

Caryn squinted at the door. Then she went to work. But the image that emerged was not a person, not even a stick figure, but an ice cream cone. Then, over the rounded scoop, she drew what looked like a hangman's mask with a single eye. Next to this figure, she drew a circle inside another circle. Placing her tree drawing next to this paper, she sketched an arrow from the double circles toward the hanged man. Then she slid the hangman drawing away. Her eyes challenged me. Had I understood? I sensed she thought *I* was the dim bulb in the room.

I reminded myself that this plain, mopey girl's issues had gotten her into a secure facility. Her diagnostic workup had described a reactive attachment disorder with psychotic features. Jax had assured me this wasn't true. I began to think it was. She rubbed her arm as if she wanted me to understand something.

I selected a test that required Caryn to fill in blanks. Jax had urged me to use it, as if he had a plan. "What you see here shows me your verbal abilities. Next to the words, write what you think they mean."

She shook her head slightly, as if she thought this was all pointless. Then she squinted as if trying to figure out what I really wanted. She spent ten minutes completing this exercise. When I looked at it, I saw nothing but nonsense. There wasn't a single word I could understand. It didn't look like a foreign language, either.

A stocky female corrections officer opened the door, battering me with the noise of kids shouting in the hallway. "Everything all right in here?"

Caryn sat back, her eyes down. The uniformed woman edged over to look at her work. I stood and blocked her. "I'm sorry, but this test is timed. I'd appreciate having no interruptions. Now we'll have to start over."

She gave me a suspicious look, but shrugged and left, closing the door. I realized there could be a hidden camera. I picked out another instrument, but Caryn seemed reluctant to keep going. She watched the door. I offered her a limited-choice personality test. She read through two pages. Instead of responding to the items in order, she underlined three words and circled five others. I asked her to sign and date it. She put a date two days away. I wasn't getting it. I hoped Jax would. Caryn grabbed back the hangman's tree and darkened the lines around the male figure's head. Her eyes conveyed urgency. She traced the date to make it bolder. I nodded as if I understood. She added a tear to the female figure's face before shoving the papers toward me to show she'd done enough. Now it was up to me.

To my relief, Jax returned. He thanked Caryn for meeting with us and told her he'd let her know when he could get her moved closer to her family. She looked at me and tapped near her eye twice before the female CO escorted her out.

Jax gestured toward the table. "Pack her papers up tight into one envelope."

I folded the papers to fit into a size 10.

"Now, shuffle your other papers around and covertly stuff this envelope under your blazer."

Mystified, I did so. We left the interview room. "Just follow my lead," Jax said. We were nearly out the last locked door when a muscular black male in a sweat-stained uniform shouted at us. "Stop, please. We need to check your items again."

Chapter Twenty-Five

I shook my head. "These test results are private." I waited for Jax to assert his legal authority. To my shock, he said nothing.

The officer held up his hand. "We have reason to believe you're smuggling contraband." Jax nodded for me to follow his order. I handed over my folder. Now it made sense that he'd wanted me to hide the envelope. But then the guard gestured toward my jacket. "All of it. We have to scan it for drug residue."

So, they'd had a camera in the room. They'd seen everything. Still, I was surprised Jax didn't object. He had a right to. I feared they'd use the crazy stuff Caryn had scribbled to put her on meds. I flashed him a look of displeasure before I handed over the envelope. Although most of Caryn's responses were nonsense, I worried they'd see the masked ice cream cone. I frowned. Jax gestured to me to cool it.

I went over to an orange plastic chair and sat in a way that expressed my frustration. I'd undertaken this evaluation as work product for an attorney. I expected that attorney to protect it, but he leaned on the desk to talk to a flirty uniformed redhead. I disliked how completely at ease he seemed with what had just happened. *It's a set up.* Danny's warning made my stomach clench. If I'd driven my own car, I might have walked out. I wanted to trust Jax, but his actions today made this difficult.

When the officer returned the papers, they were now a mess. Jax thanked him for respecting our time and guided me out before I could fire forth with what *I* thought. In the parking lot, he put a finger to his lips. Only when we'd been in the car for ten minutes beyond the facility gate did he breathe out. "It's not what it looks like."

"I hope not! Because it looks bad. You let them violate your client's rights. You *thanked* them!"

"Annie, relax. They protect themselves. It's better to act as if you have nothing to hide. If they think we got nothing from Caryn, they'll relax. We don't need their suspicion. Nor does she."

"What if they misinterpret her responses as psychosis? If I didn't know better, it would look like that to me. She might end up on meds."

Jax glanced at me. "This place isn't run that well. No staff psychiatrist will even check before I get her out."

"I hope not."

"The best way to hide what we know is to keep the pieces apart. When we return to the house—when it's safe—we'll see how it all fits."

I gritted my teeth. "So, I'm the mule."

"The mule?"

"I carry intel without knowing what it is."

"Ah." He smiled. "Like I just did."

"You?"

"I supplied autopsy photos that only you could interpret. So, yesterday, I was the mule."

I frowned. But I got it. I sat back. "That's more trust than I'm used to."

"Fair enough. And I'm an attorney. You don't like attorneys."

"Well…"

"That's all right. I don't, either."

I relaxed. He'd cleared the air. "What do you think they made of Caryn's notes?"

Jax shrugged. "They saw the scribbling of an unstable kid. Before we came, she did some drawings to make it look like she's just entertaining herself. They're probably laughing over how stupid we were to interview a crazy girl."

"This is risky, Jax. And I'm not so sure we got much, anyway. I couldn't ask her anything directly about Danny. Or about Brooke."

"She knows that." He glanced at me. "Give her a chance. We'll know soon enough."

"Why are you so keen to rescue these kids?"

Jax watched the road for a moment. Then he said, "I owe someone. Two people. An attorney and a psychologist, ironically. In the... in detention, I was considered a lost cause. But they thought I was..." He searched for a word.

"Adoptable?"

"That's Valerie's word. I don't know. But I *was* lost. Angry. Destructive. Just 12, and I'd committed a string of petty crimes."

"Why?"

"It doesn't matter. Just reacting to a bad situation." He glanced at me. "But these two decided I was worth rescuing, as you put it. They got me out of the system and saw me all the way through law school. I repay them by using my skills this way."

"Okay, but lots of kids need legal help. Why pick the ones in this dangerous network?"

"You're the psychologist. I'll let you figure that out."

"And I will."

He glanced at me. "I know. But don't tell me."

"Why not?"

"You said it on your podcast. Solving your own mystery is an energy leak, right? You flatten your passion. I'd rather care about my cause than understand why I do it."

I peered at him. I'd just learned something. He was cagey. He'd told me enough to make me think he'd been open, that he wasn't hiding something.

But he was. His clenched hands on the steering wheel belied his confidence. He was hiding something big.

Chapter Twenty-Six

A t the house, I checked my phone. I saw only a text from Natra with the hotel address where she and Ayden were heading. No mention of Kam. I took a deep breath to calm my anxiety before turning my attention to Caryn's cryptic message.

Jax had me spread her papers on the table. I'd numbered the pages, so I fixed the order.

Pointing to the date on one, Jax said, "She's letting us know when."

"When what?"

He stared at the hanging tree and then examined the unintelligible words Caryn had written, as well as those she'd underlined and circled. He pulled a scrap of paper from his pocket. "One of my other clients gave me the decoder."

"Ah! Your system. Keep info separated. That's why you weren't worried. Without the key, the officers can't understand it."

"Correct." He sat down and wrote the letters from Caryn's nonsense words into a sentence. He pointed to the first figure she'd drawn and tapped on the oddly shaped head. "Do you see it?"

I looked closely. I felt as if I were playing one of Kamryn's games. The right side was flattened while the left bulged out. "It's a D," I said. "For Danny?"

"I suspect Danny's slated for an accident. Soon."

I squinted. "If that's the plan, why did they wait?"

Jax shrugged. "Maybe it's just a scare tactic. Or maybe something happened recently and the danger of keeping him alive outweighs their potential gain."

"So, we're still stalled." I tapped the other hanging figure. "Who's this?"

"Maybe Brooke." He pointed to the way a strand of hair seemed to curl. "This looks like a 'B'."

"What if it's Caryn?" I gestured. "This curl looks like a 'C'. And she pointed to her eye. Maybe she heard they're going to do something to *her*."

Jax tapped under his own eye as if to read her behavior by mimicry. "We're missing something. I need to get her moved. How soon can you write your report?"

"I'll send Natra my notes and she can send you a digital copy tonight." I pulled up a chair next to him and looked at the *H-T-P* drawing of the prison. Caryn had spent some time on this. I pointed to the window frames. "Look! I think there's something here."

We both tried to make out what appeared to be tiny letters, but it was difficult. Jax pulled up a magnifier app on his phone and handed it to me. "Read them to me. I'll write them down."

It seemed to be more nonsense. Jax used the decoder, but there were gaps. He stared at the result.

"The first word might be 'stop'," I said. "Stop doing something."

"Stop… t…r…n.."

"Transfer! That must be it! Stop them from transferring him." I looked at Jax. "They're going to do something during a transfer." I tapped on her date. "In two days!"

He nodded. "That makes sense. We're three days from a potential hurricane. They want him in place."

I glanced through the papers where Caryn had circled and underlined words. Jax added them to his list.

"I could really use Kamryn right now," I said. "She can spot patterns and decode things like this."

"My brother could, too." Jax tapped his fingers on the paper. Then he sorted through them. He pointed to the page numbers. "They took something."

He was right. A page was missing. I looked for Caryn's drawing of the ice cream cone. It wasn't there. "I know what it is." On the other side of the hanging tree page, I replicated it from memory. "Do you think they figured something out?"

"Maybe." He picked up the drawing and narrowed his eyes. "This must be Plat-eye."

I gasped. "Plat-eye! Danny used that word. What does it mean?"

"Danny said Plat-eye? That name? When?"

Danny's safety outweighed my duty to confidentiality, so I told Jax about his statement.

Jax ran his finger around the window of Caryn's house drawing. "Does she write that here?"

I used the magnifier to make out the letters in her design. I saw 'witch'. "This must be the witch house he mentioned."

"Witch?" Jax pondered this. "No, it's not witch." He pointed. "It's *switch*. The switch house. The place where they take the kids for the sex parties."

We looked at each other. *Switch* has several sinister meanings. "If they take Danny there," I said, "he probably won't get out. Where is it?"

"The Lowcountry, but I'm not sure where."

"And who's Plat-eye?"

"One of the I Scream Men." He tapped the one-eyed mask I'd drawn. "That's what the kids say."

"So, Plat-eye is going to take Danny to the switch house? Maybe that's why Caryn touched her eye. Plat-*eye*. How can we stop it?"

Jax rested his face in his right hand for a moment. Then he said, "I have some ideas. Can you get your team together?"

"They're ready to roll, probably already in Georgia. Let me see if there's anything new." I called Natra.

"Annie," she said. "I was just about to call. Lillian Broderick wants to meet with you this evening. She says it's urgent. She has something to show us."

Chapter Twenty-Seven

We had just enough time for dinner and a discussion before Lillian's arrival. I still hadn't heard from Kamryn or Wayne, which worried me. Ayden said he'd tried them several times. "I should have gone by his house before we left."

"If they don't call tonight," I said, "I'll go back tomorrow. Wayne can be a jerk, but Kam's grudges don't last this long."

"Maybe she left her phone in Linda's car," Natra suggested. "She's like that."

"Yes, she is. She almost forgot it this morning." I breathed in to calm myself. "I'm sure she's fine. If something happened, Wayne would have called. I wish I had Linda's number, but I don't know her last name. There's nothing I can do about it now, except make a mental note to never let this happen again. Let's get down to business."

Natra had ordered dinner. Over a grilled shrimp Caesar salad, I summarized my time with Caryn. Jax had kept her papers, so I drew the images from memory and told them about Plat-eye.

"Creepy," Ayden commented. "A plat-eye's a one-eyed shape-shifter—a red eye as big as a plate. Parents used it to make kids behave."

Natra wagged a finger. "But in some tales, it's a guardian of buried treasure."

"I think this one's more likely a bad guy," I said. "We think Caryn's warning us that something bad will happen to Danny Harnett in two days. Jax is using his connections to find out about transfer times. It's not necessarily to an official facility. There's a possible Lowcountry location, but Jax doesn't know where it is."

"Should I go help him?" Ayden asked.

"He'll let us know." I told them what I'd learned—or rather *hadn't* learned—about Sullivan. "At least Jax has a connection there. If Sullivan knows anything important, he'll tell Jax. That's my impression. So, no visits to him just yet."

I could tell it bothered Ayden to hold off. He likes action. I asked him to take Mika to his room so we could prepare for Lillian.

When he left, Natra stood to clear the table. "Do you trust this attorney, or not?"

"Jax? I think so. But the jury's still out. He keeps his plans to himself, so I wouldn't say we're a team. I'm still finding my way with him."

"I got more info from my cousin about the brother, for our victimology." I gestured for her to continue.

"Carter was four years older than Jax. Married, two teenage kids. He was also a survivor of juvenile detention. They grew up with an abusive father who beat their mother into dementia. Both parents are deceased. Carter became a cop, then a detective. We know that. But this is interesting. There was talk of him being charged for corruption, but the charges were dropped. Ayden's working on getting more info. Carter resigned right after that and became the investigator for CSP, which was set up with settlement money from a JTA lawsuit. We also know that. But my cousin said Carter had recently advised Jax to dissolve CSP. He doesn't know why."

"Hmmm. That's odd. Obviously, Jax didn't accept the advice. I wonder if Valerie's aware of that."

"The settlement also bought a nice piece of property, where Jax lives. He takes care of his grandfather, apparently. The *owala*."

"That's in his favor. I do think Jax sincerely wants to help these kids. He has an agenda with JTA, if they're implicated in his brother's murder. That makes his moves more genuine but also dicey. He has secrets, that's for sure. And maybe Carter did, too."

A text chime on Natra's phone announced Lillian's arrival. She sent her the room number and texted Ayden. We had to focus on Jimmy now.

I introduced Lillian to my team and invited her to sit down. Ayden took a chair slightly behind her. Next to me, Natra posed as my clerical assistant, so she could observe Lillian's behavioral tells. I had no idea what to expect. I didn't relish telling her I'd struck out with both psychics.

Lillian seemed distracted, even annoyed. I soon found out why.

"Ah saw the name of that medium on yo'ah website," she said. "Airic. When Ah didn't hear from you Ah called him."

I mentally kicked myself for misjudging her desperation. She'd been on my podcast website, where several people had discussed Airic.

"I was just getting my notes together," I told her. "We didn't get anything with McMaster, but we're investigating something—"

"His assistant said she sent you a recordin'. May Ah see it?"

I looked at Natra. "Let's show her." I figured it couldn't hurt, but I wondered why Kisner had spoken to Lillian but not to me. I sensed Lillian thought I was hiding something.

She watched the brief recording and shook her head. "That's not mah son."

"I didn't think so."

Lillian pointed. "This boy was the'ah? You saw him?"

"Yes, I saw him. He's not a ghost, if that's what you're thinking. He was in the session. He looks nothing like Jimmy. If he had, I'd have called you right away."

Lillian took a tissue and wiped her eyes. "So, you ha'yev no leads. That woman gave me the impression yo'ah workin' with this medium."

That seemed strange. "I don't know him. I've never even spoken to him privately. He invited me to a session and sent the recording, but he didn't follow up. I don't know what he thinks about it. I've been trying to initiate a conversation, and when I do, I'll talk with him about Jimmy. Until then, I don't consider myself working with him. But I thought you had something to show us. Maybe we should look at it."

"Yes." She dug through her purse and extracted a folded piece of paper. "This. Ah found it in my husband's cah. He doesn't know Ah took it and Ah must get it back before he notices." She handed it over.

I unfolded it. My heart sped up. I handed the note to Natra and looked at Lillian. "Why would he have this?"

Lillian raised her chin. "That's yo-ah address, isn't it? Ah looked it up. You have an office in that buildin'. What did mah husband tell you?"

Chapter Twenty-Eight

Ayden rose to his feet. "He's been following you, Annie!" To Lillian, he said, "What's going on?"

She cowered.

Unnerved myself, I gestured for Ayden to sit down. Then I turned to Lillian. "I don't know your husband. I don't know why he has this address. But now I wonder why you contacted me. Did you really see Jimmy in a dream?"

Lillian's eyes watered. She glanced at Natra and back at me. "Ah did. Ah truly did. Mah son *is* missing. Ah do need help."

"But you didn't contact me as a potential investigator, did you?"

She looked at the floor. "Ah came to you because of that note. Ah thought James—that's Jimmy's fathah—brought him to you."

I tried to hide my anger. She wasn't the first client to start a case with a lie, but at least we'd caught it before we'd invested much effort. I did understand, though. If Kam disappeared, I'd storm the gates of Hell to find her and tell any lie I had to. "Who's your husband and what does he want with me?"

"He… he runs an architecture firm. Ah don't know what he wants with you. Ah only know he has yo'ah address."

"What kind of car does he drive?"

Lillian blinked at me. "A Lexus."

"Dark?"

"So, you did see him?"

"Maybe. But just the car. Start from the beginning. Tell me what happened. We'll try to figure this out together, but only if you tell me the truth."

Over the course of an hour, we learned that a judge had sentenced Jimmy to juvenile detention over skipping school and throwing some rocks off a bridge. He'd hit no one, but he got four months at a county facility. Within a week, Jimmy was moved to a more restrictive facility for bad behavior. Lillian couldn't learn the location. She suspected her husband knew, but he refused to tell her.

"He can afford a good attorney," I said. "Why would he allow this?"

Lillian broke down and sobbed out, "Ah had another dream! Two nights ago. Jimmy came back! He was naked and screamin', he just kept *screamin'*..." She put her face in her hands and wept so hard she shook. Natra retrieved a tissue box.

I wondered if Jimmy was with the I Scream Man.

"If mah husband didn't bring him to you, maybe he wanted you to investigate."

"That's possible," I said, but I didn't think so. It was a shared office space I rarely used, and he hadn't tried connecting by phone or online. If he'd been at Jax's guesthouse, watching, he wasn't interested in my fact-finding skills. He was up to something, and I intended to find out. I expected it would lead me to Jimmy.

We got no further with Lillian. I assured her I'd engage my whole team. When she left, Ayden fetched Mika while Natra got out the wine. I spotted a stack of drawings on the coffee table. They looked like Ayden's work. "What're these for?"

Natra shrugged. "He's working on his face memory. Drawing helps define them and keep then sorted."

I looked at the top one, which depicted Danny Harnett. "He's got a good memory. And an eye for what's distinct. And I keep looking past what's distinct. First, I marginalized Danny. Then I minimized Jimmy. What else have I missed?"

Ayden returned. "I need to find out about Broderick. Put me on it, Boss."

I held up my hand. "We need a plan. Jax wants you for something, too."

"Shouldn't we tell him about Jimmy?" Natra asked. "It's a Georgia juvenile case."

"Jimmy doesn't fit the pattern," I said, "but I agree. Let's call Jax."

We used Ayden's phone, since I now thought mine could be bugged. I soon had Jax on speakerphone. I summarized our conversation with Lillian.

"James Broderick," he said. "Of Broderick Architectural Design?"

"I think so."

He breathed out, and not in a good way.

"Is there a problem?"

"We think he's involved with ISM."

A chill gripped me. That man had been at my office. He'd been following me. Ayden nodded, as if he'd already concluded this.

"How?" I asked.

"Perks for services. He's got some political ambition."

"Then why would they take his son?"

"Not sure. Maybe to make him do something. If the boy was moved that quickly, the judge was in on it. This could be about you, Annie. They might be worried about your snooping. They've moved you away from Danny, but you're still on the suicide cases. And now they've seen you with me, twice. Maybe Broderick's supposed to watch you. Did you send that report to Danny's former attorney?"

"I did."

"Good. That signals you're pulling out. I'll tell the Mortons and Girards that you're off their cases, too."

"Wait a—"

"Officially. I'll camouflage your involvement."

"You don't think ISM already knows I'm in Georgia?"

"And you'll leave in the morning. We'll bring you in, get some paperwork done, as if that's what you're here for, and then you'll go. Keep your doors locked tonight."

I was sorry I'd called him. "Jax, if Broderick intends harm, he could have done something to me at any number of places. Such as the guesthouse."

"We don't know his intention, so our best maneuver is to make ISM think you're backing off. You'll finish Caryn's report and then leave. Be ready tomorrow. Early."

He ended the call. I looked at my team. Ayden scowled. "I don't like this."

"Nor do I."

"I think he's right," Natra said. "Let's formally sign off and see what happens next. We can still investigate Jimmy's case, find out what Broderick's up to. Let's just keep working."

"Okay. I think I might pay Airic a call. In person."

Ayden went with Natra to keep watch while she took Mika out, leaving me alone to finish my wine. I flipped on the TV to see the latest weather. Conditions had worsened. Like our case, the storm had twisted onto a new path, as if searching for me.

Chapter Twenty-Nine

The morning brought surprisingly clear weather. That meant nothing. Tourists in Galveston in 1900 had witnessed a gorgeous September morning transform so fast into a raging hurricane that by noon they were trapped. By evening, more than 6,000 were dead.

Kamryn still hadn't responded, and her full voice mailbox now blocked messages. That supported Natra's theory that she'd mislaid her phone. Even if she were ignoring me, she'd have cleared the messages. Wayne had also ignored me, as had his partner, JD. I left angry messages once more for both. I considered calling Wayne's neighbor, but it was too early.

A knock at the door at 7 a.m. startled me. I opened it to Valerie Raines, looking fresh in a mint green outfit with matching pumps. She entered. "He'ah I am again, Annie. Lord, it's humid out! Makes me feel like a frog. It nearly melted mah make-up."

"Where's Jax?"

"Oh, we ran into yo' PI outside. They'ah gettin' acquainted. Why, that young man's a dahlin'! Chahmin' as a bunny eatin' honey. Yo'ah lucky. A good PI is tough to find." She set down her briefcase. "I believe Jax spent the enti'ah night tryin' to decide what to do. Ah know he didn't get much sleep."

"I'm sorry—"

"Well, it's not you, hon. That's what he does for difficult decisions. He went into the ground, is the way he puts it." Valerie lifted a coffee cup and gestured toward the carafe I'd ordered. "May Ah?"

"Of course." I grabbed it and poured her a cup. "Can I order you some breakfast?"

"No, that's sweet, but Ah'm just fine. Ah ate. An empty stomach on coffee's like drivin' a cah with no steerin' wheel."

The simile eluded me. "What does it mean to go into the ground?"

"Well, that's where Puca—that's his grandfather—lives. Not 'cause Jax wants him to, mind you. Jax has a fine house, but that old man stays close to the soil. He loves his cave. Says it gives him pow'ah." She gestured in the air. "Puca sees things. So, he's in a bunk'ah on the ranch. He's a, oh...what's the word? L-somethin'."

Natra had entered with Mika. She finished the sentence: "*Owala* or *alektca.*"

"Yes, that's it!" Val reached for Natra's hand. "Hello, Ah'm Valerie. Yo'ah the dog handlah. She's a pretty dog. You must have some native blood, yo'self, Ah see it in your go'geous features. Ah'd die to have ha'yah that long."

"Do you mind the dog, or should I put her away?"

"Oh, goodness, no," Valerie told her. "She's fahn. She looks well-behaved, and nowhere ne-yah as much ha'yah as Digg'ah."

I gently redirected her. "So, he went into the ground."

"Yes, it's a ritual. Cahtah used to do it. He'd disappe'ah for three days sometimes. They take their wisdom work seriously. And let me tell you, that old man saved those boys. If not for Puca, they'd both have gone to prison young and stayed they'ah."

Natra raised an eyebrow at me. The idea that Jax had stayed up to spiritually discern a sense of direction impressed me.

"Where was their mother?" I asked.

Valerie moved some magazines to set up her laptop. "Put in an institution. Ah met her just once, when I married Cahtah. She passed just after tha'yat. But you know, we nevah lose them. You might think Ah'm as crazy as the top of a crackah box, but Ah still talk tah Cahtah ev'ry day. But now we have some business to discuss. We have a young woman's suicide note. You said you can spot a fake one?"

Her abrupt shift startled me. "I might be able to."

"Can you do it from a copy?"

"Let's have a look."

Valerie reached into her blue briefcase and pulled out a note on plain white paper. It contained a series of short sentences in red ink.

"I'm doing this because no one cares. My friends are gone and it's my fault. I know it's wrong. I might go to hell. Don't blame Barry. He tried to help. It was my decision."

I placed the note on the table. "Do you have a handwriting sample from her in another context? I'd like to compare them."

"We don't, Ah'm afraid. At least, not yet."

"I'd need to know more about her. I can try a content analysis, although there's not much here. It's hard to know what counts without context, but I'll tell you what I see." I pointed at the bottom line. "First, it's not signed. Second, she says not to blame someone named Barry. Fake notes often name a person in a favorable light who'd be suspected if the death looks staged. Ninety percent name someone who turns out to be the killer. So, find out who Barry is."

"We think it's the case workah."

"Okay. Another thing that's off is the explanation. It's rare to see an actual reason named for suicide, except when someone's enraged. Most people who simulate suicide notes for research studies believe suicidal people explain themselves, but they mostly don't. I also see a moral judgment expressed, which only deeply religious people think about."

A knock on the door interrupted us. Natra went to answer it. Ayden came in, followed by Jax. Ayden flashed me a look that said he was impressed.

"She's already at work," Valerie said to Jax.

I tapped the note. "I need context, especially from her background. And someone should analyze the paper, see if she had more like it in her room. What I see is suggestive of a fake note, but I need to know more about the note writer."

"It's Brooke," Jax said. "And she's in critical care."

Chapter Thirty

My stomach lurched. "Oh, my God. She tried to kill herself?"

"Maybe. That's why we want your take on the note." Jax introduced himself to Natra and sat in a chair next to me. Mika went straight over to him as if he were her master. Jax rubbed her neck. "I've seen this dog in action at SAR events. She's talented."

He looked tired. Dressed in jeans and a casual linen jacket, he clearly was not here as an attorney. And he carried a gun. It reminded me to make sure my Ruger and Glock were ready. Jax directed Valerie to show me the photos.

She removed a large envelope from her briefcase.

"So, you think they might have tried killing her?" I asked. "How did you get this note?"

"The person who found her is a friend of mine at the facility. One of the women I spoke with when we went. She knows I've been concerned about Brooke, so she called me last night and sent over what she could."

"And where was the note?"

"Close to her."

"She has no roommate?"

"She was in isolation. Allegedly, she'd stolen something from a CO."

Valerie laid out copies of photos. I leaned in. This was Brooke, the girl I'd been looking for. I picked up one that showed the pudgy brunette with deep marks and a purplish bulge from the cord noose. The canting groove along the neck looked right for a live hanging, but a killer could have stood behind her and pulled up on the cord. In that case, there should be signs of a struggle, such as her fingers scratching at the noose. Unless she'd been drugged. It was too soon for a tox report. "Will she live?"

"That's hard to say. She hasn't regained consciousness."

"How did she get the rope?"

Jax shrugged. "Who knows?"

"When did this happen?"

"Yesterday evening."

I looked at Jax. "After we were at Sycamore? Is this related to our visit?"

"I suspect it is. Caryn tried to tell us."

I nodded. "She did. But we couldn't have done anything, not if it happened that quickly." If this incident were related to our visit, then my attempt to see Brooke at Angel Oak had started the ball rolling. "For what it's worth, if I didn't know anything else, I'd still say that note is more likely to be fake than genuine."

"Her file just got moved up in priority for us. She's under constant care right now, but I'll let an official I trust know about potential foul play. If someone tried to kill her and didn't succeed, he or she will try again. At least she *is* alive, for now. There's a chance of saving her."

"I hope so. And what about Caryn? Isn't she at risk?"

"That's unclear. If they went after Brooke, it's probably because of what she knows about the supposed suicide pact. If that was staged, she poses a greater risk than Caryn. But our attention on anyone right now raises their risk. I need to get Caryn moved."

Jax picked up Ayden's drawing of Danny. "This is good. Looks like him." Ayden beamed.

"Okay," I said, "I think it's time for us to get to work."

Jax held up two fingers. "First, some conditions. We're concerned about Broderick poking around. No doubt he knows who your team is, and he might know his wife has consulted you. So, *I* take the lead."

"But Lillian hasn't hired you."

"That doesn't matter. Broderick's interest in you and his likely involvement with ISM puts his son on my list."

I held out my hands. "What's the other condition?"

111

"Valerie can take Natra and Ayden to the office to finish the Greenwood report and brainstorm ideas." To Ayden, he said, "You can use our resources there." Then Jax turned back to me. "I need you to come with me."

I cocked my head. "Where?"

"My house. It's twenty minutes from here. My grandfather has a message for you."

Chapter Thirty-One

I'd met shamans before. The only time one had focused on me specifically, I'd learned about a serious medical problem I didn't know I had. Treating it had saved my life. I took Jax's directive seriously.

Natra said she'd pack my stuff and take it to the CSP offices. I asked her to keep trying Kam's phone. By this time, I knew she'd either lost the phone or something was wrong. She'd have contacted one of us, even if it weren't me. I wondered if Linda had taken her phone away. I had to get back and see Wayne.

Jax and I got into his jeep. "I appreciate your willingness to do this," he said. "When my grandfather attunes to someone, it's usually beneficial."

"He said he has a message? Like what?"

Jax shrugged. "It's for you, not me."

"Valerie called him Puca."

"She gets it wrong. It's pronounced Pu-tcha, not Pu-ka. A stronger sound. He's my actual grandfather, but he's also the tribal grandfather, symbolically. He's a far-seer, *hecvs*." He glanced at me. "You know this term?"

"I don't. Is it like a remote viewer?"

"It's more ... internal. He oversees our lives, so he peers into the hearts of people we deal with. Sometimes he knows we'll meet someone before we do. He warns us."

"He warned you about me?"

"No. But he said my fate is linked to yours."

"Is that good or bad?"

"Either. He never says. We call him a peacemaker. He draws out poison so we can make peace with ourselves. Did you eat this morning?"

"Just coffee."

"Good. You'll be alert."

"How did he know I'd agree to come?"

Jax passed a car before he replied. "One thing about you, Annie. You're willing to explore. You reveal a lot on your podcasts. You're attracted to spiritual things. At least, you're open to them." He glanced at me. "Puca wouldn't invite you if he thought you'd decline."

I wondered if this *owala* could tell me about Kam's wellbeing. If I had the opportunity, I'd ask. "I've done some remote viewing. I'm not good at it, but I did a podcast on a group of viewers who found a missing mother. Does he want me to do that?"

"He just told me to bring you." Jax gave me a sidelong look. "So, now I'm the mule."

"Touché."

"He did say something disturbs you. It's all knotted up around you, and it's been there a while. He wants to untangle it so you can work more effectively. I can tell you this, from experience. If you stay knotted up, you're paralyzed. But open up and you'll come away with something."

I swallowed. This felt invasive. "How does he know me?"

"The same way I do. He listens to *Psi Apps*."

"What?"

"My nephew, Dylan, Carter's son, told us about your show. He studies with Puca. We listened to several of your episodes together. Then last week, Puca advised me to investigate the attorney on the Morton-Girard case, which I knew about from Sullivan. I discovered they were blocking you. So, I stepped in."

I didn't know whether to be pleased or disturbed. "Will you be at this meeting?"

"No. It's private. Dylan will direct you."

"Is he like Val?"

"Not at all. He's quiet. He's a real apprentice. He caught the breath."

"The breath?"

"When babies are born in our band, the peacemaker breathes on them. If one catches the breath—breathes in—he or she can become a healer."

"So, you didn't?"

"I caught it, I'm told, but I pushed it back out." Jax shrugged. "That made me a different kind of caretaker."

"That reminds me…" I checked my phone. Kam would be up by now. But there were no messages.

"Has Kamryn forgiven you yet?" Jax asked.

"I don't know. She might still be pouting. She won't pick up." I rubbed my face. I needed to refocus. "What about you? Any kids? Know what it's like to be shut out?"

Jax stared ahead.

"Sorry. That was rude. I'm taking this out on—"

"I do know." His response was so quiet I barely heard it. I sensed I'd poked him in a tender spot. He looked in the rearview mirror before he said, "Ethan's Project is named for my son."

"Jax, I didn't—"

"It's all right. There's no mystery about it. He died in a detention center, a JTA facility. I didn't even know about him until he was already in trouble. His mother was…a mess. She'd lost custody twice, so he'd been in foster care. When she ran out of options, she told me about him. By then, he was ten. I did what I could, but he was like me at that age. Angry, stubborn, destructive." He glanced at me. "He was 14 when he was killed."

I put my hand to my mouth. "My God, Jax! I'm so sorry. How?"

"The guards set up these fight clubs and forced kids into them. They'd pit the youngest kids against the oldest. Ethan went up against a 17-year-old. He was tall but not muscular. He didn't have a chance. He died from multiple blunt force injuries."

"That's horrible!"

Jax nodded. "It was. And I sued. That settlement was our seed money for Ethan's Project. But I kept looking at issues in JTA. Sexual abuse was rampant in this facility as well, but complaints were quickly erased. Carter joined me and traced the network of cover-ups to some politicians getting paid to renew the corporate contracts. So, I started my list of questionable deaths."

I wondered why Carter had tried getting Jax to dissolve the CSP enterprise. "More abuse, more lawsuits."

"Yes. We have half a dozen potential suits, but I want a crippling knockout. I need a smoking gun."

"What happened to Ethan's mother?"

Jax tensed. I sensed I'd peeled off some skin.

"She was a CO at a facility where I was... a resident. I was 15. You can figure out the rest." He glanced at me. "That's the downside to being adoptable, as you call it. Female sexual aggression is brushed off as a joke. We boys bragged about it. But there's damage. It pretty much erases your ability to trust."

My problems with a brooding child suddenly felt trivial. As if reading my thoughts, Jax said, "Kamryn's a good kid. She'll come around. Even her annoyance with you is full of affection. She admires you."

I teared up and blinked fast to keep my composure. Jax tapped the horn and pointed to his right. A black-and-white dog running near a small herd of sheep stopped and went alert. I recognized Digger. We were here. I would now meet this medicine man who thought I had knots to untangle.

Chapter Thirty-Two

L ittle about this ranch, as Val had called it, spoke of traditional Georgia aside from the long, paved driveway and thick oaks that guarded the expansive two-story brick house. Just beyond it was a fenced pasture that held a dozen black-faced sheep, shorn for summer. From under the gate, Digger came running.

"That's smart," I observed, "giving him sheep to herd."

"Border collies need to work."

Behind a barn, I spotted a compact blue helicopter on a raised helipad. Across a pond was a shooting range. "This place looks like a training ground for an assassin."

"My friends use it," Jax said. "My neighbor's a cop. Comes in handy sometimes."

A slender dark-haired young man came toward us. "Welcome," he said, his hand stretched toward me. "I'm Dylan." He bowed slightly. "I'm honored to meet you, Dr. Hunter. I've listened to all of your podcasts. I've learned a lot."

I shook his hand and thanked him. I recognized Valerie's fine features in his handsome face, but he had a light brown complexion.

Digger bounded up. I didn't see what Jax did, but the dog sat at once and remained still, panting. Jax released him from his barely contained pose and let him receive attention from me before he sent the dog back to the pasture. Gesturing toward the house, he said, "I hope you don't mind going underground. As I recall, you once investigated a case inside a cave."

"I did, but I don't like enclosed places. The things I'll do for a case don't generalize to my personal life."

"This is for our case."

Inside the house, citrus scents soften the imposing dark wood and leather furniture. It felt serene, the kind of place that welcomes after a long day. An alcove near the kitchen had been turned into what looked like a mini pub. I pointed at it. "I want a drink at that bar one day."

"Noted. I imported most of that from Scotland."

Just off the kitchen, we entered a bright room with white ceramic tile floors and lockers that suggested a high-end sauna in a salon. Not the tribal decor I'd expected. Dylan offered me a glass of dark liquid. "Holly tea. Lots of caffeine. It clears your vision."

Jax turned to me. "I'll leave you here. Dylan knows the ritual."

Dylan gestured toward a pile of folded white cloth. "You'll need to change into bleached cotton. We allow only natural fibers in the vision chamber. My mother wears this when she goes in, so it should fit you if you roll up the cuffs. It's clean."

"Your mother does this?" I'd had the impression Valerie had been merely tolerant of this spiritual exercise.

"After my father died, she came almost every day for a month. Puca got her through a rough time, even though he was grieving, too. He helped us all." He pointed to a door. "You can change in there. Then I'll take you to him. Oh, and no shoes."

When I'd changed and folded my clothes, I drank the cold holly tea, which was slightly bitter. I hoped Dylan would have warned me if it were laced with a hallucinogenic. Whatever. I'd taken the plunge. I don't get to meet a shaman—a peacemaker—every day, especially one who's "seen" and summoned me.

I made a final check on my phone. Ayden had texted his progress. He said Wayne was in the field, according to another agent. He hadn't heard from JD, and there was nothing from Kam, so he'd asked Joe to ping her phone to check its location.

I emerged to find Dylan waiting. "Am I really going into a hole?"

He smiled. "It's not as bad as it sounds. Jax made sure we could all tolerate it. And you're not locked in. If you feel uncomfortable, you can leave."

"Okay. I'm ready."

"Here's how it works. You enter and choose a seat. There are several in different positions. Take a moment to let yours call to you. He won't greet you. He'll know you're there, but you stay silent. It's like a psychomanteum without a mirror. You're there to create a spirit vision. He'll guide it. You'll hear a distant hum, and you'll feel the vision moving in a way that seems like someone else is shaping it. Whatever is blocking you will become present. It might not be pleasant. We've all been through this. One time I ran out. But I came back. He doesn't force anything. He just helps you focus so you can receive things."

"It sounds like whatever I'm here for is urgent."

Dylan shrugged. "Puca thinks so, but you'll decide. At the very least, doing this keeps you aware of what matters. Also, when you come out, you might feel dizzy, so hold on to the bars we've placed on the wall. There's a shower, a sink, fresh water, whatever you need. Have you done this before?"

"Not really. Not like this."

"Well, no matter what you experience, something will emerge. Puca has spent his whole life attuning people. He knows better than we do what we need to see." He seemed to think for a moment before he added, "You might receive something that will alter your approach, like realizing you've been driving in the wrong direction."

We went down a set of stairs to a short dark hallway. Dylan touched small white discs on the walls, three feet apart, which spread a diffuse light to show me the way. I felt cool marble at my feet. Dylan opened a door and gestured for me to enter a dark room. When I went in, he closed the door behind me.

Chapter Thirty-Three

A warm fire burned in a circular ring in the middle. Contrary to what I'd imagined, there were no rough cave walls, low ceilings, or dirt floors. The clay tiles under my feet felt clean, as if scrubbed daily, and the spacious room smelled of fresh cut hay. I saw several round drums of different sizes along one wall, and half a dozen bare wooden seats. Dylan had advised me to let one choose me.

The seated white-haired figure on the floor at the other side of the room had his back to me but seemed aware of me. His stillness seemed more attuned than if he'd greeted me.

I chose a bench to my right, close to the door, and closed my eyes to breathe in the aroma of heated lemongrass and clary sage oils. I thought I knew who wanted my attention. Sarah had said it at the Scavenger House. A redheaded girl. I'd searched for my childhood friend, Hailey, since the day she'd vanished, but amid my other concerns this felt like a distraction.

Still, I'd agreed to come, and since this was *my* vision, I had to start somewhere. If I were wrong, then I hoped whoever had a message for me would break through. I assumed that was Puca's role.

I breathed deeply, closed my eyes, and took myself back to that awful day. I'd turned fourteen, but Hailey was still thirteen. We heard about a local fifteen-year-old girl, Becca Lynn Young, who'd reportedly hitchhiked on a busy road near a popular outdoor mall. Witnesses had reported a red Ford truck, a blue Chevy Nova, and a white van with red lettering stopping for her. But she'd vanished. No lead had panned out. Two days later, Becca Lynn's body turned up on the side of a country road. Her white tennis shoes were missing, but police found one shoe a mile away in the foundation of a deteriorated barn. A week later, a blouse from another missing girl turned up there as well, in debris mixed with small animal bones.

Hailey and I scanned the news daily. We went walking near the road where Becca Lynn's body was found, looking for a red truck or white van as if we might spot the abductor. A biker rode up and pulled over. He asked if we wanted a ride. He was cute, a few years older than us, and his motorcycle seemed cool, so we said yes. "I can take one of you first," he said, "and then come back for the other." He beckoned for Hailey. She flung her red braids back and climbed on behind him. He revved the engine. But she looked scared, like she didn't want to go. Her face silently begged me to do something. I could have kicked him or pulled her off. But I didn't act. He rode off, leaving me with a lump in my stomach. I waited for two hours, but he never came back.

Tears stung my eyes as I recalled those awful times. The police searched for Hailey day and night. I sensed people blaming me. Even after the searchers gave up, I kept looking. I went into the woods, walked the tracks, and looked in deep holes and farmers' wells. Three years later, a young man named Tommy Ray Bruder was picked up, caught with a girl in a van. He admitted to the abduction and to a murder. I saw his picture. He was the biker. But no evidence besides my report linked him to Hailey, and she was never found.

Years later, I'd gone to the prison to interview Bruder. He'd sneered. Said he'd picked up girls every day. He didn't remember Hailey. But I knew he did. My pain was the caramel topping on his ice cream.

In Puca's chamber, my vision blurred, as if I were rising above and looking down. I tried to grip the seat but felt nothing in my hand. My heart raced. I wanted to stop. I heard a girl's voice, too faint to identify. I blocked it. I didn't want to know what Bruder had done to her. It *was* my fault. I didn't want to hear her accuse me of failing her.

I felt my stomach cramp. I rocked. I wanted to vomit. I remembered the tea. It was making me sick. I fought the feeling.

Suddenly, I saw Kamryn's face. The same expression as Hailey, like I'd seen in the car. She'd wanted me to get her out. But I hadn't. Just like with Hailey, I'd let her leave.

I heard the hum Dylan had mentioned. I felt hands gently grip my shoulders and wondered if Dylan had come in to support me. I saw Kamryn, but it was *Hailey's* voice that begged, "Find me." Then it was Hailey's face but Kamryn's voice, dissolving into Black Shirt. They all watched me, waiting.

I needed to find Kam. I had to do it *now*.

I stood. "I have to go!"

The old man sat silent. He hadn't moved. The door was open. I felt the need to apologize but more pressing was a sense of dread. I found my way to the steps and rushed up to the changing area. No one was there. I found a toilet, went to my knees, and vomited black tea and coffee and whatever else was inside me. This was the purge. It burned my throat, but my head stopped spinning. Weak and drained, I was able to stand and put on my clothes. I threw cold water on my face and rinsed my mouth and throat. I was sure I'd lost ten pounds.

I looked at my phone and couldn't believe twenty minutes had passed. I saw a call from Wayne. Finally! I ignored the voice message and just called him back. Before I could say anything, he blasted me. "Where's our daughter?"

Chapter Thirty-Four

I was floored. "What are you talking about? She's with you! Your girlfriend picked her up yesterday."

"Linda said she went to your place, and you told her you'd bring Kam over today. But you never came!"

Panic nearly closed my throat. "She's lying! She said you didn't have time. Where have *you* been? I've called you! I've left a dozen texts and messages!"

"I expected better from you, Ann. First, you take her to Savannah, and where are you now? Georgia again? You don't know what you're dealing with. They're dangerous. Just because you don't like my—"

"Wayne! Linda said you sent her. Kamryn got in the car and went with her!" I couldn't breathe. "If she's there and Kam isn't, then… I want to talk to Linda. Put her on the phone! Why would she—?"

The call went dead. I stared at the phone. This couldn't be happening. Was I hallucinating? But, no, I saw evidence of his call, and mine. We'd just talked. *Yelled.*

My hands shook as I pressed Kam's number. It rang six times, an eternity. No answer. I grabbed my things. I had to get back. Were they trying to take her from me?

I found Jax in the yard with Dylan and Digger. "I have to go! Kam's missing! Wayne just told me his girlfriend denied picking her up." I started toward his car but stumbled and nearly fell.

Jax caught me and guided me toward a bench. Dylan handed him a mug. He put an arm around me and urged me to drink from it. "This will clear you. Breathe."

"They took my daughter!" Tears flowed freely. Dylan handed me tissues. "This is my fault! I have to get back. I have to find her!" I cringed at her parting words. *You don't want me here!* I tried to text Natra, but my hands shook.

Jax put his hand over my phone. "Annie, tell me what you saw in the chamber."

"Kids. Kids from my past, kids from this case. Missing, dead. Waiting." I gulped. Fresh tears burned my eyes. "I felt so helpless. I got sick."

He squeezed my hand. "What do you know about the woman who took her?"

"Nothing. She's Wayne's girlfriend. Kam doesn't like her. But she wasn't some stranger. Kam got in the car..." But she hadn't wanted to.

Dylan stood in front of me with a tablet of unlined paper. On the top sheet was a drawing. "Puca says you left this. He says the girl gave it to you."

Jax took it. "This looks like a map."

I could barely see through my tears. "Of what?"

"He used your vision to draw it."

I wiped my eyes and looked. I saw a series of circles, a thick scribble, and a darkened circle, possibly a hole. I shook my head. "I didn't see this. I need to go!"

"Wait. Someone sent it. Maybe Kamryn."

My phone rang. It was Ayden. I put on the speakerphone. "Joe pinged Kam's phone," he said. "It's off I-95 in South Carolina, near the border. Not where she should be. I'm on my way to look."

Jax leaned in. "Tell us where. We'll meet you."

"Joe will send you the info. See you there."

Jax took my phone. When we received the location, he said, "It's not far. We'll take Digger. Do you have anything Kamryn recently wore?"

"In my car. Natra can bring it."

Digger jumped into the Wrangler. I called Natra to tell her about Wayne's accusation and urge her to meet us. She and Val were already in the car.

Chapter Thirty-Five

We spotted Ayden's truck at the side of the divided interstate, going south.

"This makes no sense," I said. "Kam wouldn't be out here, not unless she ran away."

Jax cut across the median. Natra soon came in behind us, with Valerie. It had started to rain. "No!" I cried. "It'll ruin the scent."

"Digger can do this," Jax assured me. He handed me an umbrella and took his dog out of the Jeep. "We also have Mika. We'll find her."

Natra handed me Kamryn's pink baseball cap, with the red *Rose Whisperer* logo I'd sewn into it. I gave it to Jax. "She wears this a lot."

Jax had Digger sit still and sniff the cap. Then he gave him the search command. The dog took off. Jax gave the cap to Natra and followed. Natra repeated this gesture with Mika and went to the right.

I called Wayne again, but he didn't pick up. I then called Kam's phone. I hoped the ringing would catch someone's attention. Valerie came out and opened an umbrella. She put an arm around my shoulder.

Digger ran back and forth near the tree line, alerting on nothing. I tensed as Natra sent Mika out, but she seemed to have the same trouble. Mika knew Kam's scent. She practiced finding her all the time. I wanted to run out there, look for her, do anything but stand here, helpless.

Jax pulled Digger in and came back. To Valerie, he said, "Watch the road. If any cars slow down, make a note of their license plate number."

I looked at him for an explanation.

"*They* might be looking for her, too."

"Why would she even be here?" I sounded hysterical. I couldn't bear to voice it, but I knew what he was thinking: they might have killed my daughter and dumped her body as a warning. I called the phone again. Ayden was fifty yards south, near Mika, but he didn't react. Jax whistled for him and gestured, so he came toward us.

Jax sent Digger out again and watched him for a few minutes before calling him in. Ayden joined us, looking puzzled. "I know we're close."

Jax's phone rang. "Dylan?" He frowned and looked toward the Wrangler. "Where's that map? The one from Puca."

I retrieved it. Jax studied it. "We're in the wrong place."

Ayden looked doubtful. "According to Joe, we're close."

Jax handed him the tablet, using my umbrella to shield it. Ayden pointed at the five circles and glanced south. "I saw something like this when I drove around. A row of highway planters. But they're too far south."

Jax looked at me. "You decide." In essence, he was asking whether I trusted the vision or the technology. Natra brought Mika back and shook her head.

I gestured. "Let's go south."

Jax put both dogs in the Wrangler and had Ayden get in the passenger seat to lead us to the planters. I climbed in back with the dogs before Jax sped off.

The planters were full of dead weeds. Each was four feet in diameter. I counted five. Near the circles on the map was a scribble that might indicate an untrimmed hedge five feet from the planters. I pointed. "There's a hole!" It was exactly where a circle had been drawn and blackened. "Let's look here."

The rain was steady now. Jax put the dogs in motion. Digger sniffed around the hole, uninterested, and moved along the hedge. Ayden followed Mika as she went to the other side.

I called Kamryn's phone.

Then Digger went alert, looking south. Jax used a hand signal to send him there. Mika and Ayden ran after them. I called her phone again, then ran in that direction.

Digger went down. He'd found something. Mika stopped, looked at

Ayden, and barked twice. Ayden ran toward Digger. Jax leaned down near his dog. Ayden handed him a rubber glove. He reached down and I saw a flash of pink in his hand.

Kam's phone!

I arrived and he showed it to me. I saw the turtle stickers she'd recently applied. "It's hers."

My text tone sounded. Natra had sent a warning. *Cops!*

I turned and saw a state trooper's car stopped behind mine. Under a green umbrella a shade darker than her dress, Valerie leaned toward them. Natra stood apart, watching.

We returned to the Wrangler to put the dogs in. Ayden offered me the front passenger seat while he got in back. Jax placed the phone in a plastic bag. We couldn't drive back because we'd have to ride on the shoulder in the wrong direction. We had to wait. Every second was torture. I wanted to check Kam's phone. I wanted to keep searching for her.

Jax watched in the rearview mirror. "He's coming. Be pleasant if he addresses you but say as little as possible."

He glanced at his phone. I saw a text. The cop pulled in front of us and stopped. He got out in that authoritative way cops have when they expect to ticket you. Rain hit the brim of his hat and spilled onto his blue shirt. He strode to Jax's open window. "May Ah ask you folks whah you stopped he'ah?"

"Looking for a cap that flew out the window," Jax told him.

Ayden held it up. "Found it."

Upon request, Jax handed over his license and registration. The cop glanced at me. "Someone visitin' from Noath Ca'olina?"

"They're my clients," Jax responded. "I'm representing them in a lawsuit."

The cop's face hardened, but he returned the license and stepped back. "You folks have a nice day now."

"Thank you, Officer Gorvich."

Jax had subtly intimidated this man. He got into his car and drove off. Jax showed me the text. Valerie had cued him up with the hat story.

I picked up the bag containing the cell phone. "I should check this."

"Do you know her code?" Ayden asked.

"No."

"Then let a professional open it. Joe might know since he set it up."

Jax held up a hand. "Let's do this carefully, away from potential spyware. We'll take it to our office. We can check it for fingerprints, too."

"What if she's still here?" I couldn't leave without knowing.

"Digger would have found her."

Ayden nodded. "Mika, too."

He was right. Mika loved finding Kam. She'd have run off to hunt if she'd caught Kamryn's scent—or the scent of a body.

Still, I touched the door handle. Jax grabbed my arm. "Annie, we'll find her. Let's stick together and use our collective resources. Puca must have known she was in trouble. That's why he sent for you. He connected with her. She's the only one who could have shown us this location. She's alive."

I nodded. I had to hope. But I cried again. I knew well enough Jax couldn't promise anything. And he didn't know how we'd find her. Then he said, "Your girl can see in a unique way. She'll be ready for an opportunity."

I was still terrified. I couldn't grapple with this mystery of why Wayne's girlfriend had taken my daughter and then lied to him about it. Or that he'd lied to me.

"I should just go to Wayne's house. She has to be there."

Ayden touched my shoulder. "Annie, let's get this phone analyzed. We don't want to risk losing data. If that fails, I'll go with you. I'll bust down his door myself."

I pulled my arms together and nodded. "Let's go then."

Natra and Valerie brought up Ayden's truck and my SUV. Ayden took a very wet Mika with him while I went to my car to put Kam's phone on a charger. Val and Natra rode with me.

Dread flooded me all the way back. Leaving South Carolina felt as if I were stretching a rubber band to its breaking point. I could only hope Kam wasn't stuck somewhere in the rain. *Hold on, Kam,* I mentally begged. *I'm coming!*

Chapter Thirty-Six

Freshly changed, we gathered in the CSP office on the second floor of the law firm. The main conference room offered large screens and the feeling of high-end technology at our disposal. It felt safe until a gust of wind against the building reminded me of the approaching storm. My heart raced.

We got Joe on a screen. Ayden had filled him in. I introduced Val and Jax, then asked if he knew Kam's lock code. Joe's tech counterpart here, Trish, prepared to help. Jax had dusted the phone for fingerprints and the battery reading approached 75%.

"I don't know the actual code," Joe told us. "But I have some clues. I told her not to use her birthday or her parents' birthdays, so that eliminates three."

"So, she used a birthday?" I asked.

"I had that impression."

"Maybe yours?"

"No. She said it was a date no one would guess."

"So probably not mine," said Ayden. "Or Natra's."

Joe checked his records. "We set it up last March."

"We have, what, ten attempts before it locks us out?"

"Five before you're locked out for a minute. But ten, I'm afraid, is going to erase it, because that's how we set it up, in case she lost it. And you know how she forgets where she put it. I've had her hooked to a back-up, but that still needs a password and might not help with recent activity."

Jax moved closer to the screen. "We can't risk losing access."

"Her best friend's birthday is October 8," I said, "so try 1-0-0-8."

Trish looked at Jax. He nodded. She tapped on the screen. *Rejected.*
Down to four.

"Try her father's," I said. "12-18."

"I don't think so," Joe said.

I gestured. "Just do it."

Rejected.

My heart stopped. "What would we *not* guess?" Kam's puzzles could pose
real twisters.

"A character in a story?" Valerie asked. "A favorite doll?"

"She loves escape movies. But there are too many." I looked at Natra.
"Has she learned any knots that go by a number?"

Natra shook her head.

"What about a year? That would be four numbers. Try the year she was
born."

I told it to Trish, and she made a move, but Natra shouted, "Wait! Try this.
0-3-1-8."

She did. The phone unlocked.

Natra smiled. "Mika's birthday. We celebrated that around the time you
gave her the phone."

Relieved, I nodded. And I wouldn't have guessed.

"There's an unsent text." Trish looked at me. "She was sending it to you."

I read it out loud. *"Nt 2 Dd 95 17 278 xit she grbg hlp."*

Ayden bent over it. "'Not to Dad' makes sense. She's telling you Linda
isn't taking her to Wayne. And they were on I-95, where we found the
phone, and h-l-p for help."

On another screen, Jax pulled up a map of South Carolina. "Let's think
from her perspective. They're on 95, going south." He pointed. "We found
her phone here. In this area, 17 and 278 run parallel to 95. She must have
seen a sign. And 278 has an exit from 95. It's near where we were."

"So, did they keep going on 95 into Georgia or did they exit onto one of
those other roads?" I asked. "I can't tell."

Natra chimed in. "She grbg...she's grabbing. Linda must have seen her

130

texting. Maybe she grabbed for it. So, either Linda or Kam threw the phone out the window. She probably couldn't finish her message."

"She placed a call to Wayne," Joe added, "right before the phone was tossed. That made it easier to track. And her GPS timeline was on."

I stared at the map. "They were going south. If Linda had grabbed it, she'd have tossed it from her side. But it went out the passenger window. It was Kam."

"Smart," Jax said. "It's a breadcrumb. Not many kids would even think to do that." He looked at me. "She knew you'd find it."

Ayden scanned the map. "She also knew Joe could locate the area, because he taught her how." He looked at me, his eyes glowing. "That vision map helped. It took us past where Joe told us."

Tears blurred my vision. "How does it help us find *her*?" I looked away.

"Look," Natra said. "Wayne's house is north, so when Linda went south, Kam would have known right away something was up. So, Linda probably said they were going to see Wayne at another location, maybe a late lunch in Charleston, or something like that. So, Kam would relax until it was clear they weren't taking the right exits. Kam knows them. She called Wayne. He didn't pick up. She guessed something was off."

Jax tapped the screen. "We should find out from Wayne what time Linda returned. Then we can calculate how far she drove. That will narrow the range."

"But if he wasn't home when she arrived," I said, "he might not know. She obviously exploited his absence, knowing I couldn't reach him. She told Wayne she'd pick up Kamryn but hadn't because I supposedly refused to let her. So, he didn't worry until this morning when I didn't show up. Linda had nearly 24 hours to do whatever she's doing. But why? I just don't understand what this is about."

"Can you tell us what Linda looks like?" Valerie asked. "Maybe she's in some offend-ah database. Obviously, she didn't cozy up to yo'ah ex for his chahm. She had a plan. She might have a record."

"She's got thick blond hair with a reddish tint," I said. "Like dyed hair. Shoulder-length. She's about five-seven, I'd say. Slender."

Ayden went to his bag. "I can show you. I drew her after she left." He presented his drawing. I looked at it. "That's close. Needs more make-up. I've seen her only twice, but the facial features are right." I handed it to Jax. He frowned and passed it to Valerie. She put her hand to her mouth. Her eyes went moist, and she shook her head. Jax pulled out his phone, tapped it a couple of times, and showed us a photo of a brunette. "Is this her?"

Ayden's eyes widened. "Yeah, yeah. Hey! Now I remember where I saw her. It was in your file, with this hair color. You know her!"

Valerie showed us a photo on her phone of a man on a motorcycle with this same brunette posing next to him. "That's Cahtah. And that's the bitch who set him up."

"Her name's not Linda," Jax said. "This is Sloane. And now we know where she's been."

This revelation cut through me. "This dangerous woman has my daughter! Why?"

Ayden took out his phone and walked away. "I'm calling Wayne."

I held my breath. I couldn't bear the short wait. He shook his head at me to indicate no success. He started to type a text when Jax said, "No! We can't tip her off. If she's with him and knows you're on to her, she might kill him. That will put Kamryn in even greater danger."

Chapter Thirty-Seven

Jax helped me to sit down before asking, "Do you know what case Wayne was working on?"

"No. But he was putting in long hours. His partner must be with him, because he's not responding, either. Ordinarily, Wayne would have me keep Kam if he had an assignment like this, but he was angry that I took her to Georgia."

Jax looked thoughtful. "What did he say when he called you? Anything out of character?"

"He was annoyed that I... Wait. He did say something odd. He said I didn't know what I was dealing with and that *they* were dangerous. He knew I had a JTA case." I looked at Valerie. "Is Sloane part of this ISM group?"

"We think she might be."

"Oh, my God!"

"I'll be back." Jax walked down the hall.

I could barely think. Valerie came over, sat with me, and took my hand. "We'll get that little girl back. She's smart. She'll know how to protect herself."

I didn't want her to *have* to. I knew she was scared, and it was my fault. *The I Scream Man.* Had Broderick come to my office to warn me? Was he in the same boat, with Jimmy missing? None of this made sense. "But no one's contacted me. They took Kam yesterday! Why haven't they called to tell me what they want me to do?"

"Maybe it's not about you, hon," Valerie said. "Maybe it's about yo'ah ex."

I stared at her. That hadn't occurred to me. But maybe they'd already pressured him. His anger had seemed overblown when he'd found me in Georgia two days earlier. But maybe it had actually been fear.

Ayden closed his bag. "I'll find Wayne and make him tell us what he knows."

"I'm going with you."

Jax came back. "You don't need to. I just got confirmation. Wayne's on an investigation of JTA facilities around Charleston. I'm sure that's why Sloane cozied up to him. Annie, maybe that's why you were hired for the clinical evaluations. So, it's likely he knows Kamryn's been taken." He came over to me. "Maybe Wayne gave you some clues. Let's take this from his point of view. We don't want to miss any signals. Maybe Sloane was with him when he called you."

I nodded, although I wanted to just get in my car and go looking. I had difficulty focusing. I closed my eyes and recounted the first conversation, at the guesthouse. Then I looked around. "He was over-reacting, but nothing else in that call seems out of place. It was brief. He just yelled at me."

Jax sat across from me. "What about the call this morning?"

I put my hand over my thumping heart. I closed my eyes again and brought up everything I could remember. Then I had it.

"He called me Ann. He's never done that. Never. He knows I hate it. I didn't know why I didn't realize it right then. Maybe he was trying to alert me. He asked me if I was in Georgia again." I thought for a moment. "But he *didn't* say he'd tried calling her. He didn't ask to speak to her or say he'd come and get her." I breathed in. "You're right. He knows they have her. He left things out because he knows I always look for what's *missing*."

Jax squeezed my arm. "Then we must be careful in how we communicate with him. For now, Sloane doesn't realize you know who she is. That's good."

I put my hands over my face. I couldn't bear this. I felt Mika's paw on my foot.

"This might be like the Broderick case," Jax said. "They use people in whatever capacity they're serving. If you're a judge, you favor them in court. If you're a politician, you ensure contracts and protection. Wayne's a SLED task force agent. He'll be forced to give them intel, or falsify documents, or help set up accidents."

I looked up. "Like with Danny?"

"Maybe."

"Wayne won't do that."

"Not even for Kamryn?"

He had me there. I'd do anything to ensure her safety. So would Wayne.

I held out my hands. "I'm the more obvious target. I could turn those cases in their favor to deflate the lawsuits."

"And you might be directed to," Valerie said. "Sloane apparently sees mo'ah value in Wayne right now. Ah'm su'ah they'ah watchin' him closely. There's much mo'ah at stake than blockin' lawsuits. We just have to learn what it is."

"And where they are," Ayden added.

Chapter Thirty-Eight

Valerie opened her computer. "Ah think Ah can help." She turned her screen so we could see. "Some JTA associates use these juvenile facilities to hunt for kids who fit the deviant tastes of those who'll pay with money or fav'ahs. They coerce othah kids into baitin' 'em. Then they take them to isolated places for sex games."

Valerie pulled up a map of the Southeastern states. On it were a dozen blue circles. "Carter identified potential locations. So, we know a few things."

"Did he leave anything?" Ayden asked. "Papers? Maps? Photos?"

Jax tapped a pen on the table. "He told me about a ledger with names that would implicate prominent people in crimes. But if he had it, someone took it. That's what I was waiting for on the night he died."

"Or he hid it," I suggested.

Jax raised an eyebrow.

Natra pointed to the map. "But they must also have a place where they keep kids they're using for leverage, like Kam. Maybe Jimmy Broderick. Did Carter tell you anything like that?"

"We think Cahtah was explo'rin' near the coast." Valerie pointed to two circled locations in South Carolina. "You know how that salty a-ya just clings? That's how Ah knew. And his clothing sometimes smelled like he'd been in a swamp."

"Even if we identify it," Ayden offered, "we don't have time to infiltrate." He glanced at Jax. "They'd be watching for that, right?"

"We can't infiltrate. I hope to find someone we can turn. We have two peripheral players, but we need someone deeper inside."

Ayden nodded. "Like a hurricane."

We all looked at him.

He moved his hands like he was playing an accordion sideways. "Hurricanes are vertically stacked systems, with the lightest winds at the top. But its own force can turn hostile and strangle it. Basically, the hurricane kills itself."

I looked at Jax. "What about this woman? What do you know?"

"Sloane Gilchrest!" Valerie's anger reddened her cheeks. "She was his pahtnah! Aftah he left law enforcement and we set up Ethan's Project, he gave Sloane some freelance work. So, she knew a lot about the law firm. When he died, she fled. We lost her trail a few times. The PI we hi'ahed to find her quit a month ago. Said his family was threatened."

"Would she know what Carter found?" Natra asked.

Valerie crossed her arms as if to keep her temper in check. "We don't know, but he trusted Sloane. He probably said somethin' about it."

"I'm heading back to South Carolina," I said. "I'm sure that's where Kam is."

Ayden's phone alerted. He held it up. "Weather." He checked it. "Storm's shifted. It's getting worse. We should put on the TV before we leave, check the roads."

Trish picked up a remote for the wall screen. The TV came on to a news channel. There was a special alert, but not for the storm. We all listened.

"...for this breaking story," a Hispanic anchorwoman was saying. "We've heard of prison riots over bad conditions, but it's rare to see one in a juvenile facility. Golden Larch Treatment Center is now on lockdown, but at least four guards were taken hostage. Several were injured. We'll report developments as they happen."

I gasped. "That's where they're taking Danny."

Jax rose. "Excuse me. I need to attend to this." He went into another room and closed the door.

"He has clients they'ah," Valerie explained.

I had to find Kam. I asked to see the weather. Trish found a channel.

There was rain along our route but no major flooding. The storm had hurricane-force winds, although it had stalled. We had time.

Natra gestured for Mika. I told Valerie I'd call Jax from the road. We grabbed our bags and went down the elevator. The rain had stopped, but a wind gust left me breathless. Ayden strode to his truck. Natra and I were halfway to my SUV when I heard a car door open to my left. Mika growled. I looked over to see a man in a gray raincoat stride toward us. I pressed my purse against me to feel my Glock.

The man came right up to me, his eyes blazing. "I'm James Broderick. I know who you are. Stay away from my wife! You will not contact her again! I don't know what you think—"

"Sir!" I interrupted. "Your wife came to me."

Near me, Mika was whining. She went to the ground in her alert pose and barked twice.

"Shut that dog up!" Broderick yelled. Natra took a defensive position over her.

Ayden called over from his truck. "What's going on?"

Broderick pulled out a semi-automatic handgun and waved it at us. My stomach clutched as he shouted, "You will stay away from my family!" Mika jumped up, barking ferociously, her fur raised. Broderick aimed at her. Natra held up her hand and shouted, "No!" I heard a shot, but not from Broderick. I looked up. Through an open second-story window, a rifle barrel jutted.

The distraction gave Ayden the opening he needed to train his Beretta on Broderick, who backed away.

Natra could barely contain Mika. The dog seemed intent on attack. Natra gripped her collar with both hands. "Get out of here!" she yelled. "Or I'll turn her loose."

Broderick rushed back to his Lexus, got in, and raced off.

My heart pounded. "My God! Is everyone okay?"

Mika continued to whine and strain at her collar. Natra made a helpless gesture. "I don't know what's wrong with her."

Jax emerged. "She wants something. Let her go."

Natra released Mika. She ran to where Broderick's Lexus had been parked. Sniffing for a few seconds, she went down in her alert position with a quick *yip*. Natra ran over. She picked up a crumpled tissue, holding it between her forefinger and thumb. "Must be Kam's."

Ayden ran to his truck.

I went after him, but he screeched out of the parking lot before I could get in. I fumbled for my keys as I strode to my own car.

"Wait!" Jax was behind me. "Don't chase him."

"It's Broderick! You said he's with ISM, and they have Kam. She's been in that car!"

"You can't go."

"But Ayden—"

"They know your car. They might shoot you."

Natra brought Mika back. "Thank you. He might've killed her."

Jax reached down to pat the dog. "I'll get an escort so you can get safely out of the state."

I shook my head. "I can't leave. Kam's been with Broderick and he's right here."

I told Natra to take Mika inside. Then I said to Jax, "You know things. You clearly have connections. If we're doing this together, no withholding."

Jax stood still, as if deciding. Then he said, "I had prior knowledge of the plan to riot at Golden Larch."

I opened my mouth in surprise. "How?"

"I heard about it at Sycamore yesterday."

"At Sycamore! Aren't you required to disclose such things?"

He shrugged. "Sometimes doing nothing is doing something."

I frowned. "*I* said that."

"I know."

"Jax! Kids might get hurt!"

"There's a minimal chance, and a riot does impede the transfer process. I weighed the risks. I'm trying to save Danny. When we deciphered Caryn's message, I decided to let things play out."

I crossed my arms. "There's more, isn't there?"

"Let's go inside. And speaking of withholding, that applies to you as well."

"My cards are on the table."

He cocked his head. "Are they? You thought Puca's map came from someone else."

He had me. But *that* had nothing to do with *this*. Kam was my priority.

Valerie saved me by opening the door. "Will you two please come in?"

Jax raised an eyebrow, suggesting he wouldn't forget and gestured for me to go first.

Inside, Mika came to me for the praise she deserved. Trish swiveled in her seat. "Over here. I've got something."

Chapter Thirty-Nine

Trish turned her screen for us to see. It was an image of the surveillance video from the carriage house paired with a photo of what looked like the same car in a parking lot outside. Valerie pointed at it. "We heard yo'ah dog and saw that nasty man outside. Ah took pictures of his car. I had a hunch it was the one you saw befo'ah."

Natra placed the tissue from Broderick's car on a table and came up beside me to look. "So, he went to your office and followed you to the carriage house. Then came here. He knows his wife came to see us. Now we know Kamryn was with him, so Sloane must have handed her off. But what's his role? And where would he take her?"

I stared at the tissue. I didn't want to think about what it implied: that she'd been crying. Perhaps they'd hurt her. She would have fought them, that much I knew. My little girl was assertive and that could get her in trouble.

"I think he just took a big risk," Jax said. "He probably shouldn't have approached you."

I gestured toward the screen. "I have a feeling Broderick knows exactly where his son is." Then I had a worse thought. "What if he's getting Jimmy back in exchange for Kam?"

"It doesn't work that way." Jax pointed to the screen. "Enlarge this, please."

Trish zoomed in. I peered at it but saw nothing significant. "What is it?"

"A sticker. It's for a gated community. I've seen it before. This lets him in and out without being stopped."

"Do you know where it is?"

"Let's enhance it."

Trish produced a result. Jax looked closely. Then he invited us to gather around the table. "We need to think this through." When we were seated, he said, "I think Broderick's an errand boy. His son is probably leverage to ensure he does what he's told."

"Like Wayne?" I asked. "You think they're holding Kam to make him do something?"

"Since they haven't contacted you, that makes the most sense. But ISM stays low-key. I think they sent Broderick to your office to find your clinical notes, but he acted here on his own. He must be spooked about his wife contacting you."

I nodded. "It seemed desperate, but—"

My phone buzzed with a text alert. It was Joe. *Snding Trish recrdng. U need to hear this.*

Trish pulled up her email and found it. She downloaded it and hit "play." It was a scratchy audio recording, but I recognized Broderick's voice. I heard "girl" and "Jimmy" clearly. The rest was muffled. There was a background voice, as if someone were speaking near him. My blood chilled. I looked at Natra. Her eyes widened and she nodded. Then we heard a female voice say, "Come *now*" before the recording ended.

"Play it again." I said. "Louder." She did so. This time I also heard what sounded like "flat" but couldn't figure out the context.

"Ah think that's Sloane," Valerie said.

I called Joe.

"It's from Ayden," he said. "He bluejacked a phone. It's poor reception, sorry. I cleaned it up as well as I could."

Natra rose and took out her phone. I suspected she was calling Ayden.

"What is it, hon?" Valerie asked me. "You look white as a bleached bone."

I closed my eyes for a second, not quite comprehending. Then I said, "I think the other voice is Wayne."

Chapter Forty

I hugged myself and sat down. I could hardly breathe. What would Wayne be doing in Georgia with Broderick, especially so close to here?

"Ayden's not answering," Natra said.

Jax told Trish to play the recording again. I listened and nodded. It was Wayne. I could've sworn he said, "We'll be there." *We!*

I felt gut-punched. "Is it possible Sloane didn't dupe him?" My voice sounded hoarse. "That he's acting *with* her? Are they taking Kamryn from me?"

Jax sat and leaned toward me. "Let's go through his phone call from this morning again. Everything."

I tried to think. I felt as if I'd stepped onto a floor I'd crossed with confidence my whole life only to now fall through. Pain stabbed me. Mika came over to lick me.

Natra stood behind me. To Jax, she said, "It was at your house. Wayne accused Annie of keeping Kamryn from him. He wouldn't listen to her say it was Linda...Sloane. He heard how alarmed she was, but he accused her of keeping Kam and then hung up."

I nodded. I'd finally found a foothold. "That's right. He hung up. He didn't keep hammering at me, he didn't threaten to send cops." I looked at Jax. "He didn't make an effort." I took a breath and closed my eyes to cover the hot tears. "Why did I let that woman take her? I didn't want to, but...I just..."

"I've got Ayden," Natra said. "He's on FaceTime." She held up the phone.

Trish moved to her computer. "Let's get your screen shared."

143

When Ayden was visible, we could see he was driving. He had a stand for his phone on his dash. His jaw was clenched.

I stood. "It's true, isn't it? That was Wayne."

"Yes."

"Ah you drivin'?" Valerie asked. "That's dangerous."

"It's slow traffic right now. If it speeds up, I'll end the call, but I need to tell you what happened, and I don't want to lose them."

Jax got to his feet. "How did you record that?"

Ayden looked uncertain. "It's a gray area, like phreaking. I mean, if someone doesn't protect their Bluetooth connection…" He looked away for a moment. "I found Broderick's car right away. Traffic slowed him down, but he was pretty far ahead. Then he took an exit. I don't think he saw me. He went into a fast-food parking lot. I drove in and parked behind the building. I went inside and looked out the window. He looked calm, which seemed weird. He just sat in his car, like he was waiting. And *then* Wayne showed up! I admit, I nearly lost it. Wayne walked over and handed Broderick his phone, so that gave me an idea. I've piggybacked it before. He uses the weakest security."

Ayden hesitated.

Valerie read his expression. "Don't worry, shugah, we'ah not cops."

He continued. "So, I got my equipment. Joe and I made this de-encryption system. It's fast, but I lost the first part of whatever they were saying. Wayne sounds distant because Broderick had his phone. Maybe Joe enhanced it?"

"Not very well," I said. "Did you catch any of it?"

"No. The wind was too strong. I saw cover near Wayne's Expedition, so I crept over and put a tracker on it."

Jax looked at me, impressed.

"I didn't have time to hide it well, but he'll only see it if he's looking for it. Anyway, they drove out at the same time. Wayne knows my truck, so I didn't follow right away. But Joe's giving me a sense of where they're going. I saw them heading north and I've already crossed into South Carolina." He shook his head. "I can't figure it, Annie."

I shook my head. "I can't, either. But please keep on them. I'm sure they know where Kam is."

Ayden looked at traffic and then back at the screen. "Wayne would never hurt her, never!"

"Maybe he's trying to take her." I barely even heard myself say it.

"Kam loves you, and Mika, and the beach, all of us. She won't let him! I like the guy, but he's not man enough for that little girl!"

"Ayden," Valerie said. "Ah don't like you out they'ah alone. Maybe you should come back."

"Traffic's breaking up. I'll check in later." The screen went dark.

I looked at Val. "Once he's on a track, you can't pull him back."

"Oh, Ah'm worried about him. Jax, send someone."

Jax shook his head. "If he's as good as he sounds, he won't approach them on his own. He's just tailing them." He told Trish to have Joe send us coordinates for Ayden's location.

"He's keeping tabs 'til we get there." Natra looked at me. "We're going, right?"

"Look," Jax said, his hands on his hips. "Not to give Wayne any excuses, but we know he's on the JTA task force. Maybe he knew from the start Sloane works for JTA and he's playing *her*. Or maybe he only discovered it yesterday, but his behavior suggests he's not worried about Kamryn. So, he knows where she is." He pointed to me. "Otherwise, he'd be just as frantic as Annie." To me, he said, "He knows you. He'll expect you to follow the breadcrumbs, right?"

I wasn't sure, but I nodded weakly.

"Annie, by now, he'd know you've seen his strange behavior. If he wanted you to back off, he'd tell you somehow. He only said that once, two days ago in Georgia. He didn't say it this morning, right?"

I held out my hands. "Then I should tell him I'm coming."

Jax glanced at the screen before he said, "Do what he did. Send a message he'd know is uncharacteristic of you or contains a covert message."

An alert on Natra's phone interrupted us. She looked at it, made a face, and said, "We have another problem."

Chapter Forty-One

The approaching storm had redirected its aim. This complicated things. A blond meteorologist sausaged into a tight purple dress stressed the need to evacuate vulnerable areas. "Hurricane Delano crossed south of Bermuda. The winds had diminished to category two at 110 miles per hour, but the ocean water is unusually warm, so it's become a category three. In response to an upper-level trough, the eye is moving toward us faster than expected, at twenty-three miles per hour. The governors of both Carolinas have urged evacuation along the coast from Charleston to the Outer Banks. Georgia's governor is watching the situation. Delano could still surprise us."

I saw only colors blending on the map as I strained to think of something Wayne and I had done with Kamryn. I needed him—and *only* him—to understand my coded message.

Jax watched me. I bit my lip. This was hard. For all my nutshell phrases for my podcasts, I couldn't land on a thing. But that wasn't an option. I had to do this. I glanced around for prompts. Desk... photos... papers... plants... monitors... Natra... map... dog... luggage... *there!* My navy overnight bag, with its zippered pockets. It reminded me of a prop in the movie Kam had referenced the day we met Jax. The line she'd quoted was, "With me. Without me." The chance of success "with me" was high, "without me" was low. Wayne had watched this movie with her a dozen times. He'd even said the line. I raised the phone and typed, "With you or without you, I'll find her." I pressed 'send' just as Natra said, "Wait!"

"What?"

"What if Wayne's …what if he's working with them?"

I shook my head. "He can't be."

"If he is," Jax said, "you'll know. They'll dictate his response."

"But he'll tell them I know he's involved."

"It's done, Annie. Let it go. Let's see what happens."

Jax couldn't know how tough that was. If wishes to change past decisions were grains of sand, I'd have a world-class beach.

Trish beckoned. "I have this photo ready. It's a little clearer." She gave Jax her seat. He leaned toward the screen. I went over to see.

He pointed. "This place, Cypress Run, is a wealthy enclave north of here. So Broderick is either using someone's car or he's a member." Jax told Trish to get the license plate checked. "Tell Doug we've had a threat here. He'll get it traced."

"Will do." She wrote it down and went down the hall to another office.

I glanced at my phone screen. Nothing. I silently willed Wayne to respond. Even if I'd miscalculated and he was now my foe, I needed intel. "Is this place—this Cedar Run—close to Charleston?"

Jax put up a detailed map of the area north of the Georgia state line. "Cypress Run, you mean. It's south of Charleston. But they wouldn't run the sex ring through there. Too public. I've heard they have a satellite location on this side of the Colleton River for special parties. It's isolated. If they want to hide Kamryn, location makes more sense. She threw the phone near the exit for 278, so they could have gotten off there and gone east to reach it."

"But she was *here*. In Broderick's car."

"We don't know when she was in the car, or where she got out."

He was right. I pocketed my phone. "Let's go, then. I need to go there."

Jax stared at me. "And do what?"

I threw up my hands. "I don't know. I just need to … be close."

Behind me, Valerie put her hands on both of my shoulders. I expected her to reassure me, but she didn't. I sensed something pass between her and Jax. She leaned near my ear. "We think that's whe'ah they killed Cahtah, somewhe'ah up the'ah."

Mika whimpered and got up. She barked and ran to the door. Then she returned to Natra, her tail pressed tight against her body.

"What's up, girl?" Natra bent down to pet her. Mika sat, shivering, and looked at the ceiling. The computer screen flashed and went dark just as a wind gust hit the building. I looked around, chilled, and met Natra's eyes.

An alert on Jax's phone drew his attention. He seemed startled. He stood up. "I need to take care of this. Then we'll decide what to do." Going into an office, he closed the door.

I looked at my phone, waiting. Natra texted Ayden. To me, she said, "He needs back-up."

"Find out where he is."

I went to the window. I just couldn't wait any longer.

Jax emerged, his face grim. "We have runaways. Three boys escaped Golden Larch. Danny's one of them."

I turned. "Danny? How? They already transferred him?"

"Apparently."

I recalled Jax's list of "runaways" who'd disappeared. "Do you think he really got away? This isn't a cover story?"

"I'm trying to find out."

"Well, Ayden's getting close to Broderick, and Broderick knows where Kamryn is."

Mika gave three short yips. Jax looked at Natra, who shrugged. "She's acting strange. I can't read her." She checked her phone and gave us a location. "He's watching a meeting in a parking lot. Broderick's there, and a limo. Wayne went a different way, so Ayden followed Broderick."

Valerie looked surprised. "Oh Jax, you know who we need."

He shook his head. "No."

"He's close to that area. Can't you forget your—"

"No!" His eyes flared. To me, he said, "Just give me a minute. I'll make some calls." He returned to his office.

Valerie crossed her arms. "He's just as pigheaded as his broth-ah sometimes."

I peered at her. "You know someone there who can help? I'll go talk to them."

"No, hon, you can't. You have to know him. He screens everyone. He's a seer, like Puca, but in a different way. Jax could get him to look into this."

Natra cocked her head. "Are you talking about Airic? A-I-R-I-C? The medium?"

Valerie looked surprised. "Yes, that's his name. Well, what he goes by, Ah guess. Cahtah was clos-ah to him than Jax. They worked on cold cases. But Jax can talk to him."

I stared at her. This was bizarre. Even disturbing. But also promising. "Jax can get a private session? At the last minute?"

"Well, not one of those intense sessions, because Airic would have to gath'ah his people, and Ah'm sure the'ah all hunkerin' down. But Jax can ask him to help us focus on the right things. If he were *willin'* to, he could."

I recalled my own session, and Black Shirt. "Why wouldn't he be?"

Valerie shook her head. "He won't tell me. They used to be as close as butter on grits, but somethin' happened. Airic is...he's..." She searched for a word and shrugged. "Asocial?"

I nodded. "He's odd. I've met him. I was there, myself, the day before you called us."

Valerie raised her eyebrows. "Whatever fo'ah?"

"Broderick's kid, Jimmy. Airic supposedly helped find a missing kid, so I attended a sitting."

Valerie looked skeptical. "He let you in?"

"Yes."

"Ah'm amazed. Did it work?"

"Not really. Not for Jimmy. But Airic recorded a guy at the session who resembles one of the kids on Jax's list. A dead kid."

Valerie hugged herself. "Goodness! How very upsettin'!"

The image of Black Shirt mouthing that desperate plea rattled me again. "I don't know if it meant anything, but that's why I was in Georgia when you first looked for me."

Valerie's mauve-polished fingers went to her mouth and her eyes widened. "Jax knows this?"

"Not exactly. I've never mentioned Airic."

"He should he'ah this." She went into his office and closed the door. We heard their muffled voices.

I looked at Natra. She was still trying to calm Mika, who remained hyper-alert. "This is weird," I said. "How can this all be so connected?" I gestured toward the closed door. "Do you think they're setting me up?"

Natra shook her head. "Valerie seems genuinely surprised. And she said Jax hasn't seen Airic. But at least Airic's actually worked on investigations."

I glanced at the closed door. "I can't wait around. I know where Airic lives. Let's just go. He'll remember me."

"Ayden needs backup."

"I'll drop you off with him. Airic's in that general area."

"You should—"

Her text alert sounded. When she read it she looked at me, confused. "Unknown."

"What does it say?"

She handed the phone to me. The text said, *Taking her to a secure facility*. I gasped. "No! Oh no!"

"What?"

I started shaking. "It's from Wayne. It's code. You know that movie. It's the *opposite* of secure!"

Valerie rushed out. "What's wrong, hon?"

"I have to go. Wherever this Cypress Grove or Hill or whatever is located, I need to find it. Now! Kam's in danger!"

Chapter Forty-Two

We made hasty arrangements. Natra took my SUV with our luggage to join Ayden, who was on the move again. I went with Jax in Valerie's car. He raced out to the interstate so fast I thought we'd spin out. But the speed made me feel we'd reach my daughter before anything bad could happen. We entered I-95 north and passed several cars. Jax wove through traffic over wet pavement as if he'd had racecar lessons. I clung to the seat. In my side mirror, I saw a flash of blue lights. "Cops, Jax, slow down!"

He ignored me, which annoyed me. We couldn't get pulled over.

The cop turned on his siren, caught up, and came tight behind us. Jax did not slow down. I took a breath and checked my seatbelt. He couldn't outrun this cop. I didn't know what he was thinking.

Jax passed a slower car and the cop kept pace. When Jax returned to the right lane, the cop pulled even with us. Jax gestured, as if he knew the guy. The cop returned the gesture and sped up, lights flashing, to pull in front of us. Cars moved over. We had an escort!

Jax touched my arm. "We'll get there."

I sat back and let him take charge. We crossed into South Carolina. Another patrol joined us, but I saw from this car's lighter color it was a South Carolina trooper. The Georgia cop turned off his lights and let us pass. Again, Jax gestured. To me he said, "It pays to have friends."

"You really *are* adoptable."

"He shoots on my range." He pointed in front of us. "That one uses the helicopter. I told them we have juvenile runaways out in dangerous weather

151

and I'm transporting a psychologist who can persuade them to surrender."

"You did? That's a stretch. I thought you never break the law."

Jax checked his rearview mirror. "I don't think I said that."

"The night we met. You said you don't go over the speed limit."

He glanced at me. *"That* night."

"Ah." I watched the road. This guy was full of surprises.

Once we had a clear shot, the cop in front of us turned off his lights. I was about to mention Airic, but Jax asked about Wayne's message. I explained about Kamryn's escape movies and the line I'd sent him. "Whenever someone in this movie said, 'We'll take you to a secure facility,' they intended to kill you because you knew things you shouldn't."

"And you're sure Wayne sent it?"

"He watched the movie with us. It can't just be a random text. And it doesn't seem like something they'd tell him to say."

Jax kept his eyes on the police car in front of us for a moment before he said, "What if they forced him to use something to lure you there?"

"The text went to Natra, as if he wanted to prevent anyone from tracing it from my phone. And I think he used a burner phone. And they wouldn't have to use him. If they told me they had Kam, I'd go."

"It doesn't sound right to me. Thinking like a father, I'd want to keep my child safe, so I wouldn't raise tension by drawing you in. Thinking like a man, I'd want you to leave it to me."

I felt the grip of panic again. "Wayne's like that, but I can't see how someone else would've used that particular line."

"Does he have a partner?"

"Yes, JD Riley. I've been trying to reach him, but he doesn't respond, either."

"What about Kamryn?"

I considered this. "She would've said 'they're taking *me*,' right? Not *her*. And the line makes sense with what I'd texted to Wayne."

"Wayne could have used a different line to signal he understood. He chose one that threw you on the offensive. Sounds like bait."

"Then why are we driving so fast?"

"Because wherever Wayne is, we'll find Sloane."

I stared at him. "Sloane? What do you mean? You can't arrest her. What are you planning to do? Kill her?"

He didn't respond.

"Jax..."

"Annie, this is between her and me. I'll help you get your daughter back, but I have my own business."

I couldn't argue. I needed him to keep driving. But now I knew we had potentially competing agendas. "If Wayne didn't send that text, he told someone else to. So, that would mean he's being forced."

Jax shrugged. "Maybe."

"You think he's part of this. He's *with* ISM."

"You said yourself he's vulnerable. P-A-L. Paid, afraid, or laid. Could any of those apply to him? Sloane could have recruited him, and there's plenty of money to be had. She certainly played Carter. Probably for months."

I couldn't contradict this. I thought of Wayne as a flawed but good person, incapable of emotional commitment but still motivated to stay within the law. Yet I'd been wrong about him before. More than once.

"So, we're going to Airic's?"

"No."

"But Airic—"

"We're not involving him. I have another idea. My brother had a Tidewater cabin up here. I couldn't say that in front of Val, and please don't mention it to her. But we can use it as a base."

I saw blue and white lights in the rearview and looked back. Another cop car was coming up fast.

"Expecting someone else?" I asked.

"No."

Jax slowed down. A call came to his phone. I tapped the answer button for him, and he listened. I heard him say, "Why?... He came himself?... Fine. Lead the way." He ended the call. "We might have trouble."

The cop behind us pulled up parallel with us and pointed for him to follow. A third cop car behind this one boxed us in.

153

Jax tapped the steering wheel. "They've been ordered to take us to Bradford Shnick, former warden of Golden Larch. He's now an administrator for South Carolina JTA. He's waiting for us."

"What?"

"Now I think that movie line was bait."

My throat felt tight. "I thought these cops were your friends."

"One is, but he can't defy an order."

"Does this Shnick know you? Didn't you win a lawsuit against JTA?"

"In Georgia. But, yes, he knows me."

"We don't need this delay!"

Jax gave me a look. We'd been blocked into a corner.

The cop led us off an exit. We soon pulled into an empty parking lot and stopped just short of a police car that sat near a black town car and a stretch limousine. I recalled that Ayden had seen a limo. I breathed out. "My God! Are we about to get whacked?"

"Stay calm. We really *are* here for the runaways. Our mission's legit."

"You think they care?"

A man in a tan suit stepped out of the limo and walked toward us with one of the officers. I saw a beefy figure get out as well and stand there. He looked like the guy who breaks your legs when you fail to pay up. As Jax opened his door and got out, I texted Natra our location, adding *Trouble*. She'd know where to look if we disappeared.

When the suited man came up, I saw why Jax had opted to speak to him outside the car. Jax was tall enough to make this man look up. Smart. Then the man told him what they wanted.

"Mr. Raines, my boss wants to speak with the psychologist."

Chapter Forty-Three

I froze. *Speak to me?*

"We're in a hurry," Jax told him.

"He'll be brief."

"We'll come in a minute."

"Just her. She doesn't need an attorney. She's not under arrest... yet."

"I'll confer with her." Jax got in and shut his door. "This is good. They're off balance. I think the boys really did run away. Go talk to Shnick. Work him."

"*Work* him? What if he figures out I don't know anything?"

"Use what you do know. Stay calm. You know kinesics. Watch the body language. Leave your phone here so they can't check it."

I took a moment to steady myself. I focused on Kam. If this helped to find her, I could do it. I got out and walked to the limo. I swallowed into a dry throat. This felt raw. The bad guys' henchmen were right here.

The beefy man outside the limo held out a hand. "Bradford Shnick. Nice to meet y'all." His Deep South good 'ol boy accent was as fleshy as his fingers. It was clear he'd rather be doing anything but pretending to be friendly to me. "Please come awn in. Sorrah fo'ah the cramped reception room he'ah, but we won't keep y'all long."

I entered the limo and nearly gagged from the mingled odor of sweat-soaked shirts, cigars, and greasy snacks. I focused on my mission as I fought back gorge and brushed corn chip crumbs off a seat. I imagined these crumbs spewing out as Shnick talked with his mouth full.

In a leather seat near the back, at the opposite door, a thin-faced man watched me. An overhead light revealed a nasty wine-red birthmark on his sallow left cheek. When Shnick got in, rocking the car with his weight, the air grew oppressive. Someone outside closed the door. I felt smothered and shifted to breathing through my mouth.

I gestured at the window. "Could we have that down, please?"

"Shu'ah, shu'ah." Shnick ordered the driver to crack the window near me. It came down an inch. Not nearly enough. I declined a drink. The glass looked smudgy. I just wanted to get this over with and get back on the road.

Shnick glanced at the thin man before he said, "We undahstand y'all're awayah we've had runaways this evenin' and y'all know 'em. Ah ya expectin' 'em to contact ya? Have y'all spoken to 'em?"

He'd said too much. He'd given me my narrative and his stupidity shored up my confidence. I *had* this. In a glance, I took in his bowed posture, his wrinkled shirt, a nervous tick in his right eyelid, and a telltale micro-sneer of disdain. Someone else gave the orders. He wasn't a leader, but he liked to pose as one. Needy. So easy to manipulate.

I wasn't a skilled liar, but Shnick was thick. He wouldn't even notice. I was more worried about the silent man who stared at me. I figured he was the real boss here.

"I interviewed one of the boys two months ago," I said. "I've performed the MMPI, the latest WISC edition, several projective tests, and—"

Shnick held up a pudgy hand with fingers too short for a man his size. "Not askin' 'bout tha'yat. What's yer hurry? Why the police escort? Ah y'all meetin' 'em somewhe'yah? Have y'all offered 'em help? How's this he'ah low'yah involved?"

"I'm concerned that they're out there without resources and we have a hurricane coming."

"They'ah hahdly 'thout resou'ces, ma'yam. Those little pickpockets, Flynn and Carl, robbed two sto'ahs. They got junk food, cig'rettes, an' some Pow-ahball tickets, like they thank they-ah gonna win somethin'."

The silent man cleared his throat. Shnick glanced at him before he continued. "Dr. Huntah, ma'am, you'd best tell us what y'all know. We'll pick 'em up. Then you can go find yo'self a nice safe spot, maybe go on home."

His mention of "safe" reminded me of the threat to Kamryn. I doubled down. "They said they knew of a house on the beach."

"Ah'd like ta check yo'ah phone, get that numbah."

"It's in the car, but they called an associate, not me. They used a burner phone, probably with fake accounts." I looked at the thin man. "Isn't that what they stole?" I was guessing, but Shnick's startled expression confirmed it.

"Withholdin' info'mation will git y'all arrested. These kids ah dangerous criminal fugitives."

"Are they armed?"

"One assaulted a CO an' stole his weapon."

The thin man sat forward. "Which beach?" His voice was weirdly tinny. I looked at him. I could imagine him forcing a kid into unspeakable acts merely with the cruelty of his washed-out gray eyes. He struck me as someone who blamed others for his perversions—*they* made him think these thoughts and feel these desires. For that, they'd be punished. "I don't know. If I'd spoken to them directly, I would've asked. They were heading to Florida, so I imagine it's south of Charleston somewhere."

"Why ah y'all rushin' to git they'ah?" Shnick asked.

"Because the beach is a bad place in a hurricane. They obviously don't understand that. They're just kids. I want to be nearby in case they contact me again." I pointed to Jax's car. "He has a friend in the area where we can wait. If the boys call, I can get to them quickly from there, perhaps persuade them to turn themselves in. I wanted to be in place as fast as possible."

Shnick narrowed his eyes. "We'll put someone on y'all."

Damn! I'd just gotten us cornered. "I'm only concerned with their safety. I wouldn't be doing this if I weren't. I'm afraid of drowning. Do you think I'd go into a hurricane if I weren't worried about them? I'd rather be home."

Shnick reached into his pocket. "We'll jus' make shu'ah." He opened his fat hand and showed me a lavender-striped shell necklace. I nearly lost it. It was the necklace I'd given to Kamryn. Her early birthday present.

My breathing quickened and I was sure the thin man had noticed. They had me. I tried to control the flood of anger that washed through me. "I understand. Give me a way to contact you."

"We'll stay with'n y'all, don't worry."

Chapter Forty-Four

Back in the car, I told Jax, "You have to drive to Airic's."

He flashed me a startled look.

"Just go. They're putting a tail on us. You don't want them following us to your brother's cabin, right? So, I told 'em we're going to a friend's house. Unless you have another friend around here that would welcome this attention, you have to go there. Right now."

"Annie—"

"They have Kamryn's necklace. They used it to threaten me."

Jax started the car and drove out. One of the cop cars followed.

I cleaned my hands with sanitizer and wished I could do the same inside my nostrils. "At least I know we've gotten close to people who've seen Kam. And she's alive."

"Trish texted me. Broderick's a member of Cypress Run, as we thought. He might have crossed paths with Sloane there."

I told Jax about the thefts and the names of the runaways.

"Good. We know who we're looking for, and their skills."

"Skills?"

"Kids in detention quickly learn who has useful skills. When I was there, we knew the thieves, the manipulators, the escape artists, the hackers and the dealers, and how to get favors from them."

I conveyed the rest of the conversation in the limo.

Jax looked at me. "You're afraid of drowning? You live on the ocean."

I shrugged. "I inherited the house. I can like it without going in it."

"Can you swim?"

"If I must." I gripped the armrest. "Okay, no, not really. Let's concentrate on what we're doing."

"Why are we going to Airic's?"

"Didn't Val tell you I was at a sitting the day before I met you?"

"She said that, but he doesn't just let people in."

"He let me in. I don't know why. But I saw something related to Mick's autopsy photos. And Airic told Lillian Broderick he's working with me. I want to find out what he meant and get his help to find Kam."

A wind gust slammed the car and we plowed into a burst of rain that the windshield wipers couldn't clear. Jax slowed down. From the set of his jaw, I could tell he wasn't keen about our new plan. I decided to broach the subject.

"What's the problem? Why don't you want to see him? Valerie said you were good friends once."

Jax stayed silent. I'd been a therapist just long enough to know when someone needs space. "Sorry. I didn't mean to—"

"I haven't spoken to him in… months. We had a disagreement. But he was right, and I'll apologize. It's important we find Kam."

"Should we let him know we're coming?"

"I'm sure Val got word to him through Dylan. She probably knew you'd steer me there."

I took a breath. He'd given in. I texted Natra. *Back on the road.* She called and I filled her in about the meeting, the necklace, and our situation.

"We've learned something, too," she said. "Joe and Trish used location services to pinpoint where Kam was. It looks like they first went off I-95 at 17, going east to where this Cypress Run is located, stayed there a while, and then got back on 95, going south."

"So, we don't have the satellite location."

"No. And we lost Broderick. Wayne knows our vehicles, so we had to pull back. Joe's keeping track of him, but the weather's interfering."

"Ok. Find this place and go wait there." I gave them the address for Carter's cabin. Jax added how to find the key and start the generator. "We're heading to Airic's. We'll meet you as soon as we can. And keep trying

JD. He's got to know something. He owes me for helping him with that pseudo-demon case."

When I ended the call, Jax glanced at me.

"JD brings me alleged paranormal cases. He's one of the few cops who don't ridicule my work. Anyway, they lost Broderick. They can still track Wayne, for now."

"That other man in the limo—did he say his name?"

"No."

"Could you identify him from a photo?"

"Definitely. He had bad skin, pale slitty eyes, and an ugly stain on his cheek. And he was losing his hair. Thin and kind of sandy gray. He had weak shoulders, sort of hunched."

Jax grabbed his phone, thumbed in his code, and handed it to me. "Look through the photos. See if he's there."

I tapped the photo icon and thumbed through several photos. Sloane's raised my blood pressure. Then I recognized the thin man. I showed Jax. "Him. Do you know him?"

"Alder Plattman."

"Plattman?" I stared at it. "Is that Plat-eye? I was just with Plat-eye?"

"Apparently."

"Creepy!"

"I think I heard Sloane mention him on the call Ayden tapped."

I nodded. "Right. She said something that sounded like 'flat.' Maybe it was Plattman. But Plat-eye fits him. A shape-shifter that torments children. Isn't he one of the I Scream Men?"

"Yes. And his keen interest in these runaways says Danny knows something very important. That's who he wants."

Chapter Forty-Five

I hoped this detour would pay off. I didn't need a delay. Jax turned off the main road.

Tall pine trees bowed to wind. A dark cloud briefly exposed the sun, itself a shape-shifting plat-eye, before returning to its pre-storm gloom. Silence crept in, exposing me to the crush of fear for my daughter. Had this creepy Plat-eye been near her? Had he touched her? I couldn't stand the image. I knew she wanted me to come for her. I seethed at Plat-eye's man now following us.

Jax pointed out in front of us. "We're getting close. Watch for runners."

"Runners?"

"Airic pays kids who live back here to run out and startle drivers."

I recalled my own near-miss on the night of the sitting. "He's a fraud?"

"No. He likes to amp up the myths. It amuses him when people spin stories about ghosts on this road. The kids get some money and tourists turn around." Jax looked over at me. "For the record, coming here was not my idea."

I held up a hand. "I accept full responsibility, I promise, no matter what happens. I know you don't want to do this."

"So, you owe me. Tell me about that map Puca drew. You thought it was from someone else. It scared you."

"It's a different circumstance, unrelated."

"No withholding, remember?"

"It's personal."

Jax snorted. "If you're worried about your secrets, don't go to Airic. He'll

162

see a lot more than you want to show him."

I hugged myself and breathed out. "Okay, okay. I thought it was a girl. Someone who disappeared years ago. A friend. We never found her. It's bothered me. That's all."

"She didn't seem present during your session?"

"I focused on her, but no."

"So, you think she's trying to show you where she…"

"I don't know. A medium told me two days ago that a girl matching her description wants to tell me something. Naturally, I assumed that's what Puca intended to show me, so I probably set myself up. Should I mention this to Airic?"

"No. Let him tell you what *he* sees. But this girl's never been present before?"

"No. I've tried contacting her, believe me. I've used every way I could to find her."

"Still, Annie, there's a theme. She's missing. You were consulted for a missing child. Now we have others missing."

I hadn't seen that connection. "And Airic supposedly helped find a missing kid, which inspired my first visit to him." I didn't add my father into this mix, but it seemed that I'd become a magnet for these cases, doing as he had done.

"Was this girl a close friend?" Jax asked.

I shifted. "My best friend. She got on a motorcycle with a stranger. She never came back."

"Ran away?"

I waited a moment to center myself. Finally, I filled in the blank. "The guy was arrested. Tommy Ray Bruder. He'd killed others. I interviewed him in prison. He gave up nothing. So, it's really not related."

Jax took a breath, like he was about to comment, but then stopped. He looked in the mirror. "Hold on. I want to lose this cop. We're coming to a good place."

We rounded a bend and Jax hit the gas pedal. I gripped the seat. He veered left around another sharp curve, throwing me against the door, then sped up on a straight part. He dodged a pothole before he took a curve to the right. Then he made a hard left toward an opening in the trees and pulled behind some overgrowth. I hadn't seen any hint of road. A minute later, the cop raced past. Jax turned again and proceeded slowly on bumpy ground, deeper into the woods. I saw puddles along the side. "Are we on a road?"

"A shortcut. Even if that cop doubles back, he won't see the opening. I can't lead him to Airic's."

"I don't remember a road like this."

"You were at a sitting. That's not where he lives. His house is in the cemetery."

I recalled the gravestones I'd seen from the parking area. "Please don't say he creeps around in some dank mausoleum."

Jax stopped again and leaned toward me. "I can turn around. I'd prefer to. Now that we don't have a tail, we could join your team."

"Are we close to him?"

"Five minutes."

"Then let's see Airic. If he says no, at least I tried."

Jax turned onto a rutted narrow path to our right. Things around us seemed visually sharper. I glimpsed a few rounded gravestones on my side. The rain had let up, so I cracked the window, letting in the smell of moss. Tree frogs' high notes mingled with agitated katydids.

Jax did the same on his side. "Feel that? The crisp air before a hurricane. It's coming. We need to get this done."

"Why does Airic live here?"

"Being with people is difficult for him. He prefers the dead. He spends a lot of time trying to communicate with them."

"I heard he has a language disorder."

Jax gestured dismissively. "He's odd and doesn't understand sometimes, so he just stares. His mother was so disturbed by his awkwardness she mostly kept him in a cage until he was four."

"My God!"

"So, his language skills were delayed. He *reads* you more than hears you. I'm used to it. My grandfather never answers directly, either. Don't be put off. He's just… unique. I'm not even sure he'll let you enter his home, even if he allowed you into a sitting. He has things hooked up for spirit communications. But we'll give it a try."

With the next turn, I saw the house. Rather, the cottage. Resembling a broad West Indies style plantation house, it looked as if it would collapse in a strong storm. At least it was raised several feet on stilts. I suspected it flooded around here with any heavy rain. The blue door, barely visible under a roof that sloped over the wraparound porch, was a surprise. I snorted. "Haint-blue? That's a repellant. I thought he welcomed ghosts."

"Ghosts, yes. Not boo-hags."

"He screens them?"

"You don't want to tangle with a boo-hag."

"I'll take your word for it."

"Airic bought the cemetery and replaced an abandoned church with a house built for his special needs. It's actually quite sturdy." He pointed up. "The attic is designed for optimum energy flow, and each room has a specific function. He has assistants, but they live across the cemetery in the log cabin you saw. And I should warn you, he has another repellant, a boo-daddy."

"A what?"

"It's a magical amulet, and it stinks. It's on a stuffed figure, his watcher, just outside the door. It's made from pluff mud, sweet grass and whatever. You won't like it." He pointed upward. "The full moon supposedly gives it power. If you're not expecting it, the thing will startle you. And don't touch it. The last time I was here, he told me Carter rigged it to emit toxic fumes."

"He makes enough from his séances to own all this?"

"He has a large circle of generous donors."

"How often did you come?"

"I usually came with Carter, maybe once a month, or Airic came down to us. He worked on Carter's cases, but he also studied with Puca." Jax parked the car near the house but kept it running and made no move to open his door. "Before we see him, here's the story. I don't want Valerie to ever learn this, or Dylan." He cut the engine and turned toward me. "On the night

Carter died, he came here first. He…told Airic he'd…done some things. That he'd been…" Jax looked at his hands and then back at me. "He was part of it. He was working for ISM. At the parties."

"My God!" I put a hand to my mouth.

Jax nodded. He didn't speak for a moment. Then he cleared his throat. "Airic told me. I didn't believe it. I said he was lying, that Carter would never participate in damaging kids. But … those three motivators. Carter was vulnerable. So, I did some digging. When Carter was a cop, he was compromised with drug deals and payoffs. I think ISM used that to blackmail him. How long he worked for them I don't know, but he must have done something that made them think he was a threat. I believe Sloane knew their plan to kill him. I think she lured him—"

Jax looked at the house. I saw Airic on the porch, a tall stick figure. His long hair and a gauzy black shirt blew around him.

"Give me a minute," Jax said.

He walked over as Airic came down the steps. The wind swept out their words, but their gestures were clear. Airic embraced Jax as if welcoming a long-lost brother. Then he waved for me to come, like he'd been expecting me.

Chapter Forty-Six

Airic sat across from me, his knees almost touching mine. He leaned forward to grip both of my hands with his boney fingers. Jax had gone outside to check the storm shutters. He'd already explained to Airic about Kamryn, the map, and our hope for direction, making my need the priority. Airic had watched the floor the whole time, as if trying to focus on each word. He'd said he knew I was coming, but when I asked him how I'd gotten into the sitting, he blinked at me, his eyes on my chin. I didn't press, nor ask about Jimmy Broderick.

We sat in flickering candlelight while the wind picked up again and banged on windowpanes. I was relieved that the bigheaded boo-daddy watcher was outside. It *had* spooked me. And it stank.

The various wires and blinking lights on Airic's devices for spirit communication made the place seem more an electronics workshop than a home. But the shelves full of items for "root medicine" on another wall added a more earthy effect. His twin-size thick foam mattress sat on the main room floor under a rumpled blue blanket, perhaps placed there to ensure he never missed a contact. Bare wooden chairs surrounded a table covered with notebooks and sketchpads. Nothing in this 15-by-20-foot room with only beams and boards for a ceiling suggested he entertained.

To Jax's narrative, I added the Black Shirt incident. Airic remembered the recording but didn't comment. As I described my experience with Puca and the map that led us to Kam's phone, he squinted at my mouth and nodded.

"You have the current," he commented. "You attract." This observation surprised me, as if he'd sensed the unique ability my father had possessed, which I'd also seen in Kamryn. At one point, Airic held up a hand. "Your dog."

I shook my head. "I don't have—"

"It protects you. He...*she*...searches. Dark brown, and some light." He gestured toward his face, then touched my knee. "She's been near you. She wonders where you are. She's... afraid for you. She finds things."

"Oh, yes." He meant Mika. He could have smelled her on me, but he wouldn't have known her coloring. "She's not mine. She lives with me." I leaned forward. "Did she find someone?"

Airic jerked his head down, tucking his chin to his chest. He gripped my hands and shook his head. I heard him mutter. The flame flickered and then bowed toward him as if gently blown. He reached down with his right hand and tapped the floor. Then he looked up. "They speak to you."

Only one paranormal method had ever worked for me, and I considered it just a form of heightened mental energy. It got results. "Can we do some remote viewing?"

Airic stood and beckoned for me to follow him down a short hallway into a smaller room that contained a table and three wooden stools. He lit candles, then opened a door to what appeared to be a closet. "This helps the flow." He pulled on a lever, which raised a trap door from the floor. A brace fell into place with a loud thud. The wind sounded as if it were in the room. I recalled what Jax had said about an attic. Airic had just opened the channel.

"Air and light mingle through purifiers." Airic gestured upward. "This room receives best." He gestured for me to take a seat on one of the stools. "You're jammed." He pointed to his ear.

On the table I saw a map, a thick tablet of light blue paper, and a collection of different types of pencils. I sat near the tablet. Airic sat across from me. "The girl will help."

"Kamryn?"

He pulled his fingers through his hair, winding it into two thick strands. "She talks, but you don't hear."

Jax came down the hall. Airic waved him toward us. "We need three."

Jax came over and put his hand on my right shoulder. Airic slid the tablet closer to me and gestured for me to choose a pencil or pen. When I picked up a dark purple pencil to help me focus on Kam, he put his hand over mine and pushed the pencil onto the paper. Then he peered at me. "Who didn't trust you?"

The question startled me. But I knew the answer. My mother. Her derision had been a hurdle my entire life. She'd always said I couldn't be trusted. I was like my father. She'd said I'd never succeed because I overthought and didn't act when I should. And for some things, she'd been right. I often hesitated. I'd let Hailey go. I'd let Sloane take my daughter. I should have stopped these things.

Airic cocked his head as if he knew my thoughts. Into my mind came the words, *you keep her here.*

I blinked hard against tears. Jax had warned me about Airic's approach, but I hadn't anticipated *this.* My throat felt tight. Airic seemed to hear something I couldn't. Then he said, "She says there was nothing you could do. You don't see what happened. You choke."

Jax put both hands on my shoulders and gently squeezed. He must have felt me trembling. I shook my head. "I should have..." Hailey's frightened face flashed at me. Then I saw Kamryn's fierce, desperate face. It still stung. "I told her to go first. It should have been me. I was older."

Airic passed a hand over his hair. He whispered, "Picked me." He seemed distressed. "Kept them."

I watched him through tears. "Kept what?" I barely heard my own voice.

Jax came around me and sat to my left, gripping my hand. "Bruder's victims. Did he take anything from them? Like a souvenir?"

I stared down at Airic's hands. I had to face this. I breathed in. I'd memorized the cases I'd linked from my own research to try to spot Bruder's MO—where he'd grabbed his victims and what he'd done to them. "They were kids. Girls. They found two, but I know there are others. He had an earring from one he'd buried."

My heart raced. I swallowed hard and picked up the pencil. I looked at Airic for direction. He stared at the table. Jax touched my arm. I tried to focus on Kam.

Find me.

Airic grabbed his hair on both sides and ran his hands downward. Hailey's braids. Focus on *her.*

I wiped my eyes. "The ones I know..." My words trailed off.

Jax squeezed my arm. "Don't think. Breathe."

I sensed a blurred image. A girl running. I felt it. Then I remembered. I *had* acted. I'd forgotten. The foggy details emerged like someone was throwing puzzle pieces at a magnetic board to form a coherent image. I'd run toward Hailey. I'd grabbed for her, to pull her off the bike, but Bruder had knocked me away. I'd fallen. I rubbed my elbow where I'd hurt it hitting the ground. Bruder had said something. I strained to hear it. Jax reminded me to breathe.

Airic rose and waved his left hand like he was swatting a fly.

"Cherry!" I pointed to my hair. "He said, 'Cherry's mine.' He wanted her for her *hair*, her red hair!" Suddenly I realized what Airic had meant. He'd kept her *braids*. That was his souvenir. He'd cut them off and kept them. Hailey hadn't been killed because of anything she or I had stupidly done. Even if we'd told the biker to get lost, he'd still have grabbed her. He'd been intent on his targeted prey. Hailey had been lost before we'd even seen Bruder. I wiped my eyes and felt Jax squeeze my arm. I nodded. I couldn't look at him.

Airic tapped the paper. "It's open!" He drew his hand in a fluid arc. "Draw."

Jax removed his hand. I touched the pencil to the paper.

Chapter Forty-Seven

My hand moved. I watched. Airic said something to Jax, but this strange process fascinated me too much to listen. I'd never had luck with automatic writing, or psychography. Supposedly, a spirit takes over your physical body to express something in words or images, like with the planchette on a Ouija board. I'd hired people who could do this to help solve crimes, but I'd half-believed it was fraud. Still, Puca's strange map had located Kamryn's phone.

I drew an oddly shaped outline that contained a circle and two wavy parallel lines, like bends in a river. Pressure on my chest made it difficult to breathe and I wanted to rise, as if to get above the surface of water. I jumped up. "Underwater! That's why the cellar flooded during your sitting. What we need is under water!"

Jax and Airic looked at me. I sensed I'd interrupted something.

Airic turned back to Jax and pointed to his face. "Don't bring him here again. Can't let him in. He came for Carter. Too late."

Jax got out his phone and touched the screen. He held it up. "Him?"

Airic looked away.

"This man came here? Airic, tell me. Did he hurt you?"

Airic tucked his arms around himself. "Ran away." Shielding his face, he seemed to lose his balance, but Jax caught him. Airic turned and grabbed his arms. "A boy came. He was going to you." Airic looked toward me. "You know him."

I sorted through possible candidates. "The kid from the sitting?"

Airic ran a hand through his hair.

Jax grabbed a chair and got Airic to sit. He leaned toward him. "Look at me. Be clear. Carter brought someone here? A boy?"

Airic nodded. "He didn't like it here. Didn't like me. Carter said he knew things. He saw things. He had a key."

This startled me. Sarah, the paratherapist, had mentioned a key. Pieces were coming together. She'd also referred to ice cream and my case "up north." If Carter had been involved with ISM, these scattered impressions pointed to one person. "Was his name Danny?" I asked.

Airic blinked at me, then said to Jax, "He wanted to make it right. He came to tell me. He wants you to know." He waved a hand as if gesturing toward someone in the room.

"Make what right?"

"The boy can show you."

I held up my drawing. "Does this look like anything?"

Airic stared at it, nodded, and pointed past my right ear. "It's in his head. Find him."

I shook my drawing. "Is this about the boy or about my daughter? Will this lead us to her?"

Airic pulled the paper from my hand and placed it on the table. He tapped it. "She sees *this*. You need her."

"What?" Now he was just frustrating.

Jax gestured for me to back away. To Airic, he said, "I'm going to take Annie to her team and then come back and get you to my house. You'll be safe there."

Airic shook his head. "Have to be here."

"Why?"

"Go, Jax. Go now. You both go. Follow the water. It's in the water. Everything is…in…water."

"Annie," Jax said. "Wait for me in the car."

"But—"

"He's getting confused. I'll be right there."

I picked up my drawing. I couldn't tell if we'd gotten some amazing tips or wasted precious time. I went to the car and looked more closely at the images. I tried to let something speak to me, but nothing rose above the tapping noise of rain on the roof. I folded and placed the drawing into the glove compartment for safekeeping. Then I texted Natra that we'd be there soon. She had nothing new to report. We were no closer to finding Kam.

Chapter Forty-Eight

It was hard going out to the main road. Jax had to maneuver around several large puddles. The day looked darker. A wind gust shot a spray of water at my window. I felt drained. To my right, I saw a shed painted haint blue with its roof badly caved in. I hoped it wasn't an omen.

Jax broke the silence. "I hate this place. It's unhealthy. It has snakes."

"Snakes?"

He shrugged. "You have drowning, I have snakes."

"Let's hope we don't get stuck in a flood."

"Are you okay?"

I put my hands in my lap and breathed out. "I'm angry."

"At me?"

"At me. All these years, I've let myself believe I was responsible for my best friend's abduction. My mother's constant berating crushed me so much I internalized the blame. That's not easy to accept."

"I've been under that psychic scalpel. It hurts."

"But it didn't get us anywhere. I still don't know where Kam is. Nothing I drew shows me."

"You just need context. Like an investigation, clues hang in the air until you can put them in the right place."

I knew that. I didn't want to wait. "Did Airic tell *you* anything helpful?"

"Maybe. If I'm reading him correctly, Cypress Run's trafficking hub is the switch house Danny mentioned, and it's near Carter's cabin."

I sat up. "We have to go!"

He held up a hand. "We've only narrowed down the area. I still don't know it's location."

"How did you figure that out?"

"Carter came here the day he was killed. He'd just been at his cabin, and he had this boy in tow. That suggests he'd been at the switch house."

"If I know him, I think the boy might be Danny. But Danny wasn't...Oh, wait!" I searched my memory. "There was a note in his record that he was at risk for escaping. So, maybe he was running away."

"And got caught. And Plat-eye's been trying to get him to say what he knows."

"Did Airic say anything about Kam?"

Jax glanced at me. "Sorry. He's a bit maddening. Sometimes, he leaps from one thing to another."

"Kam's like that, too."

In the mirror on my right, I saw a flash of lights behind us. I turned to look. "No way!"

Jax watched in the rearview mirror. "It's not a cop."

"Limo?"

"Don't think so." He pointed to the glove compartment. "My gun's in back. See if Val left her Sig in here."

I located a Sig Sauer P250 and a full magazine. Jax accelerated. I prepared the weapon and checked my seatbelt.

Jax turned left onto a narrow road that cut through tall weeds on both sides. The other car followed but kept some distance. I looked back. It was sportier than a police car. I saw a flash of red. Jax raced around a bend, throwing me off balance, and then braked so fast I slammed my hands against the dash. He tried to catch me, but I hit hard. I looked up. Directly in front of us was a wide swath of water flowing across the road. He'd nearly gone in. Lifting his foot from the brake, he edged toward it.

I grabbed the door handle. "No, Jax! Stop! We'll be swept away!" I unbuckled my seatbelt, ready to jump out. He grabbed my arm. "Sorry. I forgot. I won't."

I remained poised.

"Annie, I won't put you in danger."

175

He held his hand out for the Sig. I gave it to him, and he got out. The other car had stopped about twenty yards away. Jax raised the gun. The driver pulled toward the left into the weeds, backed up, and turned around. I knew that car. I leaned over the driver's seat. "It's her. That's Sloane's car!"

Jax handed me the gun, got in, and turned around, racing to catch up. Sloane had a surprising head start. She turned left onto the main road, going east.

I didn't care how fast Jax drove. I wanted him to force Sloane off the road so I could make her reveal where she'd taken Kam.

Something struck the windshield.

Jax gestured. "Get down. I saw a flash. Someone's shooting." He slowed to get out of range but keep Sloane in sight. She passed a silver van. So did we. She disappeared around a bend, but we found her again. She passed a blue sedan, but an oncoming black truck blocked us. By the time we got around the sedan, the road ahead was empty. A fallen tree further delayed us.

I couldn't believe it. "We lost her."

Jax turned around to look for roads where she might have gone, but I saw none. We resumed our trip to Carter's place.

"She followed us for a reason," Jax said. "We'll see her again."

When we reached the cabin, Jax pulled into a small parking area. I saw my SUV, but not Ayden's truck. A light in the window indicated that Natra had located the generator.

The one-story gray frame cabin was a basic Tidewater design with a low tin roof, narrow front porch, and four spindly columns coated with peeling white paint. I guessed it was about 600 square feet. Just a one-bedroom getaway, presumably Carter's abode while he worked the switch house parties.

"Stay alert," Jax said. "Sloane could be around here." His phone rang. His expression soon changed to anger. "When? Where?... Where's the van now?... And it wasn't a storm evacuation?... Thank you for letting me know. Please keep me informed." He hung up. "That was a Sycamore CO, the one who sent me Brooke's note. They moved Caryn this morning."

"To where?"

"Supposedly to Georgia, as I requested."

"That's good, then."

"She never arrived."

Chapter Forty-Nine

Natra opened the door and held out towels. I entered a low-ceilinged room with bare plaster walls and a pine wood floor. Nothing about it felt homey. As I peeled off my wet parka, I heard Mika barking behind a closed door.

"It's a time out," Natra explained. "She's going nuts in here."

"Where's Ayden?"

"Tracking Wayne." To Jax, she said, "The place was trashed. The lock was broken." She pointed toward a wooden table. Snack bags and soft drinks lay in a pile. "Looks like someone's camping out." She gestured toward another room. "There's something more important in here. Mika found it." She led us into a cramped, grimy kitchen with one window and a back door. Despite the poor lighting, I saw evidence of a hasty search. Dishes and pans sat haphazardly on counters and the floor. A chair was overturned, and a large butcher knife lay in the aluminum sink.

Natra turned on a flashlight. Jax took it to examine the knife and several plates. "I see dust. They weren't here recently."

"When were you last here?" I asked.

"A week after Carter died, three months ago. It wasn't ransacked. I looked around but didn't find anything. I took Carter's personal things and locked up."

"Look here." Natra indicated an area of the tile floor. "You wouldn't have noticed it. And I wouldn't have, either, except Mika kept barking the way she did in your office. She alerted right here."

Jax hovered the flashlight beam over the spot. "I don't see anything. Just some chipped grout."

Natra produced a flathead screwdriver. "I put it back, to show you." She looked at me. "Like that French detective, Macé, you mentioned on *Psi Apps* who pried up the tiles in a murder room. I noticed the grout here was lighter, like it was bleached. See how it's different? So, I pulled up this tile." She bent down to lift it out. I saw a reddish-brown stain. Jax looked stunned.

I leaned down and sniffed. "Smells like blood."

Natra nodded. "It is. I tested a small sample. Maybe your brother was killed here."

Jax went to one knee. Natra handed him the screwdriver. He chipped at three more tiles, easing them away to avoid handling them. Underneath were more dark stains that emanated a foul smell. "He must have bled here, and they thought they could just bleach it. But why would he have let them trap him?" Jax worked at lifting other tiles while taking pictures with his phone. Natra took a few to corroborate the find. I knew this had to be difficult for Jax. It was the evidence he'd sought, but this was about his brother. To give him space, I gestured for Natra to come with me to the main room.

"This is big," I said. "It proves Carter wasn't the victim of a random shooting where they claimed they found his body."

"If it's his blood."

"Seems likely. It's not fresh, but it's not from years ago, either."

Natra looked at her phone. "Ayden just sent coordinates."

Jax appeared in the doorway. "Where?"

I grabbed my parka. "Let's take my SUV. It rides higher."

He held out his hand. "Key. I'll drive."

"Unless you need me, I'll stay here," Natra said. "Mika hates all this wind and I need to calm her down."

"Good idea. You can keep us coordinated. Stay armed and stay in touch."

Chapter Fifty

Ayden's directions took us to a secluded mansion in a heavily wooded area near the river, fifteen minutes from Carter's cabin. Jax thought it had to be the switch house. Broderick's Lexus was in a parking area, next to Wayne's black Ford Expedition. I hoped his presence was a sign of his success at getting undercover and not proof of ISM using Kam to leverage him. I had to get inside.

Ayden had found a good place to watch from his truck. It was still afternoon, but the thick clouds darkened things. I sat between Ayden and Jax on the bench seat of his truck. Despite the steady rain, we had a view inside the house through a row of lit windows. The columned Gothic Revival had a two-story gallery and third-floor dormers jutting from the hipped roof. I wondered how many kids had been brought here for sex trafficking. How many did they hold captive? To me, this place was just an elegant but sinister prison.

I squinted at the parking area. A dark gray SUV and a town car sat on either side of Wayne's Expedition. "I don't see Sloane's car, or the limo."

Jax redirected my gaze toward the mansion. "Three-car garage. Could be in there."

"I saw a row of cabins, too," Ayden told us. "Probably for *private* parties. And I spotted surveillance cameras, so they must have a security command center with monitors. But no one's raised an alarm yet, not that I've noticed."

Jax looked around. "It's probably just a bare bones staff, given the weather."

Ayden offered me his binoculars. "I've seen Wayne. People are walking around inside like it's some kind of hurricane party."

I grabbed the binoculars. Hurricane parties were for crazy people who hoped to defy the odds. They usually drank a lot. Sometimes, they died. This house sat on the bank of a river, which would surely flood if Delano hit the South Carolina coast. I saw several men and two teenage boys, holding drinks.

"Do you see a way to get up to the balconies?" I asked Ayden.

"I haven't been in back, but I assume there's a fire escape somewhere."

Jax took the binoculars and scanned the grounds. He sat forward and pointed. "That van's from Sycamore." A white van sat across the yard, in shadows. I thought it looked empty.

Suddenly, Jax was out the door. He slammed it shut and strode along the tree line.

"What's he doing?" Ayden asked.

"Looking for Caryn."

Ayden shook his head. "He can't go alone." He got out. I slid across the seat to follow, but a bright flash and loud *bang* stopped me. Two second-floor windows shattered, and smoke billowed out. I heard yelling and the word, "Fire!" My heart stopped. Kam might be in there.

I exited the truck and ran against the wind across the yard. When I reached the house, I went around to the back to find a fire escape. I stopped just short of a stream of flowing water. The river had breached its bank.

A back door opened, and a skinny boy exited, followed by a man clad only in jeans who yelled at him and caught up. I stepped behind a tree. The boy struggled, but the man was stronger. I looked around and saw a thick chunk on the ground from a broken branch. I tossed it and hit the man square in the back. When he turned, the boy got away. The man followed but slipped on the wet grass and fell.

I focused on the house. I saw nothing that would get me to the balcony, so I went to the side. A short boy sprinted toward the white Sycamore van and jumped in. The lights came on and the van tore out.

Another boy climbed over the balcony railing in back. It was too high for him to jump. I yelled and motioned for him to get onto a branch further down that reached close to the edge. He made the leap and shimmied down the tree. He took off before I could question him. I tried to climb the tree, but my feet kept slipping. I was about to go back to the door from which the first kid had emerged when I heard an engine start.

I ran around the corner and saw the back of the Expedition as it left the grounds. The town car was also gone. I climbed onto the porch and peeked through a window. A pudgy man wrapped his naked body in a robe. He barked orders at someone I couldn't see. I stepped carefully to the next window and tried it. I couldn't get it to budge.

The distinct revving of Ayden's truck cut through the air. He was leaving! I ran to the edge of the wraparound porch to wave at him. A shot from behind made me duck as a bullet ricocheted off the column to my right. I jumped to the ground.

Ayden took off. I was stranded. I turned around to see James Broderick on the porch. Or rather, I saw his gun. It was aimed straight at me.

Chapter Fifty-One

I held up my hands. Broderick motioned with the weapon for me to return. I walked toward him.

"What are you doing here?" he yelled. "We know you have the kid. Talk!"

"I came for my daughter! You took her! I want to see her."

He gestured again for me to get back on the porch.

"Freeze!" Jax came up behind Broderick, his weapon ready. "Put it down."

Broderick hesitated, then bent down to place his gun on the porch. He turned toward Jax with a fierce expression, hands raised. Then Sloane emerged from the house, her gun poised. "Hold it there, Jackson!"

So, she *was* here. This confirmed that Kam must be as well. I measured my chances of grabbing Broderick's weapon.

Jax laid down his gun and stepped back. Broderick seized it and picked up his own, deflating my hope.

"This is the one," he said. "The attorney. No one will miss him." He raised the pistol directly at Jax.

I yelled, "No!" A shot rang out. Broderick jerked, staggered, and dropped off the edge. He fell to the ground five feet from me. Rain mixed with the blood that oozed from a hole in his forehead. The man was dead. I backed away, confused. Sloane had shot him.

Jax and Sloane faced each other, but she held her stance. "We're even," she said.

"Hardly! Carter's dead because of you."

"You listen to me, Jackson. I did not set him up. So, stop looking for me."

183

"You lied! He called—"

"I begged him to leave, but he said he had to keep them away from his kids. He was protecting them... and you."

I moved carefully toward Broderick's dropped gun, but Sloane trained hers on me. "Leave it!" She took a position that enabled her to shoot either one of us and gestured with her gun. "You! Get up here."

I climbed up onto the porch. "Where's my daughter? Where did you take her?"

Sloane kept her eyes on Jax. "She's not here."

"Then where is she?"

"With Wayne." To Jax, Sloane said, "I tried leading you away, but you didn't take the hint. Now both of you get the hell out of here before you blow my cover." She gestured toward Broderick. "I'll say *you* shot him, and they'll kill you when they come back."

Jax remained where he was.

I felt an urge to rush at Sloane, throw her to the ground, and beat her in the face. "I want to see inside."

Sloane raised her gun. "Leave. Now. Or she'll never see you again."

Jax guided me off the porch. I looked back to see Sloane watching us. Raised voices inside told me there were others.

"We'll get her," Jax said. "Just not this way."

I didn't know if he meant Kam or Sloane. In my SUV, I seethed over this confrontation. "I was almost in."

"They would have stopped you. If Kam's in there, she's likely in a locked room upstairs. You wouldn't have gotten very far."

"Wayne left. Did you see him take her?"

"I was trying to get in the house myself. I think Ayden went after him."

I breathed out. "I know."

Jax looked over at me. "That was close. Are you alright?"

"She shot him. She actually *killed* him. Do you think she's really undercover?"

"No."

"Then why not shoot us? Why'd she kill *him*?"

184

"I don't know, Annie. But don't trust anything she says."

I tried to clear my mind. I couldn't think about Broderick's murder. He would've killed Jax, and then me. But I was shivering. "I need to go back. There's got to be a way in."

"What we need is to find Ayden and whoever took that van."

"I think it was kids."

"Right. And they were inside the house. Maybe they caused the explosion. We find them, we get information."

I texted Ayden. No response. He also didn't answer his phone, so I called Natra to catch her up. She said she hadn't heard from Ayden.

Suddenly I saw water streaming across the road. I gasped as Jax plowed through it. We made it to the other side. He looked at me. "Sorry."

"The next snake I see, I'm throwing at you. Warn me next time."

"We can't stop for every puddle. Just don't look."

I suddenly realized Sloane had just shaken his world. In the space of an hour, his sense of his brother had dramatically shifted. Carter had been complicit with ISM, which was bad, but he'd also sacrificed himself for his family. *That's* why he'd let himself get trapped. Better that than ISM taking his loved ones hostage to control him.

Jax handed me his phone. "Call Dylan. Tell him to get his mother and sister over to my place. Then he should lock up the house, stay armed, and watch for trouble. And he should tell Airic's handlers to go get him."

I made the call. Dylan answered at once. I conveyed the instructions.

"They're already here," Dylan said, "with plenty of supplies. I'll call the handlers. And I picked up the Wrangler from the office. The hurricane shifted. It's aiming for the Lowcountry and it's coming fast. You need to get out."

"We'll try, Dylan."

When I ended the call, I said, "Hopefully, Airic will go."

"He'd better. Plat-eye knows the place. Our visit there made him a target."

185

Chapter Fifty-Two

We pulled into a space at Carter's cabin just as Ayden arrived on my right. He rolled down his window, gave a quick gesture, and yelled, "Didn't find him!"

I pointed to the house, indicating we should get inside. But then the white Sycamore van pulled halfway into a spot on our left. I saw a girl's startled face in the window before it backed up and sped away.

"That was Caryn Greenwood!" I yelled.

Jax had already pulled out. He raced after them. Ayden came up tight behind us.

I gripped my seat, my eyes on the wet pavement and red taillights ahead. Ayden sped past. The van wove to the left to block him, and nearly tipped. He honked three times and pulled wide to their right side, running into tall grass, to pass them. I held my breath until he was clear. Jax moved in behind the van. Its brake lights flared, and it angled across the road before jerking to a stop. Jax parked close. I handed him the Glock from my purse and grabbed the loaded Ruger .38 from my glove compartment.

Jax approached the driver's side. With gun in hand, he tapped on the window and ordered the driver out. The door opened. He reached in. I got out just as Danny Harnett came running from the other side with a pistol aimed at Jax.

"Let 'im go or I'll kill you!"

Jax held up his hand, stepped away, and removed the Glock's magazine. The other boy—the driver—scampered toward the trees.

"Danny, don't!" I yelled. Rain slapped my face, blinding me, but I aimed toward him. He looked at me just as Ayden jumped him from behind and gripped him in a bear hug, gun to his head. "Drop it!"

Jax grabbed Danny's wrist to angle his gun upward as his shot rang through the air.

I took a stance. "Everyone, stop! We're on the same side!"

Jax took Danny's gun. "Take it easy. We can help you."

From inside the van, I heard Caryn yell, "Jax!"

She scrambled out from the driver's side. "Danny, it's Jax! My lawyer! Stop shooting!"

Ayden let go and Danny looked at me. "What's going on?"

I placed my revolver in my pocket so I could approach, my hands open. "We're here to help. We won't turn you in. Come back with us so we can talk."

Caryn grabbed Jax's arm. "Come on, Danny. This is for real!"

He gave a curt nod, but he looked ready to flee. Ayden said he'd search for the kid who'd run off, while I drove the van back to Carter's place, with Jax behind us. My shoes were soaked through, and I was getting cold.

In the van, Danny took an angry tone. "How'd you find me?"

I looked at him in the rearview mirror. "We're after the same thing, Danny. We know about Plat-eye, just like you said, and the switch house. We were just there. I've learned some things you need to hear. We're trying to prove your innocence."

"She is," Caryn assured him. "I told you she came to see me." To me, she said, "I thought you were gonna get Brooke out. She's dead."

"No, she's not. She's in the hospital. But they took some of my papers, so I didn't understand your warning."

Caryn shrugged. "She was sure they were gonna torture her or something. She was off her meds and super paranoid."

"We hope she'll recover." I glanced at Danny again. His rigid posture said I hadn't won him over. "Why'd you take the van, Danny? They'll be looking for it."

"Key was inside."

"So, you caused the explosion."

"We done what we had ta do."

Danny directed me to park the van behind a copse of trees, to hide it from the road. "They'll come. We cain't stay long."

"They know about this place?"

"How do *you* know 'bout it? I didn't tell ya."

"It belongs to Jax's brother, Carter."

Caryn turned. "Jackson *Raines*. That's Carter's name. You were s'posed to—"

Danny made a cutting motion across his neck. His guard was up—way up. "Cain't you jus' let us go?"

I shook my head. "You won't get far. Cops are looking for you. I know you didn't do what they're accusing you of. We have to fight it. Your chances are better with us. Please, just come in and listen. We need your help, too."

As we entered the cabin, Natra gave out towels. She looked at me in surprise at whom we'd brought in. Mika, now calm, sniffed each person. Danny accepted a towel but kept his distance. I sensed he'd take off if he spotted any sign we weren't on the level. I couldn't blame him. Getting caught was a death sentence, and not necessarily in a courtroom.

"How many other kids were in that house?" I asked.

Caryn was about to respond when Danny cut her off. "We ain't talkin' till we know what's going' on."

Jax looked at me and raised an eyebrow. I sensed he wanted me to work on this kid's trust issues. I was boiling over with questions.

Jax faced Danny. "I know you were with my brother." He gestured at the mess. "Someone's been in here looking around. Why?"

Danny looked down with a slight shake of his head. "Wadn't us." He gestured toward the snack bags. "Just tossed our stuff and left."

Caryn pointed at Jax. "He won't turn us in. He's one of us. He was in juvie, too, once. He knows what it's like."

Her take-charge approach surprised me. I'd dismissed her as mousy.

Ayden entered with a short, skinny kid with large blue eyes and a flop of dark hair. "This is Flynn."

"Hey!" The kid gave a shy wave. He grabbed a towel to dry his face and scanned the room. He saw Mika in a corner. "Hey! Can I pet the dog?"

Natra assured him he could. He went over and bent down to let her sniff his hand. This kid, I knew, could be won over. He'd been on the run over the past few hours with Danny. He might know things Danny would withhold.

I flashed a look at Jax. We had to move this along. I wanted to go back to the switch house. He held up a finger.

"We need to know the layout of that house," he said, "how to get inside."

Caryn looked at Danny. "You've been there lots of times."

He gave her an angry look.

"We have to get Carl," Flynn said, still petting Mika. "They grabbed him when we set off the fireworks."

Danny glared at him. "We ain't goin' back."

Caryn sat on the arm of a couch. "That's what they wanted, the I Scream Men. Danny. I heard 'em talking. I was the bait. They'd get 'im to come and then ditch us in the river. But they *didn't* expect Flynn and his bombs. So, I got out."

"There's no alarm?" Jax asked.

"Don't know. This kid showed me how to unlock the—"

I went alert. "What kid?"

Chapter Fifty-Three

What Caryn recounted stunned me. "She was young, like, younger than us. Said she'd been in and out of the rooms. She freed me. I think she stole a knife or somethin'." Caryn paused to think. "When I told her my name, she said she knew me." She looked at Jax. "From you."

My heart jumped. "Kamryn! Was that her name?"

"Yeah, maybe. Somethin' like that."

I nearly broke down. "That's my daughter."

"She seemed to know the place. Said their security was a joke. She was pretty slick for a kid."

"She wasn't hurt in the explosion?"

"That room was empty," Flynn said. "Just a diversion. Smoke bomb, that's all."

Caryn held up a finger. "She did say her mom would come."

I put my hand to my mouth and tried to hold back tears. I nodded.

"Let's go!" Ayden said.

"We cain't!" Danny insisted.

"I can get you in," Flynn told him. "It wasn't hard. Like this place."

Danny made an exasperated noise and stalked into the kitchen.

Jax went over to the table and moved some items in place. To Flynn, he said, "Show me."

I followed Danny. He stood staring at the bloodstain. I stopped. "You saw it."

He remained silent, but his eyes watered. He wiped his face. This was my opening. "Danny, you know I'm trying to help you, right?"

He gave a curt nod. "I hate this house."

"What happened?"

He stared at the floor.

"You were with Carter." I pointed to the stain. "We know he was killed here. Did you see it?"

He wrapped his arms around his body. I leaned toward him and opened my hands to communicate sincerity. I tried a bold move. "They killed Mick. We need to find his body. He wants us to."

Danny's eyes opened wide, and he took a step back.

"You've seen something. Did Carter show you?"

"That weird guy, that magician." I wasn't sure what he meant until he added, "In the graveyard."

"Airic?"

He hugged himself tighter and shifted his weight. "Carter wanted to give 'im somethin'. That guy was creepy."

So, he *had* been there. Mystery solved. "What happened?"

"He watched me, like he knew me. He put things in my mind. I thought I seen—"

"What?"

He shook his head.

I tried a different angle. "What did you see in here?"

He closed his eyes.

"Danny, listen. We know you didn't kill Mick. But we need more. Mr. Raines is an attorney. He's building a case. That's what Carter wanted, right? He wanted to help his brother. Didn't he tell you that?"

Danny stared at the blood. "He said to take his car. He gave me an address."

"His brother's house." I pointed toward the living room.

"I didn't want to leave 'im. So, I came back."

"What happened?"

"They come from the switch house. That woman, I seen her there, so she musta knowed what Carter done. They was fighting. I seen it through the window. Then I seen Plat-eye. I had to hide."

Plat-eye! "This is important, Danny. What happened here?"

His lower lip trembled. Another tear came out. "Carter was tryin' ta help me. He wanted ta get out of this thing. He coulda left with me, but he wouldn't. Plat-eye went in, an' I heard three shots. I looked through the window and seen him here." He gestured toward the floor. "Bleedin'." He touched his head.

"Why didn't you run?"

"I tried. I took off. I wuz near over the line when they caught me."

"Did they know you were here? That you saw something?"

He shook his head. "I never told. I said I stole the car."

"But Carter hid what he'd taken, right? What did he give the magician?"

Danny shrugged and crossed his arms. "Don't know." He was shutting down. "Nothin. I didn't do what he wanted. It's too late."

"It's not too late. We're gonna figure this out. But right now, I need your help at the switch house. My daughter's there. I have to get her. Then we'll go back to the cemetery."

"No. Not there." Danny set his jaw, glanced at the bloodstain, and strode to the other room. I followed. He went over to Jax. "Don't try to go inside. I can show you where they watch the monitors. It's another house. Where Carter got the video files."

Jax went alert. "Video files?"

"The stuff they was doin'. They got cameras in the rooms. He had pictures and videos. That Plat-eye, he wants to be a senator or somethin'. He got rich people there an' taped 'em doin' stuff with kids, to make 'em do what he wanted. They called 'im the Screw. Carter had Plat-eye's records. Said it would send lots of people to prison."

Jax cocked his head at Danny. "Where are these files?"

Danny looked down and shrugged. "Carter hid 'em."

"He didn't tell you?"

Caryn rose from the couch. "That's what we came for, right? A map or somethin'."

Danny's eyes narrowed slightly. "Wadn't here."

"Is that what he gave to Airic?" I asked. "That magician."

Danny shook his head. He avoided looking at me.

Jax put a hand on Danny's shoulder. "Thank you. Whatever you can show us will help."

"Sorry 'bout yo' bro, man. He was a good guy."

"He was. He wanted to help us. And you."

Danny nodded.

"Where's Ayden?" I asked Jax. "And Natra?"

"They took Mika to look for kids in the woods near the switch house. If we need them, they're nearby. They left a two-way radio in case the cell towers quit. Ayden said it has a good range, even in wind. His weather radio said landfall's in a few hours. We need to hurry."

"We got guns." Flynn munched on some chips. "We—" He stopped, his eyes wide, as if he realized he was bragging to the wrong people.

Danny seemed agitated. "We should wait. We stole the van. They's lookin' for me."

Jax put on his coat. "We won't take the van. But we can't wait. Every inch of rain makes this whole area dangerous. The hurricane will push water up the river, and it could happen so fast we could all go under."

Danny looked alarmed. He clearly had unfinished business.

Chapter Fifty-Four

Danny insisted that Caryn not go to the switch house. She agreed to stay at the cabin with Flynn to ambush anyone who might come. She'd also keep looking for the map. I was nervous about a gun in that kid's hand, but Flynn assured me he had it under control. Just five-foot-four, he had a strutting confidence that made him seem taller. Danny tucked a Glock into his waistband.

Jax gave Caryn the key fob for Valerie's BMW, in case they had to leave. He wrote down his address and told her how to use the car's GPS system.

She seemed surprised. "You trust me with a car like that?"

"You're too smart to run."

I gave her my cellphone number. They'd stolen a detention officer's wallet and phone, which they'd turned off to avoid being traced. They also had three cheap burner phones. Carl, the missing kid, had gotten two to work. I found a moment to tell Jax what Danny had revealed about Carter. "But there's something he's not saying," I added. "He's got secrets. Be wary. He's obviously learned how to lie to protect himself." Then I texted Natra our plan and urged her to keep Ayden from approaching the switch house.

On the way, Danny described the surveillance set-up in one of the cottages. "There's eyes everywhere. We have to be careful."

A gust of wind nearly blew us off the road. Jax dodged a puddle, splashing water up the side of my SUV. He asked Danny to fill him in. "I know about Carter's involvement with people like Plat-eye."

Danny squirmed.

"And I know what they put you through. What can you tell us?"

Danny crossed his arms and breathed out. "I didn't wanna do it. They made us. Me 'n Mick was twelve when it started. They put tattoos on us, different ones for different levels." He showed me a dark blue symbol on his left forearm. "When we was ready, they made us couriers."

Jax glanced at him.

Danny cleared his throat. "We lured others into it. It got us stuff, but mostly it got us away from..." He didn't have to finish. "Mick hated it. He wanted to tell. I told him to stuff it 'cuz they'd kill us. We seen other kids disappear. But he kept grumblin'. So..." his voice changed, and he went silent.

Jax asked if he knew where they buried Mick.

Danny shifted. "They used gators. I seen it myself, twice. That's how they scared us and made us work."

"You saw them dump Mick's body in a swamp?"

"That's what they done, mostly. That's how I met Carter. He was the cleanup crew."

I glanced at Jax. Had he noticed Danny's dodge?

"Are you saying Carter killed Mick?" Jax asked.

Danny rubbed his arm. "Carter got rid of 'em. The ones they know they're gonna kill, they get some fun out of 'em. Plat-eye's one sick fuck." He glanced at me. "'Scuse me, sorry, ma'am. Carter said Plat-eye liked to watch 'em drool and choke. He got the idea from some serial killer book."

I shuddered. "Yeah, I've heard of that guy. He'd put cyanide in burgers."

"After I run, they said they was gonna pin Mick on me." He looked at me. "I thought you was helpin' 'em."

"I wasn't. But why do you think they didn't just kill you, too, since you knew the truth?"

"Carter had somethin'. Plat-eye wants it and thinks I know where it is. I said I don't, but he don't believe me. He used people like you –" he gestured toward me, "to get it out of me. Like he thought I'd tell someone. 'Specially a woman. He knows we was at that... There was lots of secrets. Bad ones. Carter knew 'em. So, when they said this week they was now gonna kill me, I thought they found his stash. But..."

Jax leaned slightly toward him. "But?"

"I think they was just tryin' ta spook me. They wouldn't've... they transferred me. I got there, so they didn't kill me on the way, like I thought. I heard 'em say they was gonna put me in a special room. I made a big fuss. Flynn helped. I guess he started up a big mess."

I realized he was talking about the riot at Golden Larch.

"So, Carter did hide things," Jax said. "He had video files. Did you see where he put them? Was it in the cemetery?"

"Don't go there. It's here."

"At the switch house?"

"Yeah, yeah. I'll show you. Then you gotta let me go. I gotta run. You cain't protect me. Not against them."

"How many I Scream Men are there?" Jax asked him.

"I seen six at one time. One was a woman. A judge, I think. That's why you cain't help me. They own 'em awl."

We passed a gate and Danny stiffened. We'd arrived. Time for action. Jax killed the car lights and located Ayden's former parking spot. He grabbed a flashlight.

The parking area near the switch house contained four cars, but not Wayne's. Danny said he'd left the car he'd stolen to flee Golden Larch half a mile away. He identified one vehicle in the lot as a warden's and said he didn't see any that Plat-eye used. I spotted Broderick's Lexus and wondered if his body was now in the trunk.

Danny led the way through a maze of hedges and puddles. The rear yard had even more water now. Finally, Danny pointed to what looked like a guest cottage, a mini replica of the mansion. The windows were dark. Water flowed just three feet from the porch.

Danny glanced at the switch house before he approached the surveillance house to look in the window. "Someone should be here. They're *always* here." He tried the doorknob. It turned. He pulled his hand away as if he'd touched a burning coal. "This should be locked." He stood aside. "Not goin' in, sorry. They ain't gonna get me again. I'll stand watch."

Jax entered and I followed. He switched on a flashlight and looked around.

Just enough light came through the front window to show desks with computers and screens on the walls, all dark.

"Danny might be right," I whispered. "Feels off to me."

Jax moved his beam across several spots. "Carter found things in here. I want to look around. If you see any flash drives or tapes, grab 'em."

I tried some file drawers. They didn't budge. I figured most stuff was digitized, but the computers would not come on.

Jax checked a switch. The room remained dark. "Someone cut the juice."

"So, we can't get access to anything." That shut down the plan to see inside the house from a safe place. I looked out the window. Across the yard, the switch house looked quiet. Two windows on the first floor glowed with light, but I saw no figures inside. I could risk it.

A text from Natra urged me to call.

"We got a kid here," she said. "Carl, Flynn's friend. We found him on the road. He said he saw a girl taken away in a black car. Sounds like Kam."

My heart stopped.

"Ayden thinks we should find Wayne. The readings are spotty. We might lose him."

I could hardly breathe. All I could manage was, "Take Carl to Carter's cabin if you're close, so Caryn can get the boys and herself away from here. We'll meet you on the road."

I conveyed this to Jax and went out to tell Danny.

The porch was empty.

I went around to the side, straight into a soaking wind gust. Wiping my face, I looked on the other side. Nothing. I went to the door.

"Jax. Danny's gone."

Chapter Fifty-Five

J ax rushed out. He skimmed his flashlight over the ground. Crouching, he pointed at disturbed mud. "These tracks are fresh. But it's just him."

"I should've kept an eye on him. He warned us he'd run."

I called Caryn. She was hysterical. "He's taken off!"

"Where's he going?"

"He said he knows what Plat-eye wants and he has to get it. He told me to stay put and he'd come back for me. I'm scared."

Jax took the phone from me. "Caryn, they're bringing Carl over. Then I want you three to leave. Drive to my house, like I told you. They'll expect you. Stay on a main road. We'll find Danny."

He hung up and called Dylan. Their conversation was short. When he handed me the phone, he said, "No one's heard from Airic, and the caretakers aren't answering."

"I'm sure that's where Danny went. Something's there. Whenever I mentioned it, he'd deflect. He doesn't trust us."

"I noticed that, too. And Plat-eye's visit there after Carter died confirms it." Jax closed the door to the surveillance room. "What Carter took isn't here. And Danny knew that. This was a ploy."

We ran through rain back to my car. Jax took the wheel.

"But how can Danny get over there?"

"Steal one of the cars, maybe. He knows how. Or he might force someone here to take him. He has a gun."

"I knew he was hiding something. But why didn't Airic tell us Carter gave him something?"

"Maybe he didn't. Airic told us 'the boy knows,' remember? He said it's in his head."

I gasped. "The map! My drawing. It's in Valerie's car. We have to get it."

"We can't, Annie. It was simple. Try to replicate it."

I grabbed paper from my glove compartment and scribbled what I could recall. Two wavy lines. An odd shape. A circle inside it. But I couldn't tell if I got the shape right, or the circle's placement. I kicked myself for this oversight.

Natra called. The kids were on the road. "But we're running into water, lots of it on these back roads, so be careful. And some cell towers are down. Joe can't get coordinates for Wayne anymore. He's south of us. That's all we know."

I told this to Jax. He remained silent.

"I should call Wayne," I said. "I have to know if Kam's with him."

A sustained wind gust hit the car so hard I thought we'd blow over. I looked at my phone. "Oh no. No service." Jax's phone showed the same status. "Got the radio?" he asked.

I turned on the two-way and tried to get Natra. No response. "They're too far from us."

"Do they know how to get to Airic's?"

"Natra knows where I went for the sitting. That's all."

"We can't wait."

"Jax! We need backup. Plat-eye has bodyguards. You saw them!"

He kept driving. "You have another gun in here?"

"Yes."

"You're the backup."

"I'm not—" A light from behind made me turn. Car lights. I squinted through the rain. "It's not Ayden's truck."

Jax stepped hard on the gas, throwing me back in my seat. "Tires okay?" he asked.

"Not really."

"Let's hope they're good enough."

I grabbed the armrest as he sped up, praying we didn't skid out. The other car caught up. This wasn't Sloane's car, either. It was an SUV.

On my right, water splashed up to my window. I gasped. Jax had gone straight into deep water over the road. I held my breath as my heart beat out a tight rhythm that nearly choked me. No time for a panic attack! Back on solid ground, I let my breath out, and looked back. "I don't see them."

Jax slowed and turned on to a smaller road.

Soon, I spotted the lights again. Jax sped up. This time I saw the water. It flowed across the road. I felt Jax decelerate.

"Just do it," I told him. "Go!"

"Hang on, Annie."

I closed my eyes but then opened them. If I were going into the water, I wanted to see. I opened the glove compartment to grab the window smasher as Jax plowed into the stream. I gripped my hands into fists to quell my panic. When we made it to the other side, I could hardly believe it. I leaned against my seat just as the back window shattered. They were shooting!

"Get down," Jax ordered.

"No." I grabbed my gun and scrambled into the back. The wind brought stinging rain, but I aimed at the car behind us and took a shot. It didn't stop them. They probably didn't even hear it, but I hoped they saw the flash.

I felt my Jeep slip and swing to the side, back into the water. I rolled the side window down. No way was I getting trapped. If we went under, we'd have a way out. I felt us yield to the current. I panted and put my fist tight against my mouth. But then the tires gripped, and we held steady. Jax applied the gas. The wheels spun. He tried again. We climbed out. I got back in my seat. I sensed from the strain on Jax's face he hadn't expected to make it. He looked at me. "Okay?"

"Jax!"

A tree came down hard on his side, breaking glass. It pushed us backward into the water. This time, the tires failed. We floated.

Chapter Fifty-Six

I grabbed Jax's arm to pull him toward me, but a branch pinned him. Panicked, I pushed on my door. It stuck. I pushed harder. It opened. A wind gust caught it and yanked the SUV, throwing me into the water. I took a quick breath before the current rolled me.

I grabbed for something to brace me and knocked my knuckles against a hard surface. Twisting around, I reached for weeds to keep from being pulled away from the bank. My lungs burned and I kicked against the tepid water. Gulping air, I pushed toward a dark hump. This brought solid ground under one foot, but the swift current knocked me back in the water. I caught the trunk of a downed tree and clung to it as rushing water tore at my sodden clothes. With a final burst or adrenaline, I pulled myself along the tree until my foot hit ground. I pushed toward the bank. All I could think was I had to survive. I had to find Kam. She expected me. She'd bragged I'd come. I had to! Even if an I Scream Man held out a hand just then, I'd grab it.

I crawled onto a bank of saw grass, coughing and spitting dirty water. I lay there until the knife-sharp jabs to my lungs diminished. I barely felt the rain. But then I remembered. Jax! I sat up and looked to my right. There was no sign of my car.

"No! No! No! Jax!"

I'd floated, but how far? Gripping the tree, I got to my feet and leaned toward the water. The wind nearly blew me over, so I flung myself back on the bank. "Jax!" My voice didn't carry. I started to shiver. Crawling backwards up the sloping bank, I tried not to think about snakes.

201

Once I reached level ground three feet from the water's edge, I stood up and looked around. I hurt all over, especially my hands. I couldn't tell where I was. I pushed my wet hair out of my eyes, but rain still blinded me and ran into my mouth.

Follow the water.

Airic's guidance popped into my head. I looked to my left toward where the current flowed. I thought I saw a glimmer of light. I called out for Jax again. No response. I hoped he hadn't been hurt. That tree had come through the window on his side. Maybe it had knocked him out. My car must have floated past me downstream.

This can't be happening, my brain said. *I can't be stranded out here with my child missing and a hurricane coming.* But if Jax were okay, surely he'd be looking for me. He'd call for me. Maybe he was and I just couldn't hear him over the wind.

Stay on your feet, I thought. *Lean forward. Move.* I pushed through a swatch of swamp grass toward where I'd seen the light. With thick foliage overhead and the sun behind dark clouds, I could barely see my way. I kept moving. Ahead of me, the grass parted. I froze and backed up. Shivering, I shouted as loud as I could, "Stop! Get back!"

It stopped.

I shouted again. The sound of rustling in the stiff grass suggested it had turned. I waited. Then, I made out the shadow of something large enough to be a gator. I watched it slip down the slope into the swollen creek. I let out my breath. I'd been lucky. I might have stumbled right into it, or worse, still been in the water. I tread more cautiously. I called Jax's name, but my voice was too hoarse to carry.

As I came around a bend, I saw the light. Two of them. Car lights, bobbing.

I hesitated. What if it were the car that was following us? But it looked smaller.

"Jax!"

No answer.

I hit an open spot and ran for several yards before the tall grass grew thick again. I saw my Jeep Liberty, lights on, caught on a fallen tree. The branches seemed to shelter it. I pushed toward it, certain Jax would be there. The driver's side door was open. I rushed to the car but found the seat empty. The windshield was fractured, and the frame badly bent. I looked under the SUV and on the other side, but I didn't see Jax. The car, slanted downward, seemed stable, although water flowed in behind the front seat. I used my sleeve to brush out fragments of glass before I warily stepped in. It wobbled but held. The door, also bent on top, wouldn't close, so I moved toward the seat's far side to avoid the rain that came through the hole in the glass.

I reached for the key to start it, then stopped. Bad idea. Whatever water might be in the engine could further damage it. I turned off the lights. This was an old vehicle, and I couldn't recall when I'd replaced the battery. I put my hand on the horn and pressed hard. I hit it again. *Jax, where are you?*

I felt around for the flashlight I'd left near the passenger seat and found it. Fighting panic, I shone the beam in the back and saw a plastic jug of water and a first-aid kit. My overnight bag was gone. I hoped Natra had grabbed it. A folded blanket that looked dry was still back there.

Turning carefully, I leaned as far as I dared between the seats. Floating debris hit the SUV, moving it, and I jerked back. I imagined alligators floating out there.

"Okay, okay," I whispered. "I can do this. I'll be okay. Nothing will happen." I had to believe that.

I slowly stretched toward the blanket and gripped it. But then it moved. I snatched my hand away and shone the flashlight. A glimpse of shiny dark scales made me freeze. The snake slithered away from the blanket to somewhere behind me. I aimed the flashlight to see where it went, but this movement rocked the car.

Stay still! I hoped the thing would stay in back, but there was water on the floor that could give it access to my feet. I told myself it was just a swamp snake, not dangerous, but that didn't work. It could be a cottonmouth. Slowly leaning toward the center, I lifted the flashlight and shone the beam across the seat. Nothing there. The snake was still back there... or under me. I was about to shout, hoping to scare it, when I felt a hand grab my left arm.

Chapter Fifty-Seven

"Jax!" I leaned out, and he reached to help me, but I pushed him away. "Snake! There's a snake in here!"

He jerked back. I lifted my feet and twisted to jump out. Then something crackled inside the car. "The radio! We need that!" I leaned over the passenger seat to grab my purse. The SUV moved backward.

Jax grabbed my knee. "Out of the car, Annie!" He bumped the open door, which snapped the supporting branch. The car rocked, coming loose.

I hugged my purse and jumped into the water. A stone gave way under my foot, but Jax caught me. He pulled me toward the bank until I found leverage and scrambled onto a clump of swamp grass. I watched, horrified, as a surge of water swept my SUV away.

Jax came out of the water and grabbed his shoulder.

"Are you hurt? Oh, the tree! It hit you."

He sat next to me. "Just bruised. Sorry about the car."

The wind slapped my wet hair against my face. "Can't deal with that right now. We're alive. We can keep going. Did you see where that car went?"

"I was trying to find you."

"Let's hope we can get Ayden, or we're screwed." I grabbed the radio and pressed the transmission button. "Hello? Are you there? Ayden?"

The radio crackled, but I couldn't make out a voice. I tried again.

Jax gripped my arm. "Let's go. Give me your flashlight. I'll cut a path. Stay behind me. We have to find the road."

The only mercy was that the rain had turned to mist, but the wind still lobbed it as stinging darts, mixed with pine needles from surrounding trees.

I pulled my parka over my face, glad I'd grabbed my purse. We still had a gun, my phone, and the radio, not to mention a couple of energy bars.

Jax stopped so abruptly I bumped his injured arm. The flashlight flew from his hand and hit the ground four feet away. He stayed where he was, so I squinted ahead. In the light beam, I saw the glistening rough skin of a wet gator, its reptilian eye focused on us. It hissed. We were too close. The only way around it was through even taller grass, with its own perils... like snakes.

Jax put his arm out to shield me. He slowly pushed me back. There was no way to run from this thing without risk of it chasing us. I felt in my purse for my gun but touched the window breaker I'd grabbed. It might work to bang the gator's snout or poke its eye, but I might also lose a hand. I took another step back.

The gator made a quick motion. I heard its teeth crush the flashlight. Jax put out a protective hand. "Don't move."

"They're near-sighted, right?"

"No. Just stay still."

I caught a faint sound. It came again, over the wind. First, a car horn and then a dog barking.

Mika!

I tugged on Jax's shirt. "Did you hear that? We need to get over there. Ayden must have heard us on the radio."

"Annie, no sudden moves."

But my team was near. Maybe they were looking for us. If we didn't respond, they'd leave. And we couldn't get around this beast!

Mika barked again. Closer. She was coming toward us. No! She was fierce but no match for a gator. I wanted to get on the radio and tell Natra to call her back, but that meant movement and noise—exactly what we had to avoid.

I had an idea. Using Jax as a shield, I reached into my purse and felt for the energy bars. I grabbed one and scratched off the wrapping. Gators had a good sense of smell, although I knew the wind might reduce it. I tossed the bar to my left and heard it hit the water. But a loud splash in the wrong place made me freeze.

Jax moved against me. "There's another one."

I peeked around him.

Mika barked again. I thought she'd found where I'd come out of the water upstream and was following my trail. I wanted to call to her, command her to stop. I had to do *something*. I couldn't let her charge into this area.

I found the transmitter button. I had to risk it.

First, I tossed my other energy bar into the water. A loud splash, followed by a ferocious bellow, made Jax push me, knocking the radio away. I reached down to grab it and heard a rumbling growl. Jax grabbed my arm, but I shook him off. Both gators were on the bank, thrashing together so close I feared they'd knock the radio into the water. That couldn't happen. I jumped at them, scooped it up, and pressed the button. "Natra! Call Mika. We have gators! Over!"

Jax pulled me backwards.

No response on the radio.

"Ayden! Natra!"

"Copy!" It was Ayden.

A loud splash made me jump. The reptiles had taken their contest into the water.

Jax grabbed my arm. "Now! Run!"

Chapter Fifty-Eight

I sprinted over the ground the creatures had occupied, passing them just as a dark shape bounded toward us.

"Come on, Mika! Come!"

She circled my legs, nearly tripping me. Natra called her from a distance. I yelled, "We have her!" Mika charged back the way she'd come.

A light beam shone toward us from upstream. I picked up speed, grateful for my team. We now had a ride.

I came into a clearing and saw a downed tree alongside a submerged road. I thought it was the tree that had smashed into us. Natra leashed Mika.

I waved a hand. "Don't hug me. I'm drenched. Long story."

She pointed toward Ayden's truck, twenty yards away. "Your suitcase is in the truck. Where's your car?"

"Downstream, submerged. Let's go!"

I headed for the truck's back door. Ayden was in the front.

"Sorry," I said as I climbed in. "I'm soaked."

"Just glad we found you. What ha–"

"Later." I grabbed a bottle of water.

Jax got into the passenger seat and gave Ayden directions.

Natra brought Mika to the open back door. I urged her to get in. She threw a towel over the wet dog to keep her from shaking all over us.

"That was close," I told her. "We had two gators there, between you and us. How in the world did you know to stop here?"

Natra grabbed a blanket for me to sit on. "We didn't. We came through the water, and someone ran onto the road. I thought it was one of the boys.

We veered away and got stuck. We'd just gotten free when Mika took off."

This surprised me. We were several miles from Airic's. How many running kids could there be, especially in this weather?

"Did you find the kid?"

She shook her head. "No. We barely saw him. No coat, dark clothes. He apparently wasn't looking for a ride."

"Seems pretty lucky it was in the right spot," Ayden commented.

I don't like coincidences, but we had more pressing concerns. "Danny went after them on his own. Did you hear anything from Caryn?"

"No cell reception."

"Right! Damn! Ayden, do they have a two-way?"

"No. I have three. One's on my belt, you have one, and the other one's in my bag." He patted something next to him. Jax looked inside. "I don't see it."

"In the side pocket."

"No."

"It was in here. No one's been... aw, crap! That kid! Flynn. He asked for something to wipe his face. He must have grabbed it."

This surprised me. "Why would he?"

"Cuz he's a *thief*? He said he was in for shoplifting, which probably means B&E."

"Okay," I said. "We'll make do with two. I'm sure Flynn and Caryn are out of range."

Jax turned toward me. "We'll head to the handlers' house, where you went for the sitting. We can cross the cemetery from there."

"You know the place. Just show us."

Ayden ploughed through multiple bands of flowing water. At one point, he had to veer around flying debris from a roof. He looked at me in the rearview mirror. "We need to do this quickly, Annie. That hurricane's blasting through soon. It's gotten stronger."

"Where?" Jax asked.

"Through Savannah or slightly north, then up this way."

"Savannah! I thought it was heading north."

"There's always a cone of uncertainty, by a good fifty miles, especially with this one. It's been twisty. Landfall's this evening. They expect extensive flooding up here."

I didn't want to think about it. The last thing I needed was another dunking. But I had to find Kam.

We passed the barn with the crushed roof, which was now nearly gone. Jax directed Ayden down another road. When I saw the lightning-split sycamore I'd missed before, I knew we were nearly there. I prayed our conjectures about Kam and Danny were right.

Suddenly, a boy on the side of the road jumped up and down, waving his arms and shouting. Ayden swerved and skidded to a stop.

Mika jumped up and barked. Natra looked back. "Who was that?"

Jax opened his door. "It's Flynn."

Chapter Fifty-Nine

The boy ran toward us. Jax let him into the back. He looked terrified. "They're after me!" he shouted. "Keep driving!"

Ayden didn't have to be told twice.

Completely drenched, Flynn panted so hard he couldn't talk. Mika licked his hand. He looked over his shoulder, his blue eyes wide. The kid was shaking. Natra dug a sweatshirt out of her bag for him. After he changed, I wrapped a blanket around him. Everything was damp but I thought it could help.

Jax directed Ayden to turn. "Take this driveway. There's a parking area." Then he looked back at Flynn. "What happened? How'd you get here?"

"Someone followed us." His blue lips trembled. "We kept seeing car lights, but Caryn didn't wanna speed. She thought it was cops. Then a big black car ran us off the road."

Jax looked at me. "They must have recognized the BMW."

"We almost crashed," Flynn continued. "Carl took off, but they caught me'n Caryn."

"Who did?"

"Two guys. They had guns. They made us go with them."

"Where's Caryn?" I asked.

"This weird house on stilts. It had all these computers. Plat-eye was there. It's close."

Had to be Airic's. "Danny, too?"

"No. Didn't see him."

I looked at Natra before I asked, "Who else was there?"

Flynn shook his head. "A skinny guy with long hair. He was hurt. His head was bleedin'. And a girl. I thought it was his daughter, but Caryn said no."

"A girl? Kamryn?"

Flynn looked out the window. "We should get out of here. It's too close."

"Look at me, Flynn. Did this girl have long dark hair?"

He nodded.

"Younger than you?"

Again, he nodded. "She was helpin' the skinny guy. They put me'n Caryn in a dark room. I got out through a window, but it was really high off the ground. I jumped and heard shouting, like they seen me, so I took off an' hid. Then I heard your truck."

Flynn pulled up his legs and hugged them against his chest. His teeth chattered. I rubbed his back and breathed out. Kam was close.

"So you don't know if Caryn got out?"

He shook his head.

We arrived at the log cabin, where this had all begun just days ago. It looked dark. Jax went to knock on the door. Flynn kept looking around, like he thought the men were still after him. Ayden watched through his window. Jax came back, shaking his head. "They're gone, but we need to get in. There's a map."

"I've got maps," Ayden said.

"Of the cemetery. It has several parts, with crossroads. We need a strategy."

Flynn sat up. "I can get you in. I bet there's a loose window or somethin'."

Jax considered this. "We'll look together. I don't want anything broken unless there's no other way."

We each grabbed a Maglite and a pocketknife from Ayden's stash, then checked our weapons. Flynn asked for a gun, but I said no.

"I know how to use it," he whined.

"Sorry, kid. I wouldn't feel safe."

Looking for a place to enter was rough in the wind. Jax and Ayden checked windows while I looked for a hidden key. Our little thief was first to spot a weakness. The padlock on the cellar access door, which looked locked, was loose. Flynn pulled it open.

"Someone's been here," I said to Jax.

"Or, maybe expected us."

"Let's be careful, then."

Mika pulled on her leash and barked. Natra directed her away. "I'll stay with her in the truck. We don't need noise. I'll keep watch out here."

The light switch didn't work, so Ayden used a flashlight to take the lead. Lower down on the steps, he stopped. "It's flooded down here. Maybe a foot."

Jax and Flynn went in. More inclined to go with Natra than back into water, I entered last. Claustrophobia threatened again, but I envisioned Kam waiting for me. I took off my shoes, left them on the steps, and pushed on. I thought about the people at the sitting who'd hoped that Airic would conjure up a ghost. I remembered Black Shirt across from me. *Find us.*

I moved my flashlight beam around the enclosed room. Airic's chair, with its restraints, sat alone in the water. The pool in which I'd seen ripples was submerged, and the chairs we'd used had been folded up and placed against a wall.

Jax slid open the door to Airic's private room and entered. Ayden looked over at me. He knew my fear of water. I signaled I was fine. He followed Jax.

Flynn stood near Airic's chair. "It's creepy in here. What's it for?"

"Ghosts."

He dashed into the other room.

Alone in the séance room, with water halfway to my knees, I felt watched. I'd dismissed this all as theater. Now I thought something could be in here. I looked around, but the darkness and the shriek of wind felt ominous. I joined the others.

With a flashlight, Jax showed us a mural that covered an entire wall. It resembled a primitive landscape painting. Clusters of tiny gray monuments rose up in random places against a long, narrow green space dotted with trees. Most of the rounded or rectangular headstones were ordinary. The size of this place looked daunting. If Carter had buried something here, we needed solid clues, fast.

I noted several connecting roads running through the place. "Someone spent a lot of time on this map."

Jax glanced at me. "The caretakers. And it's a good thing. It's easy to get disoriented, even in good weather." He pointed to where we were in relation to the graves, with access roads running parallel from the main highway to this cabin and Airic's house. He tapped a blue line along one side. "There's a stream here to the southeast, which is probably flooded. But it's some distance from Airic's house, which is right here." He put his finger on a dark square near the middle. "He lives about a quarter of a mile from here straight through the gravestones, but the road to it twists a bit." He pointed at several other markers. "This is an outbuilding for the caretaker and a garage for Airic's restored hearses." He tapped a monument. "Given the poor visibility, keep these landmarks in mind. They're good places to reconnect or take shelter."

Flynn stood to the right. He cocked his head and used a finger to trace around an area near the blue stream. "What's this?" He pointed at a group of three brown spirals near the stream.

"Trees with twisted trunks," Jax told him. "That's where the energy crackles." He touched his neck. "When you're near them, you can feel it back here."

"A vortex?" Ayden asked.

"That's one word for it. There's supposedly a stronger one under Airic's house."

I felt the urge to hurry. "What's the best way to get to the house?"

"Not by road. It's too visible."

"I say we split up," Ayden offered. "Expand our resources and cut our risk."

Jax drew a finger around the mark for Airic's house and looked at Flynn. "How many men were with Plat-eye?"

"I saw two. The ones who brought us in. One smelled like cigars. He called the other guy Vince."

"With Plat-eye, that's at least three. Did you see how many cars?"

Flynn counted on his fingers. "Two, I think. When I was in the house, I heard another one come."

"So, let's say three. That adds at least one more person to deal with, but we should anticipate there might be more. What happened to my car?"

"They made us get in theirs. They both got in with us, so they didn't drive it away. They musta left it on the road."

"Did you see an Expedition?" Ayden asked. "A black SUV?"

Flynn shrugged. "We were in a Tahoe. Caryn told me they left the key in it. If she got out, maybe she took it."

Jax looked at Ayden. "We'll leave your truck here. We can't let them see or hear it." He turned back to the mural. "Annie, you've seen Airic's house in front and inside, so you know the layout. In back, you'll find a metal ladder fastened to the wall that goes up to the attic. You know about his airflow—"

"Right! That trapdoor in the closet. That's an air chute. Can I get up through that?"

Jax looked me over. "It's tight. You might get stuck. Easier to go down it than up. Don't try the back door. In this weather, it'll be swollen and possibly locked. Use the ladder to get into the attic. That's the best way in. There's another ladder down from it into the room where you did the drawing. But be careful. There's no plaster buffer. The attic floorboards are supported by beams, but you can see between cracks. So can they."

I had an idea. "Would Kamryn fit down that chute?"

Jax nodded. "Probably. But someone should be at the bottom to help."

"Aren't we gonna help Danny?" Flynn asked. "Caryn said he was coming to the cemetery to get something. He has a car."

"What kind of car?" Jax asked.

"Don't know. He stole it from the switch house. We should look for it."

I knew what Jax was thinking but I had to find Kam. "We have something to do at the house on stilts first," I said. "Then we'll look for Danny."

The walkie-talkie on Ayden's belt crackled. He grabbed it. "Come in. Over!"

We heard nothing more. Ayden looked at Flynn. "What happened to the radio you pinched?"

Flynn's eyes widened. "I didn't—"

"We know you took it. Who has it?"

"Caryn. I gave it to her cuz she had pockets."

I pointed toward the stairs. "We need to go. We have to get closer."

Chapter Sixty

We split up. Jax took one of the radios and headed toward the caretaker's building, so he could scope the house from a side angle. Ayden and I bundled up in rain gear and went straight across the cemetery. Flynn stayed with Natra and Mika, out of the rain and wind, away from Plat-eye's crew. I hoped we wouldn't be long. Exposure to this weather was taking its toll. I knew we were all hungry and tired, but now we'd need our best resources.

The wind had kicked up. A large branch came down nearby, and I dodged flying leaves and twigs as we moved carefully along the sodden ground. My socks and shoes squished. When I stepped into a sunken area, I realized I'd have to watch above and below while also protecting my face. This slowed our progress. Ayden blocked a flying piece of jagged wood from hitting me and shielded me as much as he could from the driving wind. At times, he bent low, holding the hood of his sodden parka close to his face. The only upside to this weather was its potential to thwart our adversaries from being out here.

But they wouldn't be looking for us. Not yet. We still had an advantage. Whoever had followed us had seen my car go into the water. Plat-eye probably thought we posed no threat. He'd come for whatever Carter had brought here. He already knew the place. I figured he also knew that Danny had stolen a car. It wasn't hard to put two-and-two together: Danny intended to recover what Carter had brought here. If Caryn hadn't made it out the window, Plat-eye might use her as bait.

Since Kam was here, Wayne was too. Flynn hadn't mentioned him, but he'd said he'd heard another car come to the house.

I thought about Airic's enigmatic messages. Danny had been here with Carter. He was "the boy" who "knew things" and "had a key." He'd lied about not knowing where Carter had stashed Plat-eye's stolen items. I guessed he hoped to use them to blackmail Plat-eye and bargain for his freedom. It was the thinking of a fifteen-year-old who underestimated corruption and power. To him, the kind of lawsuit Jax could launch with those same items was abstract. Danny trusted no one to help him but himself.

Ayden stopped. "I think I see it." He pointed. "That dark shape."

I squinted ahead and protected my eyes. "Maybe." Then I saw a slight glow. "Candles or a lantern. Has to be it."

I dodged headstones and stepped in rippling puddles. Soon the dark bulk of Airic's plantation house came clear. It looked larger than I remembered. The cemetery's border stopped in the back about twenty yards from the building. We hid behind stones to watch for signs of someone guarding the place or looking for Flynn. When the area seemed clear, we dashed toward the house and ducked underneath. No alarms were raised, at least not that we heard over the wind.

I drew Ayden's attention to a dark square on the wall that looked like the cover for the air chute. I went over to open it. I couldn't move the latch. Ayden took out his pocketknife to pry it. Finally, it released, and we opened it. I tapped the metal inside, felt the dimensions, and nodded. I couldn't get through it, but Kam could. Wind prevented the cover from staying open, but if the latch were off, whoever came down could push through. I pointed toward a window eight feet up and gestured that Ayden should boost me so I could look inside.

He shook his head. He imitated climbing a ladder. I gestured I wanted a quick look, so he made a cat's cradle with interlaced fingers, and I put my muddy shoe in his hands. He lifted me toward the window. I wasn't quite tall enough to see anything, but I heard male voices. One sounded angry. I was tempted to tap on the window in case Caryn was alone. I could move her toward the chute.

A voice came over Ayden's radio. I got down so we could listen. "Is anyone… is there someone…?"

Caryn! I mouthed.

Ayden lifted his radio to speak when we heard her yell, "No! Don't!"

I made a cutting motion so Ayden wouldn't talk.

A gust of wind nearly knocked the radio from his hand. We huddled closer. Then another voice came on.

"Harnett! Give up. I know you're here. I have your girl. You know what I'll do to her. You have five minutes before you'll hear her scream."

Chapter Sixty-One

In the background we heard Caryn yell for Danny to stay away. I pointed to my eye. Ayden nodded. Plat-eye had the radio. We'd come close to giving ourselves away.

We located the ladder to the attic. I went first. The cold metal rungs were slippery, and I lost my footing twice. At one point during a strong gust, I had to cling to the side rails to avoid being blown off. But I reached the top and pushed on the narrow, half-size door, which thankfully opened inward. The sound of rain battered the roof, and in places, it leaked. But getting out of the wind was a relief. Ayden entered and shut the door. I pointed downward in front of us to the right, where the main room was located. Faint flickering light came through cracks.

With the shielded penlight, I spotted a row of ferns to the left—the "purifiers." This oriented me to where the ladder went down into the psychography room. Spirit lore held that certain types of vegetation used streaming sunlight to channel fresh air into the "receiver" room. With three skylights overhead, Airic had created quite the set-up. Wind leaned hard on the roof and a stream of water leaked through a skylight at the far left end, but the windows held. So far. Unpolished oak planks—also conductors—lined the floor. Jax had said the ground itself conducted energy.

I motioned to Ayden that I'd go first. I didn't want our combined weight to cause creaking that might alert them. The wind's noise and pressure could cover us, but I wanted to test the floor. On hands and knees to distribute my weight, I crawled toward the crack that showed the best light and found a position. I recognized the end of Airic's mattress. Angling a bit, I saw jeans-clad legs, as if someone were sitting on it. Someone small. With shoes like Kam's. My heart raced. I beckoned for Ayden to follow.

A raw shriek of wind and a quick puff to my face told me the front door had opened. I heard a voice I recognized: Shnick.

"Can't find Vince. Too dark out there."

"Then go drive around! We have to find that kid before this fucking storm floods the place."

The door opened and closed. I heard loud voices on the porch. One was female. Had to be Sloane. I pointed to the crack and mouthed, *Kam.* Ayden nodded. I used a finger to draw the outline of the house, gesturing toward the main room, and indicated where it was on my outline. Then I pointed to the location of the room where I'd go. The din of wind and rain made it difficult to convey what I wanted, but with gestures I tried to make Ayden understand that he should go outside and wait near the air duct cover.

The door downstairs opened and closed again. We waited. I heard whispering that sounded like Kamryn. She must have felt safe enough to talk, which meant the hostages were alone. This was my chance.

"We go now," I whispered. "You go outside. I'll try to get Kam out through the chute. Go help her."

Ayden left. I moved carefully toward the row of plants, and found the hole for the air passage. A chill passed through me, and my neck and ears tingled. There was a current here. Alternating metal rungs, each six inches wide, provided the means to get up and down. I turned and felt with my foot for the first one. Then I descended. Inside the closet, which felt much closer than it had looked from the outside, my penlight showed the trapdoor's outline. I recalled Airic opening it with a lever. But that was on the other side of the closet door, inside the room. I touched the doorknob to let myself out.

The front door slammed. I pulled back and went still. I heard male voices. I thought I'd lost my shot, but I decided to examine the size of the chute. I found a metal ring on the trapdoor, stood to the side in the cramped space, and lifted. It moved slightly, but it was heavy. I strained harder. It lifted higher. Finally, I managed to pull it into an upright position. Along one side, I saw a brace. It moved. I tried to catch it but it dropped into place with a *thunk.*

I held my breath. I felt for the brace, moved it, and lowered the trapdoor back onto place. Then I pressed myself against the closet wall, as far from the door as I could. I stood still.

The space was too small to effectively hide. I turned to climb back to the attic, but the sound of heavy footsteps entering the room stopped me. I withdrew my gun. Someone was close. I heard the doorknob turn. I pushed myself as far as possible into a corner and positioned my weapon. A crack of light made my heart sink. There was no place to hide. They'd find me. Then they'd find Ayden. We'd given ourselves away too soon.

A flashlight blinded me, and I held up my gun. I heard a sharp intake of breath. I touched the trigger.

Chapter Sixty-Two

To my shock, the door closed again. I heard Wayne's voice. "No one in here."

Another door shut. Footsteps receded. I breathed out and eased my finger off the trigger. I'd nearly shot my ex. There were times I'd wanted to but not right now. He'd seen me. And let me go.

Trembling, I pressed on the closet door. It moved. He hadn't locked me in. I carefully entered the room. A dim light coming in under the door helped me to see. I knew the house was small and the layout simple, which meant few places to hide. With a penlight, I explored the space and saw the table where I'd drawn the map just hours earlier. I returned to the closet and used the lever to open the trapdoor again. I carefully put the brace into place before I tapped on the metal chute. To my relief, I heard a corresponding tap from below. Ayden was there. Now for Kam.

I opened the door a crack and listened. I heard Wayne talking. Then the front door opened and closed. I hoped I hadn't lost my opportunity. But he knew why I was here. He'd let me go. Maybe he'd just cleared the way.

I stepped lightly into the hallway. Someone paced outside on the porch. Plat-eye's muffled voice barked orders. *He* was outside. I hoped Danny hadn't given himself up. That five-minute window had to be over. Against the wall, I edged my way toward the front room. I needed Kamryn to know I was there, even if I couldn't get to her before Plat-eye returned.

I saw her on the mattress. She turned her head in my direction, but I knew she couldn't see me in the darkness. I flashed my penlight twice, hoping she'd understand. She went still and sat up straight. Then she shook her head, as if to warn me. She moved away.

Now or never.

I stepped into the main room. Kam was cutting through Caryn's bindings. I went over and took the pocketknife. To Kam, I whispered, "I'll do this. Go down the hall and into the back room. In the closet is a trapdoor to a chute. Ayden's at the bottom. Slide down. It's not far. We'll be right behind you."

Then I saw Airic. He lay on the mattress in a fetal position, facing forward, his eyes closed.

"He's hurt," Kam whispered.

"I'll help him. Go."

She hugged me. "I knew you'd come." Then she scurried down the hall.

"They're trying to trap Danny!" Caryn said.

"Shh! Let's just get you out."

The front door opened. Sloane stood there, surprised.

I turned and raised my gun. "Stop!"

But she backed out. I gestured to Caryn to run, then followed Sloane out to the covered porch. I hoped to buy time for the girls. A gas lamp outside bounced light off the wooden wall that blocked the wind. Rain cascaded off the sloping roof. At the edge of the porch, Plat-eye turned toward me.

"You, too," I shouted over the wind. "Hands in the air. Lay down your weapons. Then step inside." Kam had to be down the chute by now. She was almost clear.

Plat-eye approached me. "Well, well, Dr. Hunter. I guess you *did* know where those kids were."

To my right, I heard a familiar voice. "Give it up, Annie." Wayne came up next to me, his hand out. I felt his gun pressed at my side. "We know you're alone."

Furious, I surrendered. *Alone.* I prayed they hadn't caught Ayden. And Jax.

"Bind her," Plat-eye ordered.

Wayne stepped behind me and pulled my right hand back. "Don't make trouble." I tried to believe he was undercover. I hoped. Maybe he'd covered for me inside only because I was the mother of his child and he wanted to get her out. Now he seemed to be Plat-eye's good soldier. He could have joined me and arrested them both. Instead, he treated me as a captured intruder.

Wayne pressed my hands together behind me. A thin plastic zip tie went over my wrists. Wayne tightened it but not fully. *That* was interesting. Surely Kamryn had shown Wayne how to get these off. She'd shown me, and we'd practiced together. The technique hurt, but with the right twist, it was possible. I just needed a distraction.

Sloane looked inside. "The girl's gone."

"Fuck!" Plat-eye glared at me. "Then get the freak."

"They're all gone."

I nearly caught my breath. How? Airic had seemed incapacitated.

Plat-eye grabbed me by the throat and pushed me back against the wall. "So now we have a new hostage."

I glanced at the boo-daddy at the other side of the porch. Jax had warned me not to touch it. Toxic fumes, he'd said. Did I dare topple it? Plat-eye followed my gaze. He let go of me and went over to it. Perfect! I mentally urged him to nudge it.

"Don't touch it," Sloane warned. "Carter rigged it."

My hope faded. Plat-eye rushed at me and grabbed me by the hair to drag me close to the thing. The stench rising from it made me gag.

"We'll test it on you. If he rigged it, then he hid something in it."

I struggled to break his grip. I wanted Wayne to stop him.

A shot rang out in the cemetery. A man yelled. Another shot pierced the wind's wail.

In a moment, Shnick ran up the steps. "Get inside! That kid has a gun!"

Chapter Sixty-Three

Plat-eye's grip loosened. I had my chance. I opened my elbows, clamped my palms together and hopped hard to break the tie. It worked. Hands free, I grabbed the boo-daddy and pushed its heavy form at Plat-eye, then covered my nose and jumped away. The thing hit him. He stepped back, surprised, and fell down the porch steps. It landed on him. Shnick tried to catch his pale-faced boss, knocking the head off Airic's creepy guardian just as Wayne grabbed my arm. Shnick went into a fit of coughing. I turned away.

A bullet smacked a shutter. Sloane ducked into the house. Wayne pushed me toward the open door, but I broke free and leapt off the porch.

Someone near the boo-daddy vomited. It was working! I got two steps before I fell hard to the ground. A hand around my ankle restrained me. I kicked at it but couldn't free myself.

Close by, I heard a fierce guttural yell. Then Danny stood over me, swinging a heavy branch toward my feet. Plat-eye cried out and let go of my ankle. I rolled to see Danny slam Plat-eye again with his makeshift weapon. I jumped up to help. But my gun was gone. I felt for the pocketknife. Plat-eye fended off a blow and rose up to catch Danny in a bear hug. Sloane moved in. She aimed her weapon at me. I ran to the back of the house. I had to get Kam.

But no one was at the chute opening.

I kept going, moving behind the cover of a large tree, then circled back around to try to help Danny. They seemed to have taken him inside. I had to find Jax. Rain pellets blasted my face as I ran into the wind, in the direction

225

I remembered for the outbuilding. I saw a mausoleum and stopped under its shelter to catch my breath.

A flashlight blinded me. I heard a gruff male voice. "Hold it right there!"

I blinked and shielded my eyes. I still couldn't see his face, but I made out a gun in his hand. He motioned with his weapon. "Move out. Keep your hands where I can see them."

I obeyed. I had no choice. This had to be Vince, the only guy I hadn't yet seen, the one out looking for Danny. He felt for a gun, but I had none. I knew he'd take me back to Plat-eye. I had to prevent that. I pretended to stumble and went to the ground, but he grabbed me by the back of my jacket to force me back up. I watched for a way to get free.

"I'm the caretaker," I said. "I'm trying to get to my car."

"Keep moving."

I pulled my hood close and bent forward to push into the rain. I sensed someone to my left. The gunman made an odd noise, so I turned. He'd been yanked back. I grabbed the gun he dropped as he struggled against an arm tight around his throat. He got jerked off his feet and thrown to the ground. A crouching shadow leaned over him. I picked up the flashlight.

"Jax!"

He pulled the gunman's hands together to wrap them with twine. I knelt and put my hand over the man's mouth to prevent him from calling for help. Jax handed me a rag from his pocket. I crammed it in.

"I think they got Danny," I said. "But Kam and Caryn got out. Have you seen them?"

"No."

"They must be out here. Ayden—"

"Let's get this guy out of the way."

We dragged the bound man into the mausoleum's shelter, then headed back to Airic's. Jax gestured toward the ladder. "Go up there." He melted into the darkness.

I looked around but didn't see Ayden or Caryn, so I went up. Inside, I could just make out a thin figure, seated and hunched over a crack between boards over the main room. It had to be Airic. I approached him, but felt someone grab my left hand, stopping me with a whisper. "Mom!"

I gasped. "Kam! What are you doing here? I told you to leave."

"I couldn't leave Airic. They hurt him. We all have to work together. Like an escape room!"

I gripped her arms. "Honey! This isn't a game. I'm trying to get you to a safe place. Where's Caryn?"

"She went out. I told her to go."

I couldn't believe this. Kam was still here and now they had Danny. If they searched, they'd figure out where we were.

A sudden din of wind and rain turned my attention to the door. Jax came in. He went over to Airic and said something in a low voice. Airic looked over at me. I guessed he'd just learned the fate of his boo-daddy.

I sat down, urged Kam to sit next to me, and looked through a crack. Sloane seemed to be addressing someone I couldn't see. When she raised her voice, I caught one phrase. "He's not talking."

"He knows!" That was Plat-eye. I felt deflated. The boo-daddy hadn't taken him out. But his voice sounded like sandpaper on plaster.

Sloane turned to her left. "Did you tell anyone else?" I thought she must be addressing Danny, but I heard no response. Maybe he mumbled, but a wind gust slammed the house and drowned out other sounds. Kamryn looked at the ceiling. I rubbed her back. I wanted badly to ask her what had happened, but even whispering posed a risk. We had to stick to essential communication. But I wondered why Danny was even here. He wouldn't have heard Plat-eye's ultimatum on our two-way, and Carter had supposedly buried his stash in the cemetery.

Unless he hadn't.

I leaned toward Jax, pointed downward, and whispered, "Why's Danny here?"

Airic tapped the wood. "The watcher." His voice seemed to float directly into my mind. "Carter's map."

Chapter Sixty-Four

Voices below drew my attention. Wayne entered and slammed the door shut against the wind. "Shnick's in bad shape. I pulled him to the porch, but someone should get him to a hospital."

I took some satisfaction in that. So, Shnick was out of the picture. And Jax had disabled Plat-eye's other guy, Vince. Whether we'd truly gained an advantage depended on Wayne's role.

Plat-eye made a dismissive gesture. "Did you find anything?"

Wayne held up a plastic bag and placed it on a table. "This was in the thing. It almost blew away. Be careful."

"Open it."

Jax rose to his feet and headed to the door. I made a move, but Airic held up a finger and gesture that I should remain where I was.

Wayne sliced open the bag and extracted a rolled piece of mint green paper. Plat-eye grabbed it. He looked at the contents, then swore and slammed his hand on the table. He left my visual area and yelled, "What does this say? He must have told you." I imagined Danny sitting there, sulking and unresponsive.

To Wayne, Plat-eye said, "Find that girl. She can't be far. We'll force this brat to tell us what he knows."

The door opened and shut. Wayne was gone.

"He won't," Kam whispered. I squeezed her hand and prayed she was right.

"You sure he's with us?" Plat-eye asked Sloane. "We lost our leverage."

"He's with us. Easy to turn and plenty to gain."

I cringed, as if I'd just found her in bed with my ex. She was at least half-right about him. His weakness for women like her had ended our marriage.

"Where'd his kid go?"

"With the freak, I guess. He must have shown them a way out."

Plat-eye held up the rolled paper. Sloane took it, unrolled it, and shook her head. "I can find a translator."

"We need it now!" He gestured broadly. "They might already know. That psychologist was here, so Raines must be, too. They know something. If we don't find that ledger first, game over. For all of us."

I gasped. He'd just revealed what we were looking for. A book. *The* book, with the list of compromised people. The video recordings were probably with it. No wonder he was desperate enough to endure this weather. And he was right. If we got it first, Jax would have everything he needed to put Plat-eye away and expose other participants in the sex trafficking operation.

I spotted the two-way on the table. If I could get down there undetected, I could try to contact Ayden. I hated this blind spot. I wanted to warn him to get Caryn away.

Wayne returned. "Shnick's gone. So's the Tahoe. He must have taken it."

Plat-eye swore and rushed out. I eyed the radio and considered my chances. But Sloane remained inside, watching Danny. I couldn't get around her.

Minutes ticked by. Sloane opened the door. Then I heard yelling. Plat-eye returned. But he wasn't alone. To my horror, he dragged Caryn with him. Kam caught her breath.

"Look who we have here." Plat-eye held a gun to her head and looked to his right. "Caught her in the Suburban. Want her to live?"

"You'll snuff us, anyway." Danny had finally spoken. He sounded defeated.

Plat-eye twisted Caryn's arm, making her cry out. I pulled Kamryn toward me to shield her, in case he carried out his threat.

Sloane came into view. She pointed a weapon toward Danny and looked at Caryn. "I think you know what *he* knows. We can eliminate him."

"Don't!" Caryn yelled. "Don't hurt him."

"Then tell us!"

For a tense moment I heard only the howling wind and the bang of a loose shutter. I wondered where Wayne was. He'd stop them from killing these kids. But he was still outside.

"It's in a grave!" Caryn shouted.

"Caryn!" That was Danny.

"I can show you. Carter drew a map."

Plat-eye pushed Caryn, aiming at her. "If you're lying, it's going to be very painful for you…and him." He coughed again.

Sloane pulled Caryn toward the table. She unrolled Carter's note and pointed at something on it. "Is this the map?"

Caryn looked. "Maybe. Yeah. It's like that. I'll show you." She gestured to her right. "It's over there—"

"We're not walking into a trap."

"I don't know where exactly. But there are markers. Those circles."

Sloane pointed again. "From here, where is it? And what's the name on the grave?"

Caryn put her head down as if thinking. "Eddy something…. It's a head-and-shoulders stone."

I rose to a squat, ready to go tell Ayden. They'd soon realize Caryn couldn't have been gone long enough to see such a place unless it was close. One way or the other, she'd be cornered. Airic gestured for me to remain where I was.

"What the hell does that mean?" Plat-eye asked.

Caryn used her hands to form a stone that had a shape like a head that broadened into a set of shoulders. Then she pointed to Carter's note. "See where he put the red dot? It's sort of northwest from here."

"And what's this message?" Sloane asked. "What did he write?"

Caryn shrugged. "I don't know."

Plat-eye took Sloane aside. I couldn't hear what he said, but I heard him open the door and call to Wayne. "We're taking these kids out. Bring your car over." He came back, grabbed Caryn, and pointed toward Danny. "If you're lying, I'll cut off his ear."

I heard a loud bang and a window shattered. Plat-eye ducked, letting go of Caryn. She bolted down the hall. I said to Kam, "Stay here. I'll be back."

I climbed down the ladder in back, gripping it against the wind. Slicing rain hurt my hands and smacked me hard along my right side. Once down, I saw Ayden near the chute hole, helping Caryn get out. I ran over.

A back window opened. I heard a shot and ducked. Ayden grabbed my arm to pull me around the corner, next to Caryn. She made a move, but Ayden stopped her.

"But Danny—"

"You can't go back in."

We waited. Ayden took a position to aim toward the front. I did the same for the other side. An engine started and a car peeled out.

Chapter Sixty-Five

We went to the front. Ayden shone his flashlight around the yard, now swamped. He skimmed the sodden boo-daddy, half-immersed. One car remained, a black Suburban, like a Secret Service vehicle. They'd driven off in Wayne's Expedition.

Ayden ran up the steps to the porch. I followed and saw a large rock and broken shutter. A wind gust pushed the front door at us. As Ayden drew a gun, he gestured for us to get to his right.

Cautiously, he entered. When he signaled, Caryn and I followed. The room where Danny, Sloane, and Plat-eye had been was empty. Glass shards covered the table where Sloane had unrolled the note. My gun lay there, so I grabbed it.

"They're gone!" Caryn cried. Ayden put a finger to his lips to warn her to stay quiet. The sound of steps on the porch turned me around, gun raised. It was Jax.

"What happened?" he asked.

"I threw a rock to startle them," Ayden explained, "so Caryn could get out."

"They're heading to a grave." I told him. "Caryn knows where it is. We need to get there first."

Caryn shook her head. "No. I don't. I made it up." She gestured toward Airic's equipment. "I pulled the name off *that* stuff. See. EDI... Eddy. But we need to follow them. They have Danny!"

Kamryn entered from the back. "They left."

I hugged her. "Are you okay?"

"Yeah." She leaned into me for a moment for more. Just what I needed.

"I'll get you home soon," I promised. "I'm so sorry I let you go with her."

Kam shrugged. "Dad came. But I could tell he was upset. I heard them yelling."

"That's why he wanted me here. He let me know to come get you."

She nodded. "He said he would. But then we kept going from one place to another."

"I'll get you home now, as soon as I can. Where's Airic?"

"He said he has to get something."

Caryn kept asking what we'd do about Danny.

"What did the note say?" I asked her.

She shrugged. "Just scribbles."

"What note?" Jax asked.

"It was in the boo-daddy," I told him. "I think it's about the ledger. Plat-eye said that's what they're looking for. Remember that thing Carter told you about a list of names. He must have buried it here." I turned to Caryn. "So, Danny didn't tell you anything?"

She put her hands in her pockets as if to contain her annoyance. "No. I was barely with him. He got me out of the switch house and then you guys saw us. He went with you and left from there. When he called me, he said he had to do something for Carter, but he wouldn't tell me what. Maybe he told Flynn."

"Why would he?"

"They knew each other from before. Flynn's the one who set off the riot when Danny arrived at Golden Larch."

"Will Danny play along with your story? He obviously knew you were making it up."

"I think so. He pretended I was giving away important stuff. He acted mad."

"I could go look," Ayden offered. "Stay out of sight and see where they're going."

Jax leaned on the table. "Let's try to figure this out. They're off looking for a grave that doesn't exist, so that buys us time. Unless Caryn accidentally sent them to the right place."

She looked distressed. "There's a red dot on the location. I mean, they have the map. They can see it. And I said that's where the grave is."

Jax folded his arms. "Carter always used codes. Did you see any words or symbols?"

"It was a drawing. There was other stuff, but I couldn't understand it."

"Can you reproduce any of it?"

She shrugged. "Maybe."

I retrieved paper and a pencil from a desk across the room.

Jax held up a hand. "Wait." He looked at Kamryn. "How did you send that map this morning? The one that showed us your phone's location?"

Kamryn blinked at him. I was about to say she wouldn't understand when Kam responded, "A man asked me."

My heart beat faster. "A man? What did he look like?"

"Old. He had white hair. He was nice. He asked me to draw him a map of what I remembered, so I did."

I stared at her. *That* wasn't remote viewing. "Where did you meet him?"

"He came in the room where Linda put me, before Dad came. He said he knew you, and you needed it. Did I do something wrong?"

I was speechless, but Jax took over. "Not at all, Kamryn. It worked. That's how we found you. Your drawing was helpful. And now you can help us again."

She smiled. I looked at Ayden. His eyes were wide.

Jax leaned toward Kam. "Did Airic tell you anything when you came here?"

"He said he was waiting for me. He said, 'you're nine,' even though I'm almost ten. He said it would all work now."

"So, you can help Caryn remember. There's an energy source here. Let's use it." Jax pointed to Caryn, Kam, and me. "You three, go in the back room. I'll go outside and keep the cover open. Get whatever you can." To Ayden, he said, "We may need Natra and the dog." Jax gave him directions for how to get back to the handlers' cabin.

"On it." Ayden asked Caryn for the key to the Tahoe, and she handed it over. To Jax, she said, "Don't ask."

Chapter Sixty-Six

I opened the closet door. The trap door was still up. I placed Caryn on the stool I'd used to draw my map, hoping it might help. I glanced at Kamryn and recalled what Airic had said about a "current" running through me. So, Kam had it too, whatever it was. The image of Puca visiting her in some spirit form to "catch" the map astounded me. But right now, we had to fish for Carter's map so we could figure out where Plat-eye had gone.

Caryn frowned. "I don't get it. What's this about?"

I didn't know what to tell her. "The room's an energy chamber. Let's just do what he asked."

Kamryn sat next to her, and I took the third stool. I held my daughter's hand. She turned and touched Caryn's arm.

Caryn gave me a pleading look. "We're wasting time. We should go after them. I can get that other SUV started."

"Believe me, I'd rather be running around looking everywhere we can think of, but in this weather that's not productive. It would only *feel* like we're doing something. But what we're about to do in here has worked with missing people. It won't take long. Let's just see what we get."

"It's how they found me," Kam said. "I told you Mom would come, and here she is."

Caryn nodded. "Okay." She focused on the paper in front of her for a moment before closing her eyes. I glanced at Kam. Her eyes were closed, too. She looked so sweet in her desire to help. I wondered what Airic had meant about her being nine. Certainly not her age. He had a thing about threes, and nine came from three threes. He'd clearly attuned to her, and she to him. She'd even put herself at risk to help him get out of the room.

Caryn picked up the pencil. She seemed self-conscious as she sketched, and she kept up a running commentary. "It had an odd shape, but kind of like a house with a sloping roof. And there were these little circles all around it." She drew little round circles. "And there was a red dot inside, over to one side." She picked up a red pencil to scribble it in. "That's where they went, I think. This looks kinda like the map in Jax's car, too. That had a circle, but I think it was in a different position."

I went alert. "What map?"

"Flynn found it in the glove compartment. Just a plain piece of paper, same color as this paper. It had a shape like this, only I don't think it had these circles. And I didn't see any words."

"Did Flynn keep it?"

She shrugged. "He took some other stuff, too, like tissues and lipstick, but I told him to put it all back."

I could hardly contain myself. I suddenly realized where Danny had intended to go. I went to the trapdoor, banged on the metal chute, and called out, "Jax. Come back in."

"What is it?" Kam asked. "What did you see?"

"I know where we have to go." I looked at Caryn. "I drew the map you saw in the car. Right here in this room. I didn't know what it meant, but I think Flynn does."

Caryn frowned. "He didn't say anything like that."

"Because when he first saw it, he didn't know. But then he saw the context. And he understood."

I took her drawing into the main room to meet Jax, who entered dripping wet.

"What did you get?" he asked.

I laid it on the table. "Look at the map, the shape. Remember what Flynn was doing in the cellar? Near the map on the wall?"

Jax shook his head.

"I thought it was odd. But I realize now what caught his attention, thanks

237

to what Caryn just told me. He'd seen my remote drawing, the one I left in Val's car. It was similar to this. When he saw the mural on the wall, he recognized the shape, where those bent trees are. I saw him trace it." I was kicking myself for not grasping this at the time. "Airic told us to follow the water. That's where the water is, too."

Jax studied the drawing. "This is different from yours, Annie."

"Maybe I got it wrong," Caryn said.

Kam, nearby, leaned toward it. "Turn it around."

We all looked at her.

She pointed upward. "In the attic, Airic said Carter wrote on it that it has to be flipped upside down." She looked at Jax. "But only you'd understand 'cuz he wrote it in some other language."

Jax turned it around and looked at me for confirmation.

I nodded. "That's like the shape I drew." I held up a finger. "More important, that puts the red dot in a different position. If they didn't realize they had to turn it upside down, then Carter's note sends them northwest. But what we see now is the dot in the opposite direction—which is the area where Flynn focused, and where I'd placed a circle. If Danny makes them think they're on the right track, they're heading to the wrong place."

"He'd do that," Caryn said. "He knows once they find the stuff, they'll kill him."

"I know where this is." Jax pointed to the circles Caryn had drawn. "If Carter drew this, it's a ring of stones he once set up for Airic. It's where those trees are."

"And I think Flynn knows something we need to find out."

We heard a car outside. Jax went to look out. "It's Ayden. Looks like he's alone."

Chapter Sixty-Seven

Ayden's report disturbed me. "They aren't there," he said. "Not in the truck or cellar, or anywhere around the house. Mika's gone, too."

Caryn wrapped her arms around herself. "I can't believe this."

"Does it look like they were forced away?" I asked.

"No. But Natra didn't leave a note, either. That's not like her. Danny knew about Mika. Maybe he saw us over there and told Plat-eye he needs a sniffer dog."

"She's a cadaver dog."

"Danny doesn't know that." Ayden's eyes widened. "Unless...."

I nodded. "Unless he's looking for...." I glanced at Kam and gave Ayden a subtle gesture. I saw that Jax had caught our meaning.

He put his hands together. "Here's what we'll do. We leave your truck there in case they come back. And we'll head over to this other area right now. If Plat-eye's there, it's over. But if not, we have a chance."

"I'll stay here," I said. "These girls shouldn't—"

"I'm going!" Caryn insisted.

"Airic said I have to be there," Kam added.

"It's dangerous, Kam. Why would he say that?"

"He just did. He said I'm important."

"There's shelter there," Jax said. "A solid stone shelter large enough for three or four to sit inside. As long as it's not flooded, it'll protect her while we look around."

The sound of a horn outside startled us. Jax opened the door, letting in a

239

gust of humid wind. "It's Airic. Looks like you have a ride."

I could just make out a vintage Cadillac hearse, like something from half a century ago. Resigned to the need to stay together, I urged the girls to go get in. Then I said to Jax, "I think Carter brought more here than a ledger. He was the cleanup crew, remember? I think Mick's body's here. That would explain Danny's reticence with us. It's all he's got to prove his innocence."

"I figured that. Let's get this done."

Jax joined Ayden in the Tahoe while I climbed into the hearse's front passenger seat. Its interior was customized like a limousine, with room for six. The odor of dust and the seat's cracked leather suggested this vehicle hadn't been used in a while. I noticed a coffin-size wooden box in back, nearly hidden behind a curtain, and hoped it, too, hadn't been used in a while.

Airic looked toward me, or rather, toward my hands. "It's time, Annie. We need three of three in the portal."

I did a quick calculation. We were six. If we came across Natra and Flynn, that was still just eight. I looked at Kam. Now I understood. He'd said she was nine. So, who was missing?

The Tahoe took the lead. Water splashed up the side of the hearse, making me stiffen. I swallowed. Jax had said this part of the cemetery could flood. Debris hit the windshield in blasting waves. I flinched, but Airic seemed unfazed. I looked back at Kam, huddled with Caryn. She gave a little wave to show me she was fine.

We arrived in a swampy area that held a collection of weathered gravestones. I hoped the storm had driven whatever creatures lived here into shelter. This was prime real estate for water snakes, and the creek had crested, creating a pool. Several headstones were half-submerged. The rain had turned to drizzle, as if reserving itself for a future onslaught, but the wind still whipped twigs, leaves, and Spanish moss through the air. I saw several downed trees, their roots exposed, and others bending, including the twisty spirit trees. Then I heard a dog bark.

Chapter Sixty-Eight

Kam squealed. "Mika!" Airic turned the hearse, showing a figure in the headlights that I recognized. Natra waved and came over. Kam jumped out and hugged her, but Caryn had only one concern. "Did you see Danny?" she yelled.

Natra shook her head. "Hasn't come here. But I think he will."

"And soon," I told her. "He'll run out of options, and out of time."

Mika bounded over to greet us, but Natra kept her from shaking off her wet, muddy fur.

"Let's get in the hearse," I yelled. "There's room."

Airic opened the back door so Natra could put Mika in the back, next to the casket. The rest of us found seats inside. Ayden got into the front. Jax came in back. I put my arm around Kam to keep her close. Natra went to her other side, putting us opposite Jax, Flynn and Caryn. Technically, if we counted Mika, there were nine of us, but I still wondered whom Airic had meant.

As dark as it was outside now from the thick clouds, we could still see. We were packed in, but at least we could talk without having to shout. Ayden reported from his two-way weather alert that the hurricane, at a category 2, was near to landfall and much of the coast was flooded. They expected the storm to linger, which meant a thorough drenching. We were far enough away to avoid the worst, but the powerful surge could still swamp everything here.

"We need to hurry," Jax said.

"Maybe I should take the Tahoe," Caryn suggested. "Go find 'em and tell you if they're coming."

Jax shook his head. "Too dangerous. We should assume that when they find nothing, they'll drive around and spot us."

"Natra," I said. "What happened?"

She gestured at Flynn. "This kid. He stole Mika."

"Borrowed!" he protested. "For a good reason!"

"She wanted to go out," Natra continued, "and he offered to take her. When they didn't come back, I realized he'd swiped my dog whistle, so I went looking for them." Natra looked at me. "After you left, Flynn wanted to go back inside and look at the map, so I went with him."

"I had to help Danny!" he insisted.

"I said we didn't know where he was, but Flynn said he did. Danny apparently told him about going to some weird trees, and Jax told Flynn where they were. Then Flynn showed me a map someone drew that fit with that mural, so he knew it was the right place. He thought Danny was there."

"My map." I looked at Flynn. "Do you have it?"

He pulled a blue piece of paper from his pocket. I took it and unfolded it. Jax shone a light on it. This was my drawing. I looked at Flynn. "Why didn't you just say so when we were down there?"

He shrugged. "POS."

"What does that mean?"

"Whoever breaks the pact of silence is a piece of—"

"Okay, I get it. But you knew what we were trying to do."

"Danny didn't want me to say anything. I figured I could find him on my own. He told me what to do if anything happened to 'im."

"So you know where to look?" Jax asked.

"I know there's a body. I thought Mika could show me, but I didn't know there would be other graves here."

Jax leaned toward him. "Did she find it?"

"We just got here, and… I don't know how to make her do it."

"I tried," said Natra. "She's been reluctant. She's usually fine in rain, but I think the wind's distracting her. We haven't found anything."

Jax returned to Flynn. "How did Danny think you'd find it if something happened to him?"

Flynn shrugged. "He said it was close to those trees."

"Why didn't you leave a note?" Ayden asked Natra.

"By the time I realized he'd taken her, I was on my way here. I decided to just keep going. He did show me where. I followed the roads. I figured I'd catch up and get her back, but Mika couldn't hear me yell over the wind. I ended up walking all the way here. And that's where I found them."

"We should look," Airic said. "They'll come."

I recalled how Airic had insisted he had to be here. He knew something. He apparently saw how these puzzle pieces fit.

"But we don't know what we're looking for," I said.

Airic touched his face. "It's in his head."

Jax held my drawing in the dim light. "It's too primitive. There's no way to tell from this. We need Carter's map. The ring of rocks got us here, but they don't pinpoint a specific grave. He must have written something more. Airic, did he show it to you before he put it in the watcher?"

"I saw it," Caryn said. "There was some writing."

Airic nodded. "Two words. *Uewv* and *cvto.*"

"Muscogee," Jax said. "Water and rock. That's what they mean. We found the rocks and we're near the stream." He shrugged. "Not much help."

"Follow the water," Airic repeated.

I pointed at my drawing. "What about this circle? Does this narrow it down?"

Kam leaned in. "Maybe it's a circle on a stone… Or maybe it's a ring."

"Ring!" Flynn shouted. "There's a ring. Danny said Carter gave him his wedding ring to pawn to get some money. But he pushed it in the grave so he could come back for it. That's how I'd know it was the right one. He wanted to give it back to Carter. He didn't know Carter was gonna die."

"He pushed it into the grave?" Jax asked.

"Yeah, like against the stone, down into the dirt."

"That doesn't help us locate it," said Ayden. "Especially now, with some under water."

"The boy knows," Airic said. He leaned forward and squinted out the windshield. "He has the key."

Mika jumped to her feet and barked three times. Natra tried to quiet her, but she kept whining.

Jax folded the drawing and handed it to me. "We should start looking. Share the flashlights. Start with the stones near the twisted trees. Look for anything that stands out. An oddly shaped stone. A key or circle in the design. Signs of recent digging."

"Is it a real key?" Kam asked him. "Or is it a picture or part of a name?"

"Any of those," Jax told her. He got out and the rest of us followed.

Kam tugged on my coat. "Can I go look?"

I nodded. "Like an escape room. We all use our skills. But watch for flying debris. Go partner with Caryn. Stay close to her. If you get cold or tired, go in the shelter."

She pulled her jacket close and ran to catch up.

"I saw shovels in the back," Natra said. "Maybe we should test the ground on graves near the trees."

"I'll get 'em," Ayden said. He returned with two shovels and a trowel.

I looked around. The stone shelter, large enough for several of us to sit inside, if necessary, stood close to the swollen stream. I estimated around thirty gravesites here, and from what my penlight showed on those closest to me, the epitaphs were worn and difficult to read. A few dated back a century. Still, Carter had been here only months ago. We were looking at what he'd been able to see, and he'd chosen a place to bury something he'd wanted his brother to find. I was sure the stone would be legible. I kept an eye on Kamryn. Airic stood apart, an eerie windblown form among the graves. He stared at the rising water.

To communicate, we had to raise our voices. Wind gusts wailed like wounded banshees.

Jax pointed to the ground where I noticed a line of rocks about the size of bowling balls. "Carter set these up. I'd forgotten until I saw Caryn's drawing." He waved his arm around the area. "They surround us. Inside is sacred. Puca performed a ceremony here. I should have known he'd come here."

"Maybe it's a specific rock," Ayden offered. "A ceremonial rock. Did Carter use one in any specific way?"

Jax shook his head, shrugged, and took one of the shovels.

I joined Natra to look at the inscriptions while Ayden and Jax probed places to dig. The entire area was saturated.

I went over to Airic. "Who's number nine?" I asked. "You said there were three threes."

He blinked as if he didn't understand me.

I persisted. "Is Mika, the dog, nine? Or maybe Danny?"

I barely heard him but knew from his mouth he'd said, "The boy."

I looked where he'd been watching. I didn't see anything. If Black Shirt were here, he remained invisible to me. "Where?"

Airic pointed straight at Kamryn, who'd bent down to read a gravestone near the water. She was too close. I strode over just as she stood up and called to Jax. "Does that word mean rock or stone?"

Jax looked at her. "Either one."

She pointed with a flashlight. "Over here. It's a name. Waterstone."

Chapter Sixty-Nine

We gathered near the headstone. Against a gust of wind, Jax played his light on it. Kam pointed to another one nearby with the same name, half-submerged.

Ayden crossed his arms. "I'll be damned. I wouldn't have noticed. Great job, kiddo."

I hugged Kamryn. Her skill with word puzzles had paid off.

Natra pointed at the ground. "Look at all the stones. Maybe Carter marked it."

I shone my penlight on the wet stones and asked someone with a stronger beam to illuminate it. Flynn did. He seemed to spot the pattern at the same time as me. "That's from your map!"

Jax nodded. "Seems obvious now." To Kam, he said, "You've earned your name." She beamed.

Airic gestured to Natra. "Now, the dog."

It took no time for Mika to alert at this spot, but she seemed subdued. She shied from the flooding. The Waterstone gravesite sat perilously close to the water, and part of it had eroded, although we could still dig along its west side. Ayden and Jax got to work. I leaned close. I thought I smelled decomposition, but it was difficult to tell with all the mud around us.

Mika leaned against Natra and whined. She reached down. To me, she said, "Airic will take us back to the truck. She's anxious."

I nodded toward Kam. "Take her, too. I don't want her to see this."

Kam objected when I told her. "I'll stay in the shelter."

I insisted. "You did your part, and it was important, but now I need you to do what I'm asking."

When they were gone, I focused on Jax. I knew he had to be thinking about Carter's last desperate act, here in this spot. If we were right about this grave, Carter had secured firm evidence of JTA corruption and child abuse. That same day, he'd been killed. Carter had known Mick's body would help Jax strike a substantial blow—as long as Danny remained alive to testify. And we didn't yet have Danny. Caryn's tense expression made that abundantly clear.

I grabbed the trowel and squatted to dig into the muck near the stone. I hoped to locate Carter's ring. Flynn picked up a stick and helped me. The more I pulled away, the stronger the stench grew. This decomp was fresher than the death year on this stone, 1958. I glanced up to see what Caryn was doing. She stood on the leeward side of the Tahoe. I motioned for Ayden to watch her. He patted his pocket to assure me he had the key. She might be a skilled car thief, but she wasn't going anywhere in a vehicle we might need.

As Jax and Ayden forced their shovels into the saturated dirt, I scraped away a smelly pile of sodden Spanish moss. A pungent odor escaped a small sinkhole. With a muddy hand, I shielded my nose and indicated that Jax should try there. He used the shovel tip to probe it. Ayden joined him. Soon, they hit something. Jax knelt and used his hand to scrape away the dirt. He uncovered a grimy piece of fabric. I had to look close to see the texture. It was canvas. I steeled myself against the putrid stench and helped loosen more dirt. Ayden held his flashlight over the object. We'd found a body. Jax scraped at mud until we saw stenciled letters, then a name: Cypress.

"Cypress Run," Jax said.

That was the gated community Jax had described as an enclave for the traffickers' cartel. I recalled the Cypress Run sticker on Broderick's car. Carter, no doubt, had been there as well. Maybe that's where they'd killed Mick and ordered Carter to "clean it up." He'd wrapped the body in a tarp.

We worked on getting the top layer of dirt scraped away until we could lift the wrapped object out of the hole. The weakened canvas tore, which sent us back to work widening the hole. I looked around. Airic had seen something here—"the boy." I wondered if that boy were watching.

Once more, we pulled the heavy object from the hole. I felt what I thought was a skull. Then shoulders. I'd seen waterlogged decomposing bodies before. This wouldn't be pleasant. I was glad I'd sent Kamryn away. Carter clearly hadn't meant for Mick to be here this long. The decomp would be advanced, but not too far gone for DNA or fingerprints. We managed to maneuver the corpse out of the hole and onto the side of the gravesite away from the water. I suddenly realized the water level had risen since we'd started. It seeped into the hole we'd dug, covering whatever had been placed in this grave in 1958. It would soon be submerged.

The sound of a vehicle racing toward us from the north cut through the wind. I stood, surprised that Airic had returned this fast. But the headlights were not those on the hearse. This was an SUV. Caryn disappeared behind the Tahoe. Flynn dashed toward the stone shelter. I dropped my trowel and looked for cover. Before I could move, the vehicle was on us. Sloane jumped out, her weapon ready. Wayne came around from the driver's side.

Chapter Seventy

The Expedition's lights illuminated the disturbed grave. Plat-eye emerged from the back seat, dragging Danny with him. He held a gun to Danny's head. The boy's scowl confirmed we'd found what he'd been trying to hide. With the wind-blown rain at their back, they had the advantage.

Wayne covered Sloane as she waved a weapon with a long magazine, gesturing for Ayden and Jax to toss their guns toward the Expedition. I thought she might have a Glock 18, possibly made into a lethal automatic. We could all be shot in a heartbeat. Sloane didn't seem to know I'd retrieved my gun, but I couldn't risk grabbing it. Not yet.

"Thanks for the location!" Plat-eye yelled, his voice still raspy. He gestured toward the Tahoe.

Sloane looked down at the wrapped bundle and nudged it with her foot. I knew if she opened it and found what they were looking for, Danny became instantly expendable. He'd be eliminated, his body dumped in the open grave. I was glad the other kids had run. They could escape.

There were just three of them, and Plat-eye was in rough shape. I guessed we could overpower him, but only if Wayne were truly undercover. Only if he'd expose his role to stop a slaughter. I just wasn't sure. I felt a change in the air, then colder rain.

Plat-eye pulled Danny over to the grave and forced him down near the body. Danny turned his face away and coughed.

"Open it," Plat-eye ordered. The wind made his gun near Danny's head perilous. He could shoot this kid by accident.

Danny reached down to unwrap the reeking bundle, starting at the head. The canvas seemed to stick in place, so he pulled harder. The stench, blown at me, forced me back. I didn't dare protect my nose in case Sloane thought I was reaching for a weapon. Yet even she seemed repulsed. I blinked away rain and stared, unprepared for the dead boy's damaged face.

A layer of white cheesy adipocere covered his jaw, but the grave's heavy dirt seemed to have crushed the forehead and nose. It looked like a mass of blackened tissue, with white bone coming through. I knew of a pig study in North Carolina that showed how moisture in soil drives decomposition, especially in juveniles, with insect activity finishing the job. Condensation in bagged remains like this thwarted preservation, quickly erasing a human appearance. That was bad for us. But we could still get DNA.

Danny wiped his face. Plat-eye shoved him closer. "This him?"

Danny didn't move.

"Keep going!"

I looked at Wayne, just five yards to my right. I wanted a signal. But he leaned against the wind, seemingly ready to shoot if we made the wrong move.

Danny pulled the tarp away from the chest. Raindrops tapped on plastic. I leaned in. Carter had placed something else in this grave. Danny lifted a long book-shaped object off the corpse. It was the right size for the ledger we'd heard about.

"Give it to me!" Plat-eye ripped the thing from Danny's hand. He stepped away, stowed his gun, and removed the black plastic wrapping. Despite the rain, he held the object in the headlight beam. It was a book. He opened the cover, then slammed it shut. "Got it!"

Lights appeared in the gloom, coming from the other side. I caught my breath. Airic! Sloane raised her weapon in that direction. The hearse came into view.

"Perfect," Plat-eye yelled. "Kill the geek and the boy, and get this thing into that hearse." He gestured toward the body.

Jax held up his hands. "Don't." Sloane waved him back and told Wayne, "Cover me." She took a stance.

A rock the size of a hardball hit her shoulder. She yelled and dodged a second one. I looked for the source and saw Caryn dart behind the Tahoe. Airic came straight at us, fast.

A tree branch came down nearby, tossing debris. I shielded my eyes and heard Caryn scream, "Danny!" He jumped up and ran. Plat-eye shouted. He grabbed his gun and got off a shot.

I went for my weapon, but another shot rang out and someone pushed me hard into the mud. Near me, Flynn yelled and launched himself off a gravestone onto Plat-eye's back. Plat-eye yelled, whirled, and tried to throw him off. I got to my feet and went straight at them, pushing Plat-eye into the mud before I was rammed again. I went down into water. The rising creek now half-filled the open grave.

Airic pulled the hearse into a tight circle, sliding the ungainly vehicle in the mud to cut a wide arc of risk for anyone close. I thought he'd ram a headstone. Sloane fired at him, her bullets coming fast. One headlight went out. Now I was grateful for the wind and flying debris. Even a skilled shooter needed luck.

Airic's wild trajectory forced Sloane to jump back. She bumped into Plat-eye. The book came loose and hit the ground. Flynn sprinted to retrieve it like a ball boy at a tennis match, but Wayne tripped him and sent the book flying.

The hearse was on us. Plat-eye scrambled away. I saw the rear door fly open and understood. Airic aimed to rescue the corpse. He'd need help. I went to the putrid bundle and pulled the canvas around it. Wayne aimed at me, but I put a hand out to shield myself. I heard gunshot from another direction, and saw Wayne draw back.

A barrage of stones came at us. Several hit me hard in the back. I guessed the kids had found each other. A flash of light and a loud bang showed that someone behind the Tahoe had a gun. Sloane aimed at it and took out a window. Airic blasted his horn and made another circle that forced her back.

Jax knelt to help me. I looked for the book to toss in the hearse, but a burst of wind-driven rain blinded me. Airic spun back around and slowed the hearse near us. We shoved the corpse into the back. Jax slammed the door. As Airic sped away, I slipped and fell into the hole. Water surrounded me. I realized if the videotapes were still in here, it was too late. I held my breath and felt around for another package but found only dirt clumps and rocks.

Sloane got off three shots at the departing hearse, shattering the back window. Airic kept driving. I thought Sloane's clip must be nearly depleted. I hadn't heard Wayne shoot, so he still had bullets. I looked for Ayden, but he seemed to have vanished. Then I saw Wayne and Sloane with their guns trained on Jax. He had the book. Plat-eye limped over and grabbed it from him.

"Shoot 'im," he ordered. "Shoot 'em all."

Chapter Seventy-One

I grabbed my gun, but a sharp *crack* made me duck. When I looked up, Jax was still standing. But Plat-eye lay on the ground, his hand to his chest. He yelled in pain. I ran for the Expedition to hijack it, but Sloane grabbed me by the hair and put her gun to my head. To Wayne, she yelled, "Get the ledger!" He trained his weapon on Jax as he picked it up.

Sloane moved toward the Expedition with me in tow. Wayne did nothing to stop her. He opened the passenger door for her and ran to the driver's side. A gust of wind slammed the door hard against us, taking my breath. Sloane lost her grip, so I ripped away, hit the ground, and rolled. The Expedition backed away and took off.

Jax ran to help me up. "Annie! Are you okay?"

"What happened?" I yelled. "Who shot Plat-eye?"

"Sloane!"

"What? Why?"

We heard the Tahoe start up. Jax let go of me and yelled. "Wait!"

But it tore out, following Wayne. I saw Ayden behind the wheel. Plat-eye crawled across the ground like some creature emerging from a putrid swamp. He reached for the gun he'd dropped. Jax got there first. The I Scream Man sputtered and hacked. Jax grabbed him by the front of his shirt, gun to his forehead. "Who killed my brother?"

I moved closer. Plat-eye coughed up blood. I stood shivering, watching this nasty man realize his lieutenant had abandoned him to die in the mud. He groaned, spit, and went limp. Jax stood up. He looked around and gestured toward the stone shelter. I realized we were here alone, without a

253

vehicle, as the wind screamed, and the stream became a river. One of the twisted trees had toppled. I ran for the shelter.

Water already covered half the floor inside, but the solid walls stopped the blowing debris. Even a wisp of Spanish moss felt like a shower of splinters. I sat on a hard stone seat, waterlogged and covered head-to-toe in mud. Jax stayed near the door and removed the radio from his pocket. He tried to reach someone, but no one responded. The wind still forced us to shout.

"Where did the kids go?" I asked. "Flynn had the book 'til Wayne tripped him."

"He ran toward the road. Didn't see Danny or Caryn."

I felt along my arm and shoulder where the Expedition's door had slammed me. "Ayden won't leave us stranded." I tried to dry my face with my sleeve, but it didn't help. "Did Plat-eye admit it? Did he tell you?"

"No. But she shot *him*. So, she's the assassin. And now she has the book."

"But we have the body. And Danny."

"She's not done, not with Danny."

"They can't chase him down in this weather."

Jax tried the two-way again. Nothing. He looked at me. "It's rough out there, but we could walk to the cabin. Can you do it?"

I held up a hand. "Need a moment. Took some hits. That Airic... he's got nerve."

Jax nodded. "There's more to him than people know."

"He told us he had to be here. Now we know why."

"I wish I'd listened to him three months ago. I'd have recovered the body and ledger then." He looked outside, then back at me. "Still think Wayne's undercover?"

"Don't know." I shrugged. "He aimed at me once, but I think he shoved me down to protect me."

Jax put his hands on his hips. "If he's *not* with her, she probably knows. Let's hope she doesn't kill him, too."

My stomach lurched. Wayne was savvy, but Sloane clearly had her own design. And she now had the ledger, a record she could use to blackmail a lot of important people. For all I knew, she had something on Wayne.

He'd stayed with her despite her kidnapping his daughter. Whatever linked them, he was at risk every second they remained together.

Jax held up the radio. "The wind's interfering."

"Where would Airic take the body? Maybe we can find him."

"Not here on the grounds. He doesn't know Plat-eye's dead."

"Then let's go to Ayden's truck. I can walk."

"What about the kids?"

"If they're still here, they'd have seen us. And we should leave before the water surges. We got Mick out just—"

The radio crackled. Jax acknowledged and pressed the receive button. Ayden's voice came over, broken up, but we heard enough.

"We got... cops... coming your way."

Chapter Seventy-Two

Jax and I stepped into the wind. It took my breath and stung my new aches. Flashing blue lights from the north cut through the darkness. The rain had let up, but rising water covered much more ground. The Waterstone grave hole was filled, the stone only half visible.

A South Carolina state trooper car pulled up, followed by a black Escalade. They left their lights on, aimed toward us. A tall, stocky man emerged from the SUV. He shielded his face, but I knew him at once.

"JD Riley," I told Jax. "Wayne's partner."

JD paused near Plat-eye's body. Then he strode over to us. "You folks okay?"

Jax pointed at the corpse. "His killers just ran."

JD waved a hand as if to calm us. "We know 'bout that. We'ah gonna get y'all to safety. If you'll just—"

"Where's Wayne?" I asked. "What's going on?"

"It's und'ah control—"

"Where *is* he, JD?"

"Well, Annie, Ah don't know."

I stared. "You didn't stop them?" I pointed. "They just went out the way you came!"

JD ignored me and introduced himself to Jax.

"JD!" I shouted. "What the hell? How did Wayne get past you? Is *anyone* following him?"

He looked uncomfortable. "Ah think they switched cahs, had one hidden away awf-road."

I put a hand on my hip. "Wayne's *with* her?"

"Now don't go jumpin' ta conclusions, Annie."

"So you don't really know. That woman threatened us. She killed this man. Why didn't Wayne arrest her?" I gestured toward JD. "He had you for backup."

Another SUV drove in and JD waved it toward the body. "We need to get this movin' to beat the storm. This place'll be undahwatah soon."

I could almost feel steam rising from Jax when he said, "So they got away."

JD gestured. "Jus' calm down. They won't get fah. Ah got cahs out they'ah. Wayne's handlin' it."

Jax stared at him. "You don't know the woman he's with." He looked around. "I need a car."

A tall female in uniform emerged from the patrol car and came toward us. "Everything all right, sir?"

"Fine." He turned to me. "He'ah's what Ah'm prepared to let you do, seein's how this he-ah weather's so bad. Ah'll get y'all ovah ta Bluffton—"

Jax stiffened. "No!"

I sensed he was ready to blow, so I stepped in. "We have a ride. It's parked over there." I gestured in the direction of the séance house.

"Yo' not gittin' into this he'ah chase, Annie. That'd just be risky fo' us all. This storm's hittin' through Savannah now, so—"

Jax went alert. "I need to go. That's my home. We'll give our statements later."

The patrol officer stepped forward. "I know Mr. Raines, sir. He lives just over the border. I can escort them."

JD considered this. Then he nodded. "Ah'll be in touch. Ah don't expect y'all will be goin' anywhe'ah."

"You know how to find me," I said. "I've called you enough times. I want to know the minute you locate Wayne."

"Yes, ma'am. He'll contact you, hisself, ah'm shu-ah."

"And there are kids up by the highway who escaped these guys. Send someone for them."

"You got yor daughtah?"

"Yes. No thanks to you."

We went to the patrol car. The officer loosened her slicker. Damp strands of red hair stuck to her face. "I'll sure be glad when this shift's over." She introduced herself to me as Jennifer Fawkes and said to Jax, "Didn't expect to see you again so soon." I remembered her from Sycamore Girls. Jax did know her. I let him do the talking.

He asked about the hurricane. Fawkes said it had stalled, then shifted, throwing off predictions and growing more intense. It had made landfall on the north Georgia border. "They say the rain bands stretch for over a hundred miles. I'd bet there's no power at your place."

I watched the cemetery for movement. I figured the kids would see the headlights and hide. I was tempted to ask Fawkes what she knew about Wayne's operation, but thought it was better not to open a door to questions from her. She had to be wondering what we were doing in the middle of a cemetery on such a night. She didn't need to know we'd exhumed a murder victim and harbored his accused killer. Until we got it sorted out, Danny was still a fugitive. So were Caryn and Flynn. Airic had protected crucial evidence, and the rest of us had tampered with it. Jax was skillfully deflecting her away from our business.

My stomach clenched. I suddenly realized if Airic had taken the hearse to the handlers' place, Fawkes might see the shattered window and ask to look inside. I remained tense as we neared the log cabin. Then I panicked. In the parking lot, I saw only the stolen Tahoe. Ayden's truck was gone. I sat forward, my heart in my throat. Kamryn had been in that truck.

Chapter Seventy-Three

I could barely control my nerves as I emerged from the car. But I couldn't show it to Fawkes. To my relief, Natra got out of the Tahoe. She made a gesture to show everything was cool. Jax thanked Fawkes for getting us here and said we'd follow her.

He took the driver's seat in the Tahoe, and I got into the front passenger seat. Natra sat in a back seat away from the shattered window. She'd fashioned a towel to stretch across the hole, which helped.

I turned in my seat. "Where's Kam? Where's the truck? And Mika?"

"On their way to Jax's place. Airic said he could hide the body there."

"The kids, too?"

"Yes, we have everyone."

"And Kam's all right?"

"She's rethinking her wish to see a hurricane, but otherwise, fine."

Fawkes led us out to the road and stepped up the pace. Heavy rain battered our windshield. The tall pines along the road bent toward us, as if reaching to grab us.

Natra came forward so we could hear her. "Here's what happened. Airic brought us to the truck and went back to you. Pretty soon, he was back. Danny and Caryn jumped out of the hearse, shouting that it stank so bad they couldn't breathe. I helped Airic put the body in the casket in back."

"Flynn wasn't with them?" I asked.

"He came with Ayden, right after. Danny wanted me to just drive away. He was scared they'd come for him."

"Plat-eye's dead," I told her.

"I heard. But Danny said it didn't matter."

"I thought Ayden was chasing Wayne."

"He tried. He lost them. He found the Expedition, but they'd ditched it. And he didn't realize till too late that Flynn was in the Tahoe, so that was a factor. I guess we'll sort out the stories later, but we were going to have Ayden take Mika and the kids in the truck, since it was big and didn't smell. Kam wanted to ride with Airic, but Ayden said no. Then Danny wanted to stay with the body, so Caryn said she'd go with Airic, too, if she could sit in front. Ayden said he'd circle back if we needed him, but he wanted to caravan with the hearse. They left me with this SUV. I was about to go back for you when the patrol showed up. I thought they were here to arrest me."

"JD's here." I told her. "The patrol was with him. I'd guess that's how Plat-eye's bodyguard disappeared. Wayne said Shnick was gone, but I saw his condition from the boo-daddy gas. No way did he drive off on his own. So, JD must have been watching from somewhere. I have a *lot* of questions for him, but there was no time to ask."

"So, we're all accounted for?" Jax asked. "Everyone's going to my place?"

I did the calculations. "Three here… three in the truck… and three in the hearse. Hey! That's three threes, as Airic said." So, we had nine. And Black Shirt, maybe, in the hearse. I hadn't checked the color of shirt on the corpse, but the ledger's presence with it showed we'd located Mick.

I pointed ahead. "How do you know this cop? I saw her at Sycamore."

"We're loosely acquainted," Jax said. "She dated my neighbor a few months ago. She's picked up runaways, so I steered her away from what we're doing."

I nodded. Jax had mentioned his neighbor, the cop, but I remained tense. "I'm worried she'll see the hearse."

Jax glanced at me. "You think she'd stop a hearse in weather like this?"

"It's damaged. Maybe Wayne told JD about it."

"When could Wayne have told anyone what happened back there? If JD knew Airic took the body, he'd have asked about it, right? He probably knows broadly about Sloane and Plat-eye, but he wouldn't yet know what just transpired."

Natra handed me a bottle of water from a stash in back. I opened it for

Jax. He pointed ahead. "Keep your eyes on the road. Flynn said they left Val's car out here when Plat-eye's men stopped them."

I looked back at Natra. "What else did Ayden say?"

"Just filled me in. When he saw the cops, he cut through the cemetery to avoid them. He didn't want them to see Flynn."

"Let's hope that old hearse can go the distance."

Jax looked at me. "Do you still have a gun?"

I touched it under my shirt. "Yes. Why?"

"Sloane. She'll go after Danny. He'll need protection."

"Tonight?"

"Yes."

"How would she know where he's going?"

"He's with us. She knows where I'd go."

"So, we thought Plat-eye was the mastermind, but it was really Sloane." I looked back at Natra. "What do you think?"

She shrugged. "Maybe Carter told her what he had, and she saw an opportunity."

I shook my head. "I think she's been an insider for a while. Carter just didn't realize she was using him. We have to figure out her moves, get the big picture. We should think about this from Carter's perspective. He's central." I focused on Jax. "Can I ask some questions?"

He stared ahead, his jaw tense. He said nothing. I was about to let him off the hook when he yielded. "Yes. Go ahead."

Chapter Seventy-Four

I'm not known for sensitivity, especially in such challenging conditions, but this required my therapist hat.

"All right. Let me try to pull this together." To Natra, I said, "Tell me if I miss anything." I twisted in my seat so I could address them both. "Plat-eye was part of ISM—this I Scream Man cartel. He managed its sex trafficking operation. For his own advantage, he recorded the deviant acts of powerful people. Sloane must have helped him, and they relied on corrupt cops for protection." I hesitated.

Jax nodded. "My brother, yes."

"Ok, so they leveraged Carter into a nasty position. He did the body disposal when things went south. Like with Mick. But Carter decided to ...whatever...reverse that. He was close to the most damning evidence, the bodies of kids they'd killed. He placed Mick's remains in Airic's cemetery. He also stole Plat-eye's ledger. He probably expected to retrieve them to bring them to you, but then realized Plat-eye was on to him. Somewhere along the line, he connected with Danny. He tried to send Danny to you, so you'd have a witness to a murder and cover-up. But Danny got caught. He was a liability and would've been killed, but Plat-eye needed the ledger. He thought Danny knew where Carter put it. Sloane knew at least some of this since she'd been Carter's partner."

"And more," Jax commented. "She knows how to manipulate weak men."

I glanced at Natra and choked back my own retort about Wayne. "So, Sloane watched for her advantage. She stayed close to Carter to learn what he was doing. Except... he *didn't* take her to Airic's that night. He didn't show her. Why not?"

"Maybe he figured her out," Natra offered. "Suspected her or found out something."

"He must have." Jax breathed out. "But when? He seemed pretty close to her a week before he died. And he called her that day."

"OK," I said, "that's a mystery. Let's hold it for now and focus on Danny. Carter took Danny to Airic's. Why?"

"So Danny could show me where Mick was buried," Jax offered. "Carter must have known they were coming for him. He needed a witness."

"He had Airic."

"No. Carter wouldn't do that to Airic, make it look like he helped Carter cover up something. He wouldn't want Airic implicated. It really had to be Danny, a victim who'd seen a lot. But Airic did take us to the right place. So, he knew. He also knew that Danny saw things."

"But when did Carter set up the watcher, the boo-daddy?" I asked. "That had to be earlier. No one just carries around a package of lethal gas."

"He set it up months ago, before that day."

"But then how could he hide the map to Mick's body? Wasn't the boo-daddy dangerous to handle?"

"He knew how. Maybe he drew the note as a back-up in case Danny didn't get to me."

"But Carter didn't send Danny to Georgia from Airic's," Natra pointed out. "They went back to Carter's cabin that night."

I nodded. "Yeah, that's a snag. And a big risk, getting so close to the switch house. And Danny went to the cabin today, too, looking for something. He said he was looking for a map, but how could he have seen it there at the cabin when Carter had already placed it in the boo-daddy?"

Jax leaned forward and squinted through the rain, then shone his high beams twice. I noticed a dark sedan parked on the side of the road ahead. Jax slowed and came up behind it. Fawkes made a U-turn.

"That's not Valerie's BMW," I said. "Hey, didn't we—?"

"Yes, we saw it where you first met Plat-eye." Jax got out. Fighting the wind, he went to the patrol car and pointed at the sedan. Fawkes went with him to look inside.

Chapter Seventy-Five

I gripped my seat and leaned toward Natra. "I saw that Town Car at the switch house, too. JD said he thought Sloane and Wayne had a car hidden. Maybe they swapped his Expedition for this one, and then traded it for Valerie's."

"So, they're close to the others."

"Unless they're ahead. It's hard to say who got on this road first. I'd bet on Sloane and Wayne. They tore out of there."

"So, Wayne's definitely undercover?"

"JD didn't confirm it. I'm still not sure, but JD's backup support makes me think he is. Still, JD was off-balance. I think their plan has gone sideways."

Jax returned, thoroughly soaked. He confirmed my suspicion. "Has a Cypress Run sticker. Someone from Plat-eye's team came this way. We haven't seen Val's car where I expected it to be, so I'd guess it was Sloane. She saw us in the BMW."

Jax pulled out to follow Fawkes. I told him my theory about the car switches, and he nodded. "Makes sense. So, stay alert. Watch along the road. She might hope to ambush us."

"We need to warn someone."

Jax handed me his radio. I tried to reach someone but got only static. I gave it to Natra for her to try.

"Okay," I said, "back to Carter. From him we have these things: Danny, who's a witness. The incriminating ledger, if we get it back. A murder victim, Mick. A coded map that we've figured out. But... it was cryptic. He didn't spell out the name. You could have easily missed it if Kam hadn't noticed it."

"With time, I'd have seen it," Jax responded. "He always used codes or puzzles, even when we were kids."

"Would he make *this* situation hard to understand?" Natra asked.

"No. A code meant for me would be obvious. But he wouldn't have known I'd be under the gun. Or that the watcher would have been toppled, or a hurricane was coming." He waited a moment before he added, "He wouldn't have known I'd stopped talking to Airic, either. Airic tried to tell me, but I pushed him away." Jax looked at me. "Till I brought you. Airic opened you up, so he could channel the message to you."

"Me? You think Carter's ghost sent me that map?"

Jax glanced at me. "You don't? Isn't that what your *Psi Apps* show is all about?" He looked in the rearview mirror at Natra.

I waved my hand. "Don't look at her. I'm the skeptic. My drawing could've been Airic's projection. He knew where the body was. He knows the shape of that area with the circle of rocks, and what Carter put on the grave. He'd seen Carter's map. Or the map came from Danny, who knew about the grave and the ring. It's not clearly paranormal. Remote viewing operates on natural energy."

"That's one interpretation."

I shook my head. "Then why didn't we see Black Shirt out there in the graves? I mean, we found Mick, right?"

"Spirits do what *they* want, not what we want. Do you doubt that Kamryn saw Puca?"

"Puca's alive. I accept human astral projection, especially from shamans. But if Black Shirt was Mick, a ghost of a dead boy, he should have given a sign. Something! We were doing what he supposedly wanted." I looked back at Natra. "This is what I hate about spirit stuff. Maybe this, maybe that. Nothing's clear."

I returned my gaze to the rain-blasted windshield. "Once more. Carter buried Mick, put a note into the boo-daddy for you, and tried to send Danny to you. Danny also knew where Mick was buried. Oh!" I snapped my fingers. "I know! Danny told us. There are video files, too, and pictures.

It's not just the ledger. I felt around in the grave, but no other package was there. Where would they be?"

Jax nodded. "They must be in the cabin."

"I don't think so. Danny said there was some kind of map. Could it be for another place?"

"That kid's a locked box."

"No kidding. But why? Carter wanted him to tell you stuff. Why doesn't he? Maybe he's trying to act on his own. But Airic did mention a key. So, what's missing? Possibly another map, a key, and the videos."

Natra leaned in. "Carter took Danny to Airic's to bury Mick and the ledger. Then he and Danny went back to Carter's cabin, and he told Danny to take his car and leave. Then Sloane arrived. Maybe Carter didn't show Danny anything, just told him there was a map to the photo stash."

"But would Carter leave evidence so close to the switch house?" I asked. "And in a place Sloane knew about? His behavior that day says he didn't trust her."

"He wouldn't." Jax sounded certain. "If there's a map, it's for something else, or for a place he wouldn't expect anyone to know. I'm certain he'd told Sloane about Airic, during the days when he still trusted her. So, leaving it with Airic would've been just as risky." Jax slowed to maneuver onto the interstate. It seemed ages since we'd left it to find Kam. It had been just hours.

Natra chimed in. "Danny couldn't have carried away anything physical from Carter's. They'd have searched him and the car when they grabbed him."

I took a breath. "Again, let's think from Carter's perspective. We know he left things for you, Jax. Was there another place in the cemetery that meant something to him?"

Jax shook his head. "No. That was it, as far as I know. He made it for Airic. We need to talk to Danny. You just said he might try to act on his own. He knows something he hasn't told us."

"Maybe he's a mule. He knows something but doesn't understand it."

"Either way. I can't make sense of his pact of silence. I'm Carter's brother.

Carter sent him to me. I'm Danny's best chance at shedding this murder charge. Yet he's working against me. I can't see why."

Natra shook her finger. "One more thing to keep in mind. Carter buried Mick. Danny was there. Without evidence against ISM, it could look like Carter and Danny colluded together to cover up Mick's murder. If he went to court right now, he wouldn't have much on his side."

Jax looked at her in the mirror. "If we don't stop Sloane first, it won't get that far."

"Wayne won't let her kill him," I said. "I'm sure of it."

Jax glanced at me. "If he's still alive."

Chapter Seventy-Six

We pulled onto Jax's property, away from Fawkes, and drove down a dark stretch of road. Jax maneuvered around several flooded areas. Wind forced the trees into dramatic poses, and several broken branches lay on the ground amid other plant debris. Soon, the house came into view.

I'd been here just that morning, to meet Puca. It hadn't been raining, just breezy. I didn't see Ayden's truck in the parking area, or the hearse. They had to have gotten here before us. So where were they? I wished Jax hadn't mentioned the potential for ambush.

Dim lights inside suggested candles and possibly a generator. I thought only of seeing Kamryn and shedding my wet clothes. Jax stopped, turned off the car lights, and watched the house. I made a move to open the door, but he gestured to wait. Only when Valerie came out to the covered porch and waved a flashlight did he drive closer. I heard Digger bark, then Mika. So, Ayden had arrived, at least. He must have told Val to watch for us. Natra and I jumped out at the same time.

Kamryn caught me in a bear hug as I came through the door. Relief nearly buckled my knees, but she seemed to have bounced back with her typical resilience. That, I knew, I owed to Ayden. Even if a gator were chewing on his leg, he'd have made her feel safe. Later, I could assess potential damage. Kamryn grabbed my hand. "You're all muddy, Mom! You need a bath. I brought your suitcase in. So, you have dry clothes."

Valerie had set out towels, hot drinks, and sandwiches. I breathed in the welcome scent of coffee and looked around. "Where's Ayden?"

"Why, they went right down to the garage. They had somethin' to store. Dylan took them. Airic said somethin' about threes and safety, but I never know what that strange man means. He was drivin' a hearse, of all things!"

Valerie introduced her teenage daughter, Christi, who was also thin and polished but with darker skin than Val, and dark brown hair. I recognized Carter's brown eyes and striking cheekbones.

A gust of wind hit the house. I tensed. "What's the weather news?"

Valerie waved a hand as if this storm was no concern. "Well, it came, dahlin', quick as a guvner's cover-up. We came out here 'cause it's inland and Jax is prepa'ahed. We brought plenty of food, sleepin' bags, clothes, watah, whatevah you need, although we'ah goin' easy on the genahratah. Looks like we'll all be hunkerin' down till it passes. Ah've been tryin' to make bedroom arrangements. These kids look like they'd fall asleep on a red ants' nest."

"I'm sure they would. They've been through a lot."

Christi's eyes widened. "We're hearin' about floods and accidents and all kinds of things!"

Valerie frowned. "Now, don't you bring us bad luck. This house is as sturdy as a hog farmah's fence."

Across the room, I saw Flynn telling Natra how he'd helped with Mika. I felt relieved that we'd all arrived.

Jax entered, drenched, and looked around. "Where's Danny?"

"Well, won't you be su'prahsed?" Valerie handed him a towel. "After we got 'im and his sweet girlfriend out of those smelly wet clothes, they went down to see Puca."

Christi gave him a mug of coffee. "He said he has a message for him."

"A message?" Jax looked at me. I knew it had to be from Carter. It had been *in his head* all this time, just as Airic had said. He *was* the mule. Maybe the *key* was just part of the message, like a code.

When Valerie told Jax that Ayden, Dylan, and Airic had gone to the underground garage, his expression changed to alarm. "When?"

"Maybe fifteen minutes."

Jax put down his coffee and strode down the hall. I followed and found him unlocking a gun safe to remove a 12-gauge pump-action shotgun.

Chapter Seventy-Seven

Valerie came up behind me. "The'ah's no call for that, Jax."

He ignored her.

"I'll go with you," I said.

"No."

"You need two more. Everything in threes."

"Not this time." He told Valerie to make sure everything was locked. "Every door, every window. And get yourself armed." Then he went out.

Valerie looked alarmed. "What's goin' on?"

"Sloane. She shot two men tonight, and Jax thinks she'll come here, maybe for Danny."

Valerie went to the safe and grabbed a large khaki-colored semi-auto. "Take this one, hon. It's ready. It's a .45 and packs fifteen rounds."

I patted my weapon. "I have one. That gun would knock me off my feet." I headed for the door. Kamryn held up a plate of food. "Mom?"

"Stay here," I told her. "I'll be back. We're just checking outside." I reminded myself she hadn't seen the worst of what we'd witnessed that night. I threw Valerie a look that begged her to watch over my daughter.

Natra met me at the door. "I'm still wet," she offered. "That makes three."

Valerie told us where to find the garage, and we took off after Jax.

Slicing rain stung my face when I left the porch, nearly blinding me. I had a general sense of direction but feared I'd get lost. Natra pushed past me with a flashlight. I barely saw its beam on the ground in front of us, so I crowded her.

Sensing something large nearby, I grabbed her arm to aim the beam to the right. Digger barked at us. Then he trotted in front. I silently thanked Val for this but hoped the dog wouldn't complicate things. When he went too far ahead, he circled back, like we were lost sheep under his charge. I leaned into the wind and dodged flying debris.

We moved across sodden ground with numerous puddles and several downed branches and dead birds until Natra stopped so abruptly I bumped into her. Then I saw why. We were near Valerie's BMW—the one missing from the South Carolina road. So, Sloane was here. She'd gotten this far. It felt as if she were right behind us. I looked around, but it was impossible to see anything. "Let's check it."

The car was unlocked and empty. No obvious blood on the seat. That didn't mean Wayne was still alive because she could have shot him outside during a car exchange. I felt around for a key fob. Nothing. I'd hoped to lock it to prevent her using it to leave. Having no working phone, I couldn't text Valerie to send someone to lock it up. I closed the door. "Let's go."

Digger rounded us up. I felt gravel under my feet.

Natra leaned into me. "Look! The hearse. Can you see it?"

I did. Its distinct surviving headlight was coming straight at us. Digger barked. I drew my gun. "Grab the dog. Get ready." I took a stance and aimed at the windshield. Natra shut off the flashlight. The mortician mobile kept coming. Airic might drive like that, but so would Sloane. She'd run us over. I prepared to shoot, holding my breath to steady my aim against the blasting wind. That proved impossible, so I just hoped I'd hit something.

To my relief, the vehicle slowed. I held my ground. The driver pulled to the right, exposing the driver's side door. I blinked away rain, trying to see. That wasn't Airic. It also wasn't Sloane. I strode forward as the window rolled down.

"Wayne!"

Digger barked again. Natra shushed him. I leaned in. "If you're taking the body, I can't let you."

He stayed in the hearse. "Trust me, Annie."

"*Trust* you? You put our daughter in danger, you—"

"You have her, right?"

"Yes, but—"

"I need to go, *now*. Step aside or you'll get hurt and your friends will die."

I froze. I feared for Ayden and Airic. And I owed Wayne. He'd covered for me at Airic's house. He'd left me my gun.

A loud *bang* near the house drew my attention. Natra let go of Digger and pulled out her Glock. Wayne gunned the hearse, getting past us. I aimed at the back tires, but a form came between his taillights and me. The dog. I pulled back. Someone yelled near the house. Digger ran off and Natra followed. She took the light.

Chapter Seventy-Eight

Jax needed backup. I continued along the path. With gun in hand, shielding my face, I advanced in the dark through rain that felt like the contents of many buckets all poured at once, with dozens of spikes. Several things hit me, but I couldn't see what they were. My drenched jeans hung like a massive weight and my shoes squished with every step. I knew I could easily wander onto the wrong track, so I kept the feel of gravel at my feet.

Something brushed my right leg, stopping me. A nose near my hand and a quick bark told me my guide was back. I looked around. Natra was not with him.

"Show me, Digger. Find Jax!"

At first he ran, but then circled back. I leaned down and grabbed his collar, hoping he wouldn't pull me off my feet. He seemed to understand. Despite how awkward it felt, I kept my left hand in contact with him as he moved. We arrived at a building where I smelled manure and heard bleating sheep.

"Good dog. Find Jax."

Digger sat, apparently confused. I couldn't bear the wind and pelting rain, so I entered the building. Digger barked twice but stayed outside near the door.

Valerie had said the garage was near the sheep shed. I smelled wet wool, so I was close. I didn't dare to call out. Sloane was in here. Wayne's warning suggested she had a gun. If she'd let him take the hearse, she must still trust him. So, maybe I'd been the fool. He'd just left with our most important piece of evidence.

Wind slammed the side of the barn as if trying to crash through with a battering ram. I felt my way along the sheep pen until I found a wall, then a door. I opened it and smelled exhaust. An engine had recently run in here. The hearse, probably, or maybe Ayden's truck. I found a set of stairs and quietly descended. From the raw sound of wind further down, I sensed a door was open. I came into a large room with two doublewide garage doors. In the beam of a flashlight, Jax knelt near someone, working to untie him. I went closer and recognized Dylan.

Jax looked up. "She was here."

"What happened?"

Dylan got to his feet. "We brought the hearse here. They ambushed us and tied us up."

"Where's Ayden?"

"Took off. Thinks he can catch them."

"And Airic?"

Dylan shrugged. "He was gone before they came in."

To Dylan, Jax said, "Tell Val where I'm going. Stay alert."

I looked around. "Sloane's not here?"

Dylan pointed out the open door. "With the guy who took the hearse."

"No, I saw him. He was alone."

Jax looked alarmed. "Are you sure?"

"I stopped Wayne. He gave me the impression Sloane was holding a gun on someone who'd die if I didn't let him go. She wasn't with him."

Jax retrieved his shotgun. "So, she's still here. Dylan, go tell Val to get everyone into a safe place. Then guard it." He asked if I had a weapon. I showed him. "You come with me, then."

Dylan's eyes went wide. "You think...?"

"I'll check."

Dylan handed Jax his flashlight. Jax strode out into the rain. I ran after him. The wind slammed me again, so I pulled my parka close. Digger ran up and barked. Dylan called for him.

We crossed the yard and entered a small domed building. Jax aimed the flashlight at the floor. "She was here."

I saw water droplets. "Why?"

"It leads to Puca."

"How could she know?"

"Maybe she saw Airic come this way. Or maybe Carter told her." He showed me a wet footprint. "That's a woman's." He looked at me. "And Danny went straight to Puca, too. That's why he was coming here from Carter's that night. Not for me. For Puca."

Jax opened a door and went down a short set of stairs into darkness. I hesitated. At the bottom, the flashlight showed a passageway with a very low ceiling. I'm not tall, but I had to bend a little to go through. At least it buffered the storm's noise. I swallowed my panic and stayed close to Jax. Water came over my shoes. I fought the urge to grab his shirt.

The further we went, the heavier the air grew with a muggy earthen scent that made me feel buried alive. I caught a glimpse of designs on the wall, suggesting this passageway was an extension of Puca's underground shamanic activities. I mentally counted my paces. Darkness closed behind me, shutting off escape. My pounding heart muted my footsteps.

Jax stopped and raised the flashlight. Ten yards away I saw an opening. I wanted to race to it and find fresh air, even if it came with pelting rain. My legs tensed as I prepared to run.

Jax circled the beam around it. "That door shouldn't be open."

Chapter Seventy-Nine

H e told me to stay where I was. "Don't show yourself until I say." But 'remain in place' was not an option. I watched him enter before I moved closer. Just touching the door helped me breathe, 'though my mouth went dry. I had a sudden urge to go back to where we'd entered. Too far. Too dark. Sweat formed on my upper lip. I heard Jax call out for Puca. I leaned in. No one answered.

"Annie!"

I ran into a candle-lit room. Jax held the flashlight on a figure in the corner. Caryn, gagged and bound, made the loudest noise she could muster. Jax removed the gag while I struggled with the ties around her wrists. Jax cut them with a jackknife.

Caryn jumped up. "They left! That bitch! She took Danny!"

Jax looked furious. "What happened?"

"That guy...that... Airic. He came down here. Danny was showing this old guy something, and then Airic came and then *she* was here." She pointed toward the door we'd just come through. "She was gonna shoot Danny! But the old guy said he knew what she wanted and if she left Danny alone, he'd take her."

"Take her? Where?"

"I don't know."

"Airic went, too?"

"He *helped* her! He tied me up!"

Jax grabbed her by the shoulders. "What did Danny tell my grandfather?"

I leaned closer to hear. Her story made no sense to me.

Caryn pouted and shook her head.

"Quickly, Caryn, so I can find him. Forget this pact of silence. How did Danny know Carter? What did he tell my grandfather?"

She cringed as if she expected to be hit. "Will you be his lawyer?"

"Of course. So, this stays between us. Tell me!"

She glanced at me and gave in. "Carter came to the switch house to get Mick's body. He was s'posed to take it to the gators. He knew they were gonna pin it on Danny, so he helped 'im get out. Then Carter saw 'im hitchin', so he picked 'im up and took 'im to that place to bury Mick."

"And then? Why did they go back?"

"Carter had a van from them—from the switch house. He had to get his car. He left Danny at his place and said they'd go to Georgia, but when he came back with his car, he was real nervous. He told Danny to take his car and go."

"How did Carter know Danny was innocent?"

"We just need to find him."

"Caryn!"

"Because he told him... Danny saw that...He saw that bitch kill Mick."

"He *saw* it? How?"

"He's not lying! He has it on tape. Those guys, Danny and them, they used to ... peep. They had little holes in the walls and sometimes watched when... you know. Mick said Sloane..."

"I know what they were doing. Keep going."

"Sloane... she'd requested Mick. He told Danny to watch. Danny set up a camera to record it, so they could laugh about it later. But they didn't... she just...she shot 'im. Danny told Carter. *Showed* 'im."

Jax exchanged looks with me. There it was. Carter's discovery. Sloane was the I Scream Man's assassin. And then Danny had seen her shoot Carter.

"Where's the recording?" Jax asked.

"On a thumb drive. When Carter said he'd help 'im, Danny gave it to 'im. That was right before they killed Carter. Danny thought it was his fault."

"Where did Carter put it?"

I knew Jax worried that this crucial evidence was still in the cabin, which was likely already flooded.

"I don't know. I really don't. We have to go! We have to get Danny!"

Jax held the flashlight over a piece of paper on the floor. He bent down to retrieve it. "What's this?"

"That's Danny's. Carter told Danny to memorize it and draw it for his grandfather and *only* his grandfather. That's why we went to the cabin. Carter drew it for him there, and Danny thought he was killed before he burned it. But he couldn't find it."

Jax waved it. "This is the map you were looking for?"

Caryn wiped her eyes. "I think so. The old guy knew what it was. He said he'd take the bitch there. But she wouldn't leave Danny here."

Jax softened. "All right, Caryn. It's not a map. It's a marker. I know where they went. Let's go upstairs."

On the main floor, Dylan met us, a rifle ready. "We've got a kid out there, running around."

I gasped. "Who?"

"One of the boys. The short one. He took a gun. Valerie said he was shooting outside. Natra took her dog to look for him."

Flynn. I remembered the shot that had drawn Natra back to the house. I didn't like a gun in that kid's hands, especially in the dark, with people out there. He'd finally got ahold of one and was being just as reckless as I'd expected.

Jax spoke to Dylan in another language. Dylan looked stricken.

Caryn's patience ran out. "Let's go!"

Jax gripped her shoulder. "I can't take you there. Please remain here. I know where he is." He went out. I followed. On the porch, Jax turned to me. "Stay here, Annie. Keep an eye on her."

"No."

"Then wait here. I'll come back and pick you up."

I knew he wouldn't. I gave him a moment before I went after him. When he got into his Wrangler, I jumped in the passenger side.

"Annie!"

"Just drive! And tell me what the hell you know!"

Jax started the Jeep and drove out. Then he said, "You asked me about another meaningful site. There is one. A cave on the property. We placed Carter's ashes there, and my son's. Puca took Carter for spirit cleansing. That symbol on Carter's note is painted on a wall."

"What's there that Sloane would want?"

"I'd guess the video files. Carter would stash things in a niche he carved out. He must have wanted Danny to come here and show Puca the symbol. Puca would then have given it all to me. But Danny wouldn't have known that. You're right. He was a mule, just following Carter's instruction."

"Why would Puca give them to Sloane?"

"Maybe to save Danny. She'd tried to get him at the garage, but he wasn't there. Sloane must have seen Airic go into the sweat lodge, which leads to Puca, and followed him. Maybe Carter told her about the files before he learned she'd killed Mick."

"What about Airic?"

"If he tied up Caryn, he did it to keep her safe."

"But Sloane could get the files and still shoot Danny. And..." I didn't finish.

"Yes. That's likely. Hang on."

Jax made a sharp right turn and gunned the engine to take us over a hump. We climbed a steep hill on rough ground. Water cascaded alongside me. I couldn't see out the windshield, despite the wipers running full-speed. A wind gust knocked us off course. I gripped the seat. Jax concentrated on getting up the steep grade. Finally, he brought the Jeep to an area where he could turn around. He stopped and turned off the lights but left the engine running.

"This is a back way. I don't want Sloane to see us coming. I'll scope out what's happening before we try anything. Get in the driver's seat and keep the motor running." He gestured ahead. "Be ready to go. If I don't come back in ten, get help. Just go straight down, but be careful. There's a dangerous twist where you could end up in the creek. Right now, it's more like a river."

"No thanks. Not again."

"No gators up here, at least. When you hit the line of trees, turn left. That'll get you back to the house."

Jax opened his door. I shielded my eyes and ducked away from a blast of wind-driven rain. When he closed the door, I climbed in the driver's seat. I'd once owned a Wrangler, but this one looked equipped with high-end upgrades. To get oriented, I briefly flashed the lights but saw no clearly marked road. I looked along the driver's side for markers and some sign of the creek's location, but streaming rain blurred the view. Wait ten minutes, Jax had said. I thought we must be close to the cave.

I sat up to listen. I thought I heard a gunshot, but it was difficult to tell. Wind shrieked and pressed against the Jeep. I checked my gun and placed it close, in case I needed it. I turned on the lights again to get my bearings and moved forward. I wanted to be sure I could drive it.

The passenger door opened. Relieved, I turned and looked straight into the barrel of a 9-millimeter.

Chapter Eighty

Sloane got in. "Drive!"

I moved forward. She put her weapon against the side of my face. "Faster."

I made my way down the hill, alternating gas with brakes, hoping I'd find the right track. Jax had said to go straight. I looked in the rearview mirror but saw only rain. I wondered if he even knew I'd been carjacked.

Sloane grabbed my gun, opened the window, and tossed it. "So you don't do something stupid."

My heart dropped. My only recourse seemed to be to crash the Jeep, but that could injure or kill me, too. I didn't know this terrain. I breathed in to steady my voice. "Where are we going?"

"Just drive."

"Did you hurt them?"

"Shut up!"

"Wayne won't let you get away with this."

Sloane snorted. "Makes no difference now."

Jax was right; Sloane knew what Wayne was up to. I had to warn him. Continuous blasts of wind hit us. I turned the wheel fast, hoping to throw her off balance, and found a gun in my face. "I can kill you and take the car myself. Keep that in mind."

I held up a protective hand. "Okay. What do you want me to do?" I had a daughter. I had to be careful, for her. She was still waiting for me to come back and eat the food she'd fixed. I seethed against this woman who'd kidnapped and scared her. I wanted to ram my fist hard into her face, rip out her hair, and stomp on her throat. This was the second time tonight she'd outwitted me. I had to find some advantage.

"Move!" Sloane gestured forward. "That way."

I stepped on the gas. I noticed we had a quarter of a tank of fuel. The measure of my life unless I had an opportunity—a solid one. Once we hit a paved road, I thought I'd jump out. But that had risks too. She might even back up and put a bullet in my head.

Wind kept pushing me. I clung tight to the steering wheel and hoped the tires weren't worn. We went down a steep incline that seemed like the one Jax had driven up. I held my breath. I imagined the others dead in the cave. I hoped Jax wasn't among them.

In front, I saw only slivers of light as rain came in a torrent. A downed tree appeared in the headlights. I stepped on the brakes. Sloane lifted her weapon. I moved around it.

Finally, we came to a flat area. I picked up speed. A line of trees along the right, bent from the force of the wind, suggested we'd come to the long drive that connected Jax's house to the main road. He'd told me to turn left. Sloane pointed right. Away from my chance to get help.

I drove a few minutes more before she ordered me to stop. She peered ahead. "Drive. Slowly." I complied but watched for a place to upend the Jeep. I could jump out here and run. She'd never find me. My heart pumped. I had to act.

Sloane leaned forward. I peered through the rain and saw movement ahead, and a flash, like car lights. We were close to the main road. My heart sped up. I had to get out. Sloane lifted her gun. "Stop. Put it in park. End of the line."

I raised my arm, but she slammed my hand down hard. She aimed at my head.

"Drop your gun!"

The commanding male voice startled us both. A light-colored gun barrel appeared between the seats, angled toward Sloane. She sat back. Flynn, partly under a blanket, held both hands around the grip of that enormous .45 Val had tried to give me. Sloane twisted toward him. I stomped on the gas pedal and pulled the Jeep into a tight circle that threw her against the door. She raised her gun, but I hit it upward as she fired, deafening me, then turned the Jeep with my left hand into a sharper angle. My ears rang.

Sloane grabbed for the steering wheel, but Flynn yanked her hair hard. He climbed between the seats, crouching to shove her head back and hit her in the face. She threw him at me, knocking my hands off the wheel, but he shouted and pushed off me to land another blow. As Sloane opened the door, I turned sharply to make it slam shut. Then I turned hard to the right, throwing her the other way, Flynn on top of her.

"Get off me!" she yelled.

I spun the Jeep and prepared to twist it again, but it caught on something and ran aground. Flynn hit the windshield. I opened the door and grabbed Flynn's shirt to pull him out. Sloane jerked him back in, but he hit her and scrambled over her to exit the other side. I ran toward the back, bumping into him behind the Jeep. He shouted, "I dropped it!"

I pushed him to the ground. "Stay down."

The engine raced. Mud flew from under the tires, spattering us. Sloane had taken the driver's seat. She was trying to flee. The back-up lights glowed. I pulled Flynn out of the way. The bumper knocked me to the ground.

Sloane turned the Jeep around. Its lights flashed on the .45 on the ground. I jumped up and ran for it. Sloane tried to hit me, but I ducked away, slipping in mud and missing the gun. Flynn grabbed it and took a wild shot. I stayed down. The Jeep went over me, but the tires missed me. I got up. The red taillights lit up. I saw Flynn near the passenger side, so I ran to the driver's side and opened the door.

Sloane punch me in the jaw, but Flynn came in. He pushed Sloane out. She landed hard at my feet, on her hands and knees. I stomped on her gun hand, making her let go. She recovered, pushed me, and ran.

I chased her. Another set of lights to my left illuminated Sloane's fleeing figure. I dove and hit her hard, bringing her down. Rain battered us both. I climbed onto her back and slammed her face into the mud. "That's for my daughter!" She tried to roll me off, but I pinned her left arm behind her.

She yelled and cursed. I gripped her hair and slammed her head once more.

Someone grabbed me around the waist to pull me away. I twisted to get free. "Flynn, let me go!"

"Annie, stop!"

I blinked away rain to see Wayne. And JD.

Chapter Eighty-One

Wayne helped me up while JD bent to pull Sloane to her feet. Despite the weather challenges, he got cuffs on her.

I tried to get free. "What are you doing? I'm not letting her go with you!"

"It's over, Annie."

Another police car pulled up. Jennifer Fawkes got out. JD placed Sloane into her car.

I turned on Wayne. "What's going on? Where's the hearse?"

He guided me to the Wrangler's passenger side. "Get in. Stay here. I mean it! I'll be back."

I was relieved to be out of the rain, but still ready to act. In the car lights, I saw Wayne talking to JD. He gestured toward me. Then I remembered Flynn. I looked in back. Not there. Or anywhere near the Jeep. I feared he'd seen the cops and run. I'd been so intent on beating up Sloane I hadn't seen them approach. But he had.

Fawkes's car pulled away. I strained to see through the rain. It felt as if Sloane were driving, like she'd won. I imagined her gloating at me through the window. I grabbed the door handle to get out, but then let go. It was out of my hands. I felt as powerless as the day the killer drove off with Hailey. Sloane might be in cuffs in a locked police car, but she was still lethal. There should be a whole parade of security around her. They had to know that. Surely Wayne did. He'd seen what she'd done.

Wayne returned and got into the driver's seat. "I'll get you over to the house. JD will follow us. I assume Kamryn's there."

I froze. "You can't take her."

"I'm not here for that."

"Sloane expected you. She was watching for you."

Wayne threw me a look. "Until you messed it up."

"Messed it up! I didn't ask her to get in the car! She was about to shoot me!"

Wayne held up a hand. "Sorry, Annie. I just wish you hadn't gotten into this."

"No? If I hadn't—"

"Okay! Yes. You got Kamryn out. I'm grateful. And, yes, that was my fault. You don't have to tell me that. But I protected her. She didn't get hurt."

He started the car.

I panicked. Flynn was out here, in the rain. "Wait, wait!"

"What?"

But I couldn't tell him about Flynn, or any of these kids. I pivoted. "You think that cop can handle her?"

Wayne glanced out the window. "Sloane's cuffed, with no weapons. Our command post is set up just over the border. Others are there."

"And where's the hearse?"

"Same place."

"With the body?" I grabbed his arm. "It was a set-up, Wayne. Danny Harnett didn't kill that kid. Search her. Carter Raines had incriminating video files, too. She might have them."

"She's in custody. We'll find whatever's on her."

I kept my eye out for Flynn, but the scrappy kid had vanished. Headlights behind us told me JD was following. Even if Flynn thought I was driving the Jeep, he wouldn't come near JD's SUV. That kid had saved me, and I was abandoning him. I couldn't think of anything to do. I hoped he knew how to find his way back.

"Take this road," I said. "It goes to where I'm staying."

"The Raines house. I know."

Right. He'd met Jax. He'd come on this property with Sloane. "They helped me get Kam back." I was beginning to hurt.

"So, she's okay?"

I wanted to say no, make him feel guilty. But now wasn't the time. "She's safe."

"I never meant for either of you to be in danger. I kept my eye on her."

"Did you? Even when your girlfriend kidnapped her? That bitch had her for hours. She must have been terrified."

"She's not my girlfriend. She approached me; I went out with her."

"Was she living with you?" I hadn't intended to sound so sharp, but something boiled up inside me.

Wayne gave me a look that said *this is why we didn't get along.* "She was not living with me, and Kamryn only saw her twice. I'm surprised Kam got in her car. That's not like her."

I felt a twinge of guilt. "She was mad. At us. At me. She wanted to stay at the beach for the hurricane. Sloane arrived just as Kam was trying to punish me for sending her away."

Wayne shook his head. "I guess she got her wish."

"Go faster, please."

"Why?"

"I think Sloane hurt some people. I need to get them help."

"Where?"

"I don't know how to get back there. But someone at the house will."

Wayne increased his speed, but rain and wind made it difficult to see ahead. "Just so you know," he said, "I *was* undercover. I dated Linda…Sloane…for a few weeks. She hinted there was money to be had in the juvenile system if I wanted in."

"She targeted you. Why?"

"She likely wanted eyes on our investigations, but I figured out she also wanted access to you."

I sat back. "What?" Then I realized. "Danny! She wanted to know what he told me."

"Maybe. She did want that kid but hear me out."

I frowned. "Okay."

"She approached me nearly two months ago. JD thought I should play along, see where it led, so I showed an interest in Sloane's connections. She introduced me to people like Plattman. And they were aware of you." He glanced at me. "I think they had you on these cases to give them another way in. As you've probably guessed, they ensure loyalty by leveraging families. That's why I wanted you to stay out of Georgia. You weren't doing what they expected, so they tried to shut you out. They thought I could persuade you, but then you met these lawyers." He gestured around us. "Long story short, we realized they knew Sloane. With that link, you might have figured out who Linda was, and we didn't want her exposed. We thought she could get us close to some significant corruption."

"Wayne, she knew you were playing her."

"I know. It was close. I was fine as long as she needed me, but it was gonna end tonight."

"She would've killed you."

"I had backup, Annie. We were ready, although I admit, I underestimated how callous she is. Did Plattman die?"

"Yes." I leaned toward Wayne. "And she killed Broderick, the guy you met in the parking lot near Savannah. Right in front of me."

He looked at me. "Sorry. I really am. But what were you—?"

I waved it off. "Just keep her in custody. I never want her near Kamryn again. Or me." Then I relented. "Thanks for helping me. And Kam."

"Nearly blew my cover. I slipped Kam a knife so she could help the other kids. Then you came." Wayne looked at me askance. "I didn't expect you to make a frontal assault."

"No choice. Sloane caught me."

"Just relieved we didn't find Danny here. She wants him bad."

"She did find him, Wayne. She took him to a cave."

He glanced at me. "Where?"

"Where I need to go ASAP."

I sensed from the blurred form of buildings ahead we were near the house. "So, what did Sloane want with me?"

"Your case in Georgia."

I did a double-take. "What?"

Wayne pulled up to the house. I looked at the porch. I needed to get Dylan, but I had to hear this.

"We identified Sloane's contacts and put the screws on. A caseworker admitted she blackmailed him into killing a kid at a juvenile facility there. Told him to make it look like suicide. Said he'd tell us about others if he got a deal."

"I knew it!"

Wayne gestured toward the house. "Find out where to go. We'll help."

I got as far as the covered porch when I saw another set of lights. A truck. It was Ayden. He drove straight to the porch and got out. The other door opened, and Ayden grabbed the passenger and pulled him up the steps.

I felt a wash of relief. "Oh, my God! Flynn!"

"Found him on the road."

"We have to get inside, quick!" Flynn shouted. "Right now!"

Valerie opened the door. "What's goin' on out he'ah?"

Wayne came up the steps.

Flynn fled into the house.

"Wayne!" Ayden shouted. "You got a problem!"

Chapter Eighty-Two

"Everyone, just get in he'ah!" Valerie ordered. "So I can shut this da'yam do'ah!"

I entered and saw Flynn hovering against a wall, his eyes wide in the flickering candlelight. Ayden followed and gestured for Flynn to come over. He shook his head.

I quickly introduced Wayne and said, "He's undercover. They just arrested Sloane."

"What?" Val said. "They got her?"

Dylan came in from the hall. I tried to direct things. "Dylan, you need to show us how to get to your father's cave. Wayne and his partner will help."

Ayden held up a hand. "Wait! Wayne has to go after that cop that took Sloane. Now!"

"She's one of them!" Flynn shouted.

Wayne frowned at him. "One of who?"

"With the I Scream Men. She helps them. I saw her take kids." He touched his head. "The red hair."

For a second Wayne looked frozen. Then he left. Ayden followed.

Dylan looked confused. "What's going on? Where's Jax?"

"Do you have medical supplies?" I asked.

"Of course."

"Grab them. Just in case. Especially bandages." I offered a brief version of events. "I don't know what happened in the cave, but we have to go see. Did Natra come back?"

"She's in the guest wing with the girls."

"Please tell her to stay alert. And armed."

Dylan left and returned with a black medical bag.

"Do you have an SUV?" I asked. "The Jeep needs gas."

Ayden entered. "We'll take my truck. I gassed up. Let's go!"

On the way, Ayden told us Wayne and JD went after Fawkes. Then he said that after the ambush in the garage, he'd gone looking for the hearse. "Can't think why she didn't just shoot us," he said. "When I couldn't find the hearse, I drove back and saw Flynn trying to hitch a ride. In this weather. Crazy kid. He thought if he stayed here, they'd grab him."

"He saved my life." I described what I'd just been through.

"You didn't go in the cave?" Dylan asked.

"No. Jax told me to stay with the Jeep, to be ready."

"But they must have come up here in a car. Why didn't Sloane just take that one?"

"Dylan, I don't know. I didn't see anyone but her and she told me nothing. I don't even know if anyone's hurt, but I did hear a shot, and no one's come back."

Dylan showed Ayden where to turn, and we climbed again over the rough terrain. Water streamed down over the road, making me nervous about a washout. I couldn't see anything in front of us. I clung to the seat. "God, I hope Sloane hasn't gotten away. I had a feeling that cop was hovering too much. She volunteered to escort us here and she was still here for the arrest. Like she was waiting."

"Do you think they circled back?" Dylan asked. "Would they go to the house?"

"I don't know, but Val and Natra can both shoot."

"And Flynn, apparently," Ayden added.

I shook my head. "He's a rascal. Thank God."

Dylan directed Ayden around an upward sloping curve. "Take it easy here. It's precarious."

Ayden stepped hard on the brakes and threw me forward. A figure stood in the light beam.

"It's Airic!" Dylan got out.

Ayden peered through the windshield. "This can't be good."

I searched for a flashlight in the back. Dylan returned and opened the door but stayed outside. "Danny took my mother's car over the edge, into the creek. He's hurt. The car's stuck and the creek's flooding. Jax is down there. He needs a rope."

Ayden gestured toward the back. "I have one. Hope it'll reach."

"Then stay with Airic. I'm going up to the cave to get Puca."

Ayden drove slowly until Airic waved for him to stop. We got out and fought the wind to get to the edge of the road, where I saw the drop-off. I stepped back. A light about twenty feet below indicated where they were. I waved my flashlight.

Airic, drenched, stood at the edge and stared down.

I helped Ayden with the rope. He peered over the edge. "This won't work. I can't get the truck close enough."

"There's a tree." I pointed. "We can tie the rope to it."

"Then *you'll* have to go."

I looked at the rushing water. "You should. You climb cliffs."

"You can't pull me back up. But I can pull you."

He was right. Airic couldn't do this, either, and Dylan was searching for Puca. There was no time to indulge my phobias. I grabbed the rope to tie around me. Facing Sloane's gun hadn't seemed as daunting as this. Ayden had once taken me rappelling, so I knew a few things about footing and balance, but I hadn't enjoyed the free-fall effect. And these wet rocks were slippery, not to mention how painful the blinding rain was. I mentally vowed to change my name to Indi-Annie Jones. I'd earned it.

I let Ayden lower me over the edge and when I felt for purchase, I scraped my knuckles. Bracing my feet against the rock wall, I leaned into the rope and walked down slowly. The cliff blocked the wind, which brought some relief. I slipped once but caught myself before Jax guided me onto a ledge next to the BMW. It was stuck at an awkward angle. Water rushed through a broken window, threatening to dislodge it.

The ledge felt just as precarious. I quelled my panic by helping Jax untie and transfer the rope to the car. Danny was slumped inside, in the front.

Jax beckoned for me to get in. "He's unconscious," he yelled. "I need to slide him out so I can put on a sling, but I can't dislodge him. Can you get into that space?" He pointed to the water-filled footrest area for the passenger seat. It looked like a mini maelstrom. I stared.

Jax moved my face toward his. "Keep watching me. Climb over the seat and I'll guide you. I won't let you go."

I nodded. We both knew if the car let go while we were inside, his holding my hand wouldn't do us much good. I gripped his arm and stepped onto the passenger seat.

"Turn around. Go slowly." Jax held my right hand. I felt myself shaking. I wanted to open the door and get out. Instead, I got on my knees and pushed one leg back until I felt the whirling water. The car moved. I jumped. Jax gripped my hand. "You're doing fine. Reach behind his legs and try to twist him so I can pull him out the window."

Danny leaned against the door. The airbag had deployed, pinning him near the shattered window. I let go of Jax's hand so I could get further into the footrest. Water lapped up to my chest. I held my breath and felt for Danny's legs. Pulling his left leg close to his right, I nearly had him but got a face full of gritty water filled with debris. I coughed hard and let go so I could get onto the seat. I needed a moment. I spit out seeds and pine needles.

I took another deep breath and went back down, grabbing Danny's legs to shift him around. He seemed stuck, so I leveraged myself and jerked hard. I felt him move and realized Jax had gotten out to prepare him to go through the window. I came up and gulped down air. Jax was ready to pull Danny out. I got on my knees on the passenger seat to offer support. Danny slid through the window. I climbed through and helped Jax secure him in the makeshift sling. The kid was slender but taller than me, so it was tough.

Jax leaned toward me. "I'll come back for you. Stay here." I held the flashlight as I watched him move Danny's limp form along the rope. Two lights above us told me Dylan was back. I returned to the car to help anchor it against the added weight on the rope. Relieved to be out of the wind, I waited, still shaking. I gripped the steering wheel to steady myself. The car moved. I went still.

"The rope will hold, the rope will hold," I said. But I didn't believe it. I climbed back out. I couldn't see very far, so I touched the rope. I felt movement. Jax was still on it. How far along I couldn't tell.

The car moved again, straining the rope. I thought the knot had slipped. I looked up for some sign they'd gotten Danny out but saw only rain. It struck me that maybe Jax couldn't do this. Maybe Danny was too heavy, or the incline too sharp, or the rocks too slippery. So many things could go wrong. So many things had already gone wrong.

Strong hands squeeze my shoulders. Relieved, I turned. "Jax, thank God!" But no one was there.

Chapter Eighty-Three

I felt my shoulders. The impression had been vivid. I stepped back and looked around. Just then the BMW dislodged, made a noise of metal scraping rock, and floated across the creek. It slammed into a rock on the other side. I went to my hands and knees, terrified the ledge might go next. I crawled to find the end of the rope—my lifeline. I still had the flashlight but couldn't see anything in the water. I reached down. Nothing there. *Jax will be back*, I told myself. *He's coming.* I hunkered down and tucked my arms in, like a rabbit with no place to run. My jacket did nothing to shield me.

Then Jax bent over me. "Annie, let go." Only then did I realize I clung tight to my perch, drenched and shaking. My fingers were too stiff to maneuver the end of the rope he'd brought, so he tied it around me and helped me get across the water. Somehow, we both made it up to the top. Ayden was there, but his truck was gone. So were Airic, Dylan, and Danny.

Ayden helped me climb over the edge. "Are you okay, Annie?"

I nodded. I couldn't talk. I wanted to cry.

"Let's get inside." Jax guided me up a slope into a cave, out of the rain. I put my hand against a wall to ground myself. I wasn't Indi-Annie after all.

"Dylan took the others to the house," Ayden told me. "He'll be back."

The cave dulled the racket outside. Jax helped me sit on a stone bench. He produced a roll of bandages and wrapped my bleeding knuckles. I coughed and hugged myself, then looked at Jax. "What happened?"

"Carter left the video files in here. Puca gave them to Sloane, but Danny nicked the car fob from her and took off. Sloane shot at him and blew a tire. He went into the creek. I don't know how she found you. Maybe she saw me, and realized I'd come a different way."

"I told Jax what happened to you," Ayden said.

Jax squeezed my hand. "I'm so sorry. I thought you left because I'd taken too long."

"So you know she was caught."

"Yes."

"Let's hope she didn't get away. I told Wayne to search her for the files." I looked around. "Where are we?"

Jax turned on his flashlight and showed me the cave. "This was Carter's place. Where he and Puca came."

"Puca's okay?"

"Yes, thanks to Danny. I think she would have killed them all, but when he ran, she left the cave. Puca and Airic went deeper inside, where I found them."

I looked at Jax. "Someone was down there. At the car. Someone moved me just before it went in the water."

Jax nodded. "Things like that happen here."

The truck's horn announced Dylan's return. Ayden drove us back as Dylan told us Danny's condition. He had a head wound and concussion, probable cracked ribs, and a dislocated shoulder.

"Should we get him to a hospital?" I asked.

Jax shook his head. "Puca will take care of him."

"I hope he's got enough magic to go around. I think we all need some."

At the house, Valerie said she'd heard nothing from Wayne. Without cell service, I had no way to text him, and he couldn't call us. Whatever turned up with Fawkes, we'd have to wait.

I managed to get a brief tepid shower with the generator turned on. It felt great to get the mud out of my hair and put on dry clothes. In a large common room, Natra attended to my cuts and scrapes, with anxious licks from Mika. "Kamryn seems fine," she assured me. "She's excited by all this new stuff. I finally got her to sleep."

"Thanks for watching her. I'm glad Wayne really *was* undercover. I don't think I could have explained to her that he'd..."

"Yeah. She'll need debriefing, though."

"I know. I'm just not sure how much to tell her."

Natra raised an eyebrow. "She's ready. She understands your work. And she heard things from Caryn about Danny. Caryn pulls no punches."

"That's what I'm afraid of."

Natra wrapped my hand. "Can't protect her forever, Annie. Kam knows why we were in the cemetery."

"You're right. I'll talk to her. We'll have time while we wait out the storm. I just hate drawing her into all this."

"She's in. And she wants to be. See it as an opportunity to connect."

Valerie entered and handed me a mug.

I held up a hand. "No coffee for me. I need to sleep."

"It's not coffee."

I looked over at the door. Puca stood there. He bowed toward us and touched his hand. "This heals." Then he left.

Natra nudged me. "I'd drink it if I were you."

I'd asked for magic and now I had it. I sipped the sour brew as Valerie told me where she'd put everyone. Puca and Dylan, "our medicine men," would watch over Danny. I was sure Caryn would be nearby. It didn't surprise me that Ayden had opted to bunk in his truck, because he loved extreme weather. Flynn, still jumpy about the cops, was with him.

"Your sweet daughter's in a double," Valerie added. "I thought you'd want to be close to her."

"Thanks. Just show me where."

I entered the room as quietly as I could. I heard Kam breathing. I shielded the flashlight beam to get just enough light to see her face, then leaned to kiss her. She took a quick breath.

"Mom!"

"I'm here. Go back to sleep."

"Is everyone okay?"

"We're all here now."

"Even Dad?"

"I saw him. He's all right."

"I was waiting for you. I have to tell you something."

She pulled me close and whispered a word I didn't understand. I shook my head, so she repeated it. "*Onowa*. My name. Jax said it means wide awake. I see more."

I smiled. "That's a good name for you. And I'm so proud of you, how you helped. Everyone's impressed."

She smiled. "I like Airic. He's sweet."

I ran my hand through her silky hair. "You can see him in the morning."

I lay down next to her. I wanted to sleep, but I ached all over and my mind raced. I worried that the wind would damage the house. That Danny wouldn't recover. That Sloane would escape and kill Wayne or return to finish us off. Every sound kept me alert as the storm's most intense phase blew through. Mostly, I couldn't shake the feeling that we'd missed something obvious. Something important.

Chapter Eighty-Four

Forceful winds raged outside, but when I left the room, the dark house felt quiet. Having slept badly for a few hours, I followed the aroma of coffee into the spacious kitchen. The generator was running, but the place felt damp.

Valerie looked tired. She said she'd kept watch. She wasn't about to miss the chance to shoot Sloane, should the opportunity present itself. I accepted a cup of coffee as she recounted everyone's status. Most were asleep.

She rubbed my back. "How're y'all doin', hon?"

"Just glad to be dry. If I had a car, I'd take Kam and drive to the closest sunny place."

"The hurricane's blowin' out of he'ah soon. It's already weak'ah. We'll get some relief. The landline still works if you need to make a call."

Natra came up from downstairs. Mika padded over to greet me. She smelled like a wet dog. Valerie filled a mug with hot water for Natra's tea and asked, "How's the boy?"

"Fighting a fever."

"Should we try to get him to a hospital?" I asked.

Valerie made a dismissive gesture. "This is our hospital. Dylan studies Muscogee medicine with Puca and he's had an internship at the medical center."

Natra picked out a dog treat for Mika. "We're in good shape. They're doing whatever a doctor would do. Probably more. He woke up in pain and Puca gave him something to put him under. Dylan got his shoulder back into place. They treated Jax as well. That tree left a nasty bruise. How's

301

your hand?"

"It hurts. A lot. But I'm not complaining."

"Oh!" Valerie exclaimed. "With all this craziness, Ah forgot to tell you. Ah located that little Jimmy Broderick."

I stared at her, astonished. "You did?" It seemed like years ago we'd taken his case.

"Ah pulled in fav'ahs and made a few threats. He's in one of those awful boot camps out west. The poor kid. His fathah put 'im the'ah, can you imagine? Some kind of vile maneuvah to punish his wife. He blackmailed a judge to make it happen. But we'll get the boy back faster'n you can shoot a pea at a panda."

I didn't know how fast that was, but I thanked her. "At least we have a good outcome for one of these kids. Sort of. His father's dead. But it sounds like that could be a good thing. The man was pretty nasty."

"Ah heard about that. Ah think we'll get more good outcomes. Y'all've nevah seen Jax in court."

"A strong criminal case will help."

Valerie held up a mug in a toast. "We'll get that bitch. Then the rest will—"

A loud knock at the door startled us. Mika barked. I looked at Valerie.

"Well, it can't be *her*, hon. She'd no mo' come to the do'ah than a finch would eat a fish. Probably just a neighbah needin' help."

Digger ran up from downstairs. Natra herded the dogs away as Valerie opened the door. I stood nearby. She turned and looked at me. "Ah think it's fo' you."

Wayne came in. I could tell from his muddy clothes he'd had no rest or time to change. Valerie took his wet jacket. Her face remained tense.

To me Wayne said, "I'd like to see Kamryn. Then we need to talk."

"She's asleep."

"I won't wake her. I just want to see her." Wayne looked at Valerie. "You might want to get Mr. Raines. This concerns him as well. I'd like to discuss it with all of you."

I took Wayne to where I'd bunked with Kam. When I opened the door, she sat up, her hair in tangles.

"Dad!"

She jumped out of bed and ran to embrace him. "We're in a hurricane! Did you see? And we were in Airic's attic and I rode in a hearse. I helped them find things!"

He hugged her. "I'm proud of you, Kam. I can't wait to hear all about it."

"There's some breakfast in the kitchen," I told her. "When you're ready, Christi can help you."

I didn't like the grave expression on Wayne's face. When we returned to Valerie, she ushered us into a spacious office, filled with law books. Jax, Natra, and Ayden were seated around a room that smelled like leather polish. Everyone looked dead tired but alert.

Wayne took a seat and accepted a cup of coffee. He apologized for seeming to be working with Sloane. He repeated what he'd explained to me about meeting her.

"Well, did you lock that woman up?" Valerie asked.

Wayne examined his hands. I glanced at Ayden. We knew this tell. It meant bad news. Wayne looked up. "You won't like this, but we don't have her in custody."

Jax sat forward. "But you *had* her."

Wayne held up a hand. "She has connections. And protections. We're not just dealing with Sloane. We're dealing with a network of officials invested in protecting their secrets. She's the wall between them and us. Her attorneys got a judge to use the weather conditions to allow her to be put in their charge. She claims she's been operating undercover for Carter Raines. With your authorization."

Chapter Eighty-Five

Valerie stood, her eyes blazing. "That's a lie! That bitch killed mah husband!"

Wayne nodded. "Hear me out, please, because I need your help. I got the gist. She's making certain claims, and her legal team is using the same evidence for her innocence that could prove her guilt. You know how logic can go both ways. She says she worked as an investigator for your law firm, alongside Mr. Raines. Truthfully, her need for a cover story in the event of an arrest probably saved your lives. If she'd killed one of you, her story would fall apart. But she had a plan."

I nodded. That's why she hadn't shot me in the car, or Jax back at the switch house.

Valerie drew herself up as if she wanted to spit something out, but Jax motioned for her to wait. She sat back down, her face a mask of fury. To Wayne, Jax said, "We employed her as a subcontractor for a limited time, at Carter's recommendation. She duped us all, including him. But she's not working for us now."

"She says she helped Mr. Raines get proof that Alder Plattman was running an underage sex trafficking operation and blackmailing high-placed officials. I suspect the judge who allowed her this temporary freedom is among them."

I knew Jax couldn't reveal that Carter had not exactly been an undercover operative.

I sat forward. "Did she say this stuff to you, Wayne, when you were with her?"

"No. To me, she presented opportunities for money and power. She can say she stayed quiet about her status because she was watching for corruption in SLED."

"She's saying *you're* a dirty cop?"

"She could. I certainly acted like one." He pointed around the room. "Right now, we're all vulnerable to accusations. Theft of human remains, concealment of evidence, conspiracy to aid a killer. Annie, she could accuse you of assault. You roughed her up pretty good. Need I add more?"

Jax narrowed his eyes. "We saw her shoot two men. You witnessed one of them."

"She'll say the shootings were justified. She was protecting you. That's what I gather she's claiming."

"The hell she—"

Again, Wayne held up his hands. "I'm just telling you the hurdles we face. Do you have Danny Harnett here? She thought you brought him here. Annie said he was up in some cave."

"He's our client," Valerie said. "We know whe'ah he is."

"I should take him into protective custody."

"No." Jax glanced at me, then back at Wayne. "For all we know, you're still working with her. Maybe she's waiting outside for you to come back with him."

Wayne put down his mug. "Thought you'd say that. And that's fine. As long as you keep that kid safe. I never saw him here, so I can't say I did."

"That body is evidence," Ayden said. "The kid we exhumed."

Wayne's jaw tightened. "There's more bad news, I'm afraid. Fawkes took Sloane to where we parked the hearse at our command center."

I shook my head. "She has everything, doesn't she?"

"They took it, yes. I'm sorry. The body and the ledger." He looked at me. "You said she had digital files, too."

Jax crossed his arms. I wished I hadn't said anything.

"Wasn't the hearse guarded?" Ayden asked.

"Yes. But a team posing as SLED agents confiscated it." Wayne shrugged. "Fawkes helped them. So, we lost it. For now. It's on the record, so Sloane can't easily destroy it, but she's in the driver's seat. And that's why I'm here. We can help each other. We need evidence, solid evidence that she can't spin. Something she doesn't yet have."

I held up a finger "Wait! You told me you have the CO who orchestrated the staged suicides."

Jax and Valerie looked at me, then Wayne. He explained about the info he had for our Georgia cases before he added, "But that's he-said-she-said. No actual proof against her. Not yet, anyway. And he could back out if someone threatens him. Which they will."

"The coroner here can add some weight," Jax said. "He knows about the cover-up. But he's vulnerable, too."

"Okay, that's something. What else?"

Valerie interrupted. "You said we'd help each othah. What will you do fo' us?"

"I assume you'll be launching civil suits. We'll support you. We can all succeed if we pool our resources. But if we can't even get her to trial, we all lose. Your kid, Danny, will be the one on trial."

Jax got to his feet. "We've lost our advantage. We had a body. We had records. Now she has them. And she'll have a formidable legal team, with connections to judges who'll show her leniency. We have to discuss this before we can give you an answer. Even if you're telling the truth, clearly people around you have been bought. My brother is dead because he trusted Sloane. I won't give her any more advantages."

Wayne stood. "I understand. I wanted you to know the complications. And I'm sorry for what happened."

"Thank you for coming to tell us. It's been rough for us all. If you'll excuse me." Jax walked out.

Valerie rose. "Ah'm with Jax. And Ah'm furious." She looked at me. "I'll let you show Agent Worth out." She left the room.

"If it means anything," Ayden said to Wayne, "I believe you."

"I appreciate that." Wayne looked at me.

I hugged myself. "I'll talk to them. This is a big setback, after all we went through. We had what we needed, and now we don't. And you're right.

CHAPTER EIGHTY-FIVE

We're all caught in her web. She's been shrewd. We need a solid case."

When we came out, Kamryn threw herself at Wayne. He told her he had to leave, but he'd see her soon. At the door, Wayne said, "I wish I had better news, but this is why I stuck with her so long. She's a connection to a large network of child molesters, among other things. If we get her with an airtight case, they'll distance themselves and cut her loose. She won't have the resources she has now. We think she'll turn on them to save herself."

"I know. Jax knows it, too. He just has to process this. He won't like making any deal with her."

"Does the landline still work here?"

"I think so."

"If you learn something we can use, leave a message with our dispatch for me to contact you. Use a code. Maybe from that movie you used before. Say you're…what was it?… June something?

"June Havens."

"Right. I'll know what it means. And please keep Kamryn safe. Conditions are improving, but I'd prefer that you stay here a while."

I closed the door behind Wayne and locked it. Leaning against it, I felt the wind trying its hardest to blow the place down. I thought about hurricane stories I'd heard where people felt safe inside a building, only to be trapped in a sudden devastating wave. I sensed one still coming for us.

I turned around. Jax stood there. "Let's talk."

Chapter Eighty-Six

I looked toward the kitchen. "I should find Kam first."

"She's downstairs."

"She's allowed?"

"She said you told her she could see Airic."

"I did. Is he all right?"

Jax gestured for me to come back in the office we'd just left. He closed the door.

I folded my arms, ready for his anger. "I understand how you feel about Wayne. I'm angry, too. And it's hard to know whether to trust him. But I think he's on the level. He's gotten good stuff for our suicide cases."

"And let Sloane get away."

"Because he was bringing me back here, to get help for you. Otherwise, he'd have been with her. Maybe dead, too, because Fawkes might have shot him. Like you said, the person you least expect. She was monitoring *us*. Maybe that's why she was dating your neighbor. Well-paid or getting laid."

"Annie, we can't be sure Wayne knew nothing about Fawkes. He could be playing on your wish to give him the benefit of the doubt."

I half-sat on the arm of a couch. "Okay. Yes. I see your point. I'm just as upset as you that Sloane got away, and just as nervous."

"So, I have a favor to ask."

I gave him a look that said, *Really? Another one?*

"I know. You've done plenty, and this one isn't small. But it doesn't involve water."

Mystified, I gestured for him to continue.

"I want Kamryn to help me with Airic."

I frowned. "What do you mean?"

"I've been trying to talk with him about what Carter told him that day. He just repeats things that make no sense. And now he's annoyed, so he's withdrawn."

"How's Kam supposed to help?"

Jax paused. "Remember when I said Airic doesn't invite strangers into his private séance circle?"

I stared at him.

"I think Puca made it happen for you."

"What?" My heart sped up.

"Puca knew you from your podcasts. He told Airic you'd contact him, and he should let you come. He said you have a daughter with a special kind of talent."

We were back in the chill zone. I drew my arms closer. "I don't understand. He didn't know us."

"He's a far-seer, Annie. And you've discussed Kamryn's neurodivergence in some podcasts. How did you even know about Airic?"

I thought back. "I'm not sure. Maybe the team-sourcing comments on the website."

"I think Puca planted it. Last night, I heard him with Airic. When Plat-eye brought Kam to Airic's house, he was waiting for her. He knew about her. And she thinks like him, with that keen dexterity. That's why she's so good with puzzles. Like in the cemetery. She can see multiple ways to a solution."

"That name you gave her."

Jax cocked his head. "Yes. That was Puca's name for Carter. He thought like them, too. His mind seemed tangled to me, often confusing, but he had a unique way of solving problems. He was a good detective."

I shrugged, unsure where this was going. "But what do you want her to do?"

"I've watched her with Airic. He pays attention to her. He *looks* at her. That's rare. This morning, it hit me. We have *three*. Kamryn, Carter and Airic. Put those three minds together and we might figure out what Carter intended."

I stared. "No, Jax! I didn't even want her in the cemetery. I don't need her contacting …ghosts!"

"More like asking her to figure out what Airic knows from Carter. Like Wayne said, we need something Sloane can't spin in her favor. So far, we have nothing. She'll win."

I felt cornered. My stomach tightened. Airic's help had brought us things. He'd freed me from suffocating guilt. With a trembling voice, I asked, "What do we need to know?"

"Where this key is. Puca said Carter had sent Danny here with a symbol from the cave. Puca knew Carter had stored something there. He was going to take Danny after the storm, but Sloane arrived. You know what happened after that."

"So, maybe Sloane got the key, then."

"Puca said there was only a small box. I think he meant a storage device. The video files. And Airic keeps telling me there's a key. Like it's still missing."

"Can't Puca figure out what he means?"

"He's deep in meditation. Working on Danny wore him out. And Danny's out of it, too."

"Can't we wait?"

"Not if we hope to figure this out before Sloane does."

"Maybe I can do it. Airic might talk to me."

Jax crossed his arms. "You can try."

"I'm sorry, Jax. I just don't want Kam traumatized any more than she's been. She found that grave. She already helped."

"Before you decide, go down and watch them. You'll see what I mean."

I'd made up my mind, but I was curious. Kam was friendly, but she didn't generally connect with people she'd just met. It took her a while. I'd viewed her protection of Airic at his house as mere concern. Jax implied it went deeper—a bond with a likeminded soul. And I'd love to view her tousled intellect as a talent. I'd seen it as a drawback. I'd tried to fix it, maybe because it connected her to my father's disturbing mind. I went downstairs.

Natra stood at the doorway of the room to which Jax had directed me. When I came close, she gestured. "Kam's found a friend."

I quietly told her what Jax had asked, hoping she'd side with me. Instead, she nodded. "She wants to help. She's a problem-solver, a good one. Like you." She pointed into the room with her chin. "Watch."

Chapter Eighty-Seven

I stepped closer. Kamryn sat cross-legged on a couch, talking with large gestures to Airic, who was wrapped in a dark blue blanket. Mika lay at his feet. He rocked a little but listened closely to Kam's rambling. I realized that his peculiar disorder might give him the ability to roll her knotted mental threads into separate distinct balls. He understood her. My eyes moistened. This isolated misfit who thrived in thin spaces had found warm human contact from a kindhearted child. And she'd found a more receptive ear with him than with me. I'd been trying to get her to be someone she wasn't, exactly as my mother had done to me. I felt chastened.

Kam saw me and waved for me to come in. I walked over and she rose to her knees on the couch.

"Mom!" she cried, her eyes wide. "Airic says he can show me how to see ghosts!"

Airic bowed his head and looked at the floor, as if I'd broken the spell. Jax was right. These two were mentally merged.

I pulled up a chair. "Well, maybe we can do that now." I gestured to each of us. "We have three. That should work."

Airic cocked his left ear toward me but kept his eyes on the floor. Mika raised her head.

I hadn't asked for this, but it was at my door. Even if I couldn't keep Kam out of this awful situation, I could at least guide the flow of information. I reached over and touched Airic's hand. Kamryn beamed her approval.

"So, are we talking about Mick? Airic, have you seen him?"

Kam perked up. "Who's that?"

Okay, bad start. "Let me try again. First, we need some information. Airic, do you remember when Danny came to your house with Carter?"

Airic rocked and nodded.

"What did he see?"

"Graves. He saw graves."

"And ghosts?" Kam asked.

Airic shook his head. "Danny doesn't see. Doesn't want to. Can't."

Kamryn glanced at me before she pressed him. "Some people can't see them? Can my mom?"

I didn't want him to answer this, but then again, I did. I wanted him to state that Black Shirt, a specter, had shown himself to me.

"She tries. They're close. They talk."

Kam's mouth opened. She regarded me with wide eyes. "At that bird house. Where that woman was talking to you. Maybe that kid *was* a ghost."

I had to stop this before we digressed. Jax needed information. "Back to Danny. There's something in his head, right?"

Airic grew animated. "In his head. It's in his head. I told you." He touched his cheek.

"So you know what Danny saw."

"Graves."

I saw what Jax meant. Airic talked in circles.

"What does Danny *know*? What's in his head?"

"He doesn't know."

"So, it's something he saw but doesn't remember? Maybe hypnosis might get at it?"

Mika got to her feet and whined. She trotted out. Airic seemed to stare at something across the room. "Doesn't know."

I wanted to shake him and ask, *so what's in his head, then?*

"Is it the *other* guy?" Kamryn asked. "Mick? What's in *his* head?"

Airic rocked. "Mick. It's in his head. Danny doesn't know."

Great, I thought. *We'll need a full-on séance to consult his ghost.* But at least we'd progressed. "Airic, what do we need to do? How can we get Mick to tell us?"

He squinted, almost looking me in the eye before he dropped his gaze. "Mick's dead."

Kamryn gasped and looked at me in alarm. Exactly what I'd been trying to avoid. Airic seemed to have shut us down, so I tried another tack. "Did Danny tell you about a storage device? A thumb drive? Something Carter had?"

Airic shook his head. "You need the *key*. It's in his head."

"Okay, so Danny saw a key. He knows where it is."

"Doesn't know."

"But *you* know?"

He glanced briefly at my hands before looking away. "Carter said don't tell."

We'd advanced one more baby-step. I tried again. "When I drew the map, you told me to follow the water. We found the water. You said there's a key. We thought the key was the map Carter drew. With all the circles. Is that right?"

Airic shook his head and rubbed his right hand.

"Then, there's an actual key?"

He tapped his face three times and repeated, "In his head." He sounded impatient.

Kam looked like she was counting under her breath. I realized she was saying the phrase in different ways. "Oh!" She sat up. "Not in his *head*, but *in* his head. *Inside*. Where? In his *mouth*?"

Airic patted his face again, rocked and nodded.

I leaned toward Airic. "In Mick's mouth? The boy in the water?"

He grew animated. "In the water. Follow the water."

My shoulders dropped. We'd lost Mick's body to Sloane. If the key was in his mouth, she had it already, or soon would.

Jax came in and knelt next to me. "Airic. He's not in the water. You brought Mick here. We put him in the hearse, remember?"

Kam looked at Jax with a frown. She'd missed all of that. I grabbed her hand. I wished Jax would be more sensitive. But I realized the stakes. And I knew she'd figured some things out on her own.

CHAPTER EIGHTY-SEVEN

Airic shook his head. "No."

"Yes. You drove up to us in the cemetery and we put it in the hearse. It was wrapped in a tarp."

Now Natra stepped in. "We put it in the casket, because it smelled so bad. You brought it here."

"No."

"Maybe that's the one in the water," Kamryn said. "The other Waterstone."

"In the water." Airic glanced briefly at me. "He showed you."

A cold rush filled me. "Oh, my God!" I put my hand to my mouth. "I know. It's the missing boy." I squeezed Jax's shoulder. "That's who we brought here. The autopsy photos that Sullivan put in Danny's file, the ones I thought were Mick. *That* boy was bludgeoned in the face. But Mick wasn't. We thought it was de—" I looked at Kam, who listened intently. "We were mistaken. Carter must have put the ledger with *that* kid, the missing one. He must have done it at Cypress Run. That's why he used that tarp. He picked up Mick from the *switch* house. That means Sloane has the other boy. Not Mick."

Jax gripped Airic's arm. "Is Mick still in the water?"

Airic nodded. "I told you." He lifted his right hand, pointing to the spot where he'd been staring. "See?"

I looked but didn't see anything. Kamryn squinted and shook her head.

Jax stood. "I have to get that key."

Chapter Eighty-Eight

He left the room. I leaned toward Kamryn and said, "Thank you, sweetie," before running after him.

"Jax! You can't."

He stopped and turned. "I have to."

I stood firm. "You can't. It's a crime scene. Let law enforcement handle it if you want to use it in court. *They* have to exhume the body and *they* have to find it. Otherwise, Sloane can say you had it all along and you planted it. Or that Airic did. You can't go back."

"Sloane might realize she has the wrong body. Maybe she already does."

"It's too decomposed for her to know, but she won't even look. She just wants to keep it out of your hands. The ledger was with it. She won't question it."

"Unless she knows there's a key. Carter called her that day. We don't know what he told her."

Caryn appeared in a doorway. "Will you guys stop? You woke up Danny."

Jax strode past her into the room. I followed.

Danny looked pale in the light of a kerosene lamp. He sat against a large pillow. Caryn went to his side and glowered at us. "You're not s'posed to disturb him."

"'s okay." Danny spoke so quietly I barely heard him. "Thanks for saving me. Sorry 'bout the car."

Jax sat on a stool next to his cot. "Danny, I need to ask you something. I'll be brief."

"My head hurts but okay."

"You know we didn't bring Mick back here, don't you?"

Danny hesitated. He touched his mouth. Then he nodded.

"Why didn't you tell us?"

He shrugged. "Didn't know who to trust."

"Did Carter put something in his mouth?"

Danny blinked. "I didn't see what he done. I didn't wanna watch."

"Did he tell you anything about a key?"

Danny closed his eyes. He looked like he hurt. Then he opened them. "Just drew that map. Told me to find his grandfather so I could get the files he hid... but..."

"But what?"

"She didn't get it. That woman. Not what I gave Carter. She got Plat-eye's stuff."

"So there are two storage drives?"

Danny shrugged and flinched.

Jax waited a moment. "Let me get this straight. There's a drive with Plat-eye's files, which Carter brought *here*, and there's yours that's still... somewhere. And you recorded Sloane killing Mick, right?"

Caryn nudged Danny. "I already told him."

Danny breathed in before he nodded. "She killed Mick."

"It shows her doing this?"

"Yeah. And she tells 'im he's stupid."

"Does she know about this recording?"

"Don't think so, 'less Carter told her. But I don't think he done that. When I shown it to him, he seemed upset. Said he'd get me out. Then he did the next day. He already had the other files. He told me 'bout 'em."

"And you saw her again at Carter's place, right? When he was shot."

"With Plat-eye." Danny adjusted his position and grabbed his shoulder with a grimace.

"Can't we do this later?" Caryn asked. "He needs meds."

Jax raised a hand. "Just...one more... Danny, how do you know Sloane didn't get your thumb drive?"

"The color. She got a silver one. Like a cigarette lighter. Mine was red.

An' it wadn't here. Carter still had it an' he never got back here.''

Jax got to his feet. "All right. We're going to go find it. That's the evidence we need for you. Get some rest." He gestured for me to leave with him. We were almost to the door, before Danny called out.

"Wait!"

Jax turned.

"It was like that. The thumb drive I used. I stole it from the switch house. It was shaped like a key. That's what I give 'im."

Jax smiled. "Thank you, Danny." He strode out.

In the hall, I grabbed him. "So now we know. Let's call Wayne. He should exhume the body, but you should be present. Make a deal with him. Don't tell him the location, just tell him what you need and that you have to be there."

Jax shook his head. "It's under water. There's no reason for them to go back there. They removed Plat-eye's corpse. They don't know what Carter did."

"Wayne does! He saw the body in the tarp. Jax, you're going to regret it if you try to do this on your own. Don't take the wrong step now. In fact, you can't, because Mick's grave is under water. There's no way you could dig it up. Wayne can bring equipment. He can put a guard on the place. Even Wayne, who was right there, doesn't know where to look. He doesn't know the Waterstone connection, and he won't see the second stone. You can use that. Just work it out with him."

Finally, Jax seemed to accept that we had no other choice. He couldn't mismanage his brother's dying gift. His attorney mind kicked in.

I called the dispatcher with my code name. When Wayne called back, Jax and I talked with him together. He hesitated about the deal, but finally said he'd start arranging it. Then I looked for Kam. It was time for me to treat her as part of our team.

Chapter Eighty-Nine

The calm that replaces a hurricane is deceptively numb, perhaps so we can adjust to the damage. That morning, Hurricane Delano twisted south, disrupting itself just as Ayden had described. Some Lowcountry areas, though flooded, were accessible. The storm subsided.

Wayne and JD took our statements about the Plattman shooting and organized an exhumation in record time. We told them about the other body that needed an identity. Wayne knew Sloane was gathering her resources, so we had to hurry. To my relief, JD told us they'd located Carl and the boys who'd fled the switch house. They'd also arrested Vince, who'd weathered the storm in the mausoleum. Wayne had organized a quick search of the switch house property, but full processing for signs of Mick's blood had to wait.

Ayden returned to OBX to assess damage to our houses, while Jax and I took Airic home. On the way, we located my SUV, *sans* snake, and Jax promised to get it repaired. I doubted there was much he could do.

Water had seeped into Airic's house from various leaks, and the boo-daddy had blown away, along with three shutters and some roofing slate. Otherwise, it was habitable. He had a generator.

Both Waterstone graves were underwater. That area had become a pond. Wayne had arranged for equipment to drain it enough to pull out the body. As Mick's grave came into view, I saw a wavy line of stones similar to the adjacent grave for the other missing boy, albeit displaced somewhat by water. The set resembled the parallel lines I'd drawn on the psychographic map. Had it never rained, we'd have seen them. Carter's clues had actually been obvious to anyone who knew what to look for. Jax would have spotted them without my map. But if he'd seen them when Carter had first buried these victims, he'd never have met me or needed my map.

I watched the pump, recalling the water in Airic's séance room. I'd thought an accomplice had caused it. Now I wasn't sure. It had flooded suddenly, the way this place had.

We had Mick's autopsy photos to identify the body, although we knew that three months in the ground could make this challenging. I told Wayne about the ring that was supposedly in the grave near the headstone and asked him to look for it. Danny had confirmed he'd placed it there. Jax fretted over potential damage to the thumb drive from immersion. Finding the body was important, but we needed undeniable proof that Sloane had committed this murder. With her influential resources, Danny's report would not be enough.

A team of diggers uncovered a black vinyl body bag. I moved over to stand with Airic, holding a laptop for testing the video file. I didn't want to see another decomposed boy.

Airic was calm, as if he'd been waiting for the completion of Carter's plan. Carter had chosen his confidantes well; Airic and Danny had both kept his secret until they knew he'd want them to tell. Briefly, Airic looked my way. "I like your daughter, Annie. You can bring her any time."

I felt a flood of pride. "She'd be thrilled to come."

Wayne bent down to unzip the bag. He checked his phone, where he had the photos. Jax put a hand over his mouth and nose before he leaned in. Finally, Wayne gestured affirmatively. I breathed out. They'd found Mick. *We'd* found Mick. We'd found *them*. My eyes watered. Soon, Mick's family would learn his fate and could bury him properly. *That* lawsuit would be another thorn for Jax to stab, hard and deep, into the elephant's foot.

A forensic investigator took multiple photos. Wayne extracted something from the corpse's mouth. Then he walked with Jax toward me. I fired up the laptop.

It appeared that Carter had wrapped Danny's thumb drive in plastic to seal it against moisture. He'd probably hoped to stash it in his cave with the other files but had run out of time. On the day he brought Mick's body here, with Danny's "key" still in his pocket, he must have realized he'd never go home again. He'd had to stash the evidence against Sloane where Jax—and no one else—could find it. I guessed he'd buried both victims here at the same time in side-by-side graves. So, he'd also had the ledger then. The kid with the damaged face from ISM abuse had offered a convenient way to avoid explaining bullet holes in Mick's head. Danny must have felt helplessly trapped as he watched the fraudulent case against him build.

Wearing plastic gloves, Wayne plugged the flat red USB key into the laptop. We waited for the icon to pop up. Nothing showed. I breathed in. I couldn't believe we'd finally retrieved it only to have it fail. I looked at Airic. He gazed toward me, almost meeting my eyes, and seemed unruffled.

"Try it again," I suggested.

Wayne ejected it. Jax looked at me. This was what he'd worried about.

Wayne reinserted it. The digital folder icon appeared. We all breathed out.

Wayne opened it. The icons for dozens of video files popped up, along with some documents. Jax gave me a look that conveyed we might have more than we thought. He identified a clip labeled 'SG' and Wayne opened it. The film was blurry, but Sloane's voice was clear. Mick shouted. She insulted him. We heard a gunshot. Then a second one. The incident was over in a few seconds. The contents were just as Danny had described.

Wayne seemed satisfied. "We got her. No self-defense or protection of others. This will spin her story a different way and give the evidence against her more weight. She was Plattman's partner, and whatever we trace to him will implicate her. We'll keep excavating this area to see if we find any others."

Wayne copied this file to the laptop, cautioning Jax against using it until they built their criminal case. Then Wayne opened another video file. Then another. "Looks like we have some other interesting items. Excuse me." He beckoned JD over. They looked at several other files. Their comments indicated that Danny's stolen thumb drive offered a mother lode. These might be the same files Carter had copied onto the storage drive he'd placed in the cave. Maybe we'd lost nothing to Sloane.

Wayne removed the thumb drive. He placed it into an evidence bag, closing it with tape before he returned the laptop and shook hands with Jax. I knew Jax wanted those other files for his own insurance, but he didn't ask. I suspected Trish had loaded software that would automatically transfer whatever Wayne had opened.

One of the diggers at the grave shouted for Wayne and pointed to his phone. Wayne checked his own. He showed a photo to Jax. I leaned in. In mud they'd pulled from the other Waterstone grave lay a gold ring. Carter's wedding ring.

"We'll get that to you when we're done with it," Wayne said. He nodded to me and left to join JD. Airic hugged Jax, and Jax hugged me.

"Thank you," he said. "I owe you."

"I know. Wait'll you see my bill."

He smiled. "I'll happily pay. But we're not finished. We still have Morton and Girard."

"I'm ready. Or I will be after I collect my team."

It was tough to say good-bye after all we'd been through, but I rented a car and took Natra, Mika, and Kam back to the Outer Banks. Ayden was already at work on my repairs. The hurricane had diminished as it moved north, but the fierce wind had still taken bites from my house. Kamryn set about pruning what was left of her damaged roses.

The next week, Jax came to OBX to go over our Georgia cases. He gave Kamryn a framed certificate and a reward from Ethan's Project for her courage and ingenuity. She was thrilled. She wanted to use the money for the sea turtle project.

Jax filled us in. Caryn had been allowed to go home. Flynn still had time left in detention, but Jax had negotiated a safer place. He was working on a foster placement for the feisty kid with a couple that raised service dogs. Perfect. And Jax had rejected a settlement offer for Danny. Wayne had confirmed they had a solid case against Sloane, which exonerated Danny. After the dust settled, Jax expected to get much more. "That kid's pretty damaged," he said. "He's got a long road ahead. He deserves every penny of what we can make JTA pay out." He planned to keep Danny in a protected place.

I told Jax I'd gotten something important, too. "You helped me appreciate my daughter's gifts. That's significant. I'm letting her be who she is."

Before he left, Jax made it clear he hoped to work with me on future cases. I sensed—I hoped—there could be something more.

Amid all this, we had to debrief. I included Kam in the forensic discussions, especially Joe's digital items, which pleased her. Wayne reluctantly agreed with this decision. But the paranormal debriefing came later, when Kam was in bed.

Chapter Ninety

Natra, Ayden, and I gathered on my second-floor deck. A light, salty breeze made it seem as if there'd been no drama or destruction along this beach. I brought out a nice red blend from the Devil's Advocate label. We laughed together. Then I got serious.

Just a week before, we'd had several kids who'd needed help. We'd achieved our goals. First, of course, we'd found my daughter and brought her safely home. Also, Jimmy Broderick was returned to his mother, and we'd kept Danny safe. We expected to ensure appropriate verdicts in the staged suicide cases. The families would be able to sue the facility, and several caseworkers would likely go to prison. Brooke had improved, denying she'd written a suicide note, which had launched another investigation. What had happened to her supported her report about the other two girls.

For the Agency, we'd expanded our investigative reach through Jax and Valerie into Georgia, and I'd added a potential paranormal consultant for other missing kid cases. I looked forward to seeing Airic under better circumstances.

But we hadn't answered all our questions.

Before I sat down, Ayden spoke up. "You win. You saw a ghost. You have to admit it."

I passed him a glass. "If you mean Black Shirt, there's too much ambiguity. You know the rule. We examine it carefully." As a skeptic, I'm alert to wishful thinking and other unconscious biases. No matter how uncanny something seems, I look first for other explanations.

Ayden preferred the benefit of the doubt. "Black Shirt told you to find him. He turned out to be Mick."

"Not conclusively." I cleared my throat. "I saw a guy in Airic's session who mouthed something that looked like 'Find us.' I did ask Airic if he'd been invited, but Airic didn't confirm anything. He said he'd entered his trance right away that evening and didn't remember who was there. And the film was fuzzy. Even Joe thought the image wasn't clear, despite his superimposition. He said only that there was a strong resemblance to Mick's autopsy photo."

Natra sipped her own wine and smiled. She'd grown up with shamans and thin spaces. She thought my need for clarity impeded my goals. But I thought a true ghost manifestation *could* be decisively confirmed. Why not? Others made such claims. That's what *I* needed.

Ayden didn't let up. "What about the map from the viewing session? The things you drew were what we saw. Wasn't that from Carter, a dead guy?"

"It could have been from Airic. He'd seen the graves with the rocks. He knew about the sacred area. Or, it came from Danny, who was highly stressed and who buried the ring that ended up on my drawing. *If* I drew a ring. To me, that's just basic *psi* energy."

Natra chimed in. "Don't forget the drawing that helped us find Kam's phone. She described Puca."

I held out my hands. "You already know what I'll say. It's the same explanation as Jimmy's appearance in his mother's dream. He was alive. Strong emotional energy can produce such things. Remote projections are *psi* energy. Unusual but still natural. Don't forget the CIA's remote viewing experiments. They got impressive results, without ghosts. I don't accept a maybe as a yes."

Ayden shook his head. "So, you don't think you saw a ghost."

I took a sip of wine. "It's like the other times we've had these experiences. In retrospect, I can't say I did or didn't. Even the things that Sarah, the paratherapist, seemed to hear were intriguing, but I can't definitively say a ghost was present, not even with Kam's report. I'll admit only this: we might have had paranormal influence in this case, especially in light of the unsettled weather. I hope we did because it improves my prospects for other ventures. But… I can't say beyond all doubt that I've seen or been directed by the ghost of a deceased person. If they're so clear to Airic and Sarah, why can't they be that clear to me?"

Ayden exchanged amused looks with Natra. "We just had a lot of connected coincidences."

"Some. Maybe. But some circumstances were contrived. Look. If Black Shirt was Mick's ghost and he wanted so badly to be found, why not show up at the cemetery and point out his grave? Especially when we dug up the wrong one? I didn't see him, did you? If he can enter a séance and urge me to find him, he can show me where he is when I'm standing where he's buried. Right? Even if he exhausted all his spirit energy to get me there, he could at least have pushed or poked me."

"Maybe he tried," Ayden said, "but the wind interfered."

"Actually," Natra said, "I do agree with Annie. I'm willing to believe spirits were there, especially the way Mika and Airic acted. But I don't get why they can seek help but not point us in the right direction. Like that one case we had where the supposed ghost told a psychic he knew his killer but then couldn't name him. If you can say the first part, you can say the rest."

Ayden looked as if she'd just abandoned him. He shrugged. "Okay, then. The challenge is still before us. That's fine. What's our next case?"

"First, we settle our current cases. We have two in Georgia, and possibly Brooke's. Wayne's given me hope for a good resolution, but it will depend on what happens with Sloane, so we might need more evidence. When I know our next move, you're the first one I'll call."

We spent the rest of the evening talking about what we'd all been through, happy to be home. What I didn't reveal was my plan to visit Airic again. I wanted to learn more about Kam's unique gift and possibly develop it. But I also had unfinished business. He'd seen a redheaded girl who seemed to know me, and I still had a cold case with a missing child whom I wanted to find.

Acknowledgements

I want to thank Lee Lofland, who gave me the opportunity to write a short story for a Writers Police Academy anthology, *After Midnight*. That started the ball rolling. Paranormalists Mark and Carol Nesbitt gave me ideas and methods, along with opportunities for paranormal investigations. "Natra" introduced me to sniffer dogs, and cyber security specialist Joe Pochron became my go-to for all things digital. Steve Myers and Juilene Mcknight allowed me to use my MFA experience to more fully explore my characters – especially in Ireland! – which grew into this novel, the first in the series. My agent, John Silbersack, gave me invaluable guidance, and Verena Rose at Level Best Books proved to be an enthusiastic editor. Susan Lysek and Sally Keglovits read the early drafts and became my cheerleaders, while Rachael Bell provided the spooky Savannah experience, complete with characters.

About the Author

Katherine Ramsland has played chess with serial killers, dug up the dead, worked with profilers, and camped out in haunted crime scenes. As a professor of forensic psychology and an investigative consultant (like her main character, Annie Hunter), she's always vigilant for unique angles and intriguing characters. She spent five years working with "BTK" serial killer Dennis Rader to write his autobiography, *Confession of a Serial Killer*, and has been featured as an expert in over 200 true crime documentaries. The author of 69 books, she's been a forensic consultant for *CSI, Bones* and *The Alienist*, an executive producer on *Murder House Flip* and A&E's *Confession of a Serial Killer*, and a commentator on *48 Hours, 20/20, The Today Show, Dr. Oz, Nightline, Larry King Live, Nancy Grace* and other shows. She blogs regularly for *Psychology Today* and once wrote extensively for CourtTV's Crime Library. She's become the go-to expert for the most extreme, deviant and bizarre forms of criminal behavior, which offers great background for her Nut Cracker Investigations series.

SOCIAL MEDIA HANDLES:
  Blog: http://www.psychologytoday.com/blog/shadow-boxing
  Facebook: **https://www.facebook.com/Kath.ramsland/**
  Twitter: **https://twitter.com/KatRamsland**
  Instagram: https://www.instagram.com/katherineramsland/

AUTHOR WEBSITE:
www.katherineramsland.net

Also by Katherine Ramsland

Track the Ripper, Riverdale Avenue Books

The Ripper Letter, Riverdale Avenue Books

The Blood Hunters, Kensington

The Heat Seekers, Kensington

How To Catch a Killer, Sterling

Heartless: Iowa's Bloody Murders, Notorious USA

Murder Alley: Nebraska Fiends and Felons, Notorious USA

Cold-blooded: Kansas Murders, Notorious USA

Confession of a Serial Killer: The Untold Story of Dennis Rader, the BTK Killer, University Press of New England

Haunted Crime Scenes, with Mark Nesbitt, Second Chance Books

Blood and Ghosts: Paranormal Forensic Investigators, with Mark Nesbitt, Second Chance Books

The Mind of a Murderer: Privileged Access to the Demons that Drive Extreme Violence, Praeger

The Forensic Psychology of Criminal Minds, Berkley

The Devil's Dozen: How Cutting Edge Forensics Took down Twelve Notorious

Serial Killers, Berkley

The Human Predator: A Historical Chronicle of Serial Murder and Forensic Investigation, Berkley

The Criminal Mind: A Writer's Guide to Forensic Psychology, Writer's Digest

The Forensic Science of CSI, Berkley

Ghost: Investigating the Other Side, St. Martin's Press

Lightning Source UK Ltd.
Milton Keynes UK
UKHW030630200922
409139UK00001B/143